JAMES TYNION IV * RIAN SYGH * WALTER BAIAMONTE

THE BACKSTAGERS™

VOLUME ONE: REBELS WITHOUT APPLAUSE

BOOM! BOX™

THE BACKSTAGERS Volume One, May 2018. Published by BOOM!
Box, a division of Boom Entertainment, Inc. The Backstagers is ™
& © 2018 Rian Sygh & James Tynion IV. Originally published in
single magazine form as THE BACKSTAGERS No. 1-4. ™ & © 2016
Rian Sygh & James Tynion IV. All rights reserved. BOOM! Box™
and the BOOM! Box logo are trademarks of Boom Entertainment,
Inc., registered in various countries and categories. All characters,
events, and institutions depicted herein are fictional. Any similarity
between any of the names, characters, persons, events, and/or
institutions in this publication to actual names, characters, and
persons, whether living or dead, events, and/or institutions is
unintended and purely coincidental. BOOM! Box does not read
or accept unsolicited submissions of ideas, stories, or artwork.

For information regarding the CPSIA on this printed material, call:
(203) 595-3636 and provide reference #RICH – 788195.

BOOM! Studios, 5670 Wilshire Boulevard, Suite 400, Los Angeles,
CA 90036-5679. Printed in USA. Third Printing.

ISBN: 978-1-60886-993-0, eISBN: 978-1-61398-664-6

THE BACKSTAGERS™

CREATED BY JAMES TYNION IV AND RIAN SYGH

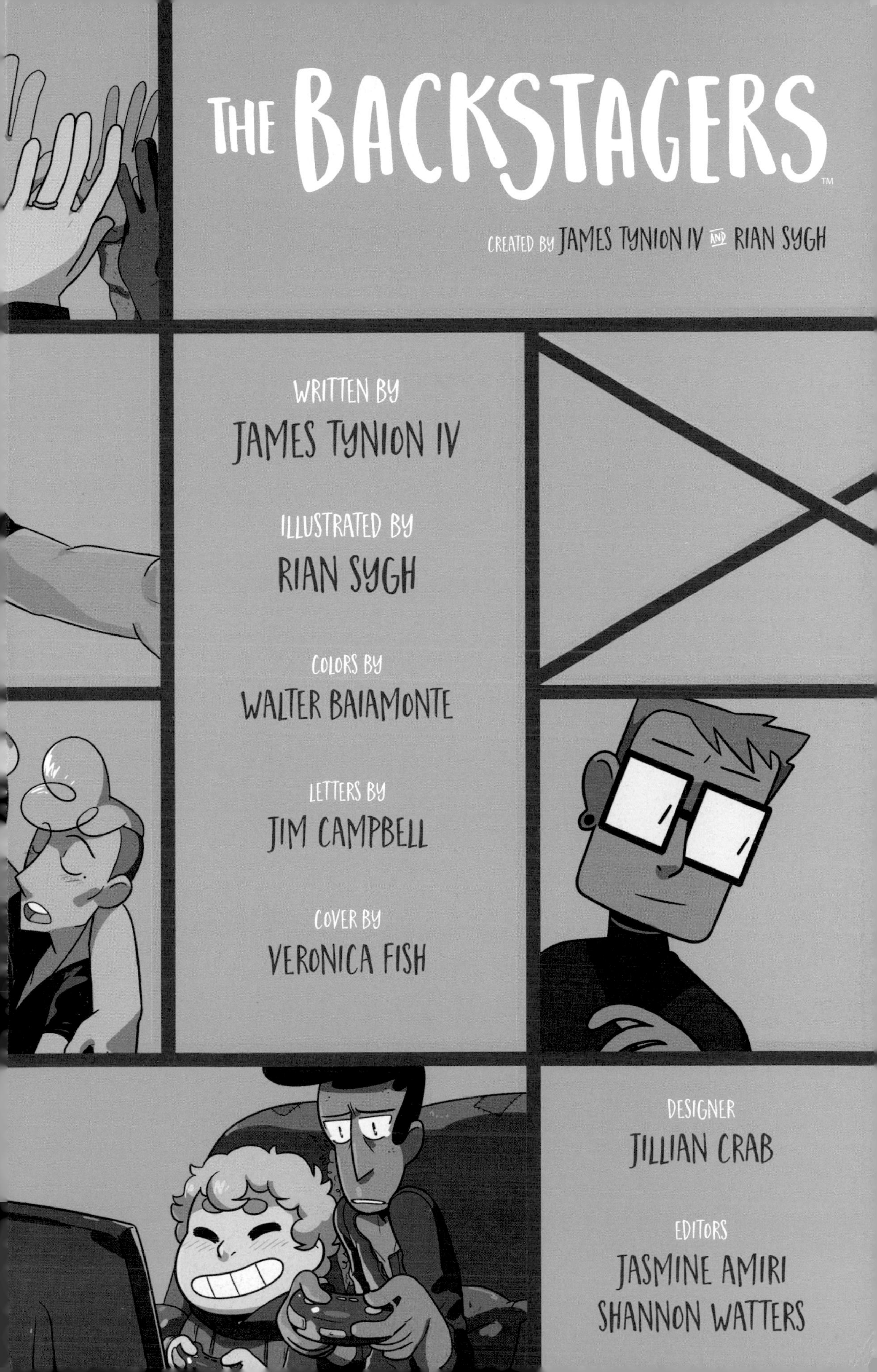

WRITTEN BY
JAMES TYNION IV

ILLUSTRATED BY
RIAN SYGH

COLORS BY
WALTER BAIAMONTE

LETTERS BY
JIM CAMPBELL

COVER BY
VERONICA FISH

DESIGNER
JILLIAN CRAB

EDITORS
JASMINE AMIRI
SHANNON WATTERS

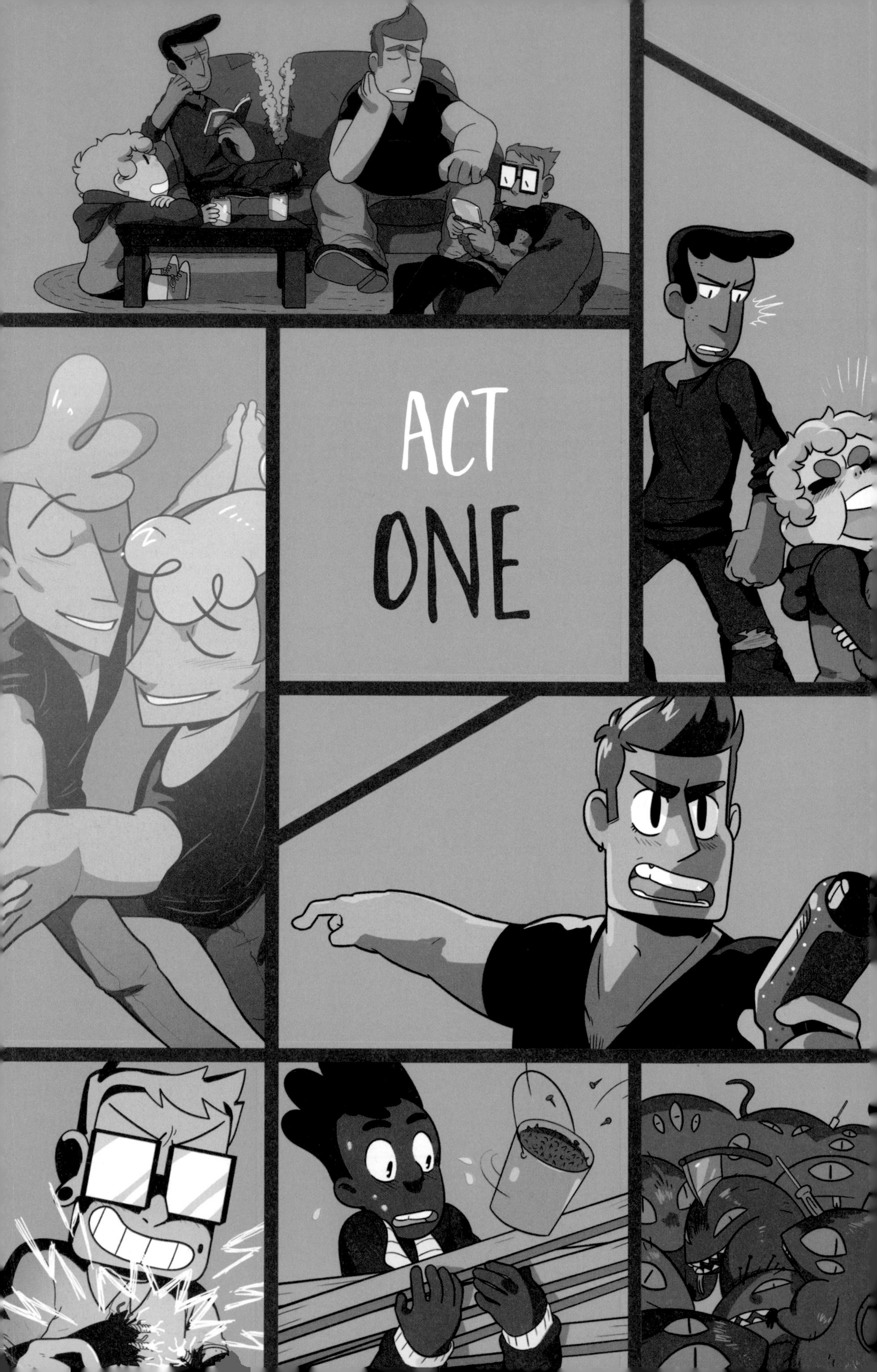
ACT ONE

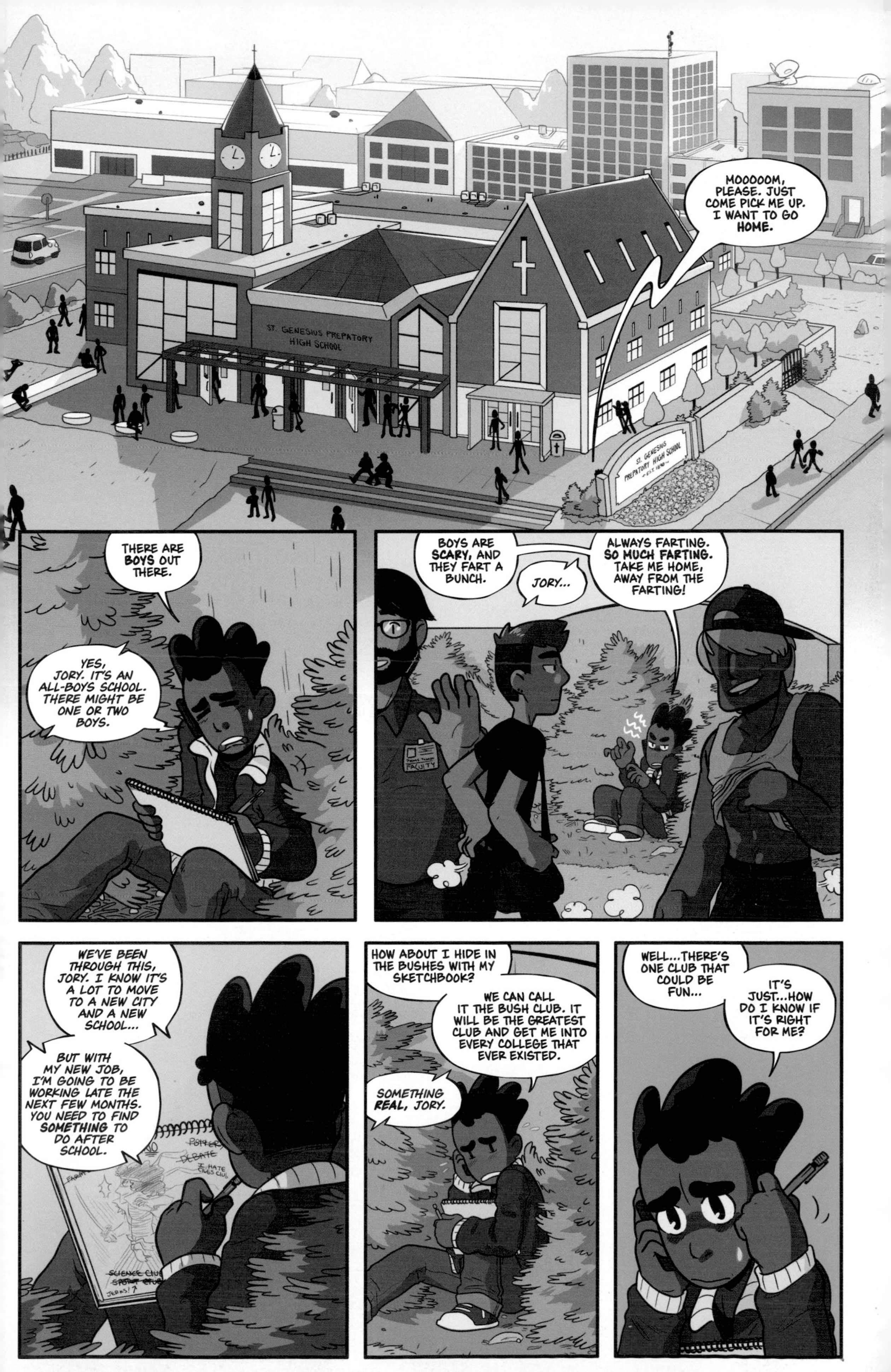
ST. GENESIUS PREPATORY HIGH SCHOOL
ST. GENESIUS PREPATORY HIGH SCHOOL
MOOOOOM, PLEASE. JUST COME PICK ME UP. I WANT TO GO HOME.
THERE ARE BOYS OUT THERE.
YES, JORY. IT'S AN ALL-BOYS SCHOOL. THERE MIGHT BE ONE OR TWO BOYS.
BOYS ARE SCARY, AND THEY FART A BUNCH.
JORY...
ALWAYS FARTING. SO MUCH FARTING. TAKE ME HOME, AWAY FROM THE FARTING!
WE'VE BEEN THROUGH THIS, JORY. I KNOW IT'S A LOT TO MOVE TO A NEW CITY AND A NEW SCHOOL...
BUT WITH MY NEW JOB, I'M GOING TO BE WORKING LATE THE NEXT FEW MONTHS. YOU NEED TO FIND SOMETHING TO DO AFTER SCHOOL.
HOW ABOUT I HIDE IN THE BUSHES WITH MY SKETCHBOOK?
WE CAN CALL IT THE BUSH CLUB. IT WILL BE THE GREATEST CLUB AND GET ME INTO EVERY COLLEGE THAT EVER EXISTED.
SOMETHING REAL, JORY.
WELL...THERE'S ONE CLUB THAT COULD BE FUN...
IT'S JUST...HOW DO I KNOW IF IT'S RIGHT FOR ME?

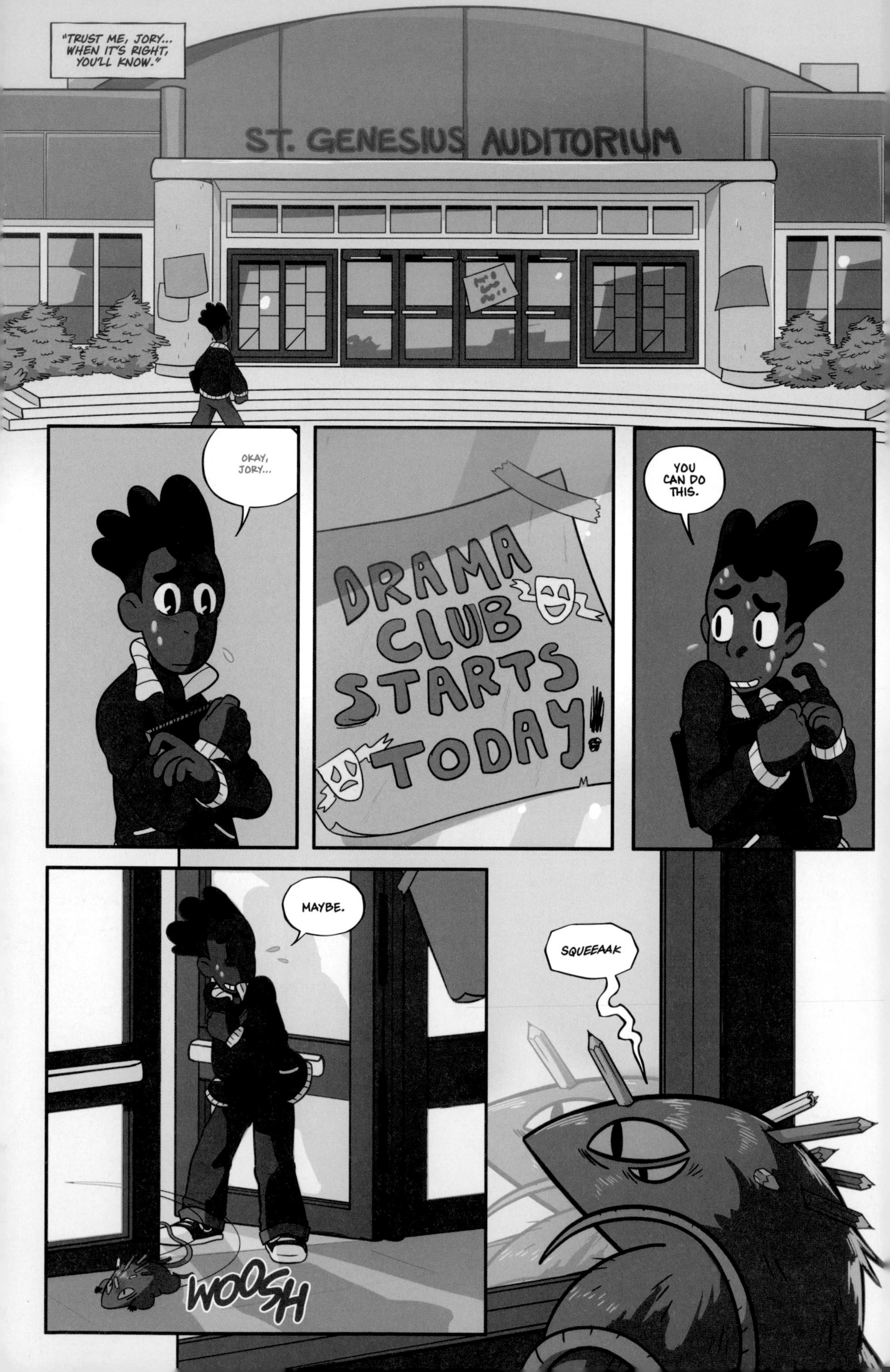
"TRUST ME, JORY... WHEN IT'S RIGHT, YOU'LL KNOW."
ST. GENESIUS AUDITORIUM
OKAY, JORY...
DRAMA CLUB STARTS TODAY!
YOU CAN DO THIS.
MAYBE.
SQUEEAAK
WOOSH

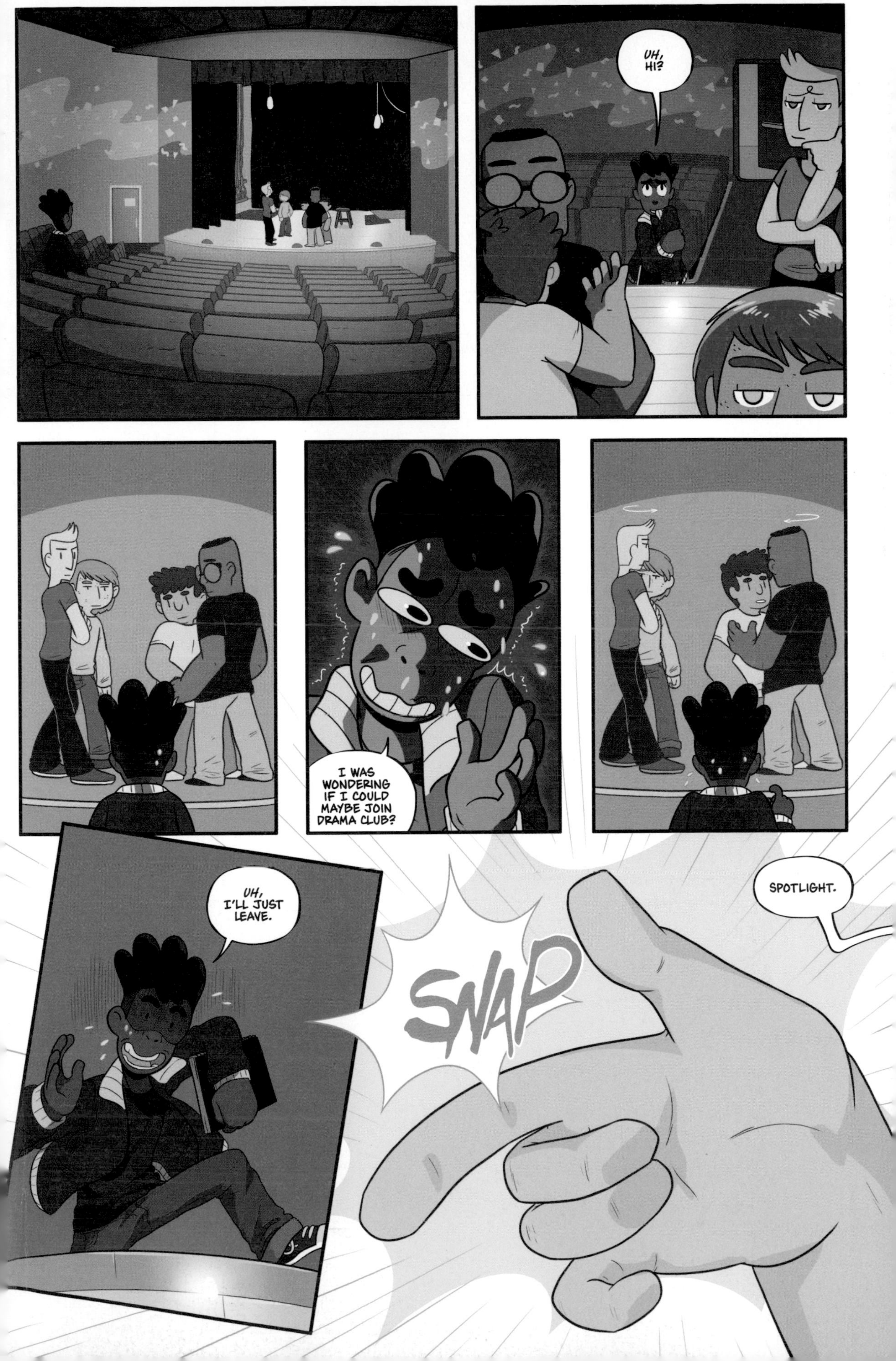
UH, HI?
I WAS WONDERING IF I COULD MAYBE JOIN DRAMA CLUB?
UH, I'LL JUST LEAVE.
SNAP
SPOTLIGHT.

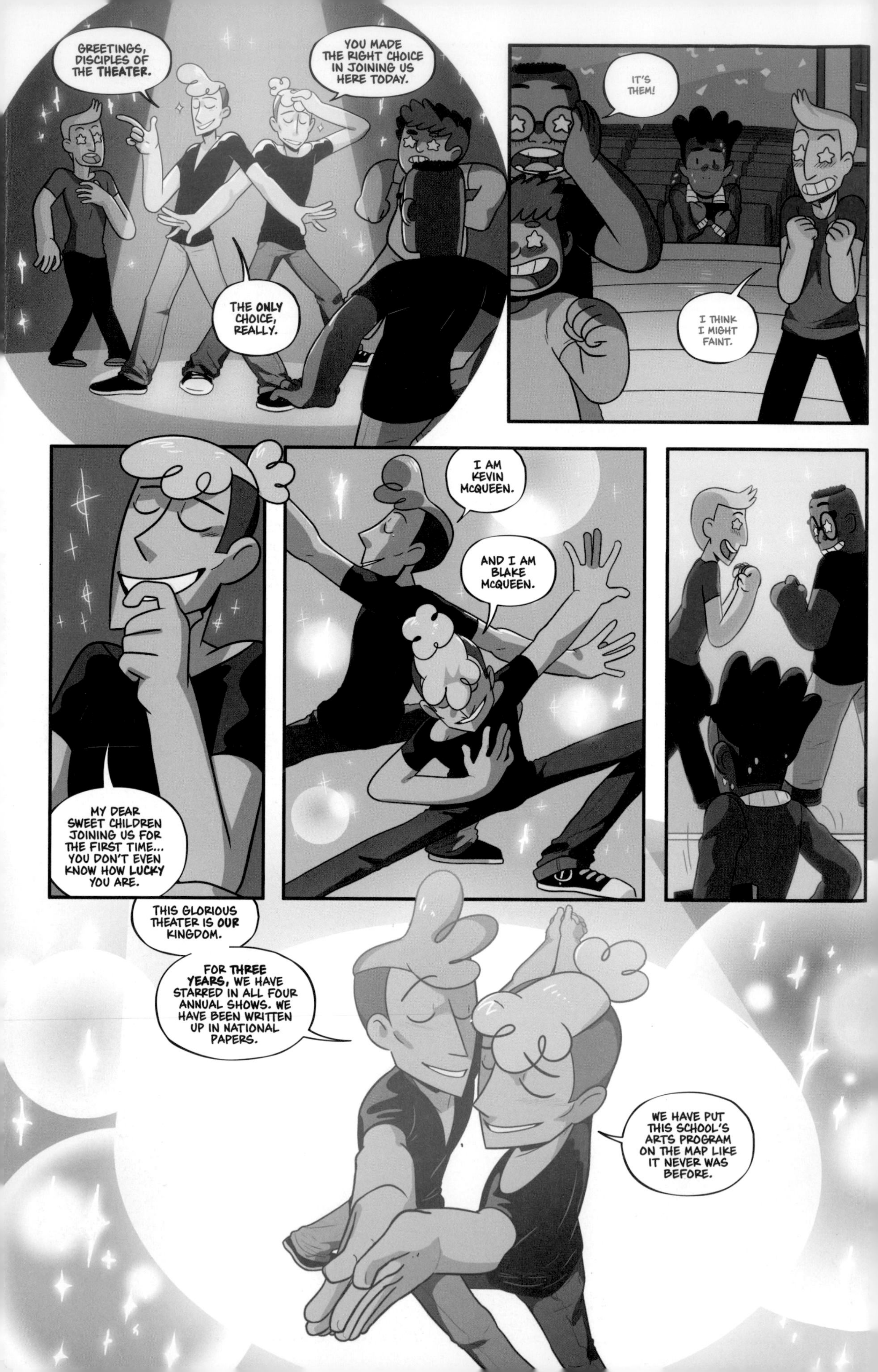
GREETINGS, DISCIPLES OF THE THEATER.
YOU MADE THE RIGHT CHOICE IN JOINING US HERE TODAY.
THE ONLY CHOICE, REALLY.
IT'S THEM!
I THINK I MIGHT FAINT.
MY DEAR SWEET CHILDREN JOINING US FOR THE FIRST TIME... YOU DON'T EVEN KNOW HOW LUCKY YOU ARE.
I AM KEVIN McQUEEN.
AND I AM BLAKE McQUEEN.
THIS GLORIOUS THEATER IS OUR KINGDOM.
FOR THREE YEARS, WE HAVE STARRED IN ALL FOUR ANNUAL SHOWS. WE HAVE BEEN WRITTEN UP IN NATIONAL PAPERS.
WE HAVE PUT THIS SCHOOL'S ARTS PROGRAM ON THE MAP LIKE IT NEVER WAS BEFORE.

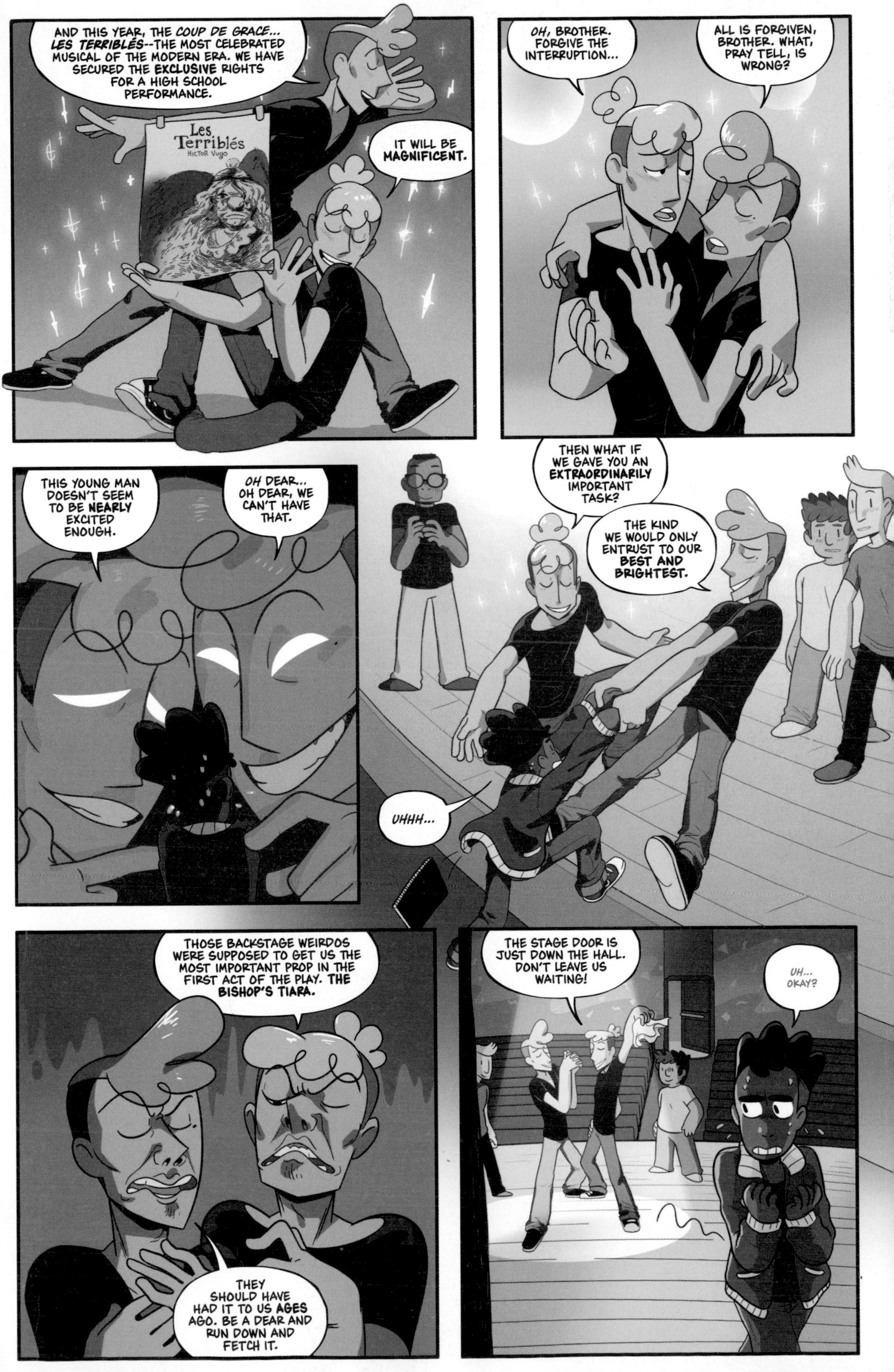
AND THIS YEAR, THE COUP DE GRACE... LES TERRIBLÉS--THE MOST CELEBRATED MUSICAL OF THE MODERN ERA. WE HAVE SECURED THE EXCLUSIVE RIGHTS FOR A HIGH SCHOOL PERFORMANCE.
Les Terriblés
HICTOR VUGO
IT WILL BE MAGNIFICENT.
OH, BROTHER. FORGIVE THE INTERRUPTION...
ALL IS FORGIVEN, BROTHER. WHAT, PRAY TELL, IS WRONG?
THIS YOUNG MAN DOESN'T SEEM TO BE NEARLY EXCITED ENOUGH.
OH DEAR... OH DEAR, WE CAN'T HAVE THAT.
THEN WHAT IF WE GAVE YOU AN EXTRAORDINARILY IMPORTANT TASK?
THE KIND WE WOULD ONLY ENTRUST TO OUR BEST AND BRIGHTEST.
UHHH...
THOSE BACKSTAGE WEIRDOS WERE SUPPOSED TO GET US THE MOST IMPORTANT PROP IN THE FIRST ACT OF THE PLAY. THE BISHOP'S TIARA.
THEY SHOULD HAVE HAD IT TO US AGES AGO. BE A DEAR AND RUN DOWN AND FETCH IT.
THE STAGE DOOR IS JUST DOWN THE HALL. DON'T LEAVE US WAITING!
UH... OKAY?

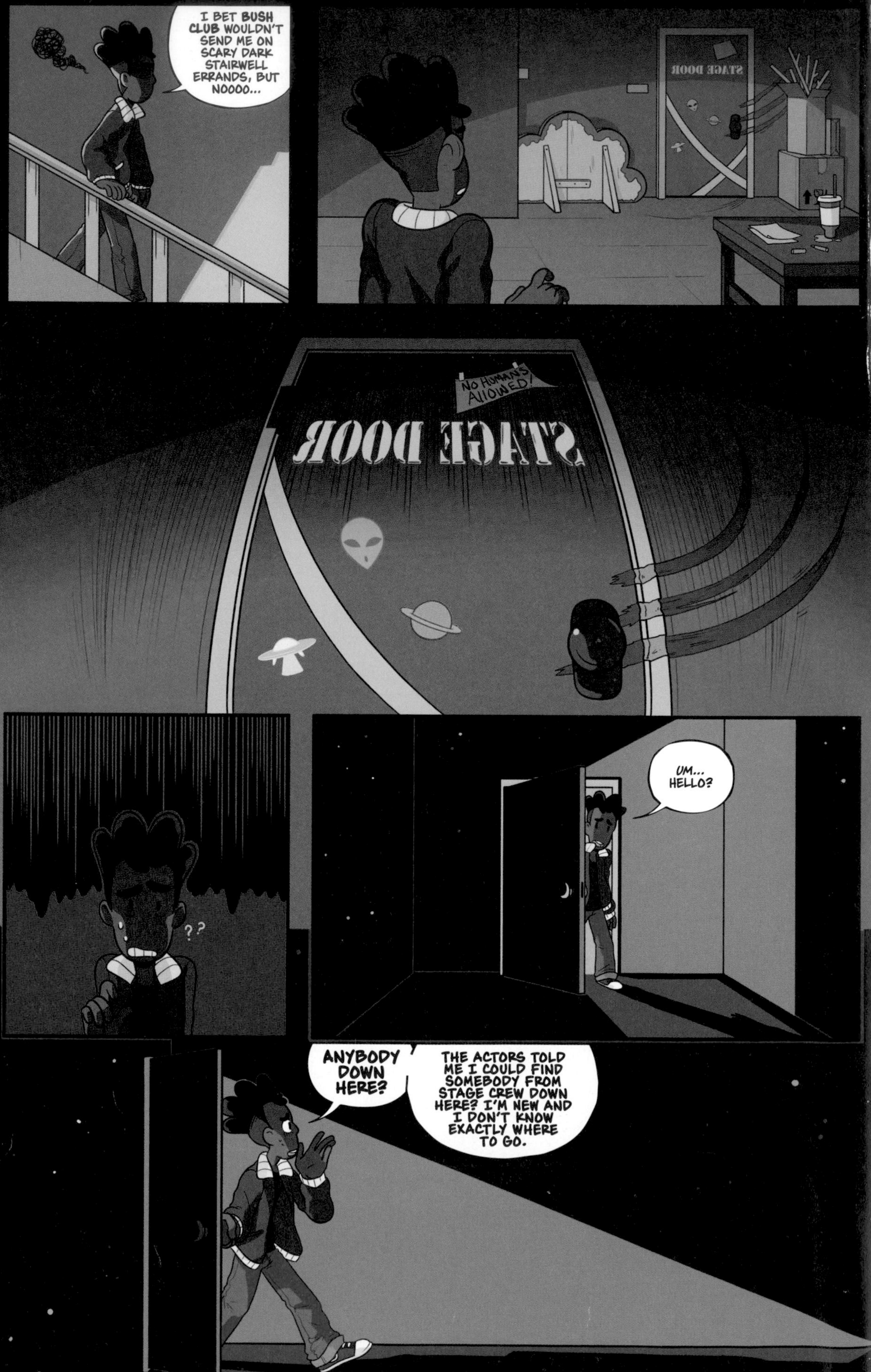
I BET BUSH CLUB WOULDN'T SEND ME ON SCARY DARK STAIRWELL ERRANDS, BUT NOOOO...
STAGE DOOR
NO HUMANS ALLOWED!
STAGE DOOR
??
UM... HELLO?
ANYBODY DOWN HERE?
THE ACTORS TOLD ME I COULD FIND SOMEBODY FROM STAGE CREW DOWN HERE? I'M NEW AND I DON'T KNOW EXACTLY WHERE TO GO.

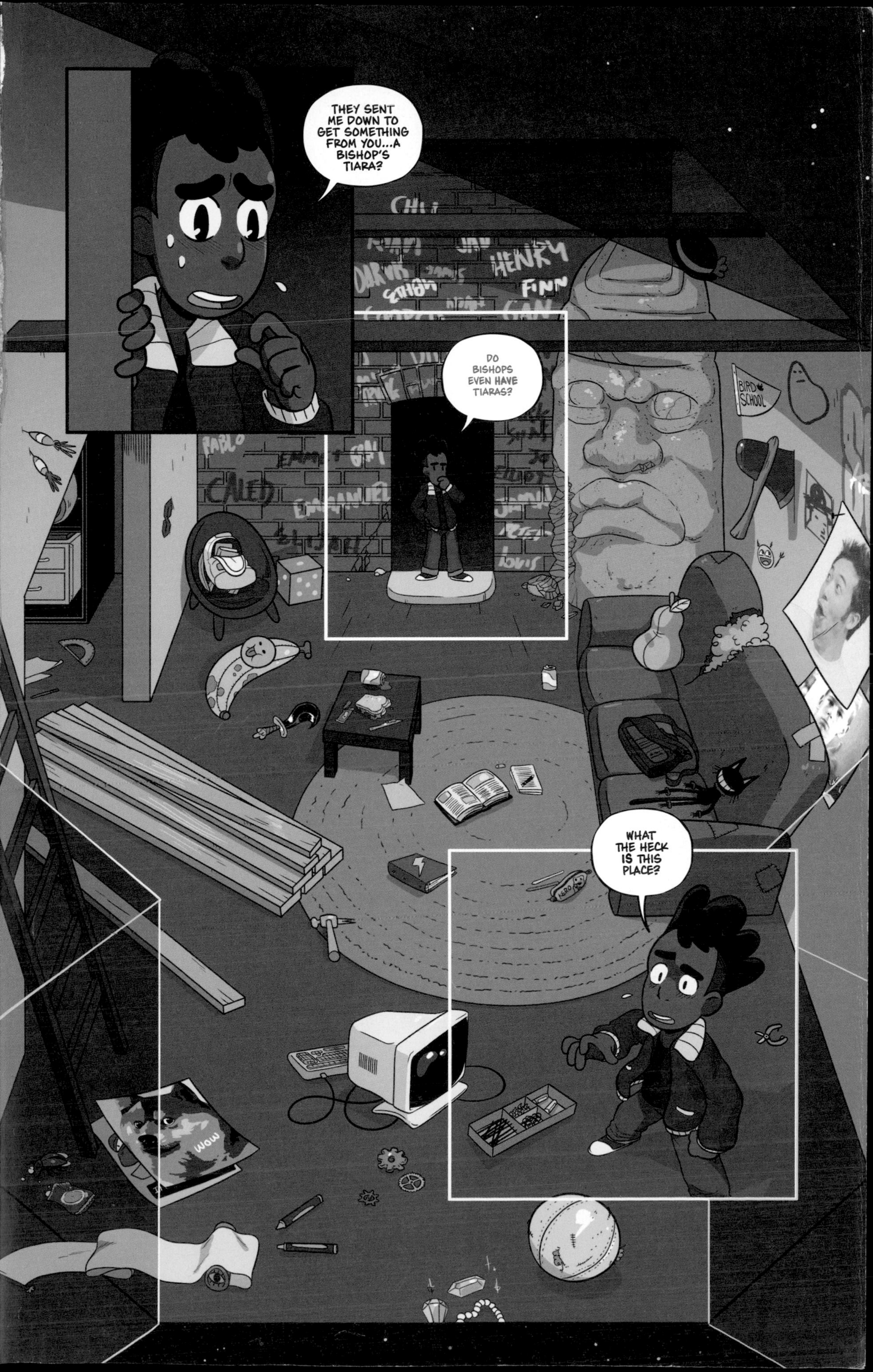
THEY SENT ME DOWN TO GET SOMETHING FROM YOU...A BISHOP'S TIARA?
DO BISHOPS EVEN HAVE TIARAS?
WHAT THE HECK IS THIS PLACE?

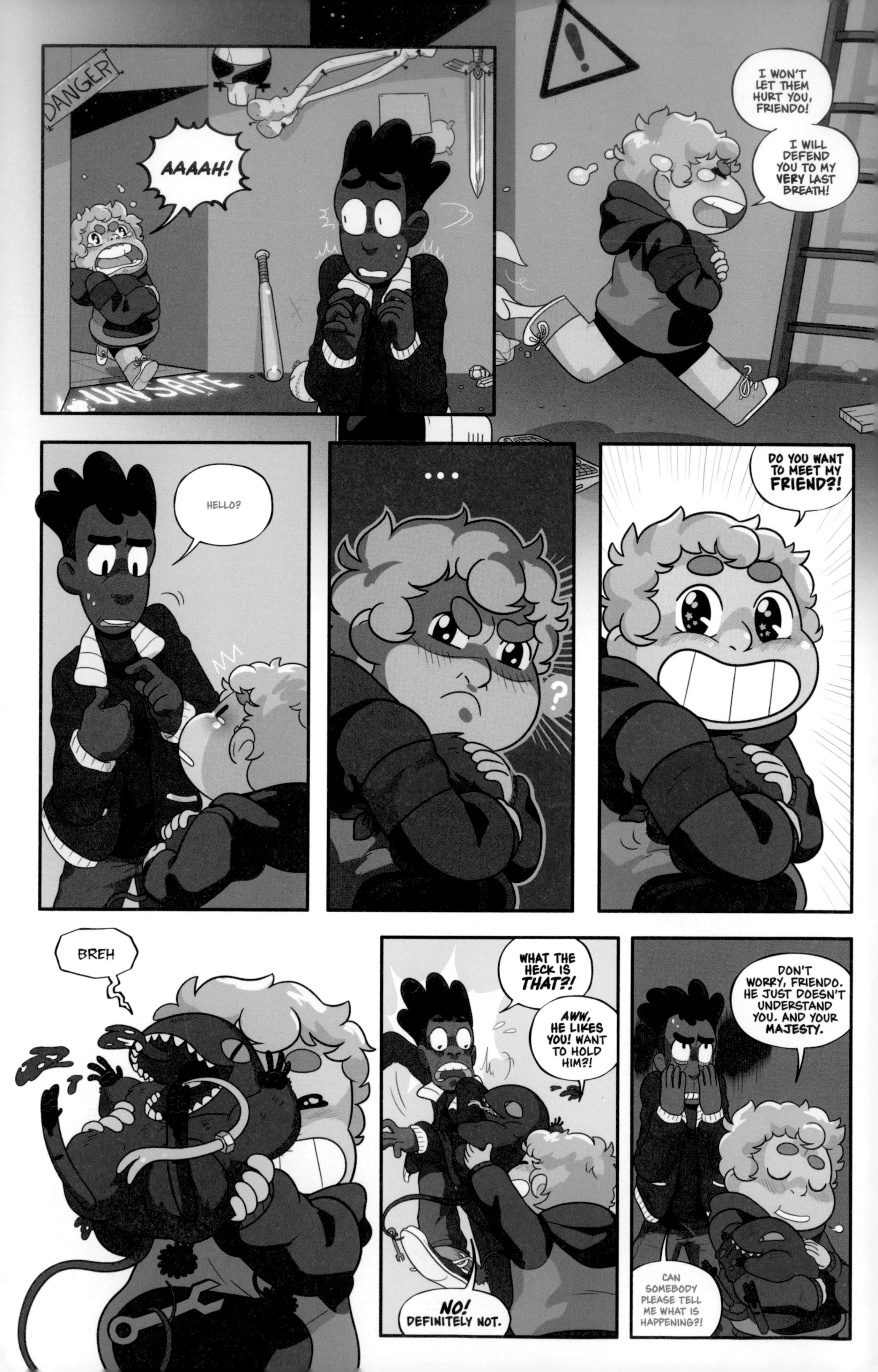
DANGER
AAAAH!
UNSAFE
I WON'T LET THEM HURT YOU, FRIENDO!
I WILL DEFEND YOU TO MY VERY LAST BREATH!
HELLO?
...
?
DO YOU WANT TO MEET MY FRIEND?!
BREH
WHAT THE HECK IS THAT?!
AWW, HE LIKES YOU! WANT TO HOLD HIM?!
NO! DEFINITELY NOT.
DON'T WORRY, FRIENDO. HE JUST DOESN'T UNDERSTAND YOU. AND YOUR MAJESTY.
CAN SOMEBODY PLEASE TELL ME WHAT IS HAPPENING?!

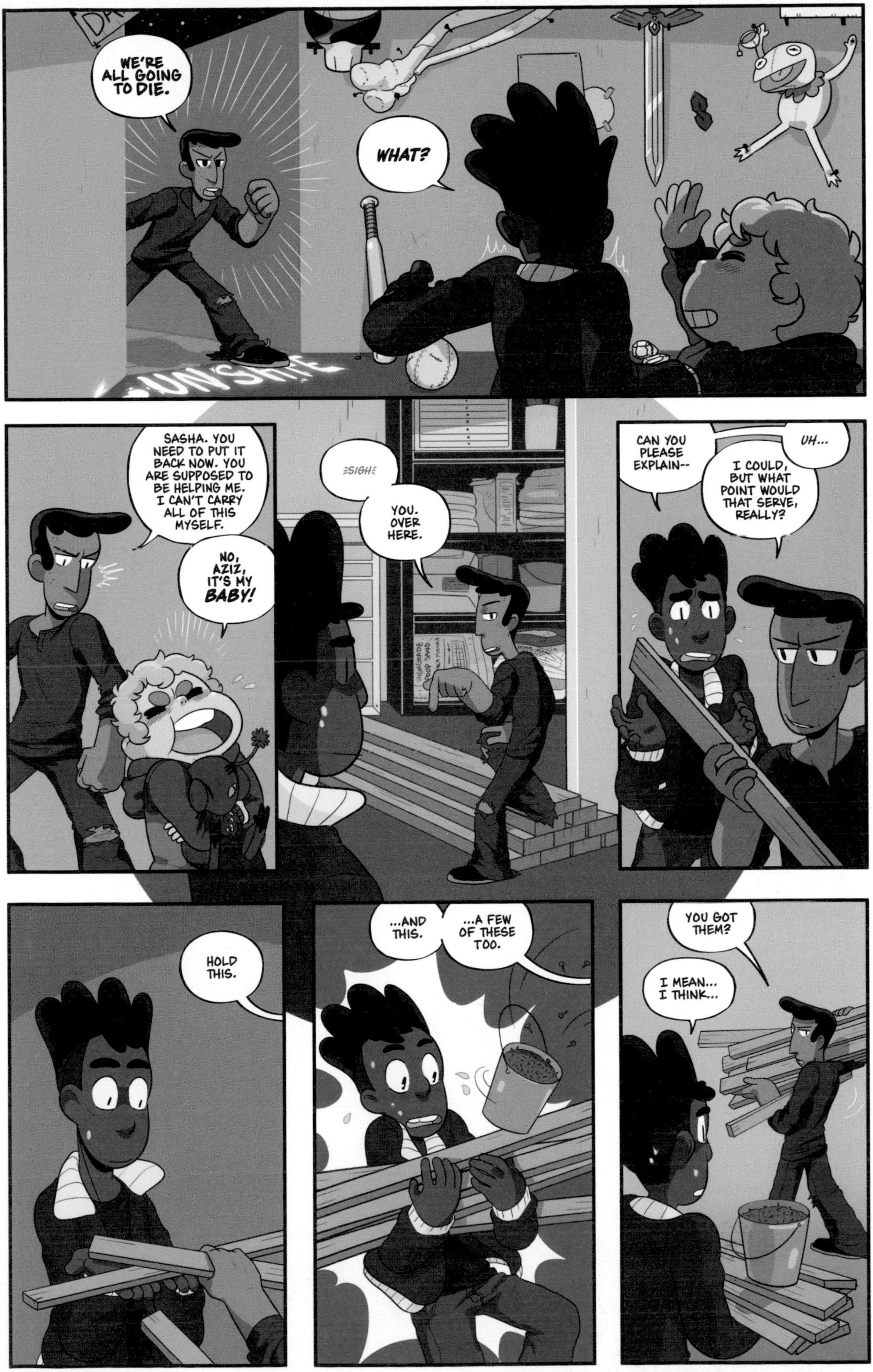
WE'RE ALL GOING TO DIE.
WHAT?
SASHA. YOU NEED TO PUT IT BACK NOW. YOU ARE SUPPOSED TO BE HELPING ME. I CAN'T CARRY ALL OF THIS MYSELF.
NO, AZIZ, IT'S MY BABY!
SIGH
YOU. OVER HERE.
HIGHGRADE POOP SAND
CAN YOU PLEASE EXPLAIN--
UH...
I COULD, BUT WHAT POINT WOULD THAT SERVE, REALLY?
HOLD THIS.
...AND THIS.
...A FEW OF THESE TOO.
YOU GOT THEM?
I MEAN... I THINK...

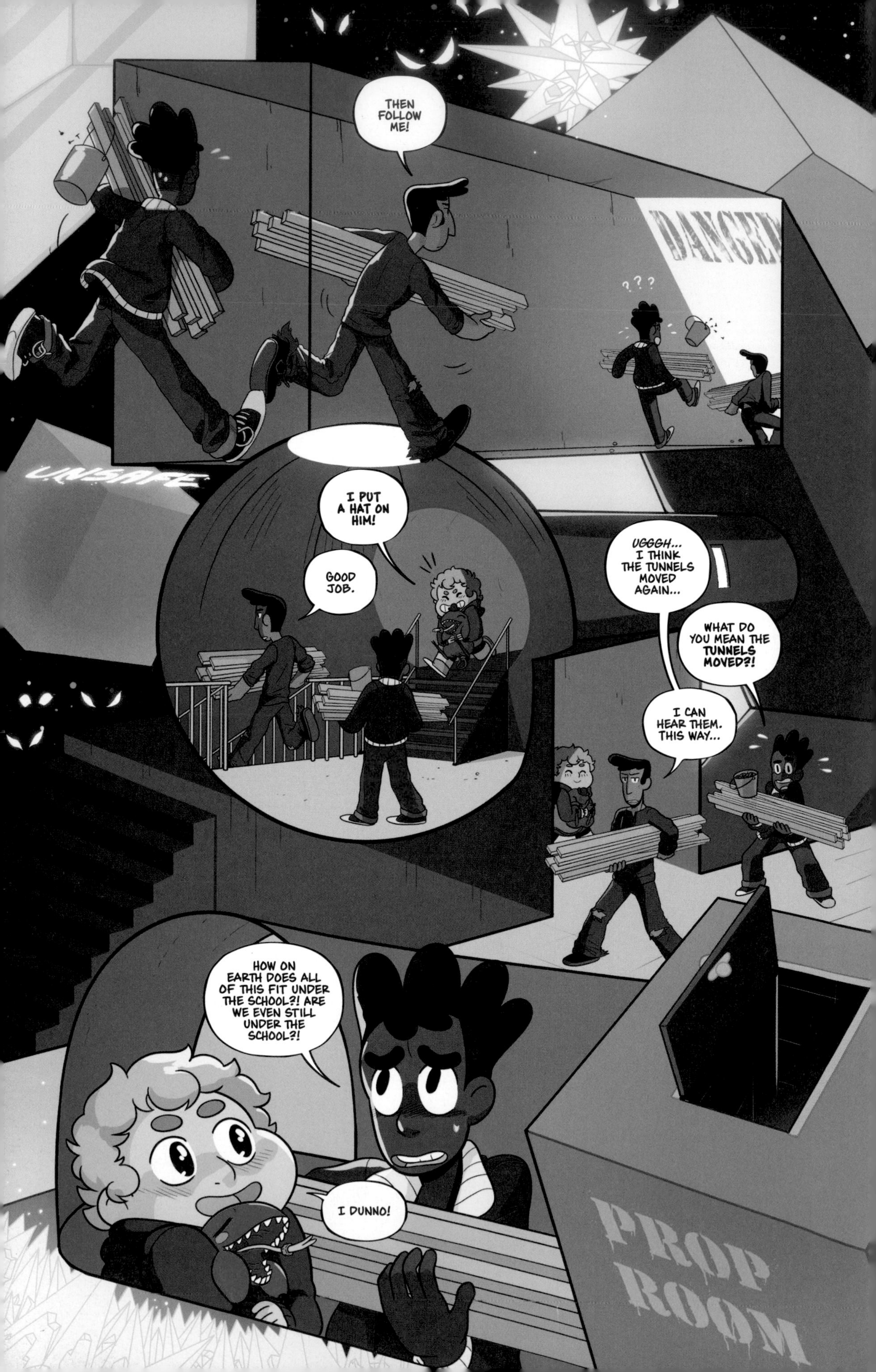
THEN FOLLOW ME!
DANGER
???
UNSAFE
I PUT A HAT ON HIM!
GOOD JOB.
UGGGH... I THINK THE TUNNELS MOVED AGAIN...
WHAT DO YOU MEAN THE TUNNELS MOVED?!
I CAN HEAR THEM. THIS WAY...
HOW ON EARTH DOES ALL OF THIS FIT UNDER THE SCHOOL?! ARE WE EVEN STILL UNDER THE SCHOOL?!
I DUNNO!
PROP ROOM

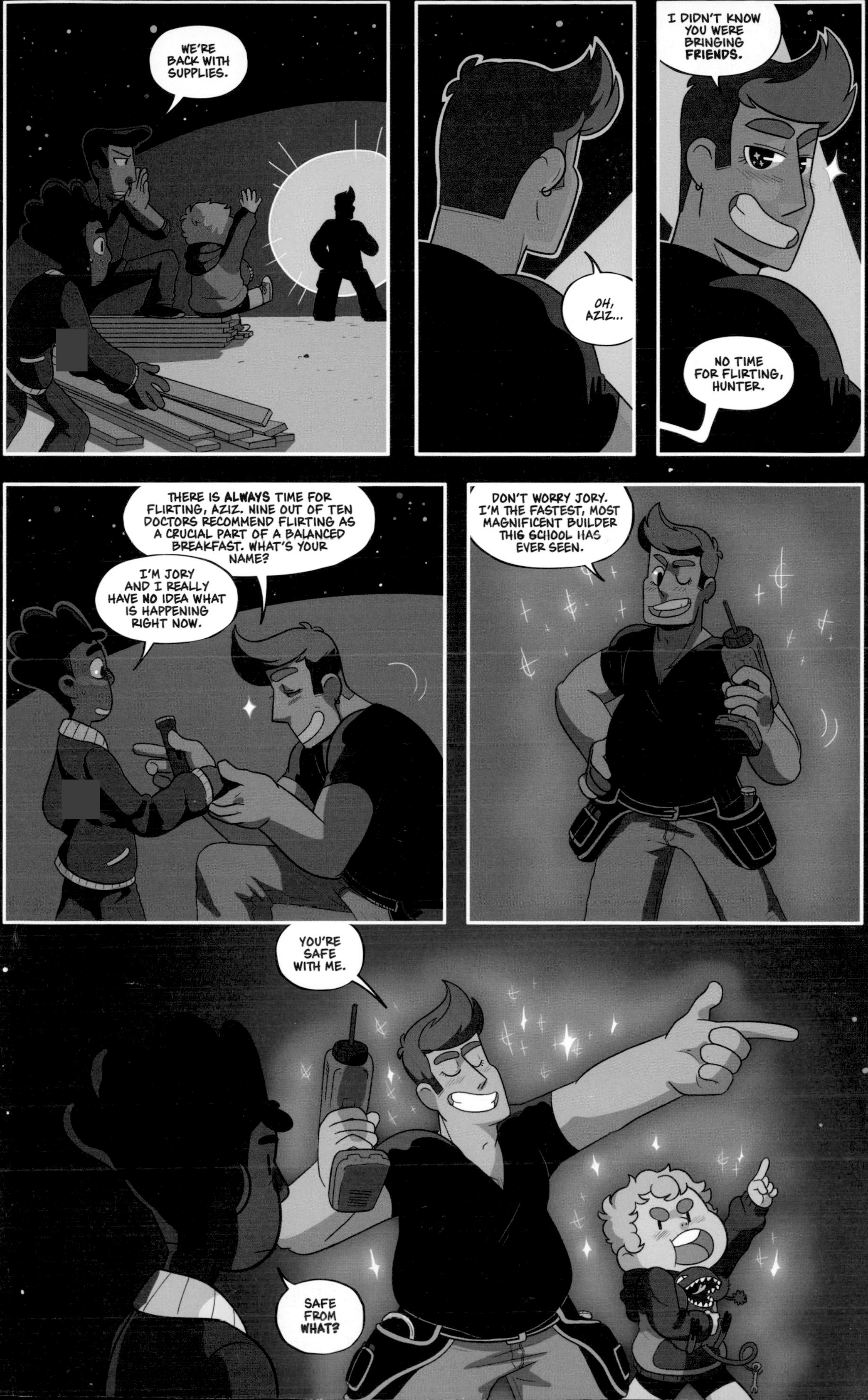
WE'RE BACK WITH SUPPLIES.
OH, AZIZ...
I DIDN'T KNOW YOU WERE BRINGING FRIENDS.
NO TIME FOR FLIRTING, HUNTER.
THERE IS ALWAYS TIME FOR FLIRTING, AZIZ. NINE OUT OF TEN DOCTORS RECOMMEND FLIRTING AS A CRUCIAL PART OF A BALANCED BREAKFAST. WHAT'S YOUR NAME?
I'M JORY AND I REALLY HAVE NO IDEA WHAT IS HAPPENING RIGHT NOW.
DON'T WORRY JORY. I'M THE FASTEST, MOST MAGNIFICENT BUILDER THIS SCHOOL HAS EVER SEEN.
YOU'RE SAFE WITH ME.
SAFE FROM WHAT?

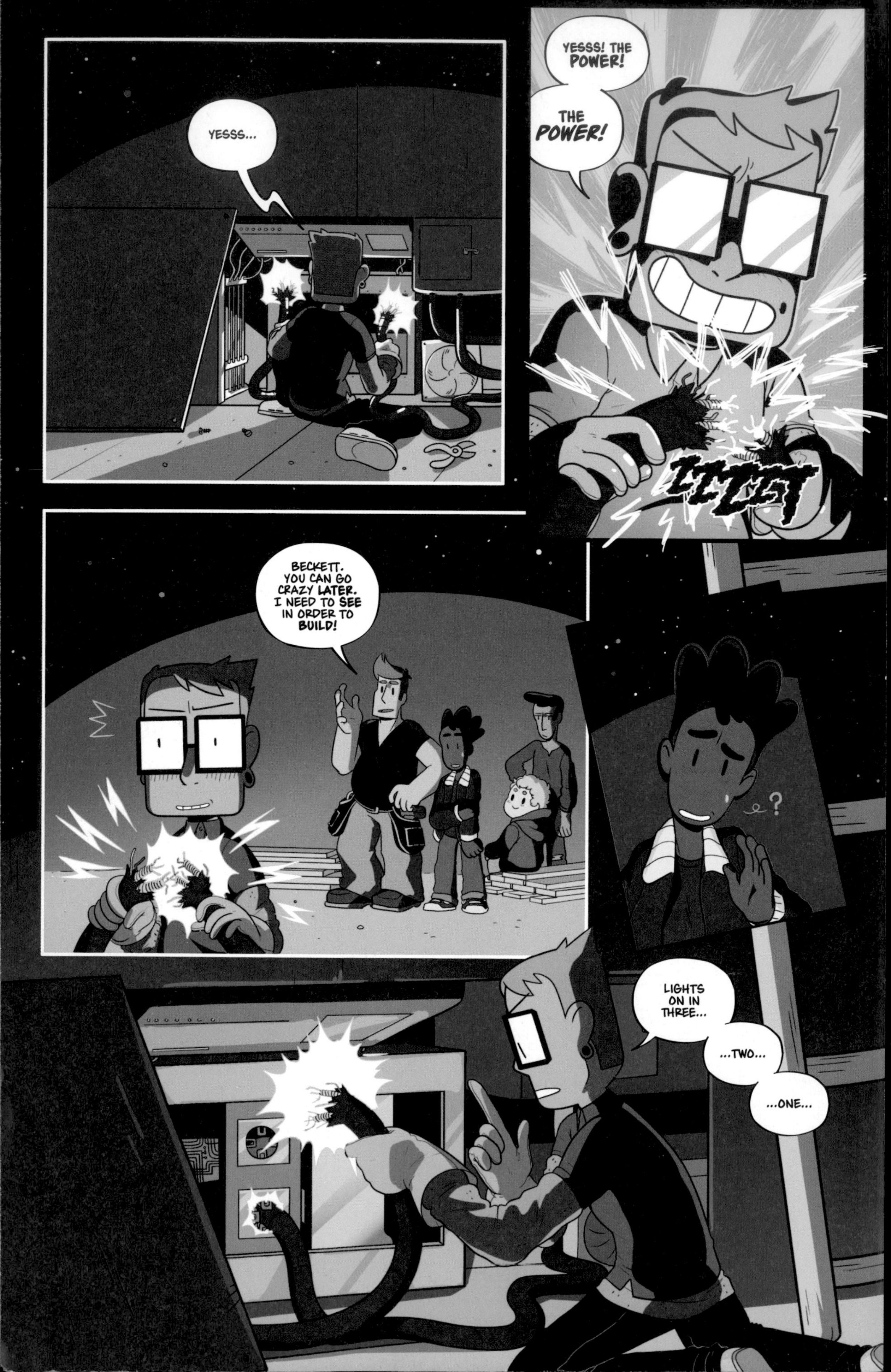

YESSS...
YESSS! THE POWER!
THE POWER!
ZZZZT
BECKETT. YOU CAN GO CRAZY LATER. I NEED TO SEE IN ORDER TO BUILD!
?
LIGHTS ON IN THREE...
...TWO...
...ONE...

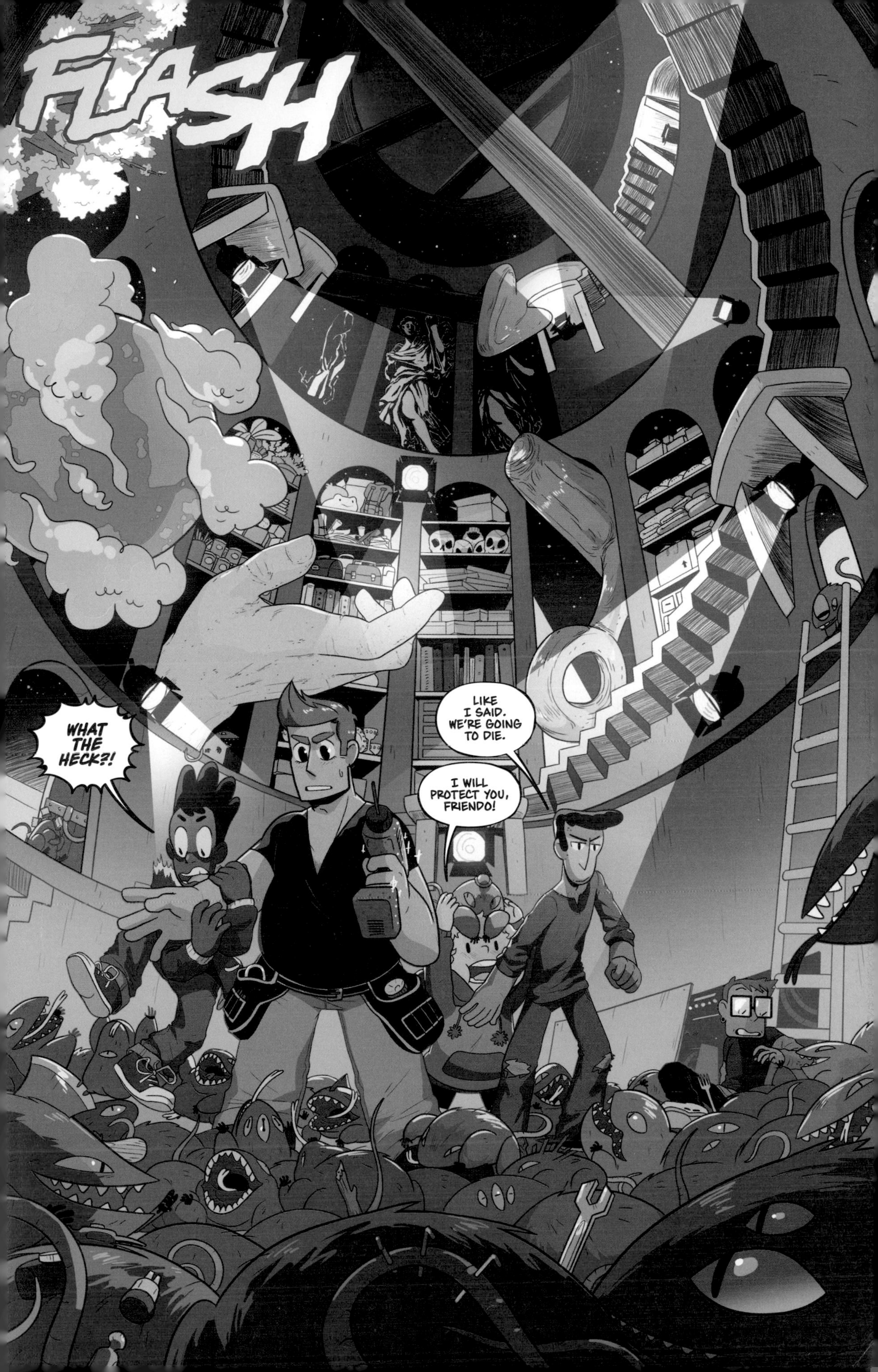
FLASH
WHAT THE HECK?!
LIKE I SAID. WE'RE GOING TO DIE.
I WILL PROTECT YOU, FRIENDO!

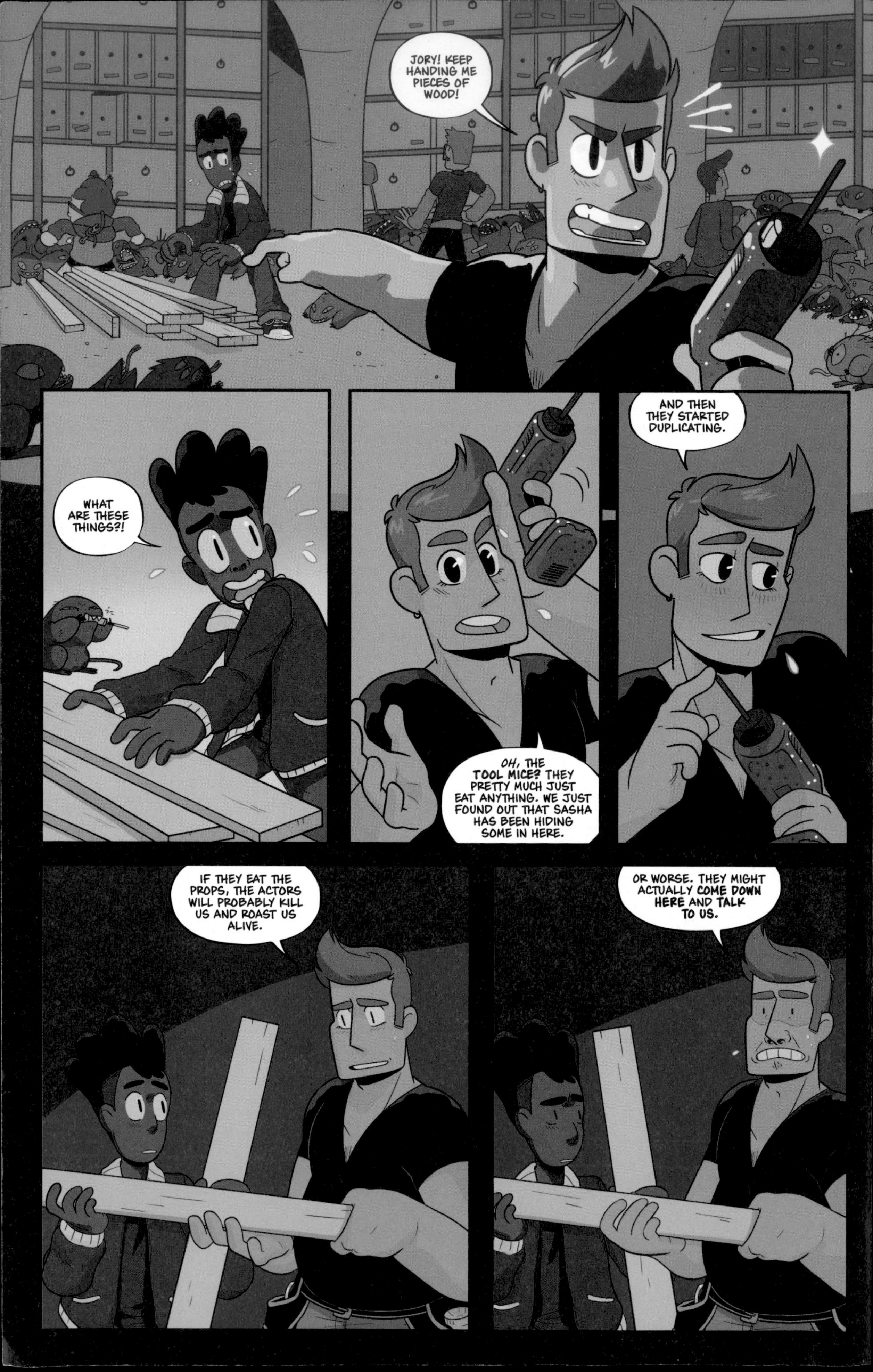
JORY! KEEP HANDING ME PIECES OF WOOD!
WHAT ARE THESE THINGS?!
OH, THE TOOL MICE? THEY PRETTY MUCH JUST EAT ANYTHING. WE JUST FOUND OUT THAT SASHA HAS BEEN HIDING SOME IN HERE.
AND THEN THEY STARTED DUPLICATING.
IF THEY EAT THE PROPS, THE ACTORS WILL PROBABLY KILL US AND ROAST US ALIVE.
OR WORSE. THEY MIGHT ACTUALLY COME DOWN HERE AND TALK TO US.

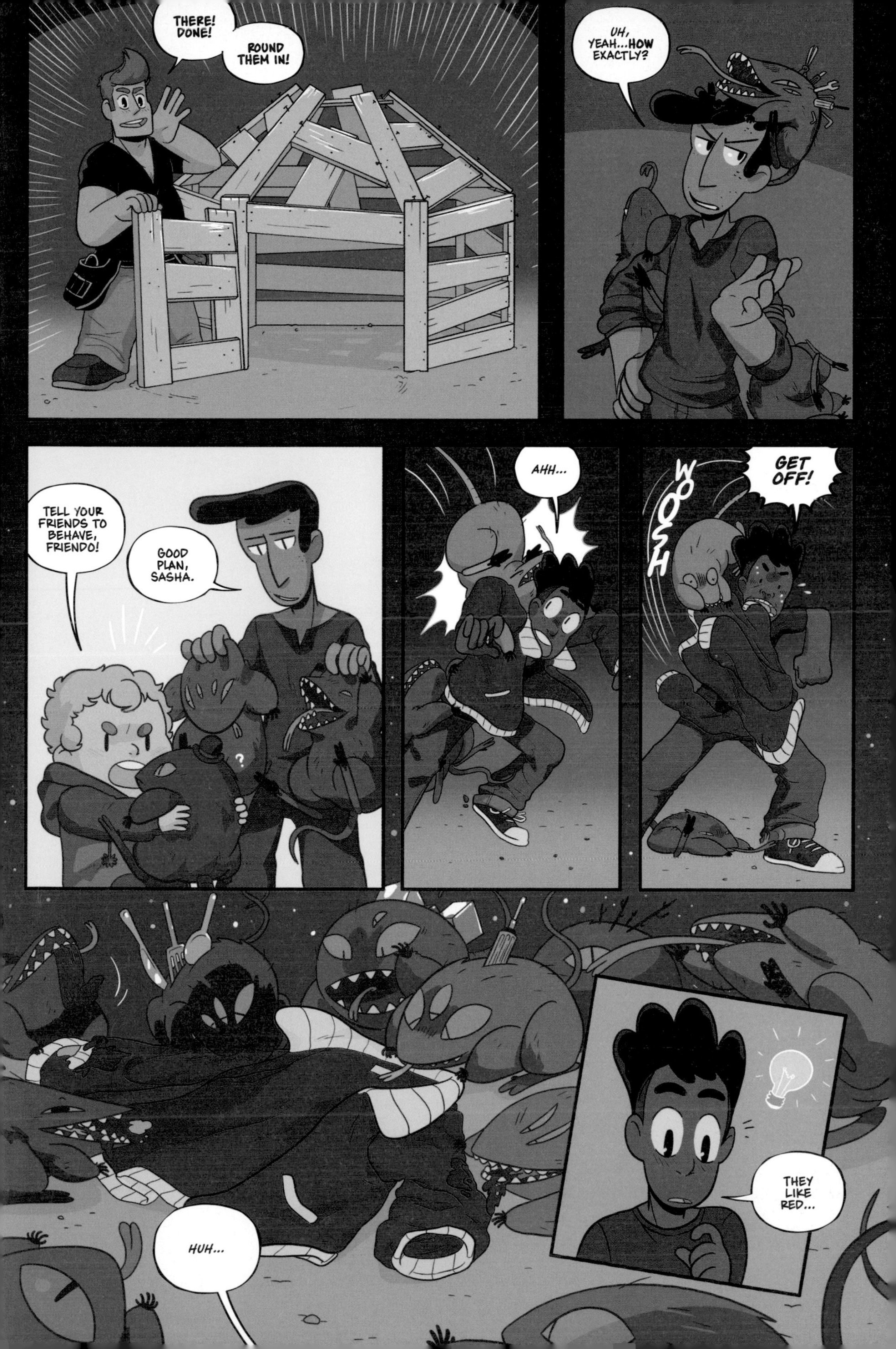
THERE! DONE!
ROUND THEM IN!
UH, YEAH...HOW EXACTLY?
TELL YOUR FRIENDS TO BEHAVE, FRIENDO!
GOOD PLAN, SASHA.
AHH...
WOOSH
GET OFF!
HUH...
THEY LIKE RED...

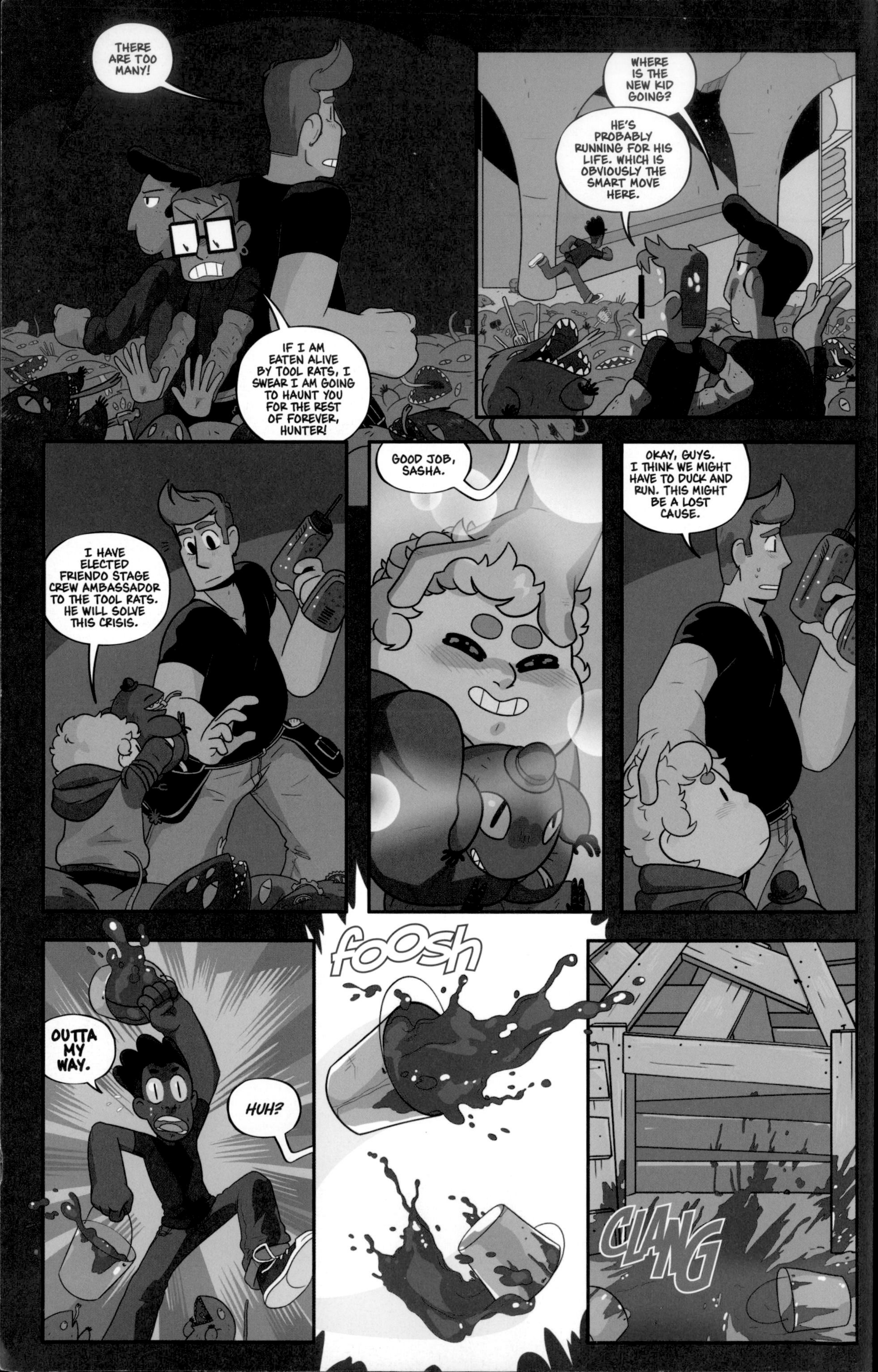
THERE ARE TOO MANY!
IF I AM EATEN ALIVE BY TOOL RATS, I SWEAR I AM GOING TO HAUNT YOU FOR THE REST OF FOREVER, HUNTER!
WHERE IS THE NEW KID GOING?
HE'S PROBABLY RUNNING FOR HIS LIFE. WHICH IS OBVIOUSLY THE SMART MOVE HERE.
I HAVE ELECTED FRIENDO STAGE CREW AMBASSADOR TO THE TOOL RATS. HE WILL SOLVE THIS CRISIS.
GOOD JOB, SASHA.
OKAY, GUYS. I THINK WE MIGHT HAVE TO DUCK AND RUN. THIS MIGHT BE A LOST CAUSE.
OUTTA MY WAY.
HUH?
fooSH
CLANG

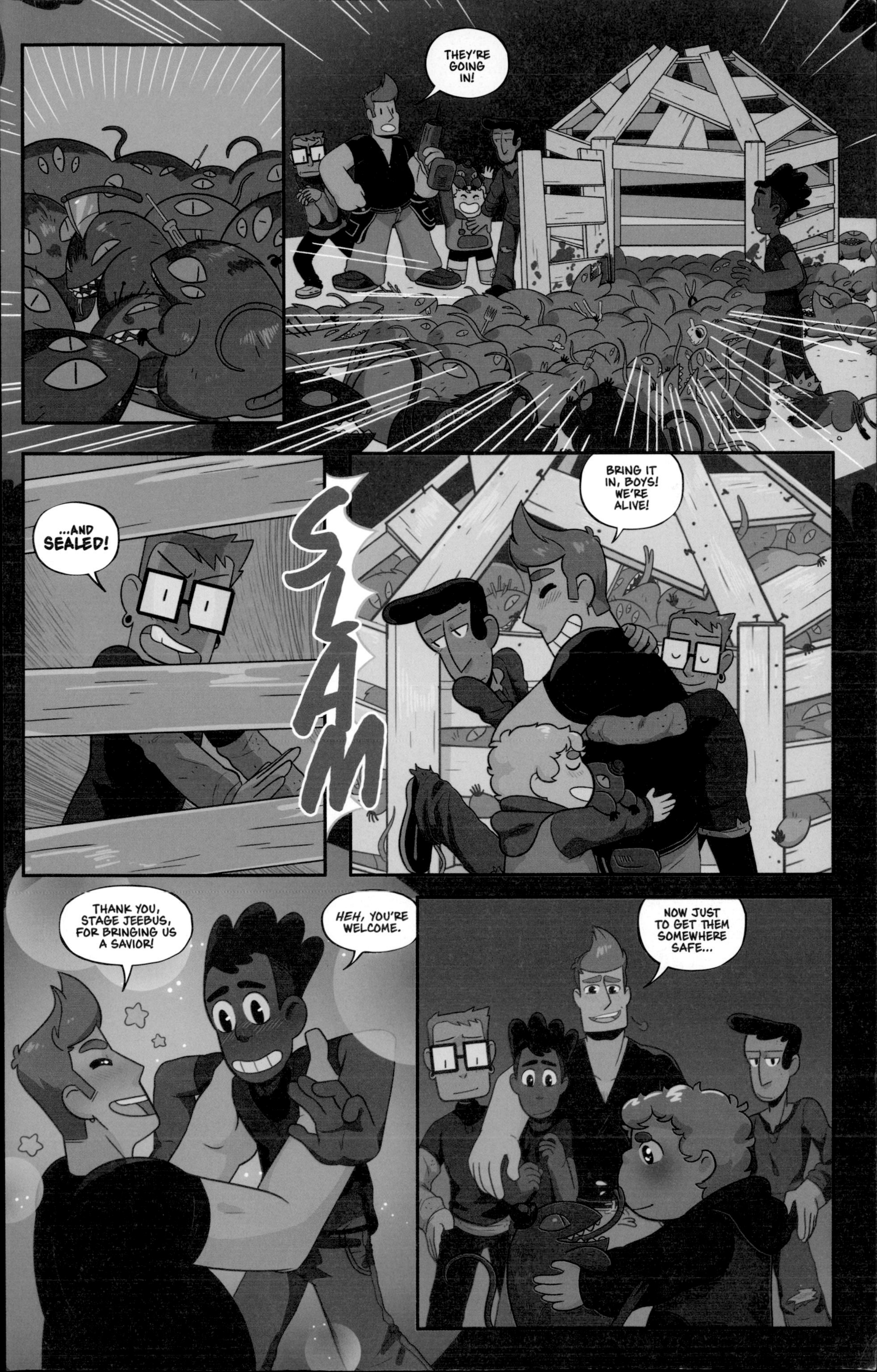
THEY'RE GOING IN!
...AND SEALED!
SLAM
BRING IT IN, BOYS! WE'RE ALIVE!
THANK YOU, STAGE JEEBUS, FOR BRINGING US A SAVIOR!
HEH, YOU'RE WELCOME.
NOW JUST TO GET THEM SOMEWHERE SAFE...

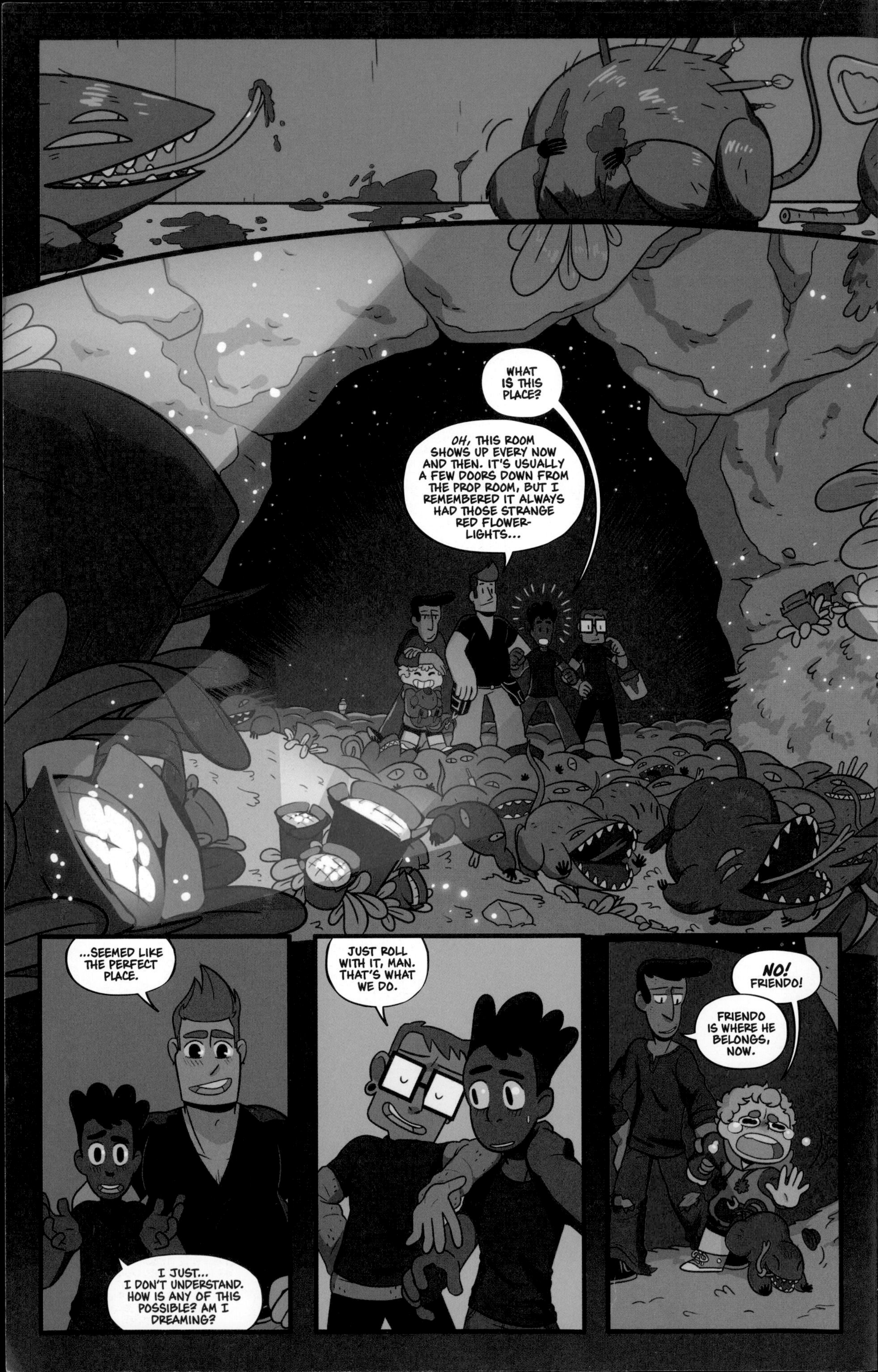
WHAT IS THIS PLACE?
OH, THIS ROOM SHOWS UP EVERY NOW AND THEN. IT'S USUALLY A FEW DOORS DOWN FROM THE PROP ROOM, BUT I REMEMBERED IT ALWAYS HAD THOSE STRANGE RED FLOWER-LIGHTS...
...SEEMED LIKE THE PERFECT PLACE.
I JUST... I DON'T UNDERSTAND. HOW IS ANY OF THIS POSSIBLE? AM I DREAMING?
JUST ROLL WITH IT, MAN. THAT'S WHAT WE DO.
NO! FRIENDO!
FRIENDO IS WHERE HE BELONGS, NOW.

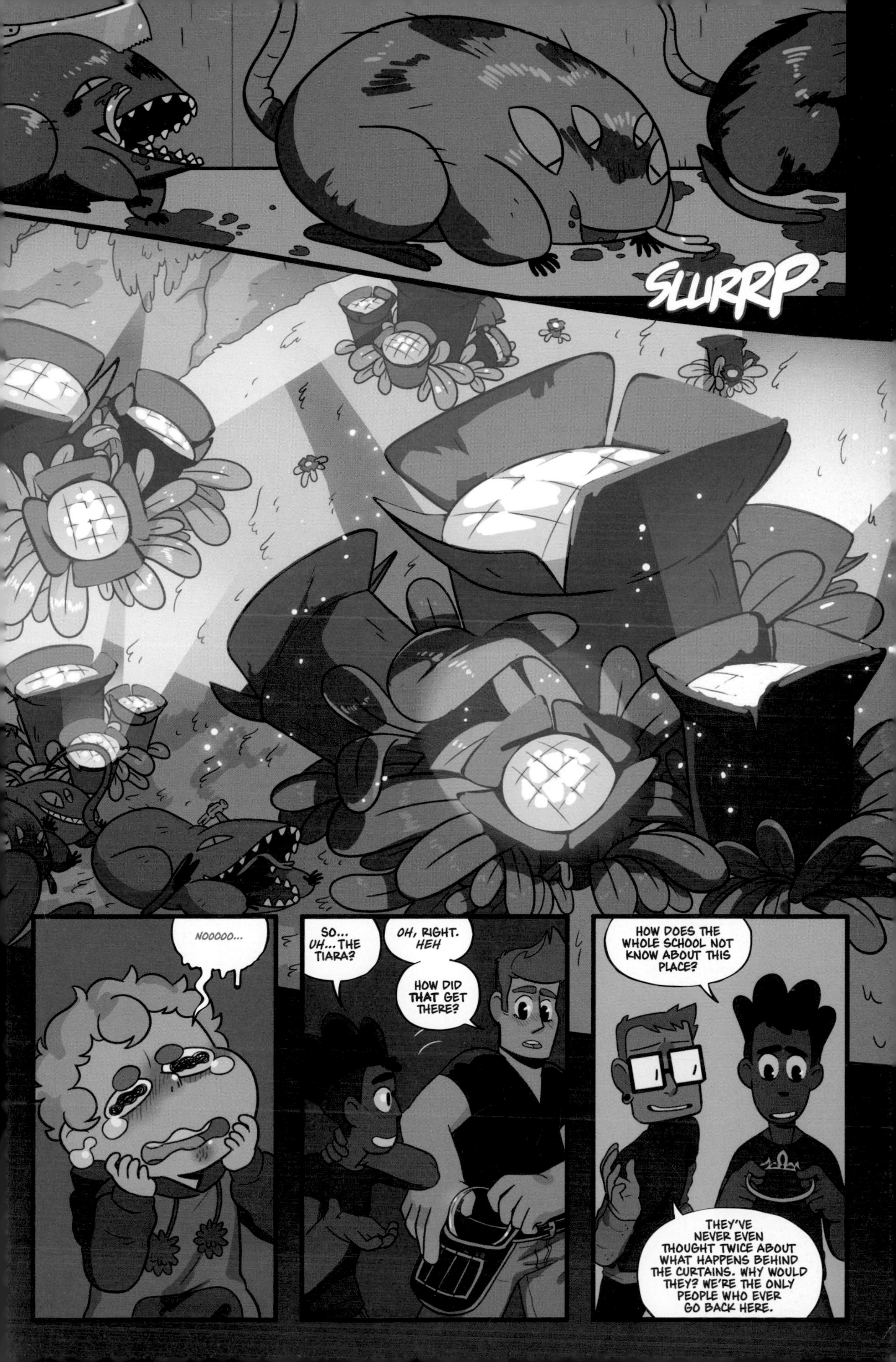

SLURRP
NOOOOO...
SO... UH... THE TIARA?
OH, RIGHT. HEH
HOW DID THAT GET THERE?
HOW DOES THE WHOLE SCHOOL NOT KNOW ABOUT THIS PLACE?
THEY'VE NEVER EVEN THOUGHT TWICE ABOUT WHAT HAPPENS BEHIND THE CURTAINS. WHY WOULD THEY? WE'RE THE ONLY PEOPLE WHO EVER GO BACK HERE.

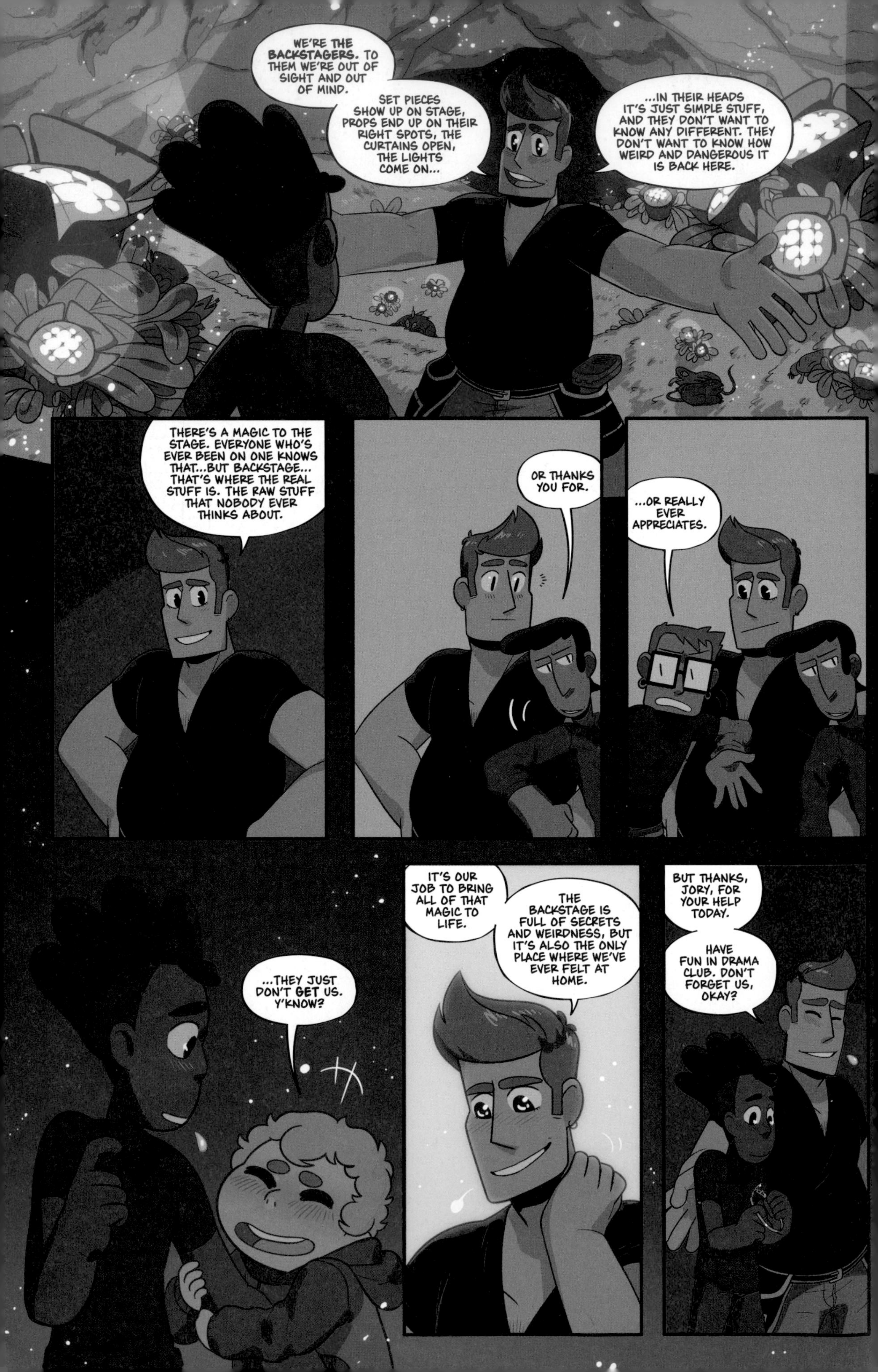

WE'RE THE BACKSTAGERS. TO THEM WE'RE OUT OF SIGHT AND OUT OF MIND.
SET PIECES SHOW UP ON STAGE, PROPS END UP ON THEIR RIGHT SPOTS, THE CURTAINS OPEN, THE LIGHTS COME ON...
...IN THEIR HEADS IT'S JUST SIMPLE STUFF, AND THEY DON'T WANT TO KNOW ANY DIFFERENT. THEY DON'T WANT TO KNOW HOW WEIRD AND DANGEROUS IT IS BACK HERE.
THERE'S A MAGIC TO THE STAGE. EVERYONE WHO'S EVER BEEN ON ONE KNOWS THAT...BUT BACKSTAGE... THAT'S WHERE THE REAL STUFF IS. THE RAW STUFF THAT NOBODY EVER THINKS ABOUT.
OR THANKS YOU FOR.
...OR REALLY EVER APPRECIATES.
...THEY JUST DON'T GET US. Y'KNOW?
IT'S OUR JOB TO BRING ALL OF THAT MAGIC TO LIFE.
THE BACKSTAGE IS FULL OF SECRETS AND WEIRDNESS, BUT IT'S ALSO THE ONLY PLACE WHERE WE'VE EVER FELT AT HOME.
BUT THANKS, JORY, FOR YOUR HELP TODAY.
HAVE FUN IN DRAMA CLUB. DON'T FORGET US, OKAY?

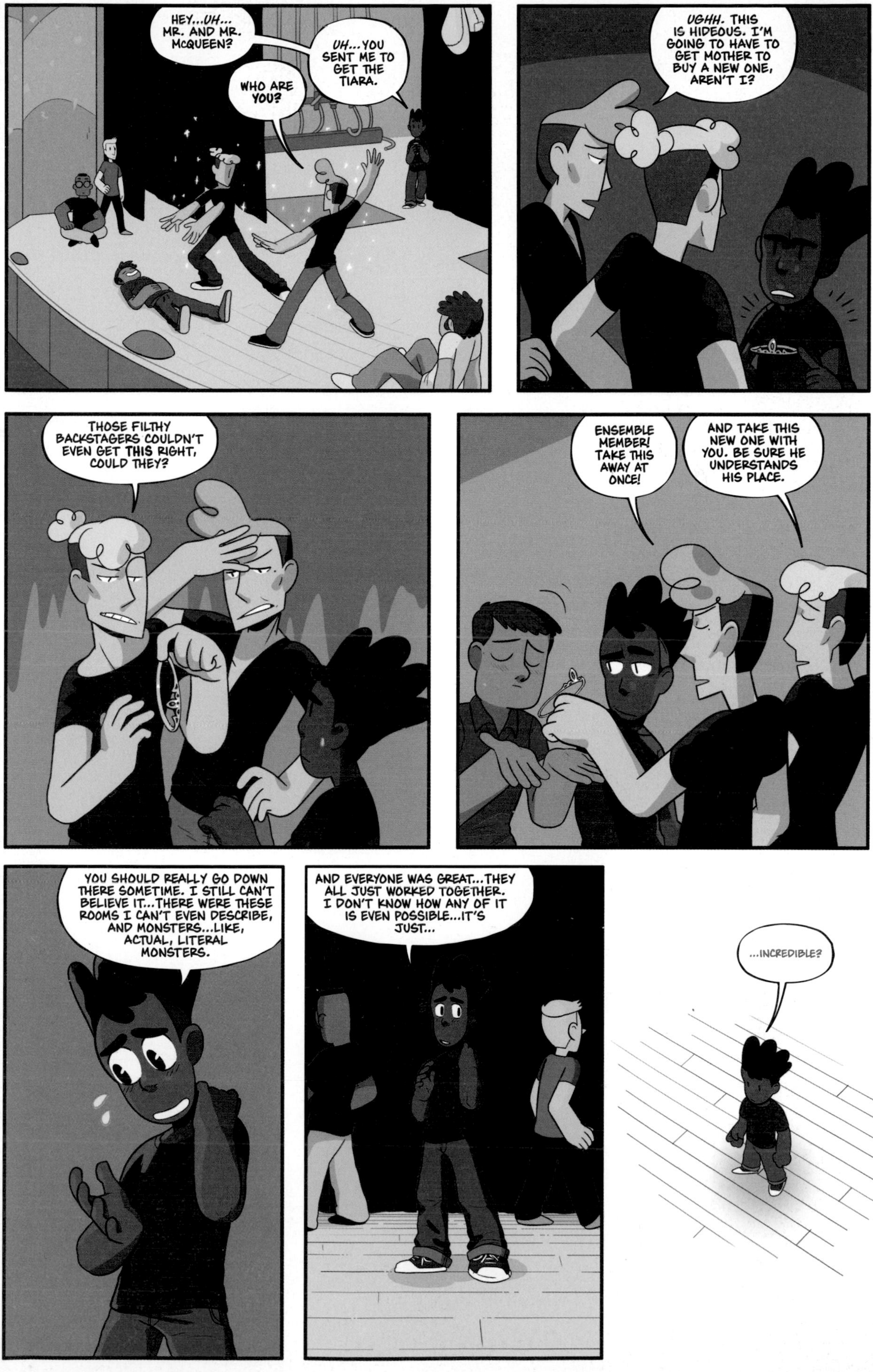
HEY...UH... MR. AND MR. MCQUEEN?
WHO ARE YOU?
UH...YOU SENT ME TO GET THE TIARA.
UGHH. THIS IS HIDEOUS. I'M GOING TO HAVE TO GET MOTHER TO BUY A NEW ONE, AREN'T I?
THOSE FILTHY BACKSTAGERS COULDN'T EVEN GET THIS RIGHT, COULD THEY?
ENSEMBLE MEMBER! TAKE THIS AWAY AT ONCE!
AND TAKE THIS NEW ONE WITH YOU. BE SURE HE UNDERSTANDS HIS PLACE.
YOU SHOULD REALLY GO DOWN THERE SOMETIME. I STILL CAN'T BELIEVE IT...THERE WERE THESE ROOMS I CAN'T EVEN DESCRIBE, AND MONSTERS...LIKE, ACTUAL, LITERAL MONSTERS.
AND EVERYONE WAS GREAT...THEY ALL JUST WORKED TOGETHER. I DON'T KNOW HOW ANY OF IT IS EVEN POSSIBLE...IT'S JUST...
...INCREDIBLE?

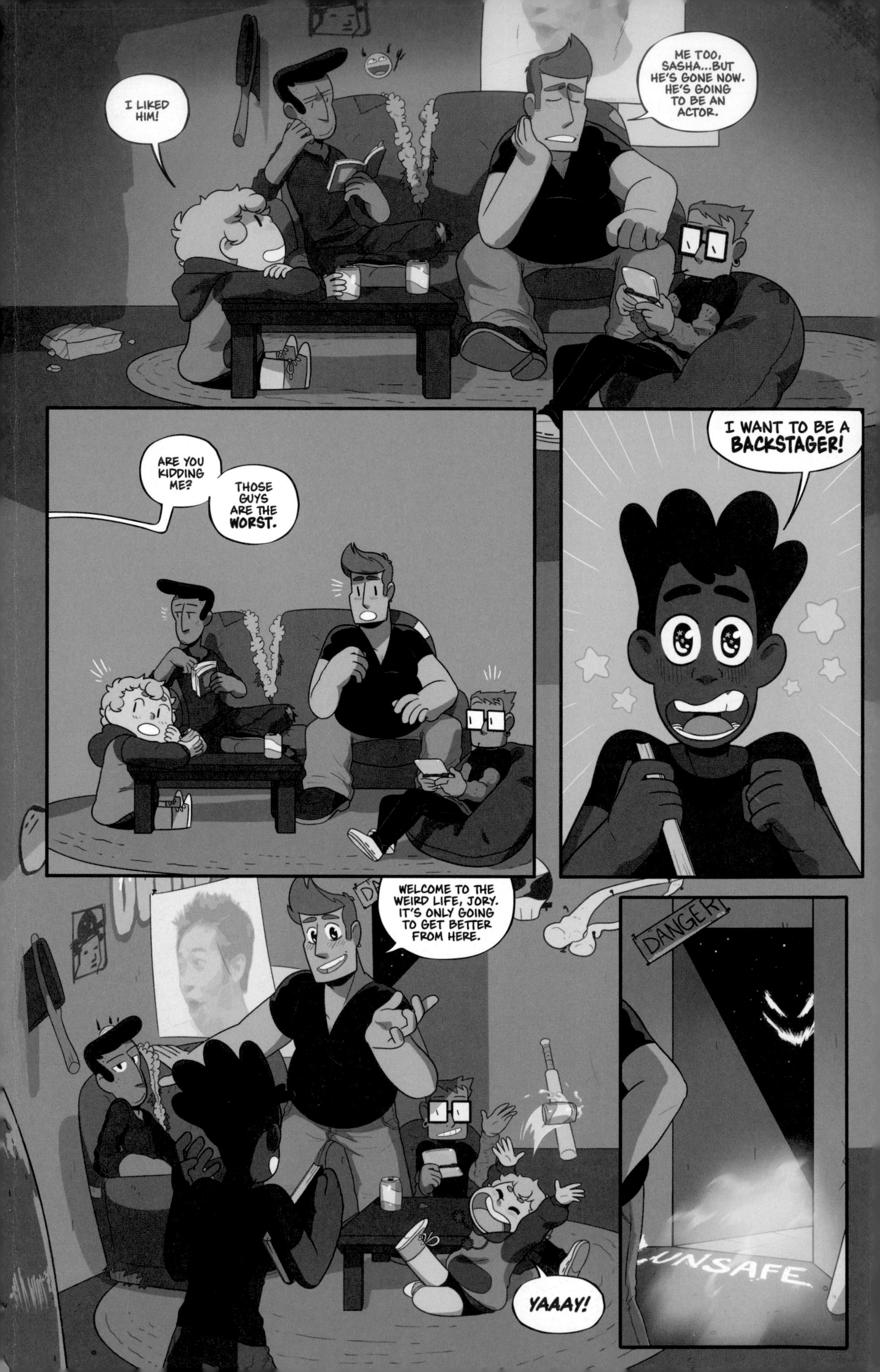

I LIKED HIM!
ME TOO, SASHA...BUT HE'S GONE NOW. HE'S GOING TO BE AN ACTOR.
ARE YOU KIDDING ME?
THOSE GUYS ARE THE WORST.
I WANT TO BE A BACKSTAGER!
WELCOME TO THE WEIRD LIFE, JORY. IT'S ONLY GOING TO GET BETTER FROM HERE.
YAAAY!
DANGER
UNSAFE

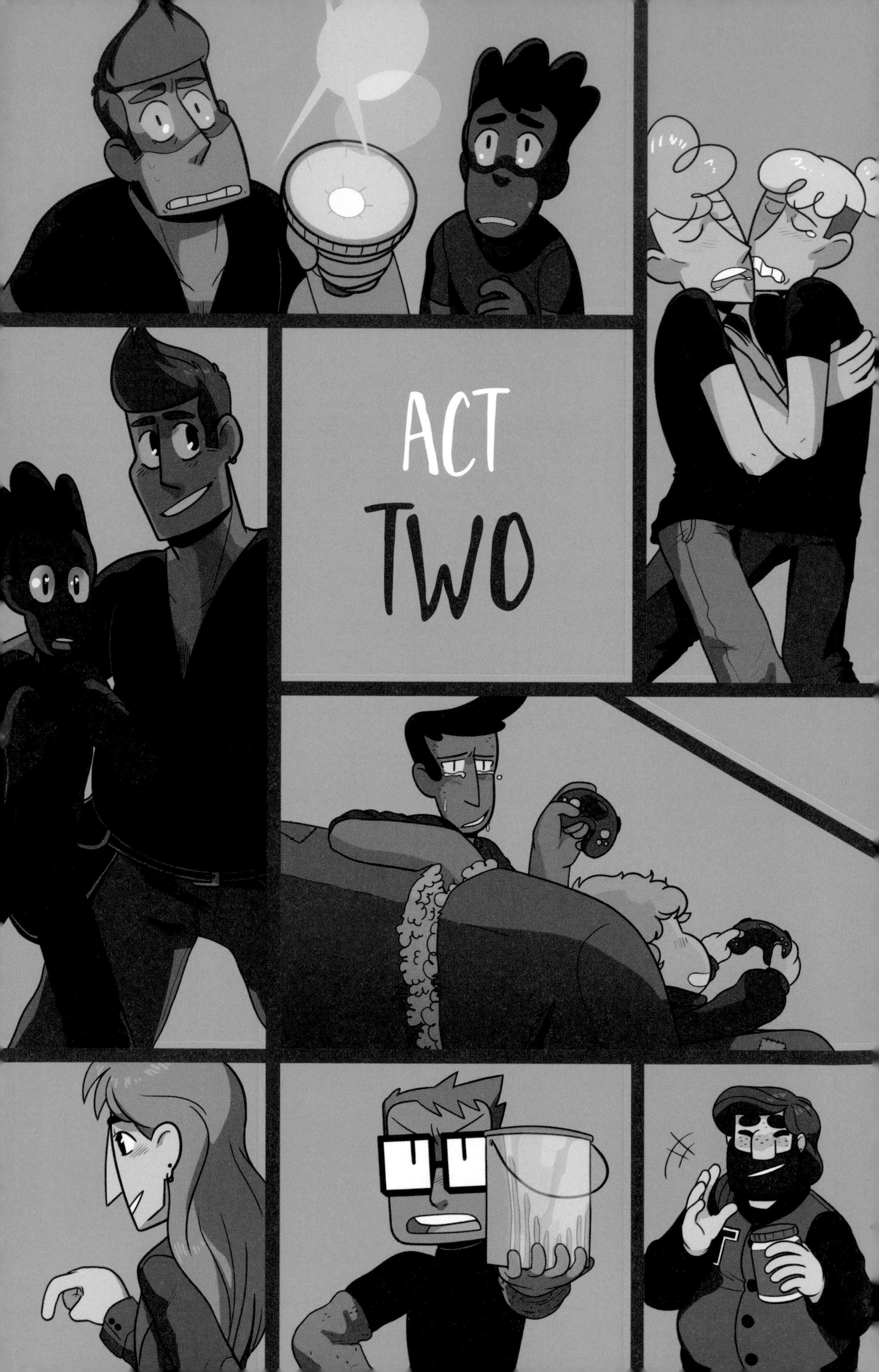
ACT
TWO

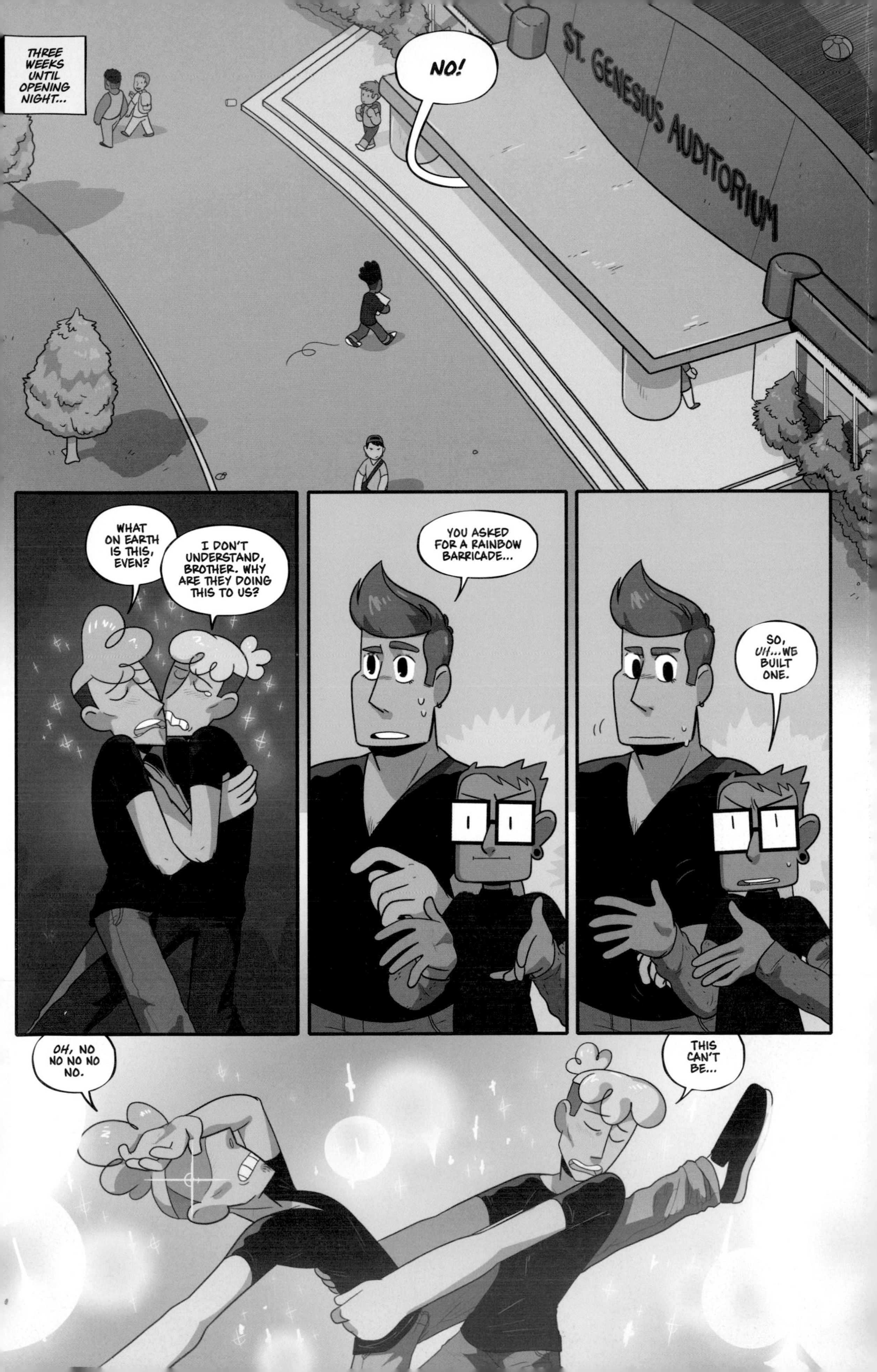
THREE WEEKS UNTIL OPENING NIGHT...
ST. GENESIUS AUDITORIUM
NO!
WHAT ON EARTH IS THIS, EVEN?
I DON'T UNDERSTAND, BROTHER. WHY ARE THEY DOING THIS TO US?
YOU ASKED FOR A RAINBOW BARRICADE...
SO, UH...WE BUILT ONE.
OH, NO NO NO NO NO.
THIS CAN'T BE...

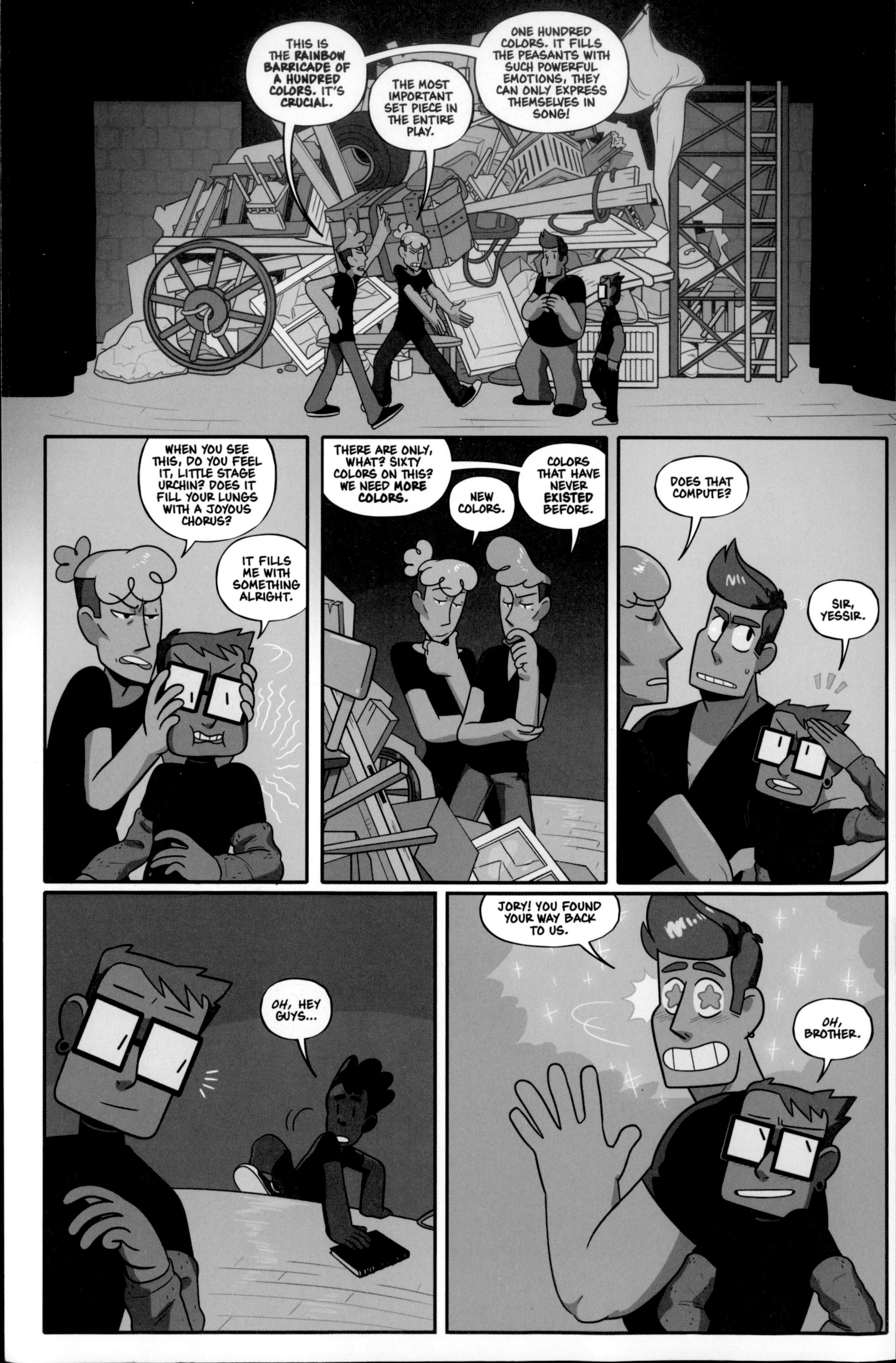
THIS IS THE RAINBOW BARRICADE OF A HUNDRED COLORS. IT'S CRUCIAL.
THE MOST IMPORTANT SET PIECE IN THE ENTIRE PLAY.
ONE HUNDRED COLORS. IT FILLS THE PEASANTS WITH SUCH POWERFUL EMOTIONS, THEY CAN ONLY EXPRESS THEMSELVES IN SONG!
WHEN YOU SEE THIS, DO YOU FEEL IT, LITTLE STAGE URCHIN? DOES IT FILL YOUR LUNGS WITH A JOYOUS CHORUS?
IT FILLS ME WITH SOMETHING ALRIGHT.
THERE ARE ONLY, WHAT? SIXTY COLORS ON THIS? WE NEED MORE COLORS.
NEW COLORS.
COLORS THAT HAVE NEVER EXISTED BEFORE.
DOES THAT COMPUTE?
SIR, YESSIR.
OH, HEY GUYS...
JORY! YOU FOUND YOUR WAY BACK TO US.
OH, BROTHER.

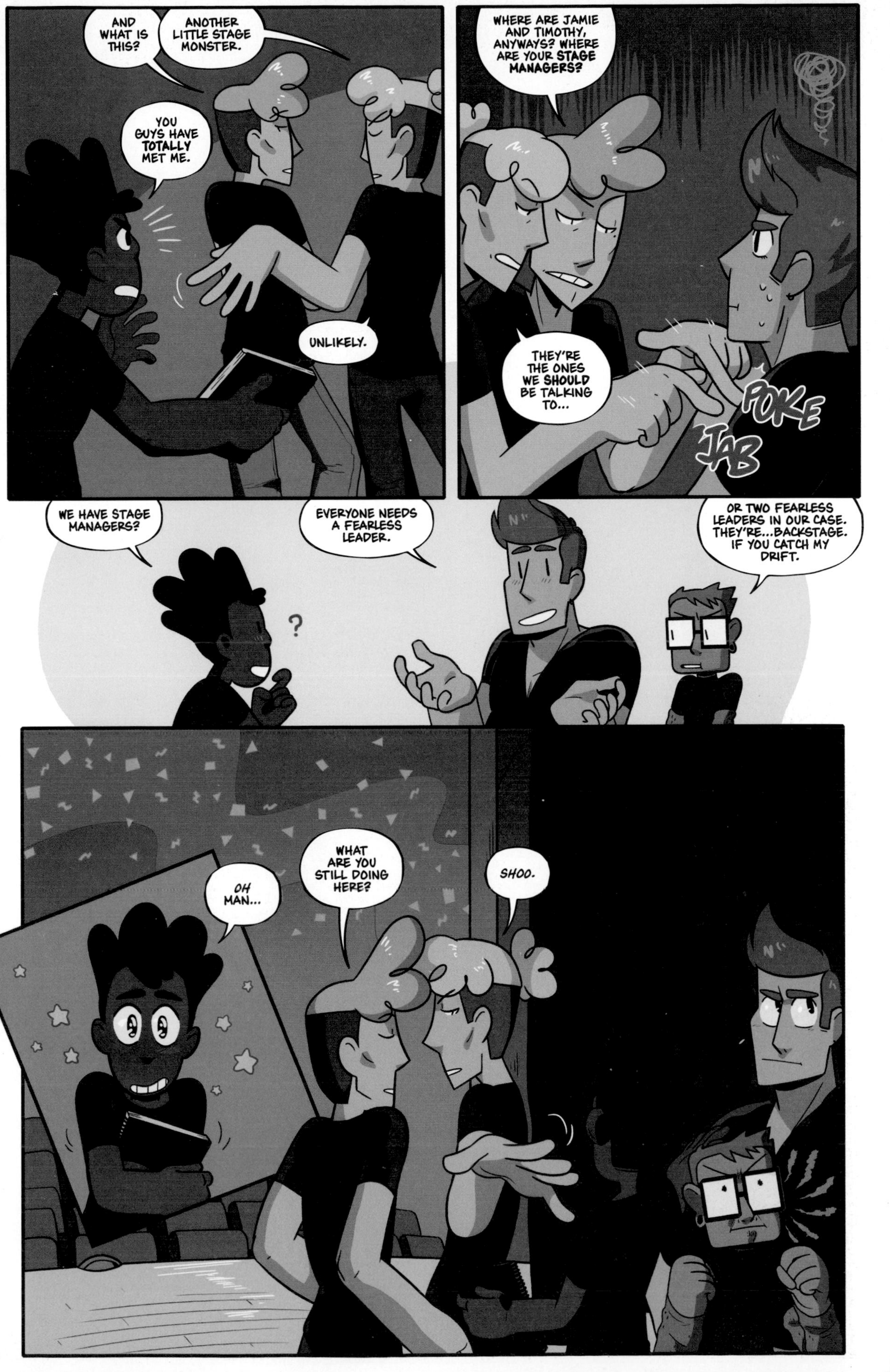
AND WHAT IS THIS?
ANOTHER LITTLE STAGE MONSTER.
YOU GUYS HAVE TOTALLY MET ME.
UNLIKELY.
WHERE ARE JAMIE AND TIMOTHY, ANYWAYS? WHERE ARE YOUR STAGE MANAGERS?
THEY'RE THE ONES WE SHOULD BE TALKING TO...
POKE
JAB
WE HAVE STAGE MANAGERS?
EVERYONE NEEDS A FEARLESS LEADER.
OR TWO FEARLESS LEADERS IN OUR CASE. THEY'RE...BACKSTAGE. IF YOU CATCH MY DRIFT.
?
OH MAN...
WHAT ARE YOU STILL DOING HERE?
SHOO.

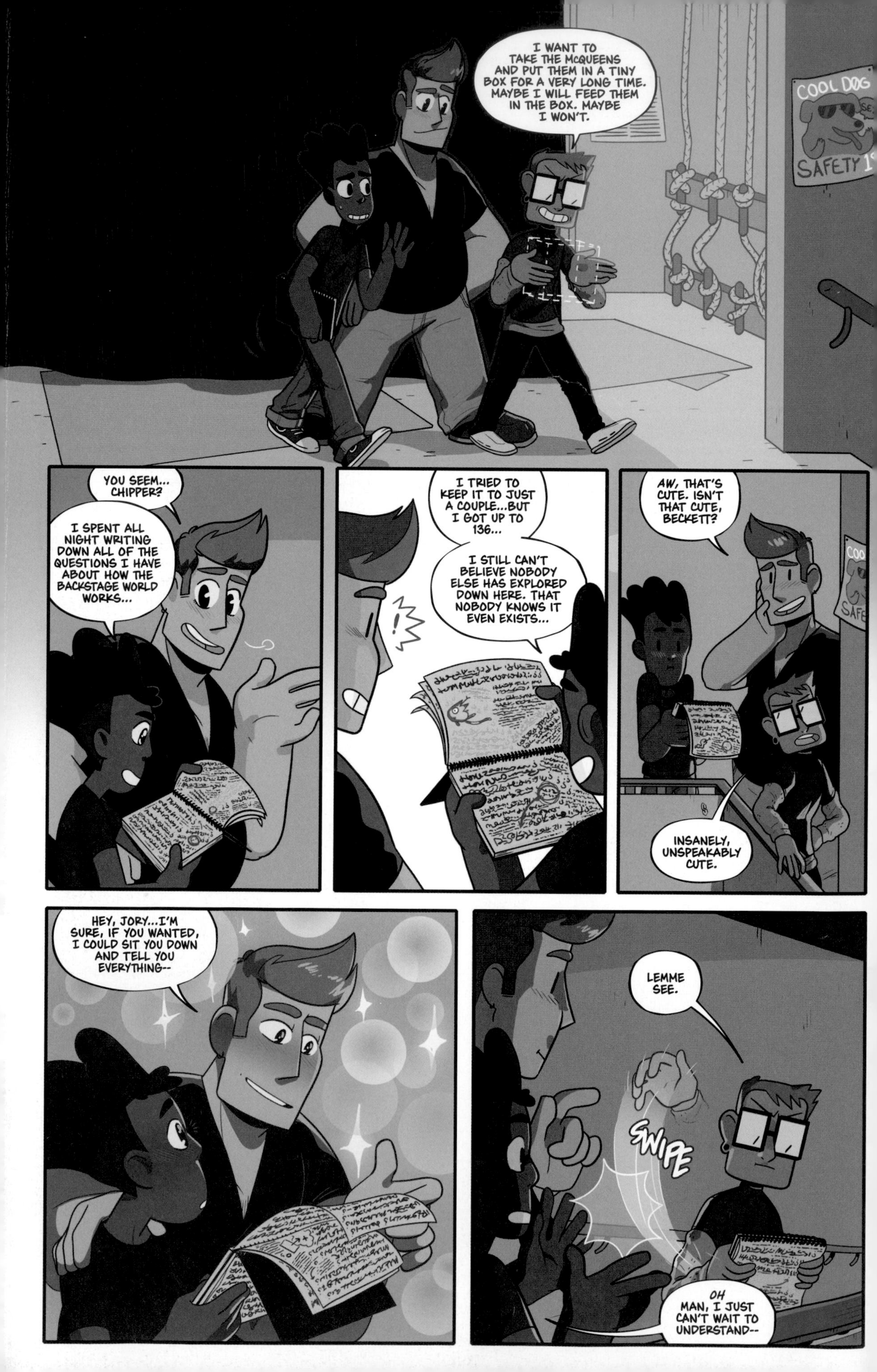
I WANT TO TAKE THE McQUEENS AND PUT THEM IN A TINY BOX FOR A VERY LONG TIME. MAYBE I WILL FEED THEM IN THE BOX. MAYBE I WON'T.
COOL DOG
SAFETY 1ˢ
YOU SEEM... CHIPPER?
I SPENT ALL NIGHT WRITING DOWN ALL OF THE QUESTIONS I HAVE ABOUT HOW THE BACKSTAGE WORLD WORKS...
I TRIED TO KEEP IT TO JUST A COUPLE...BUT I GOT UP TO 136...
I STILL CAN'T BELIEVE NOBODY ELSE HAS EXPLORED DOWN HERE. THAT NOBODY KNOWS IT EVEN EXISTS...
AW, THAT'S CUTE. ISN'T THAT CUTE, BECKETT?
INSANELY, UNSPEAKABLY CUTE.
HEY, JORY...I'M SURE, IF YOU WANTED, I COULD SIT YOU DOWN AND TELL YOU EVERYTHING--
LEMME SEE.
SWIPE
OH MAN, I JUST CAN'T WAIT TO UNDERSTAND--

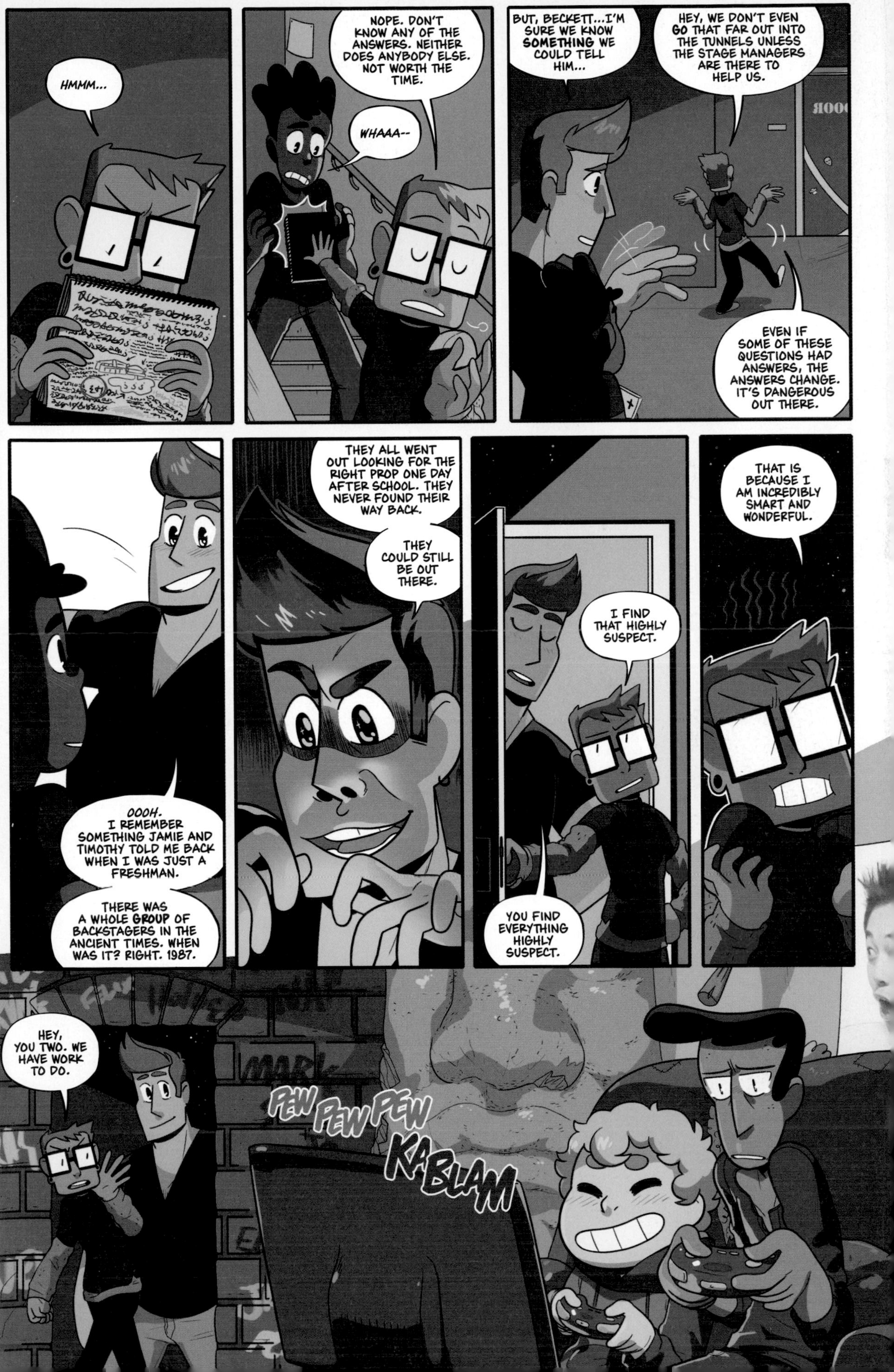
HMMM...
NOPE. DON'T KNOW ANY OF THE ANSWERS. NEITHER DOES ANYBODY ELSE. NOT WORTH THE TIME.
WHAAA--
BUT, BECKETT...I'M SURE WE KNOW SOMETHING WE COULD TELL HIM...
HEY, WE DON'T EVEN GO THAT FAR OUT INTO THE TUNNELS UNLESS THE STAGE MANAGERS ARE THERE TO HELP US.
EVEN IF SOME OF THESE QUESTIONS HAD ANSWERS, THE ANSWERS CHANGE. IT'S DANGEROUS OUT THERE.
OOOH. I REMEMBER SOMETHING JAMIE AND TIMOTHY TOLD ME BACK WHEN I WAS JUST A FRESHMAN.
THERE WAS A WHOLE GROUP OF BACKSTAGERS IN THE ANCIENT TIMES. WHEN WAS IT? RIGHT. 1987.
THEY ALL WENT OUT LOOKING FOR THE RIGHT PROP ONE DAY AFTER SCHOOL. THEY NEVER FOUND THEIR WAY BACK.
THEY COULD STILL BE OUT THERE.
I FIND THAT HIGHLY SUSPECT.
YOU FIND EVERYTHING HIGHLY SUSPECT.
THAT IS BECAUSE I AM INCREDIBLY SMART AND WONDERFUL.
HEY, YOU TWO. WE HAVE WORK TO DO.
PEW PEW PEW
KABLAM

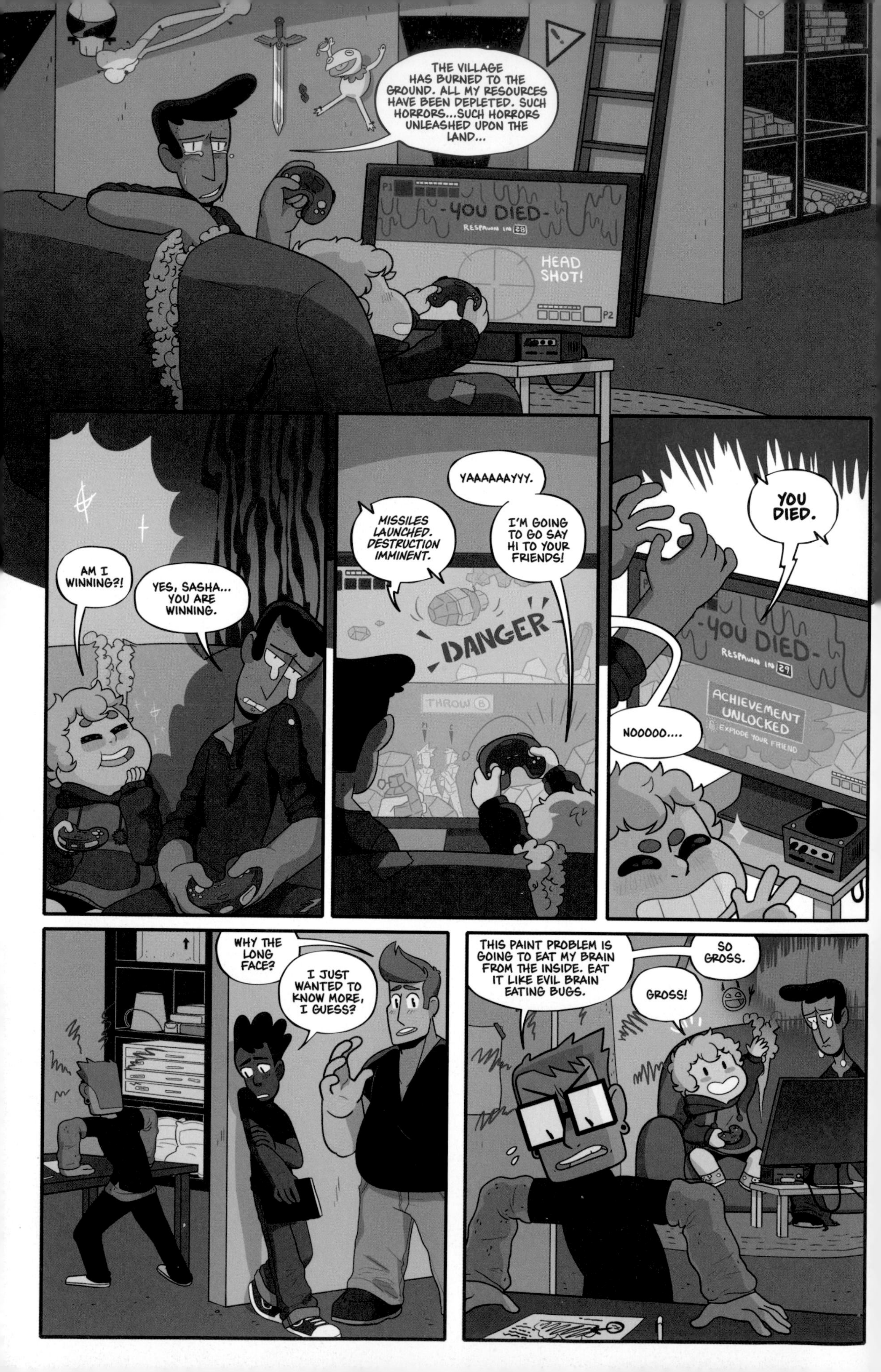
THE VILLAGE HAS BURNED TO THE GROUND. ALL MY RESOURCES HAVE BEEN DEPLETED. SUCH HORRORS...SUCH HORRORS UNLEASHED UPON THE LAND...
P1
-YOU DIED-
RESPAWN IN 28
HEAD SHOT!
P2
AM I WINNING?!
YES, SASHA... YOU ARE WINNING.
YAAAAAAYYY.
MISSILES LAUNCHED. DESTRUCTION IMMINENT.
I'M GOING TO GO SAY HI TO YOUR FRIENDS!
DANGER
THROW B
YOU DIED.
-YOU DIED-
RESPAWN IN 29
ACHIEVEMENT UNLOCKED
EXPLODE YOUR FRIEND
NOOOOO....
WHY THE LONG FACE?
I JUST WANTED TO KNOW MORE, I GUESS?
THIS PAINT PROBLEM IS GOING TO EAT MY BRAIN FROM THE INSIDE. EAT IT LIKE EVIL BRAIN EATING BUGS.
SO GROSS.
GROSS!

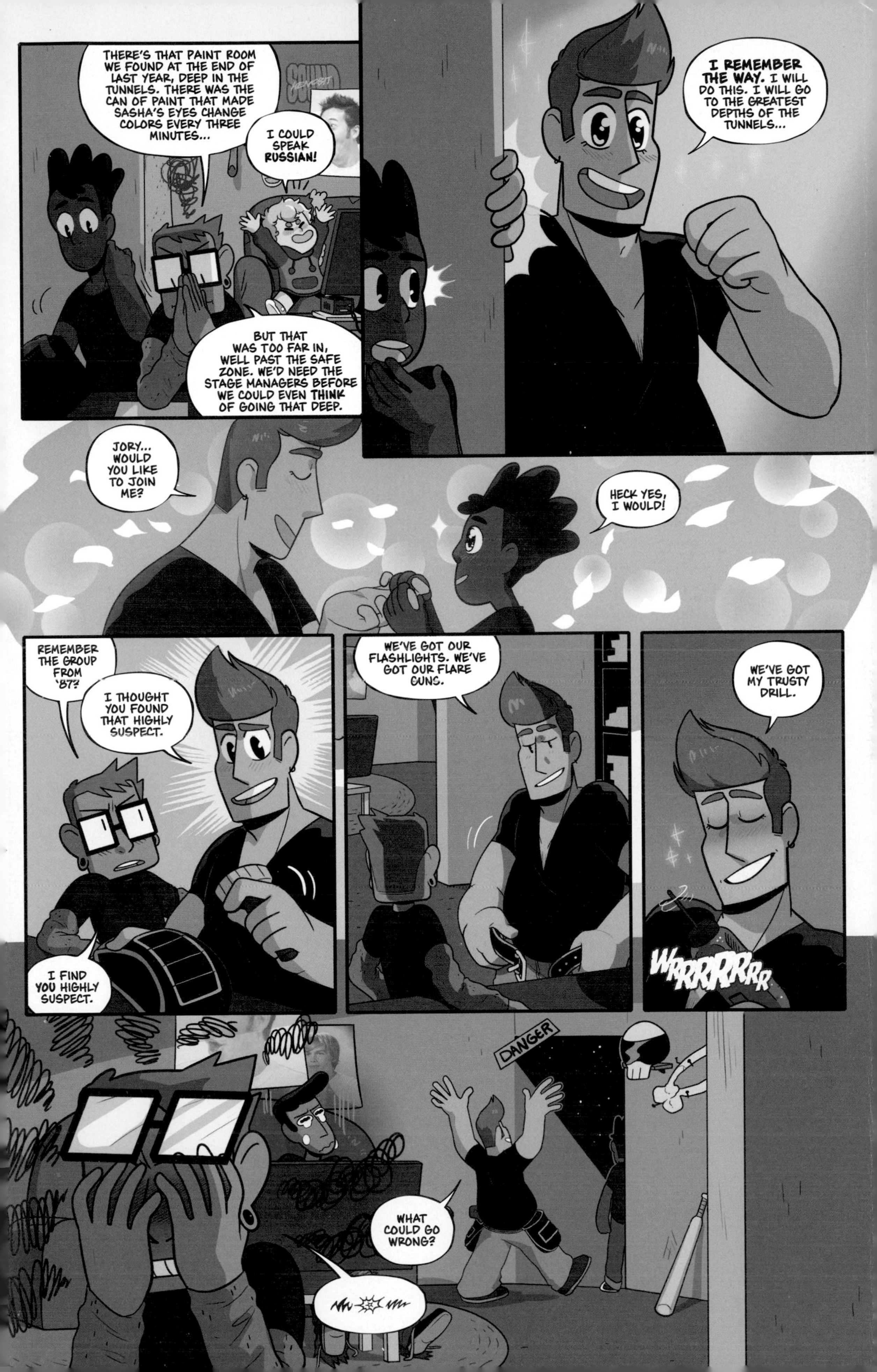

THERE'S THAT PAINT ROOM WE FOUND AT THE END OF LAST YEAR, DEEP IN THE TUNNELS. THERE WAS THE CAN OF PAINT THAT MADE SASHA'S EYES CHANGE COLORS EVERY THREE MINUTES...
I COULD SPEAK RUSSIAN!
BUT THAT WAS TOO FAR IN, WELL PAST THE SAFE ZONE. WE'D NEED THE STAGE MANAGERS BEFORE WE COULD EVEN THINK OF GOING THAT DEEP.
I REMEMBER THE WAY. I WILL DO THIS. I WILL GO TO THE GREATEST DEPTHS OF THE TUNNELS...
JORY... WOULD YOU LIKE TO JOIN ME?
HECK YES, I WOULD!
REMEMBER THE GROUP FROM '87?
I THOUGHT YOU FOUND THAT HIGHLY SUSPECT.
I FIND YOU HIGHLY SUSPECT.
WE'VE GOT OUR FLASHLIGHTS. WE'VE GOT OUR FLARE GUNS.
WE'VE GOT MY TRUSTY DRILL.
WRRRRRRR
DANGER
WHAT COULD GO WRONG?

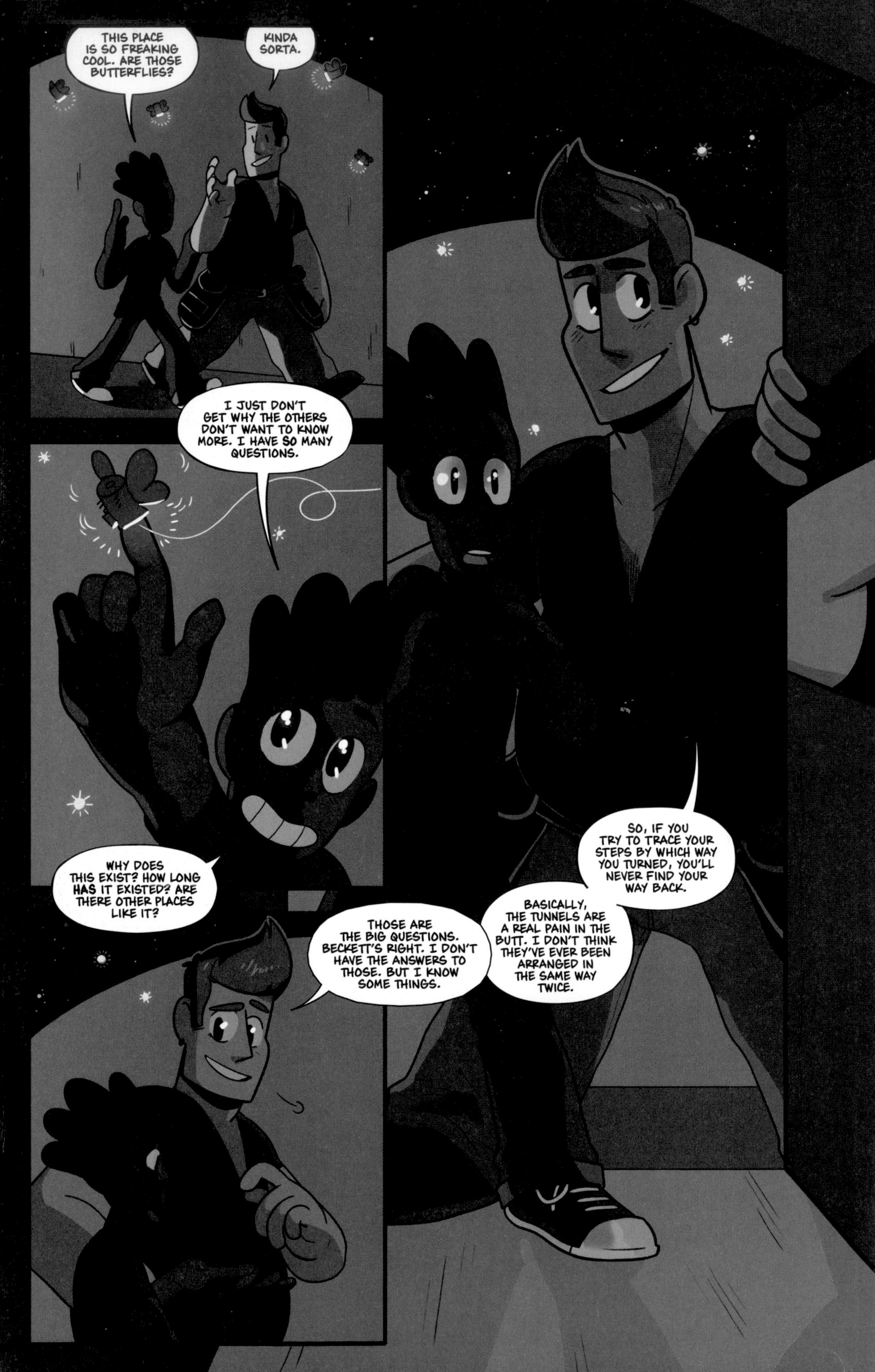
THIS PLACE IS SO FREAKING COOL. ARE THOSE BUTTERFLIES?
KINDA SORTA.
I JUST DON'T GET WHY THE OTHERS DON'T WANT TO KNOW MORE. I HAVE SO MANY QUESTIONS.
WHY DOES THIS EXIST? HOW LONG HAS IT EXISTED? ARE THERE OTHER PLACES LIKE IT?
THOSE ARE THE BIG QUESTIONS. BECKETT'S RIGHT. I DON'T HAVE THE ANSWERS TO THOSE. BUT I KNOW SOME THINGS.
BASICALLY, THE TUNNELS ARE A REAL PAIN IN THE BUTT. I DON'T THINK THEY'VE EVER BEEN ARRANGED IN THE SAME WAY TWICE.
SO, IF YOU TRY TO TRACE YOUR STEPS BY WHICH WAY YOU TURNED, YOU'LL NEVER FIND YOUR WAY BACK.

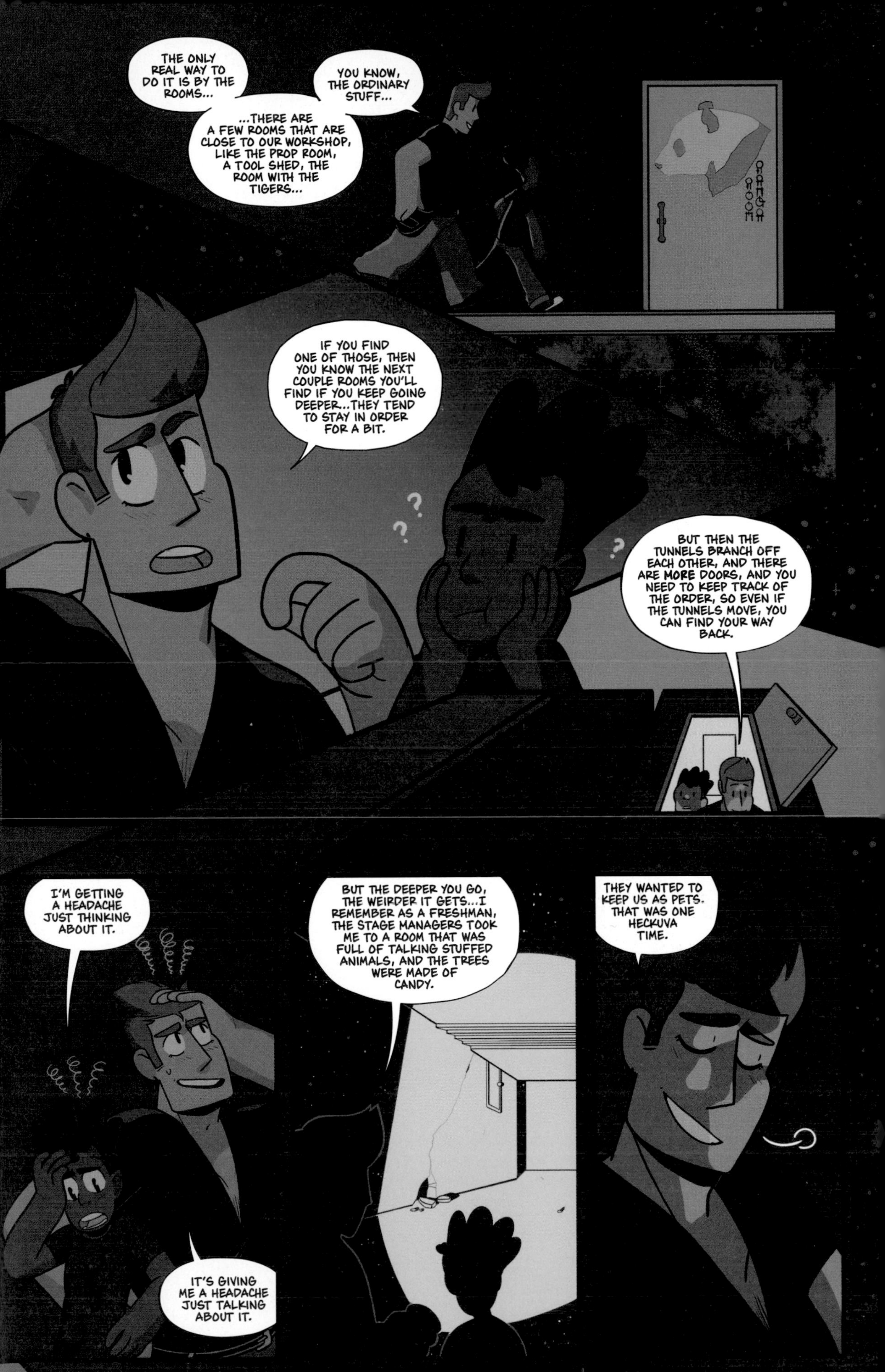
THE ONLY REAL WAY TO DO IT IS BY THE ROOMS...
YOU KNOW, THE ORDINARY STUFF...
...THERE ARE A FEW ROOMS THAT ARE CLOSE TO OUR WORKSHOP, LIKE THE PROP ROOM, A TOOL SHED, THE ROOM WITH THE TIGERS...
IF YOU FIND ONE OF THOSE, THEN YOU KNOW THE NEXT COUPLE ROOMS YOU'LL FIND IF YOU KEEP GOING DEEPER...THEY TEND TO STAY IN ORDER FOR A BIT.
?
?
?
BUT THEN THE TUNNELS BRANCH OFF EACH OTHER, AND THERE ARE MORE DOORS, AND YOU NEED TO KEEP TRACK OF THE ORDER, SO EVEN IF THE TUNNELS MOVE, YOU CAN FIND YOUR WAY BACK.
I'M GETTING A HEADACHE JUST THINKING ABOUT IT.
IT'S GIVING ME A HEADACHE JUST TALKING ABOUT IT.
BUT THE DEEPER YOU GO, THE WEIRDER IT GETS...I REMEMBER AS A FRESHMAN, THE STAGE MANAGERS TOOK ME TO A ROOM THAT WAS FULL OF TALKING STUFFED ANIMALS, AND THE TREES WERE MADE OF CANDY.
THEY WANTED TO KEEP US AS PETS. THAT WAS ONE HECKUVA TIME.

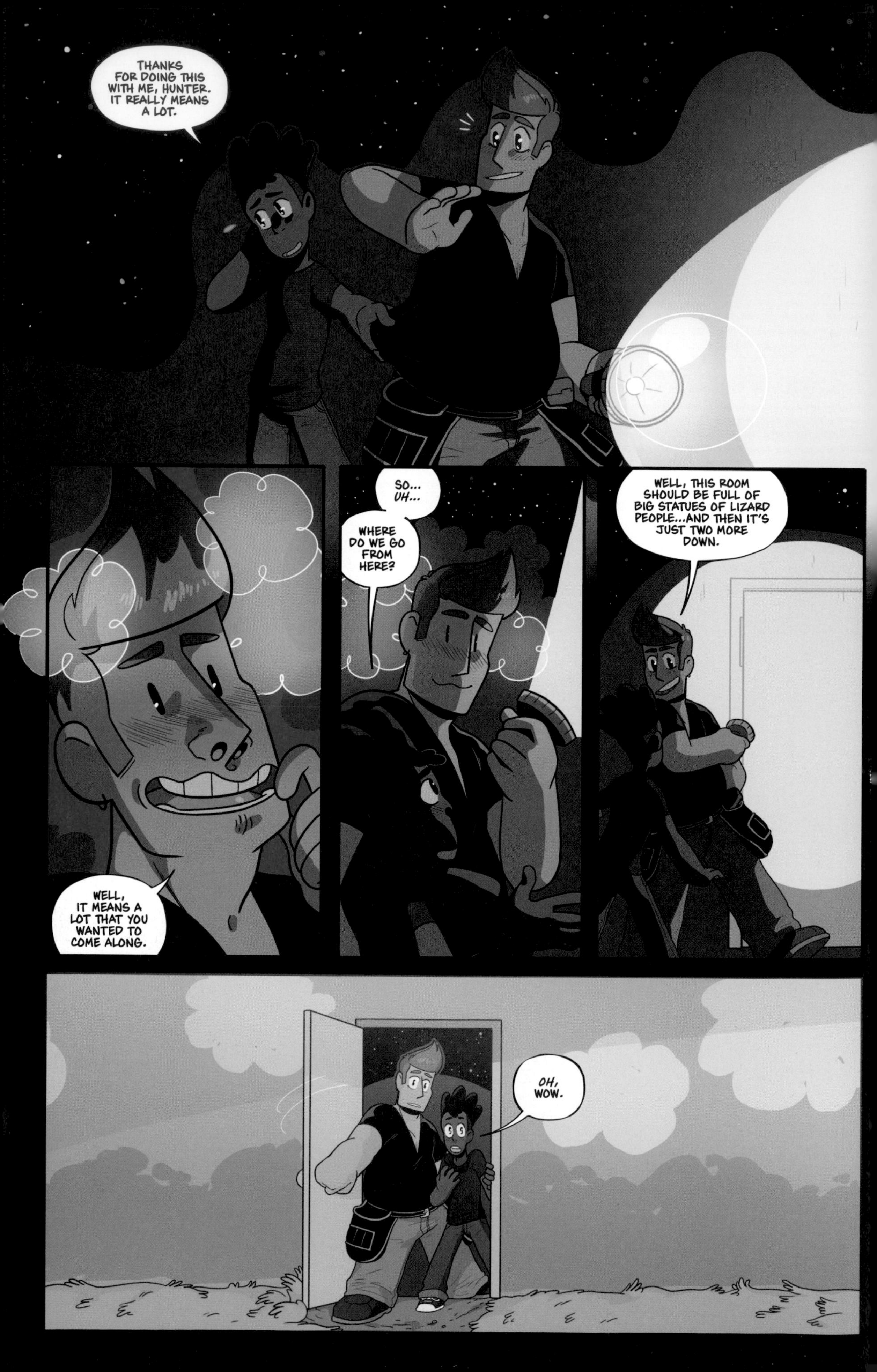
THANKS FOR DOING THIS WITH ME, HUNTER. IT REALLY MEANS A LOT.
WELL, IT MEANS A LOT THAT YOU WANTED TO COME ALONG.
SO... UH...
WHERE DO WE GO FROM HERE?
WELL, THIS ROOM SHOULD BE FULL OF BIG STATUES OF LIZARD PEOPLE...AND THEN IT'S JUST TWO MORE DOWN.
OH, WOW.

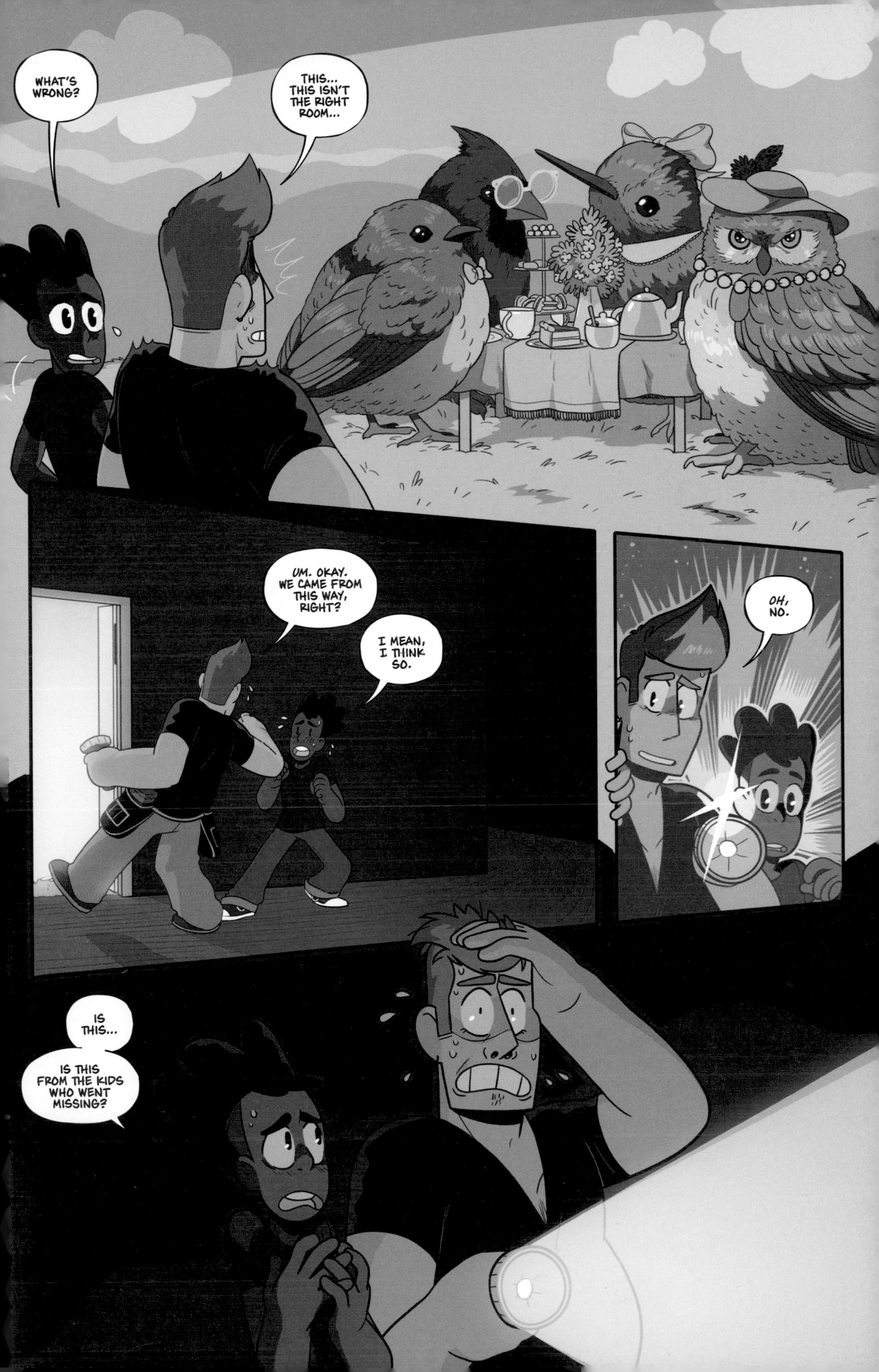
WHAT'S WRONG?
THIS... THIS ISN'T THE RIGHT ROOM...
UM. OKAY. WE CAME FROM THIS WAY, RIGHT?
I MEAN, I THINK SO.
OH, NO.
IS THIS...
IS THIS FROM THE KIDS WHO WENT MISSING?

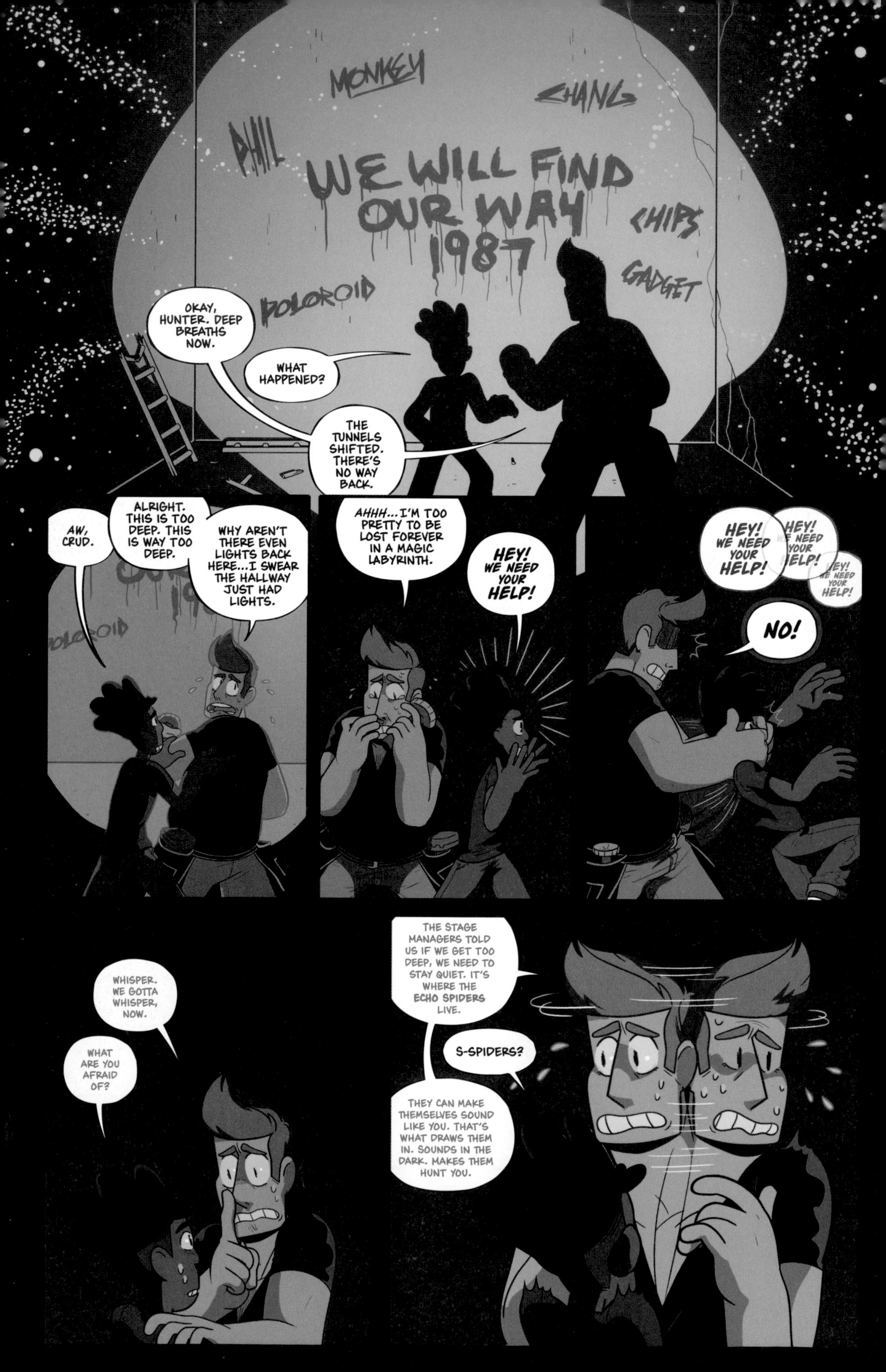
MONKEY
CHANG
PHIL
WE WILL FIND OUR WAY 1987
CHIPS
GADGET
POLOROID
OKAY, HUNTER. DEEP BREATHS NOW.
WHAT HAPPENED?
THE TUNNELS SHIFTED. THERE'S NO WAY BACK.
AW, CRUD.
ALRIGHT. THIS IS TOO DEEP. THIS IS WAY TOO DEEP.
WHY AREN'T THERE EVEN LIGHTS BACK HERE...I SWEAR THE HALLWAY JUST HAD LIGHTS.
AHHH...I'M TOO PRETTY TO BE LOST FOREVER IN A MAGIC LABYRINTH.
HEY! WE NEED YOUR HELP!
HEY! WE NEED YOUR HELP!
HEY! WE NEED YOUR HELP!
HEY! WE NEED YOUR HELP!
NO!
WHISPER. WE GOTTA WHISPER, NOW.
WHAT ARE YOU AFRAID OF?
THE STAGE MANAGERS TOLD US IF WE GET TOO DEEP, WE NEED TO STAY QUIET. IT'S WHERE THE ECHO SPIDERS LIVE.
S-SPIDERS?
THEY CAN MAKE THEMSELVES SOUND LIKE YOU. THAT'S WHAT DRAWS THEM IN. SOUNDS IN THE DARK. MAKES THEM HUNT YOU.

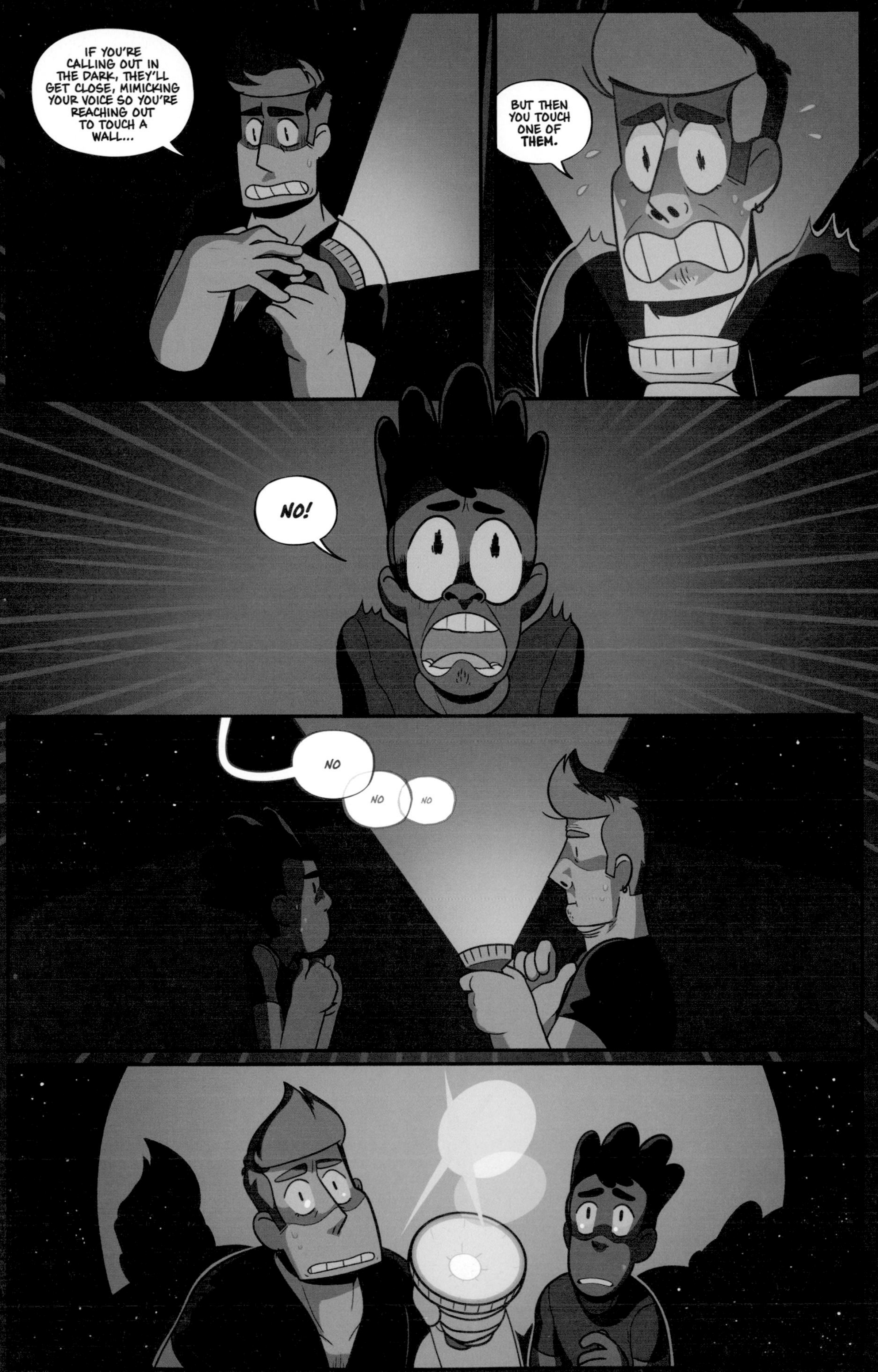
IF YOU'RE CALLING OUT IN THE DARK, THEY'LL GET CLOSE, MIMICKING YOUR VOICE SO YOU'RE REACHING OUT TO TOUCH A WALL...
BUT THEN YOU TOUCH ONE OF THEM.
NO!
NO
NO
NO

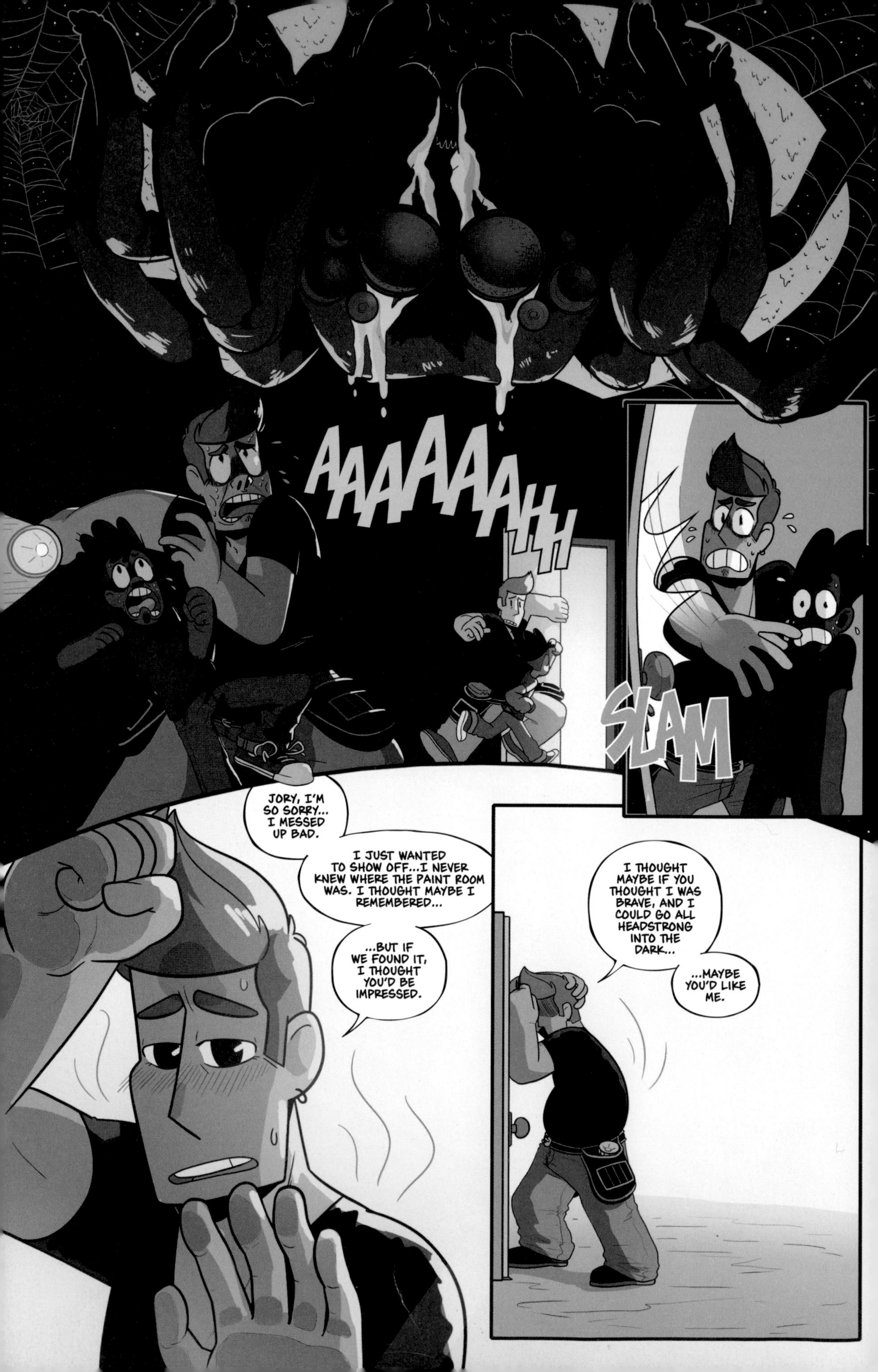
AAAAAAAHHH
SLAM
JORY, I'M SO SORRY... I MESSED UP BAD.
I JUST WANTED TO SHOW OFF...I NEVER KNEW WHERE THE PAINT ROOM WAS. I THOUGHT MAYBE I REMEMBERED...
...BUT IF WE FOUND IT, I THOUGHT YOU'D BE IMPRESSED.
I THOUGHT MAYBE IF YOU THOUGHT I WAS BRAVE, AND I COULD GO ALL HEADSTRONG INTO THE DARK...
...MAYBE YOU'D LIKE ME.

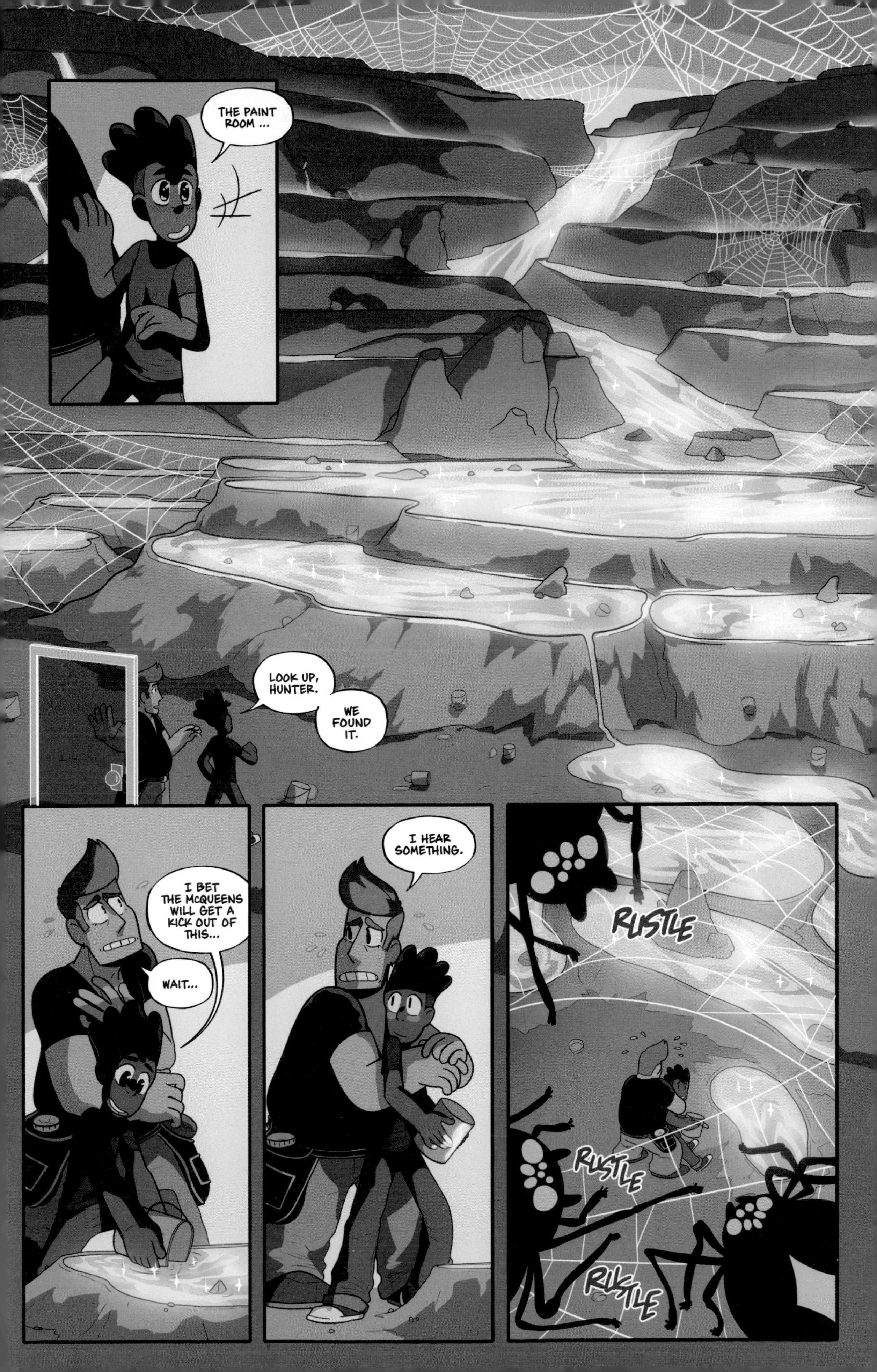
THE PAINT ROOM ...
LOOK UP, HUNTER.
WE FOUND IT.
I BET THE MCQUEENS WILL GET A KICK OUT OF THIS...
WAIT...
I HEAR SOMETHING.
RUSTLE
RUSTLE
RUSTLE

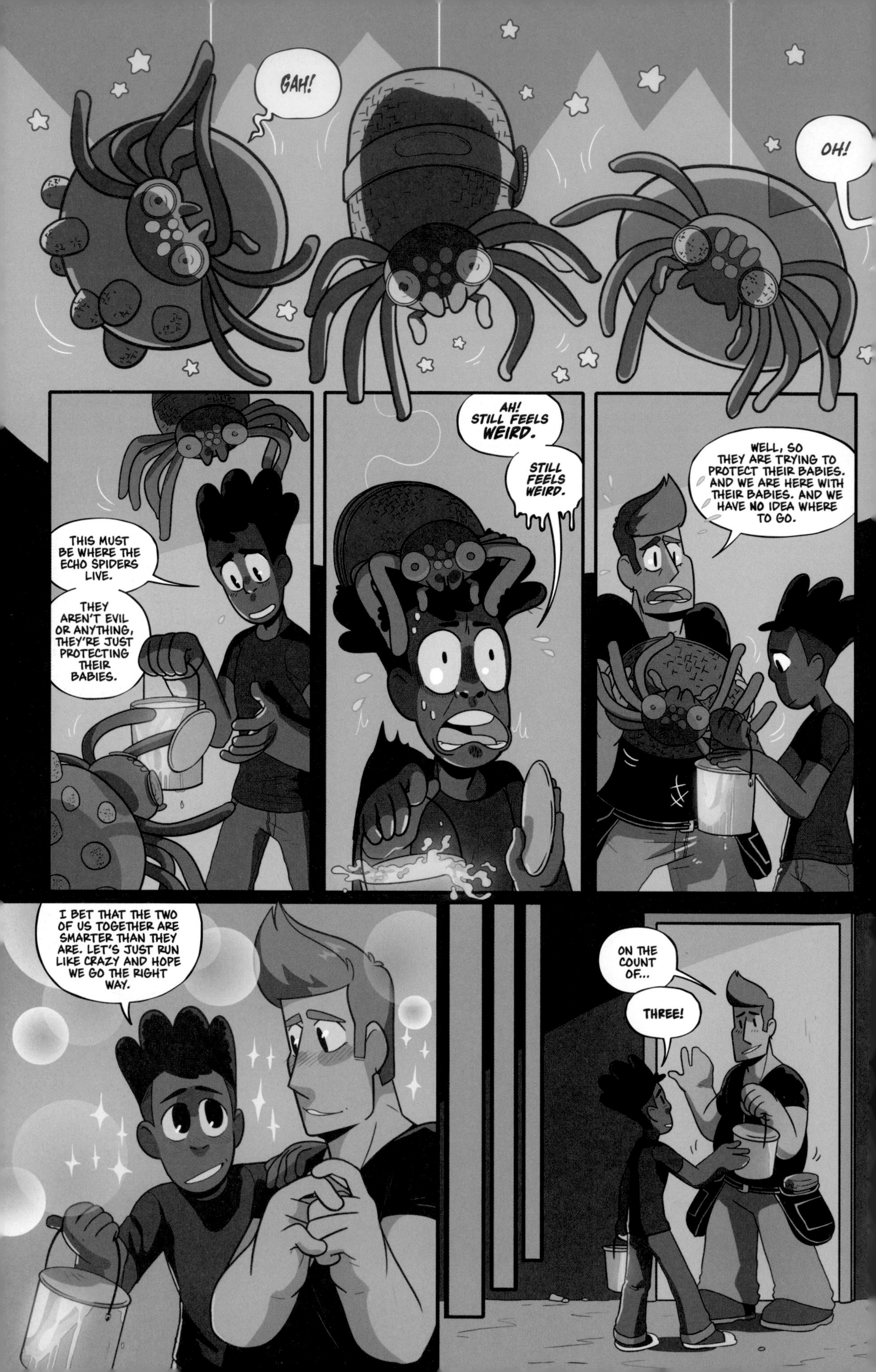
GAH!
OH!
THIS MUST BE WHERE THE ECHO SPIDERS LIVE.
THEY AREN'T EVIL OR ANYTHING, THEY'RE JUST PROTECTING THEIR BABIES.
AH! STILL FEELS WEIRD.
STILL FEELS WEIRD.
WELL, SO THEY ARE TRYING TO PROTECT THEIR BABIES. AND WE ARE HERE WITH THEIR BABIES. AND WE HAVE NO IDEA WHERE TO GO.
I BET THAT THE TWO OF US TOGETHER ARE SMARTER THAN THEY ARE. LET'S JUST RUN LIKE CRAZY AND HOPE WE GO THE RIGHT WAY.
ON THE COUNT OF...
THREE!

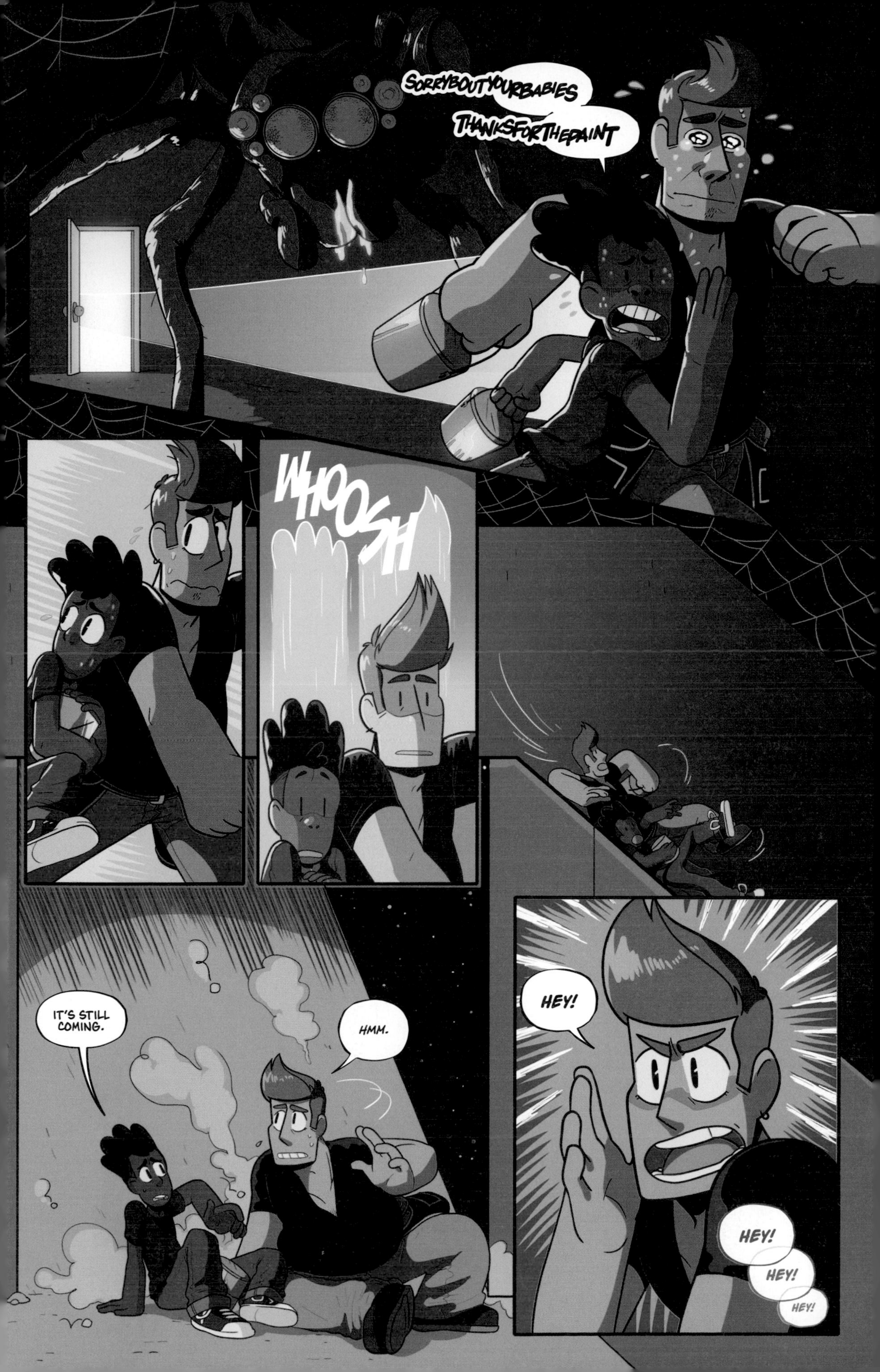
SORRYBOUTYOURBABIES
THANKSFORTHEPAINT
WHOOSH
IT'S STILL COMING.
HMM.
HEY!
HEY!
HEY!
HEY!

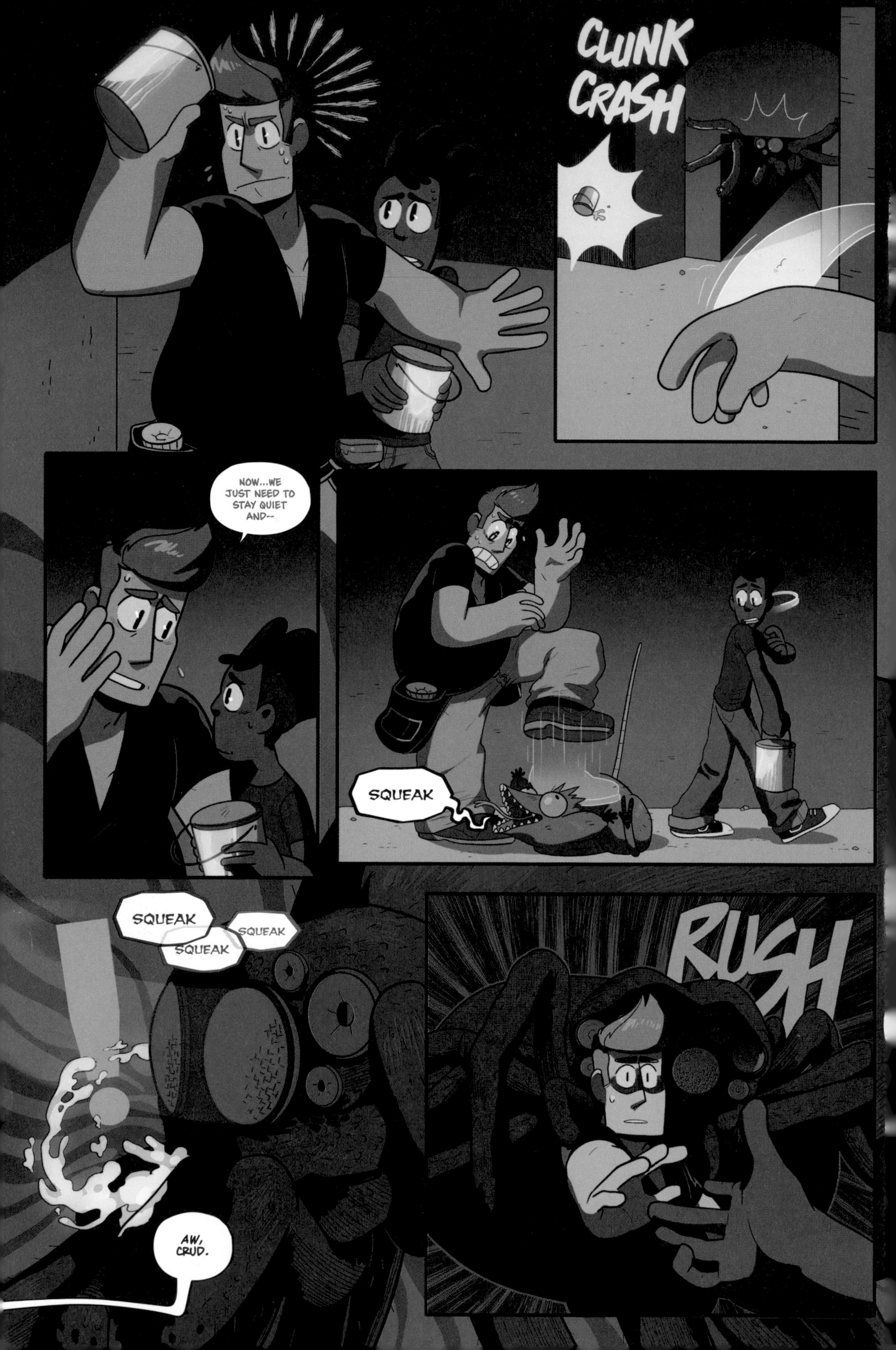
CLUNK
CRASH
NOW...WE JUST NEED TO STAY QUIET AND--
SQUEAK
SQUEAK
SQUEAK
SQUEAK
AW, CRUD.
RUSH

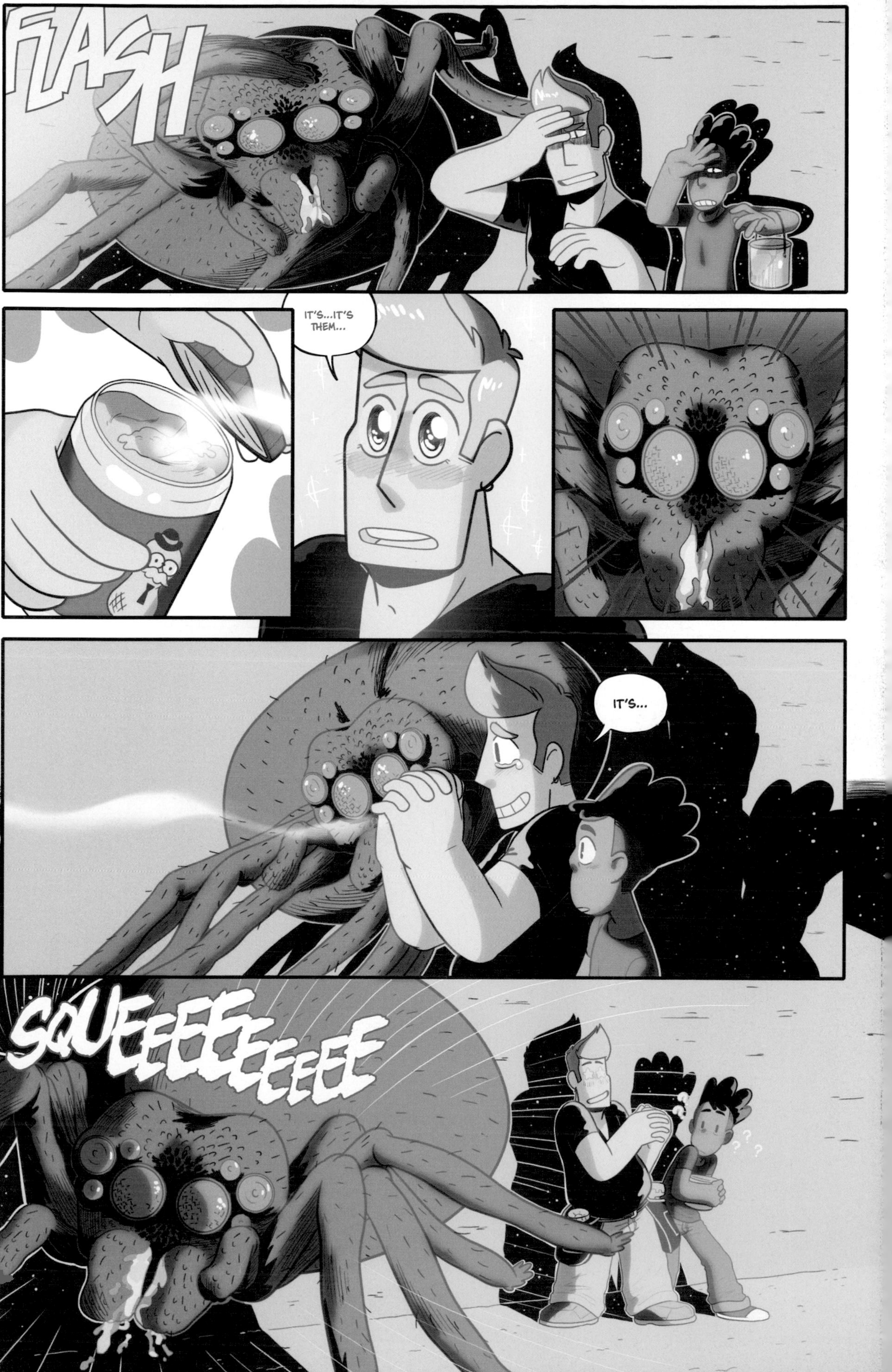
FLASH
IT'S...IT'S THEM...
IT'S...
SQUEEEEEEEEEEE

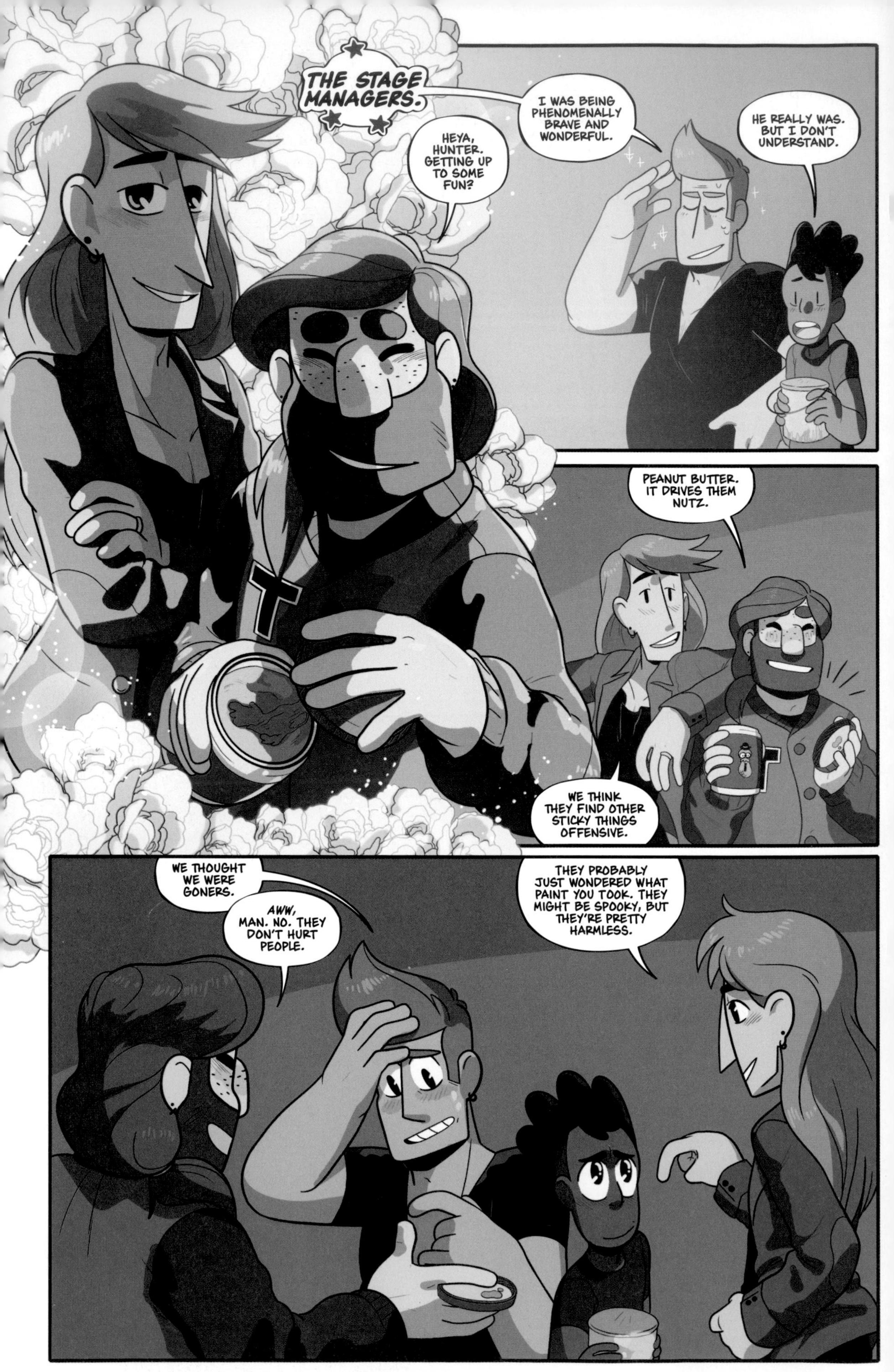
THE STAGE MANAGERS.
HEYA, HUNTER. GETTING UP TO SOME FUN?
I WAS BEING PHENOMENALLY BRAVE AND WONDERFUL.
HE REALLY WAS. BUT I DON'T UNDERSTAND.
PEANUT BUTTER. IT DRIVES THEM NUTZ.
WE THINK THEY FIND OTHER STICKY THINGS OFFENSIVE.
WE THOUGHT WE WERE GONERS.
AWW, MAN. NO. THEY DON'T HURT PEOPLE.
THEY PROBABLY JUST WONDERED WHAT PAINT YOU TOOK. THEY MIGHT BE SPOOKY, BUT THEY'RE PRETTY HARMLESS.

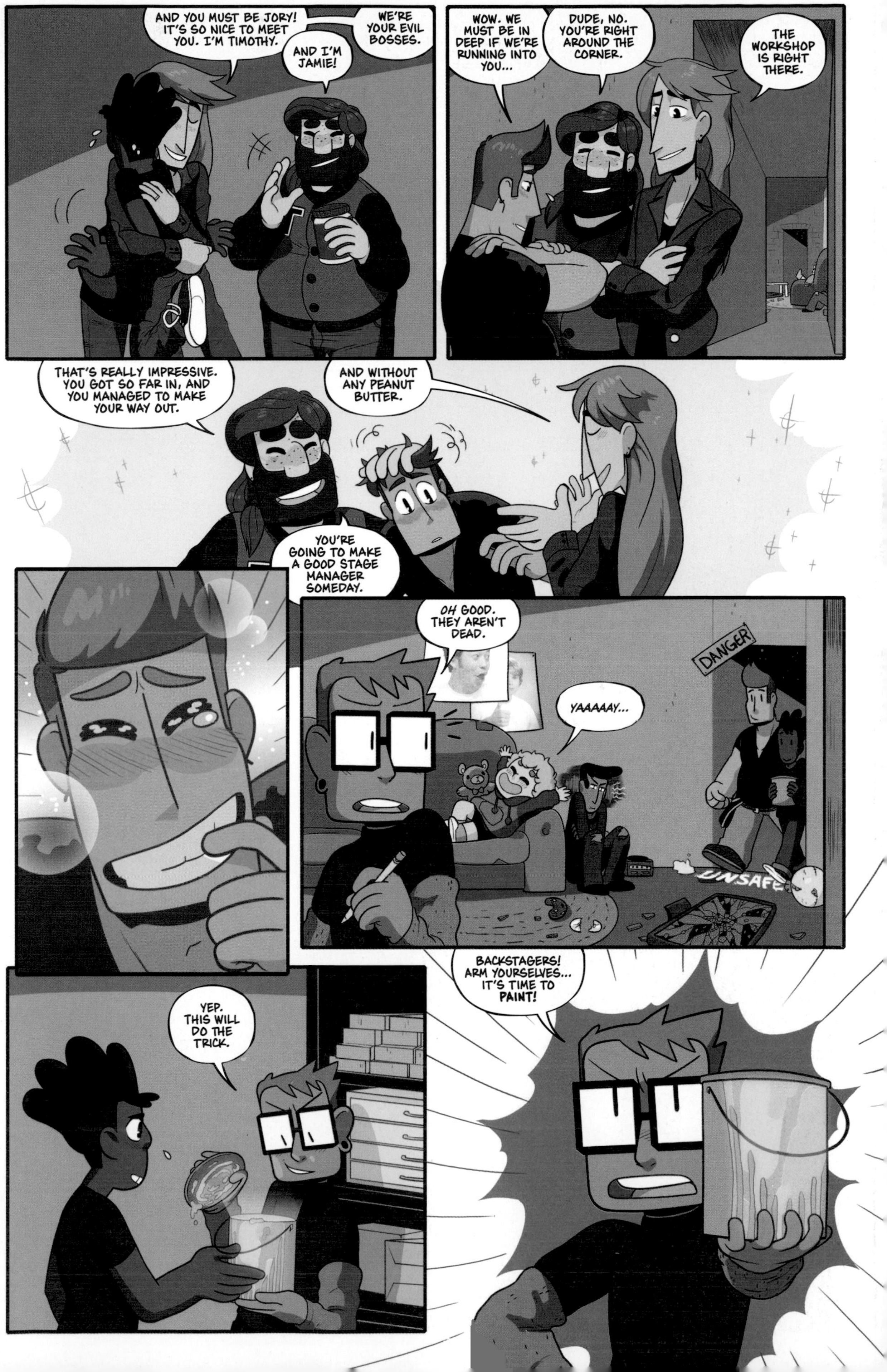
AND YOU MUST BE JORY! IT'S SO NICE TO MEET YOU. I'M TIMOTHY.
AND I'M JAMIE!
WE'RE YOUR EVIL BOSSES.
WOW. WE MUST BE IN DEEP IF WE'RE RUNNING INTO YOU...
DUDE, NO. YOU'RE RIGHT AROUND THE CORNER.
THE WORKSHOP IS RIGHT THERE.
THAT'S REALLY IMPRESSIVE. YOU GOT SO FAR IN, AND YOU MANAGED TO MAKE YOUR WAY OUT.
AND WITHOUT ANY PEANUT BUTTER.
YOU'RE GOING TO MAKE A GOOD STAGE MANAGER SOMEDAY.
OH GOOD. THEY AREN'T DEAD.
DANGER
YAAAAAY...
UNSAFE
YEP. THIS WILL DO THE TRICK.
BACKSTAGERS! ARM YOURSELVES... IT'S TIME TO **PAINT!**

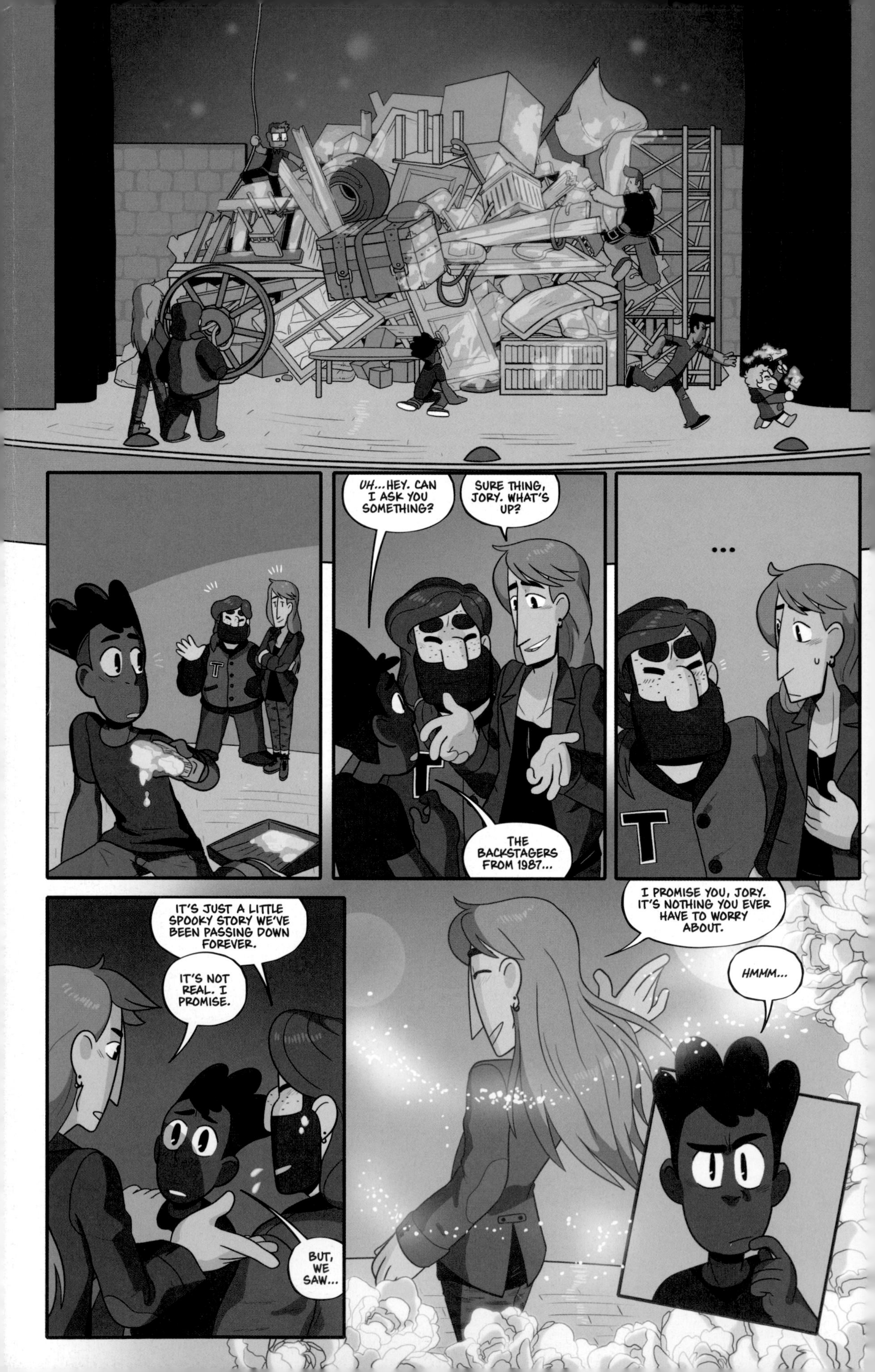
UH...HEY. CAN I ASK YOU SOMETHING?
SURE THING, JORY. WHAT'S UP?
THE BACKSTAGERS FROM 1987...
...
IT'S JUST A LITTLE SPOOKY STORY WE'VE BEEN PASSING DOWN FOREVER.
IT'S NOT REAL. I PROMISE.
BUT, WE SAW...
I PROMISE YOU, JORY. IT'S NOTHING YOU EVER HAVE TO WORRY ABOUT.
HMMM...

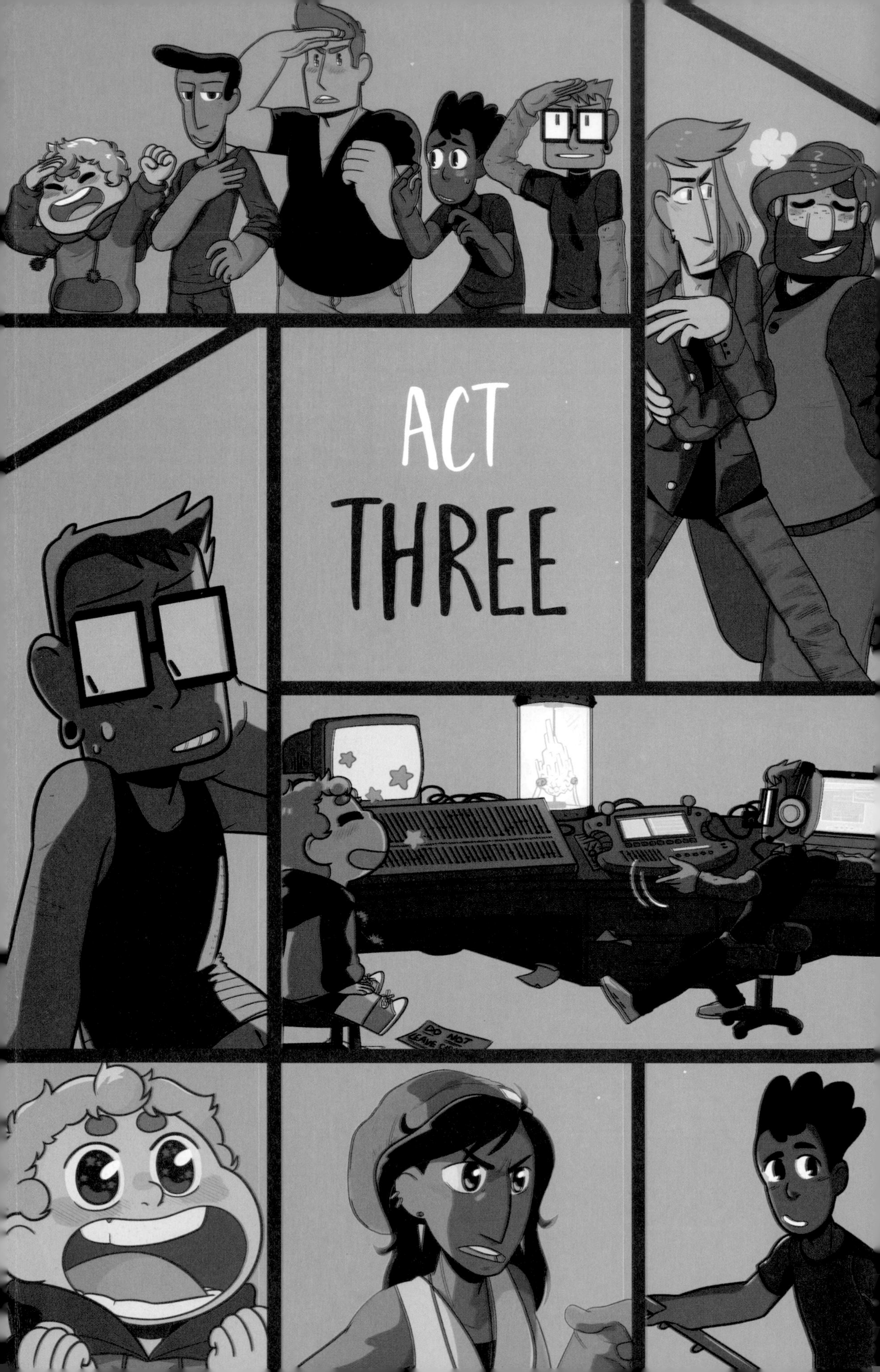
ACT THREE
DO NOT
LEAVE

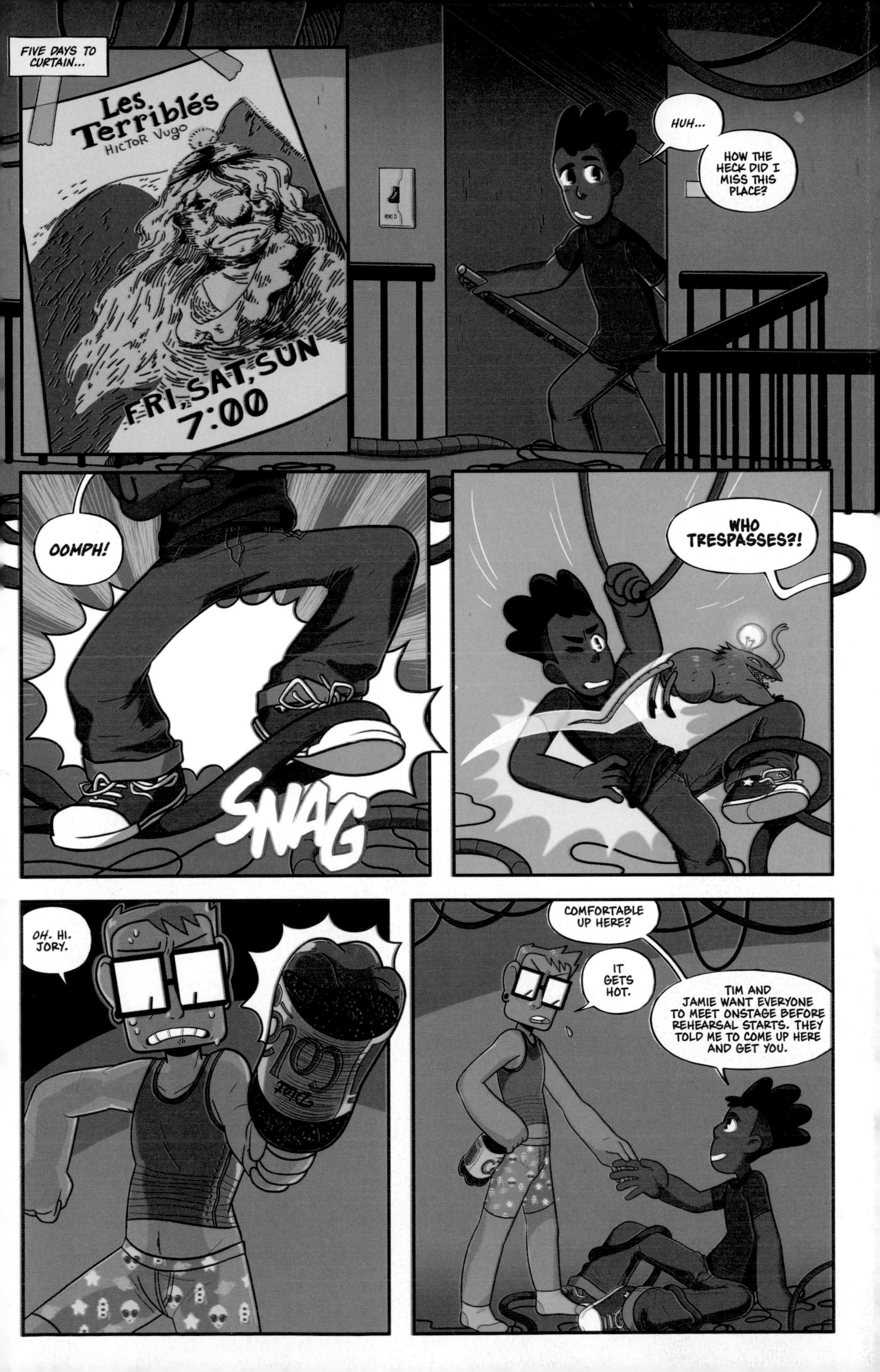
FIVE DAYS TO CURTAIN...
Les Terriblés
HICTOR VUGO
FRI, SAT, SUN
7:00
HUH...
HOW THE HECK DID I MISS THIS PLACE?
OOMPH!
SNAG
WHO TRESPASSES?!
OH. HI. JORY.
COMFORTABLE UP HERE?
IT GETS HOT.
TIM AND JAMIE WANT EVERYONE TO MEET ONSTAGE BEFORE REHEARSAL STARTS. THEY TOLD ME TO COME UP HERE AND GET YOU.

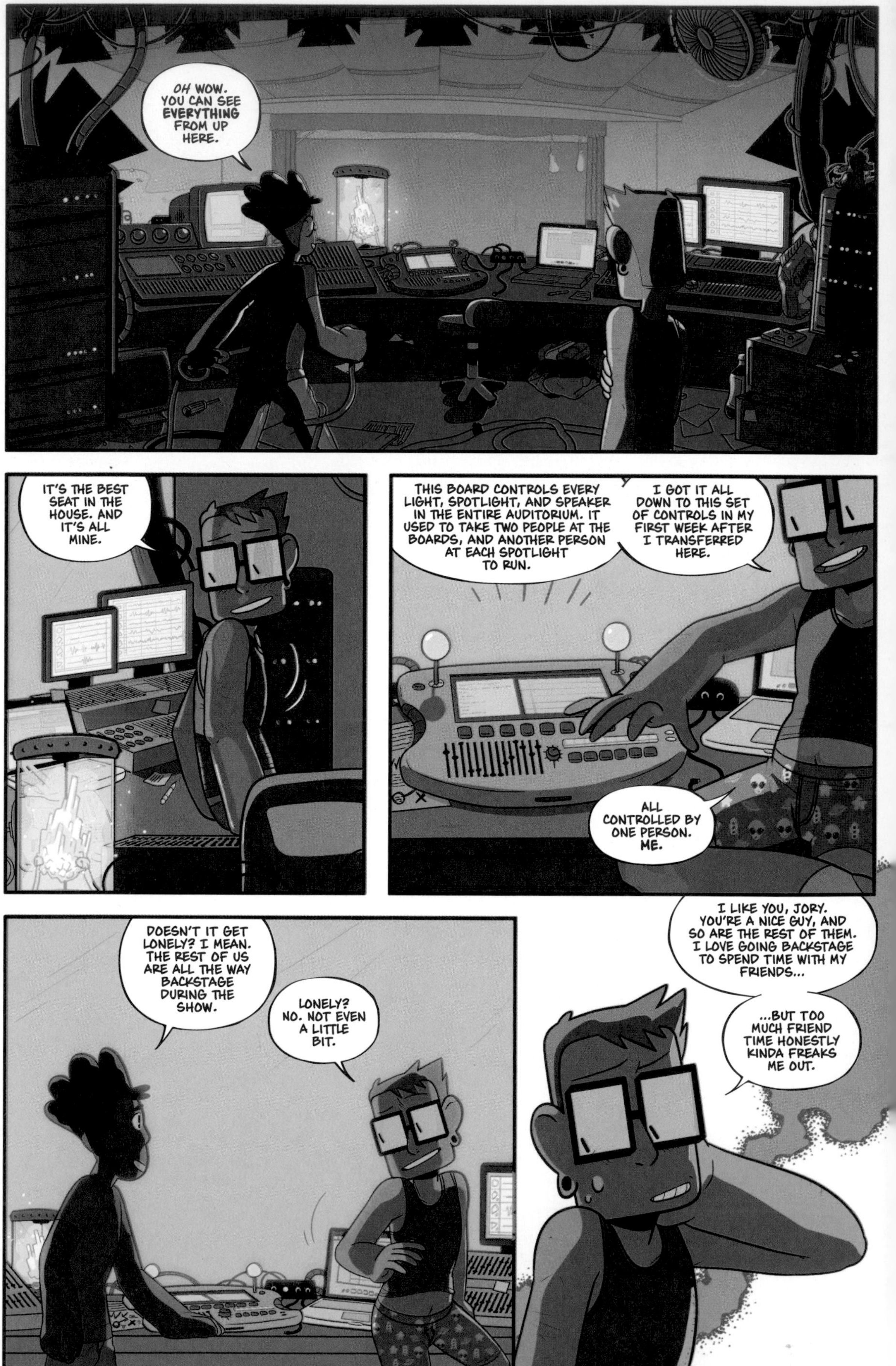
OH WOW. YOU CAN SEE EVERYTHING FROM UP HERE.
IT'S THE BEST SEAT IN THE HOUSE. AND IT'S ALL MINE.
THIS BOARD CONTROLS EVERY LIGHT, SPOTLIGHT, AND SPEAKER IN THE ENTIRE AUDITORIUM. IT USED TO TAKE TWO PEOPLE AT THE BOARDS, AND ANOTHER PERSON AT EACH SPOTLIGHT TO RUN.
I GOT IT ALL DOWN TO THIS SET OF CONTROLS IN MY FIRST WEEK AFTER I TRANSFERRED HERE.
ALL CONTROLLED BY ONE PERSON. ME.
DOESN'T IT GET LONELY? I MEAN. THE REST OF US ARE ALL THE WAY BACKSTAGE DURING THE SHOW.
LONELY? NO. NOT EVEN A LITTLE BIT.
I LIKE YOU, JORY. YOU'RE A NICE GUY, AND SO ARE THE REST OF THEM. I LOVE GOING BACKSTAGE TO SPEND TIME WITH MY FRIENDS...
...BUT TOO MUCH FRIEND TIME HONESTLY KINDA FREAKS ME OUT.

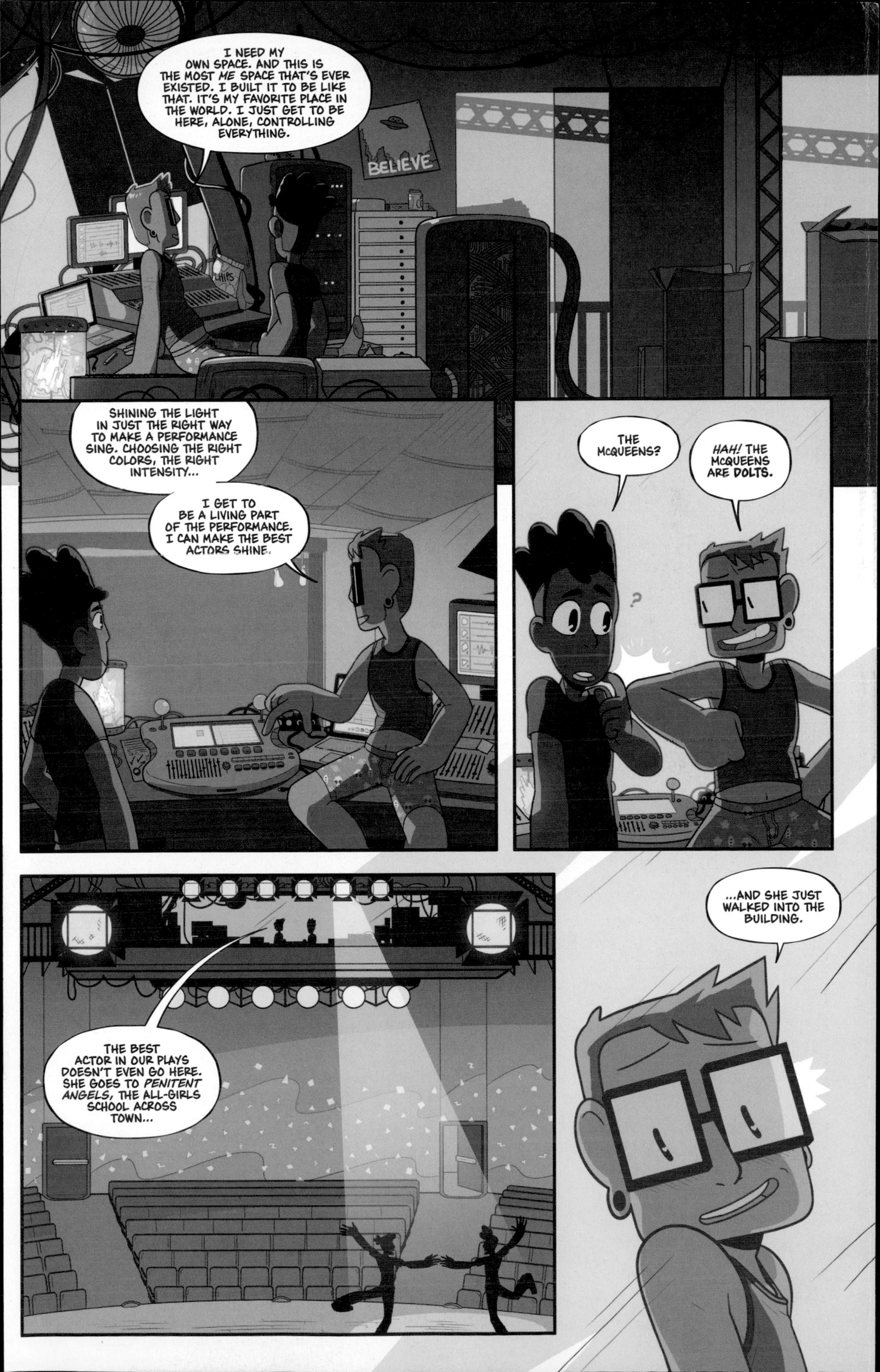
I NEED MY OWN SPACE. AND THIS IS THE MOST *ME* SPACE THAT'S EVER EXISTED. I BUILT IT TO BE LIKE THAT. IT'S MY FAVORITE PLACE IN THE WORLD. I JUST GET TO BE HERE, ALONE, CONTROLLING EVERYTHING.
BELIEVE
CHIPS
SHINING THE LIGHT IN JUST THE RIGHT WAY TO MAKE A PERFORMANCE SING. CHOOSING THE RIGHT COLORS, THE RIGHT INTENSITY...
I GET TO BE A LIVING PART OF THE PERFORMANCE. I CAN MAKE THE BEST ACTORS SHINE.
THE McQUEENS?
HAH! THE McQUEENS ARE **DOLTS**.
?
THE BEST ACTOR IN OUR PLAYS DOESN'T EVEN GO HERE. SHE GOES TO *PENITENT ANGELS*, THE ALL-GIRLS SCHOOL ACROSS TOWN...
...AND SHE JUST WALKED INTO THE BUILDING.

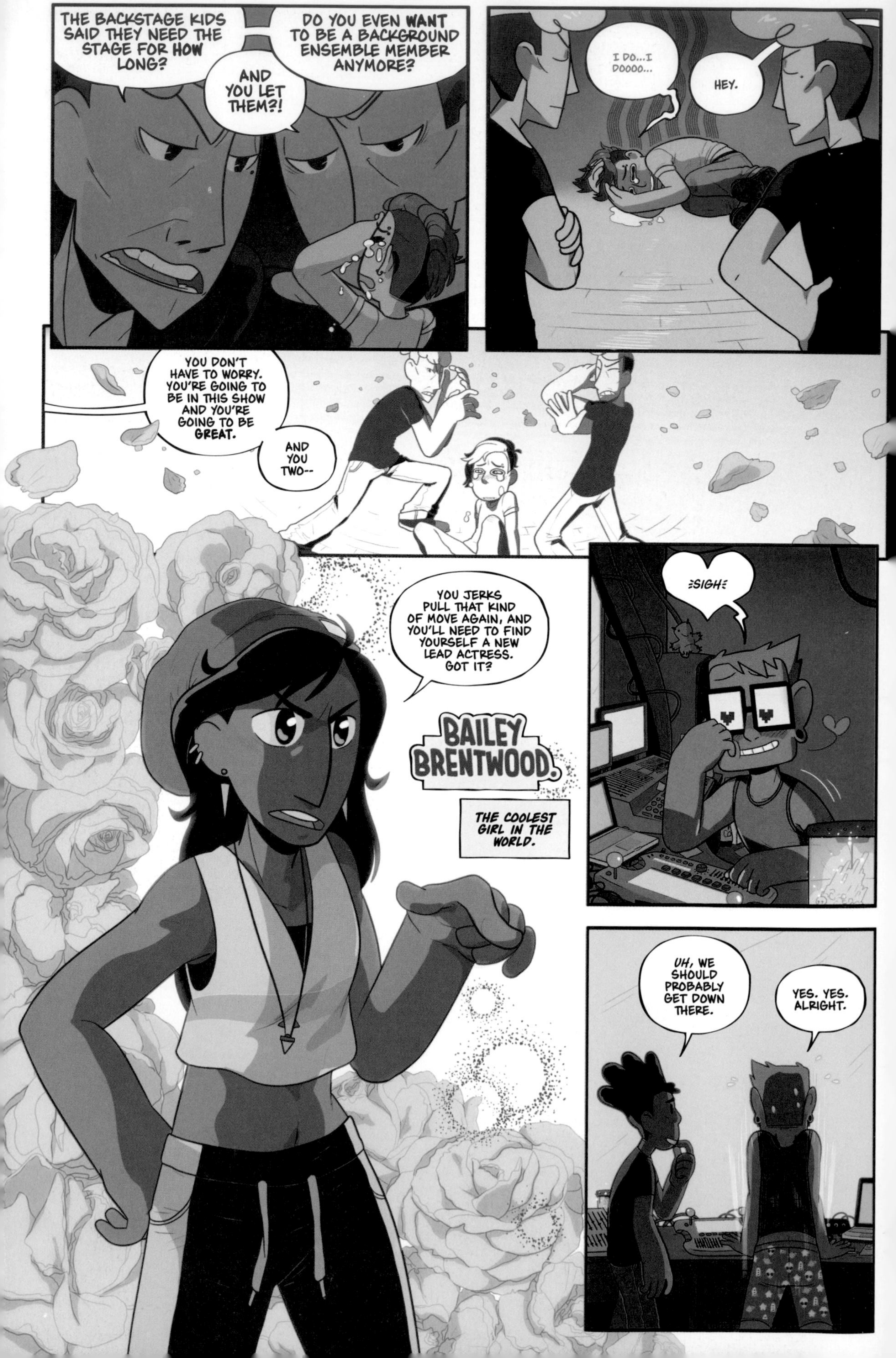
THE BACKSTAGE KIDS SAID THEY NEED THE STAGE FOR HOW LONG?
AND YOU LET THEM?!
DO YOU EVEN WANT TO BE A BACKGROUND ENSEMBLE MEMBER ANYMORE?
I DO...I DOOOO...
HEY.
YOU DON'T HAVE TO WORRY. YOU'RE GOING TO BE IN THIS SHOW AND YOU'RE GOING TO BE GREAT.
AND YOU TWO--
YOU JERKS PULL THAT KIND OF MOVE AGAIN, AND YOU'LL NEED TO FIND YOURSELF A NEW LEAD ACTRESS. GOT IT?
BAILEY BRENTWOOD.
THE COOLEST GIRL IN THE WORLD.
SIGH
UH, WE SHOULD PROBABLY GET DOWN THERE.
YES. YES. ALRIGHT.

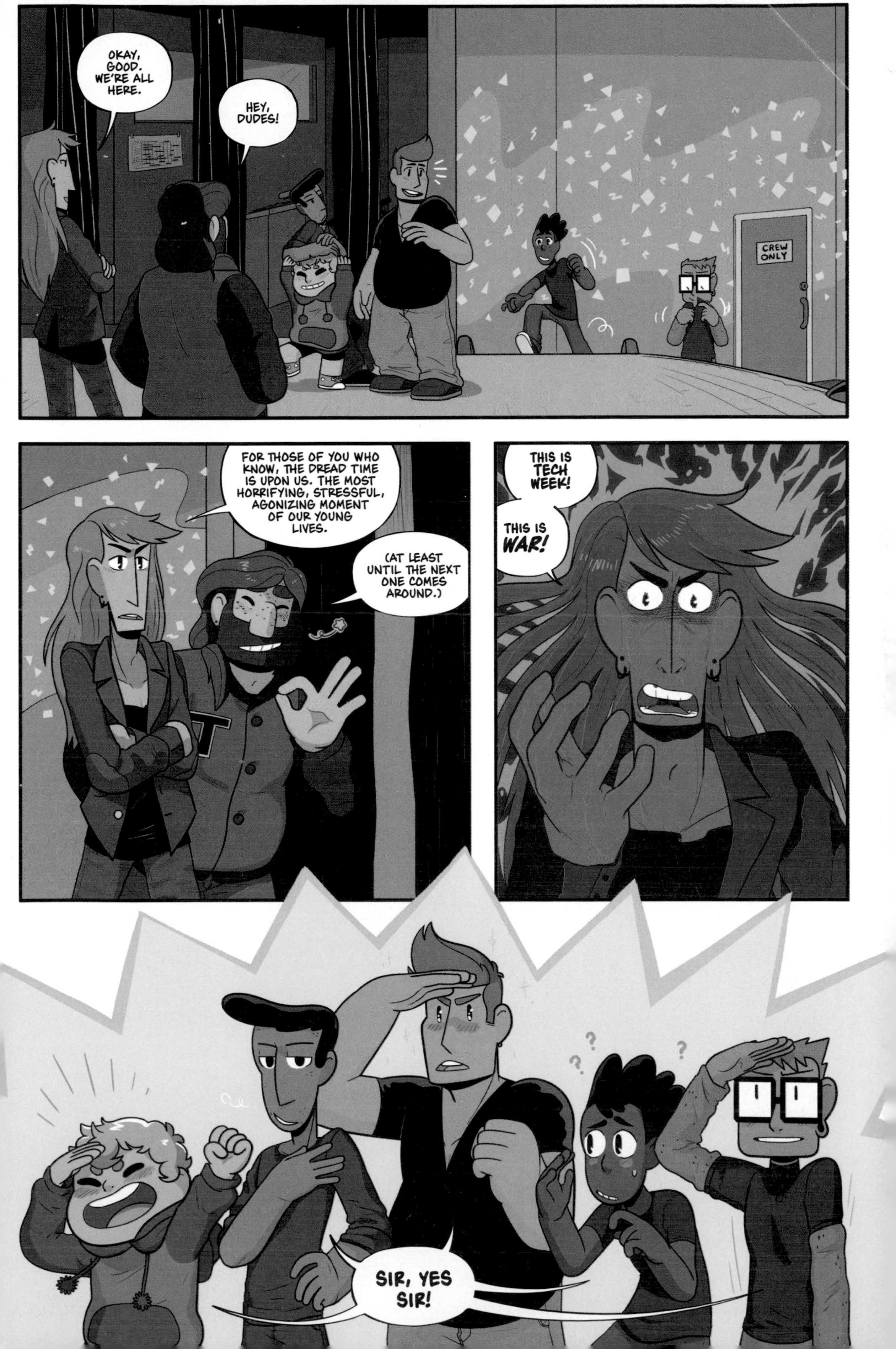
OKAY, GOOD. WE'RE ALL HERE.
HEY, DUDES!
CREW ONLY
FOR THOSE OF YOU WHO KNOW, THE DREAD TIME IS UPON US. THE MOST HORRIFYING, STRESSFUL, AGONIZING MOMENT OF OUR YOUNG LIVES.
(AT LEAST UNTIL THE NEXT ONE COMES AROUND.)
THIS IS TECH WEEK!
THIS IS WAR!
SIR, YES SIR!

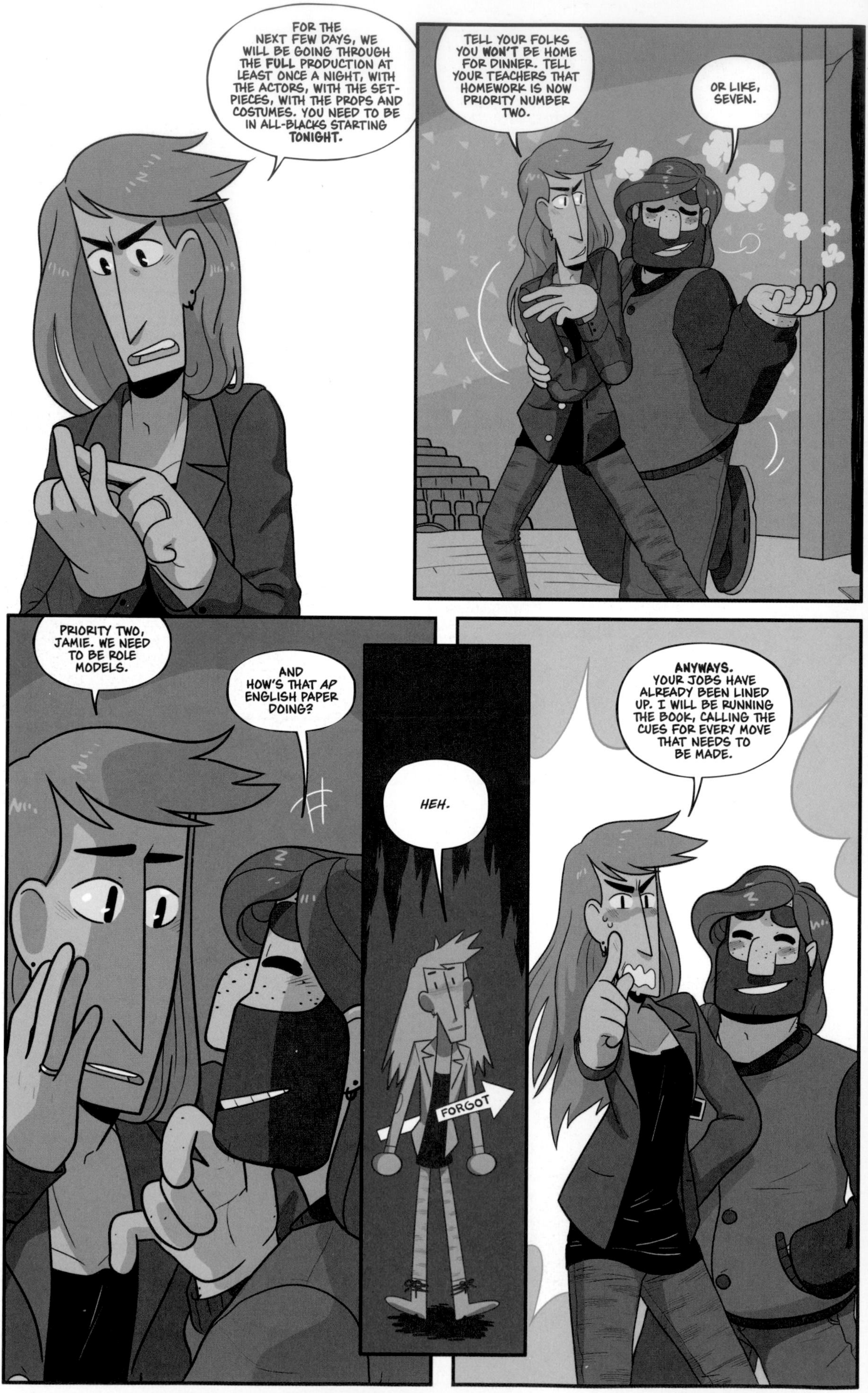
FOR THE NEXT FEW DAYS, WE WILL BE GOING THROUGH THE FULL PRODUCTION AT LEAST ONCE A NIGHT, WITH THE ACTORS, WITH THE SET-PIECES, WITH THE PROPS AND COSTUMES. YOU NEED TO BE IN ALL-BLACKS STARTING TONIGHT.
TELL YOUR FOLKS YOU WON'T BE HOME FOR DINNER. TELL YOUR TEACHERS THAT HOMEWORK IS NOW PRIORITY NUMBER TWO.
OR LIKE, SEVEN.
PRIORITY TWO, JAMIE. WE NEED TO BE ROLE MODELS.
AND HOW'S THAT AP ENGLISH PAPER DOING?
HEH.
FORGOT
ANYWAYS. YOUR JOBS HAVE ALREADY BEEN LINED UP. I WILL BE RUNNING THE BOOK, CALLING THE CUES FOR EVERY MOVE THAT NEEDS TO BE MADE.

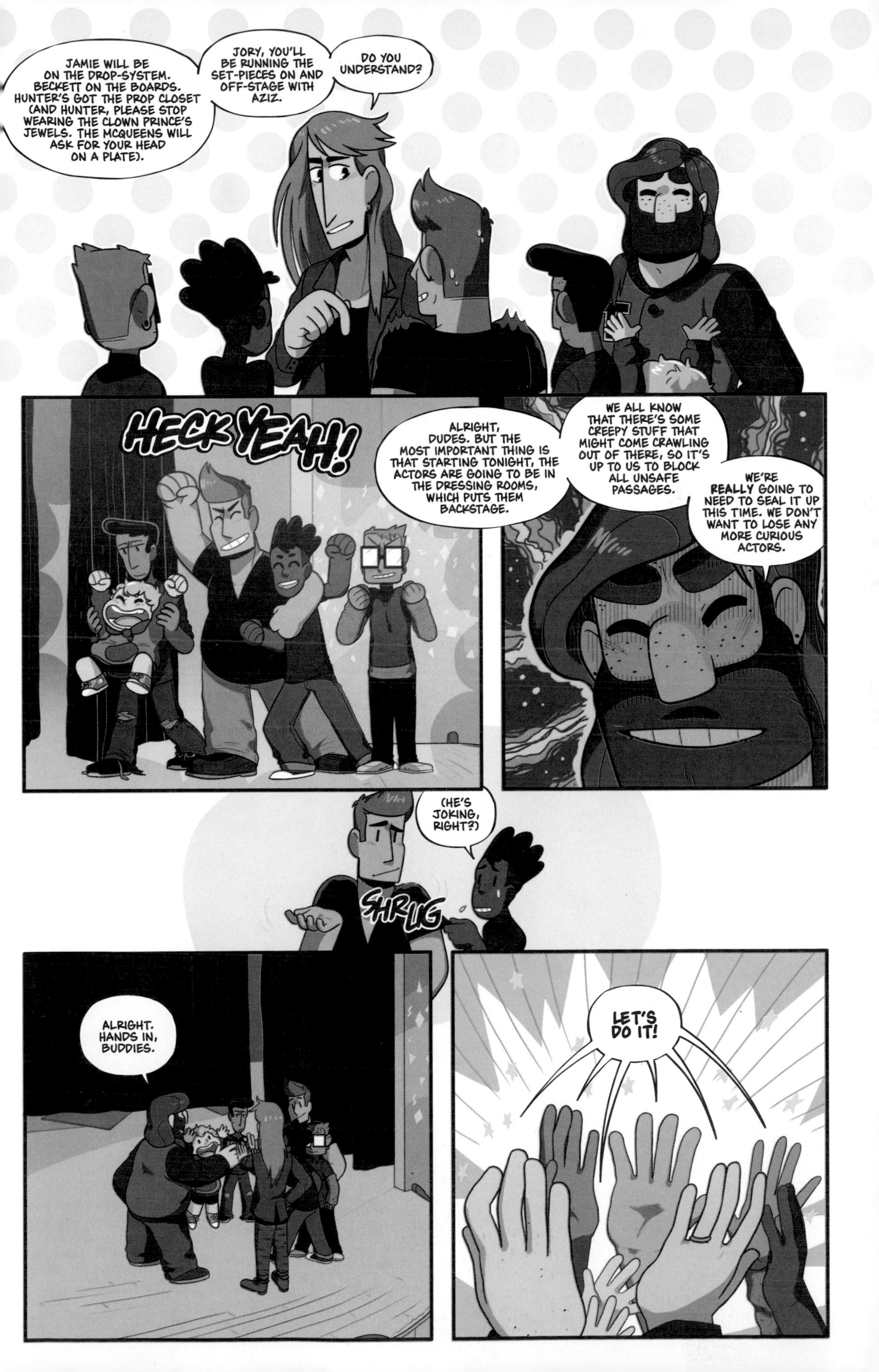
JAMIE WILL BE ON THE DROP-SYSTEM. BECKETT ON THE BOARDS. HUNTER'S GOT THE PROP CLOSET (AND HUNTER, PLEASE STOP WEARING THE CLOWN PRINCE'S JEWELS. THE MCQUEENS WILL ASK FOR YOUR HEAD ON A PLATE).
JORY, YOU'LL BE RUNNING THE SET-PIECES ON AND OFF-STAGE WITH AZIZ.
DO YOU UNDERSTAND?
HECK YEAH!
ALRIGHT, DUDES. BUT THE MOST IMPORTANT THING IS THAT STARTING TONIGHT, THE ACTORS ARE GOING TO BE IN THE DRESSING ROOMS, WHICH PUTS THEM BACKSTAGE.
WE ALL KNOW THAT THERE'S SOME CREEPY STUFF THAT MIGHT COME CRAWLING OUT OF THERE, SO IT'S UP TO US TO BLOCK ALL UNSAFE PASSAGES.
WE'RE **REALLY** GOING TO NEED TO SEAL IT UP THIS TIME. WE DON'T WANT TO LOSE ANY MORE CURIOUS ACTORS.
(HE'S JOKING, RIGHT?)
SHRUG
ALRIGHT. HANDS IN, BUDDIES.
LET'S DO IT!

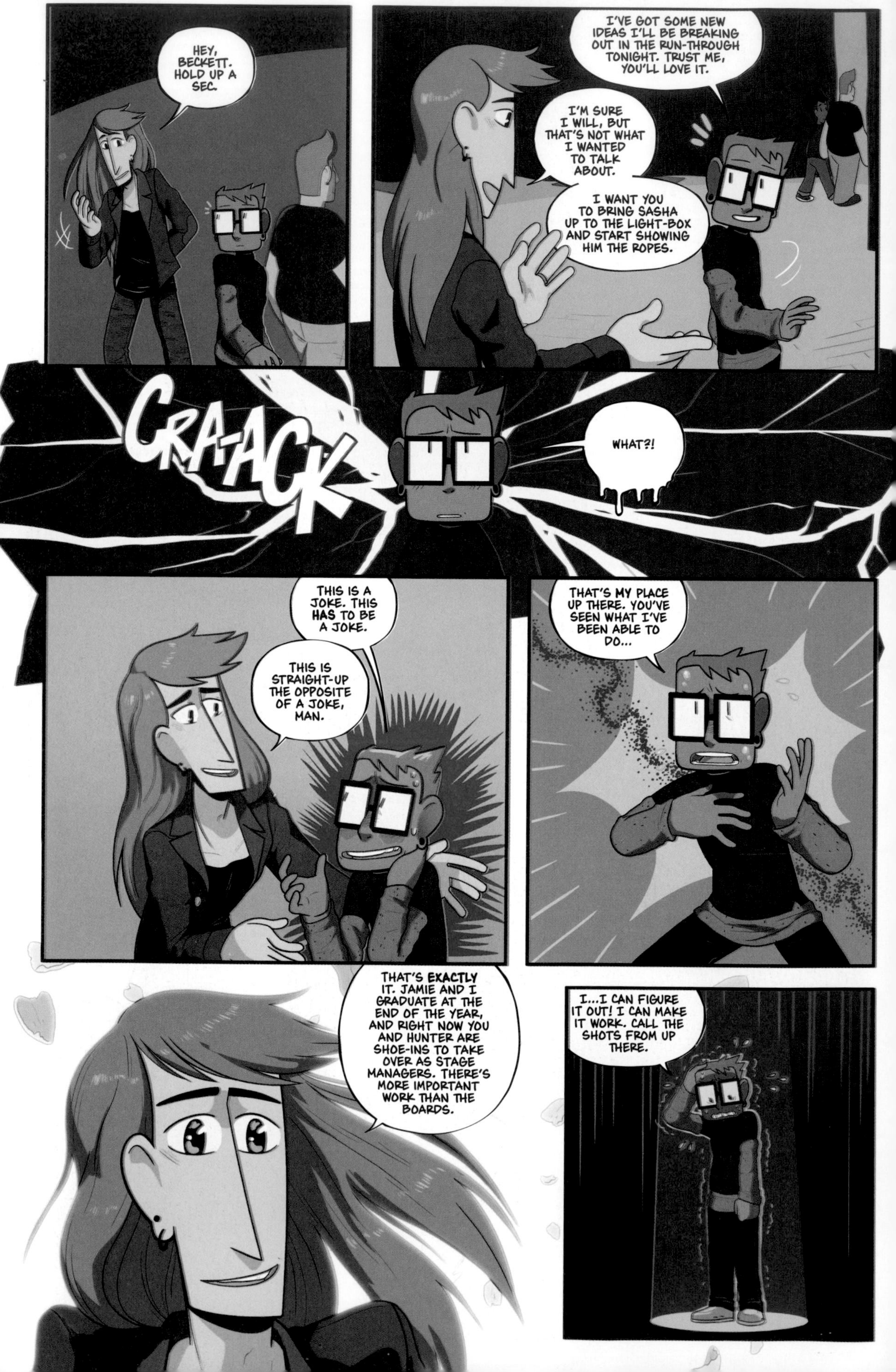
HEY, BECKETT. HOLD UP A SEC.
I'VE GOT SOME NEW IDEAS I'LL BE BREAKING OUT IN THE RUN-THROUGH TONIGHT. TRUST ME, YOU'LL LOVE IT.
I'M SURE I WILL, BUT THAT'S NOT WHAT I WANTED TO TALK ABOUT.
I WANT YOU TO BRING SASHA UP TO THE LIGHT-BOX AND START SHOWING HIM THE ROPES.
CRA-ACK
WHAT?!
THIS IS A JOKE. THIS HAS TO BE A JOKE.
THIS IS STRAIGHT-UP THE OPPOSITE OF A JOKE, MAN.
THAT'S MY PLACE UP THERE. YOU'VE SEEN WHAT I'VE BEEN ABLE TO DO...
THAT'S EXACTLY IT. JAMIE AND I GRADUATE AT THE END OF THE YEAR, AND RIGHT NOW YOU AND HUNTER ARE SHOE-INS TO TAKE OVER AS STAGE MANAGERS. THERE'S MORE IMPORTANT WORK THAN THE BOARDS.
I...I CAN FIGURE IT OUT! I CAN MAKE IT WORK. CALL THE SHOTS FROM UP THERE.

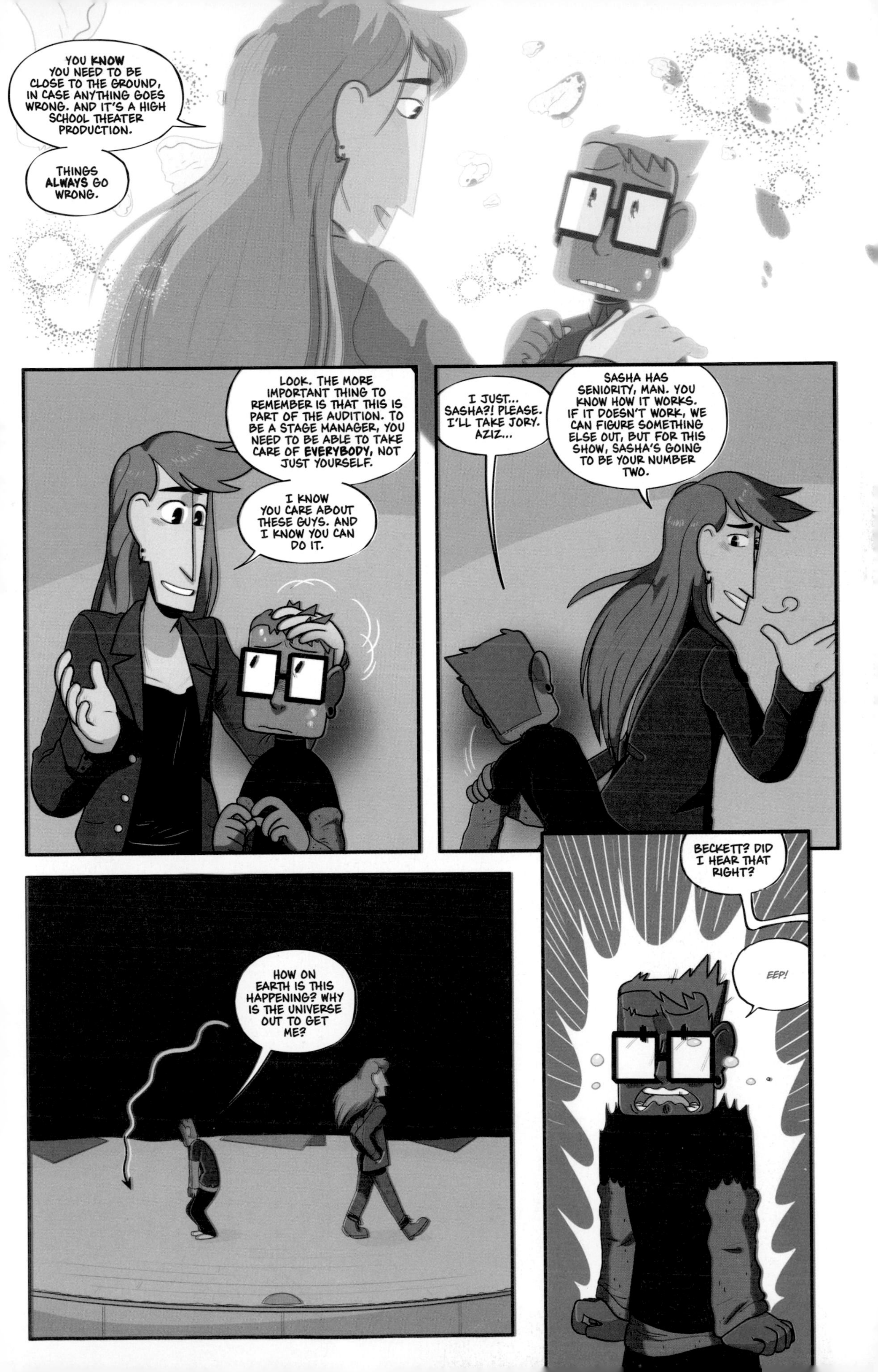

YOU KNOW YOU NEED TO BE CLOSE TO THE GROUND, IN CASE ANYTHING GOES WRONG. AND IT'S A HIGH SCHOOL THEATER PRODUCTION.
THINGS ALWAYS GO WRONG.
LOOK. THE MORE IMPORTANT THING TO REMEMBER IS THAT THIS IS PART OF THE AUDITION. TO BE A STAGE MANAGER, YOU NEED TO BE ABLE TO TAKE CARE OF EVERYBODY, NOT JUST YOURSELF.
I KNOW YOU CARE ABOUT THESE GUYS. AND I KNOW YOU CAN DO IT.
I JUST... SASHA?! PLEASE. I'LL TAKE JORY. AZIZ...
SASHA HAS SENIORITY, MAN. YOU KNOW HOW IT WORKS. IF IT DOESN'T WORK, WE CAN FIGURE SOMETHING ELSE OUT, BUT FOR THIS SHOW, SASHA'S GOING TO BE YOUR NUMBER TWO.
HOW ON EARTH IS THIS HAPPENING? WHY IS THE UNIVERSE OUT TO GET ME?
BECKETT? DID I HEAR THAT RIGHT?
EEP!

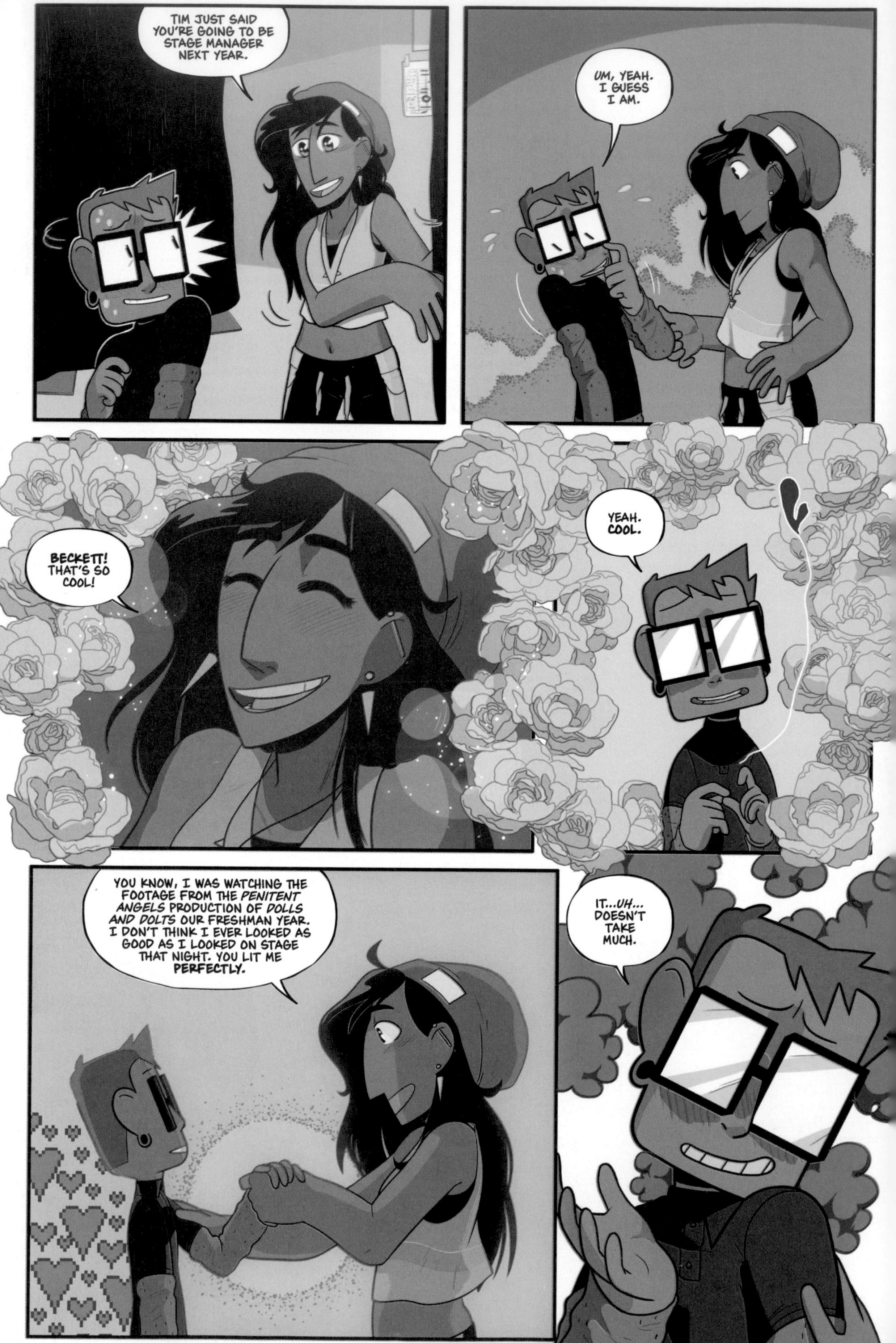
TIM JUST SAID YOU'RE GOING TO BE STAGE MANAGER NEXT YEAR.
UM, YEAH. I GUESS I AM.
BECKETT! THAT'S SO COOL!
YEAH. COOL.
YOU KNOW, I WAS WATCHING THE FOOTAGE FROM THE *PENITENT ANGELS* PRODUCTION OF *DOLLS AND DOLTS* OUR FRESHMAN YEAR. I DON'T THINK I EVER LOOKED AS GOOD AS I LOOKED ON STAGE THAT NIGHT. YOU LIT ME **PERFECTLY.**
IT...*UH*... DOESN'T TAKE MUCH.

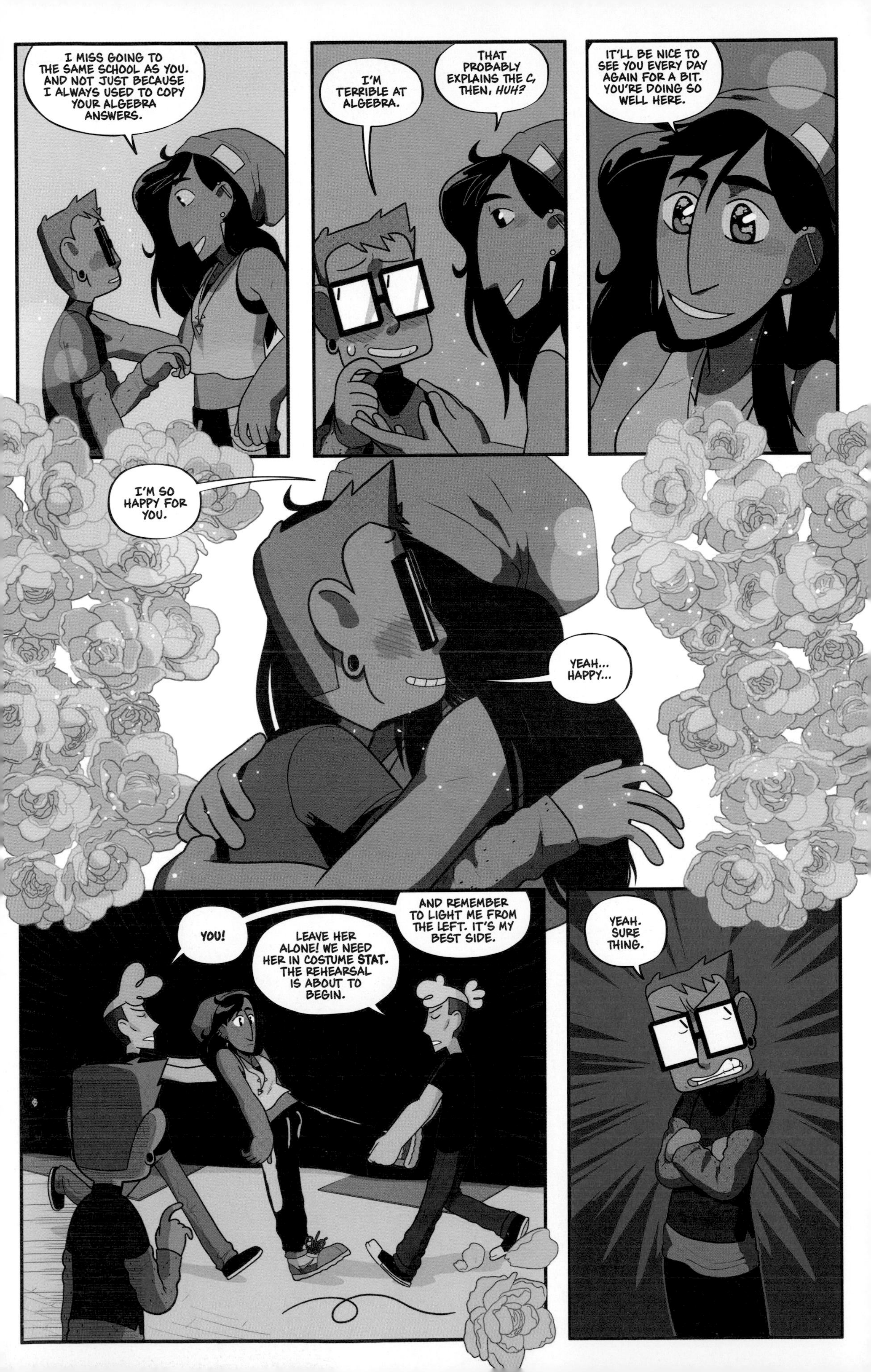
I MISS GOING TO THE SAME SCHOOL AS YOU. AND NOT JUST BECAUSE I ALWAYS USED TO COPY YOUR ALGEBRA ANSWERS.
I'M TERRIBLE AT ALGEBRA.
THAT PROBABLY EXPLAINS THE C, THEN, HUH?
IT'LL BE NICE TO SEE YOU EVERY DAY AGAIN FOR A BIT. YOU'RE DOING SO WELL HERE.
I'M SO HAPPY FOR YOU.
YEAH... HAPPY...
YOU!
LEAVE HER ALONE! WE NEED HER IN COSTUME STAT. THE REHEARSAL IS ABOUT TO BEGIN.
AND REMEMBER TO LIGHT ME FROM THE LEFT. IT'S MY BEST SIDE.
YEAH. SURE THING.

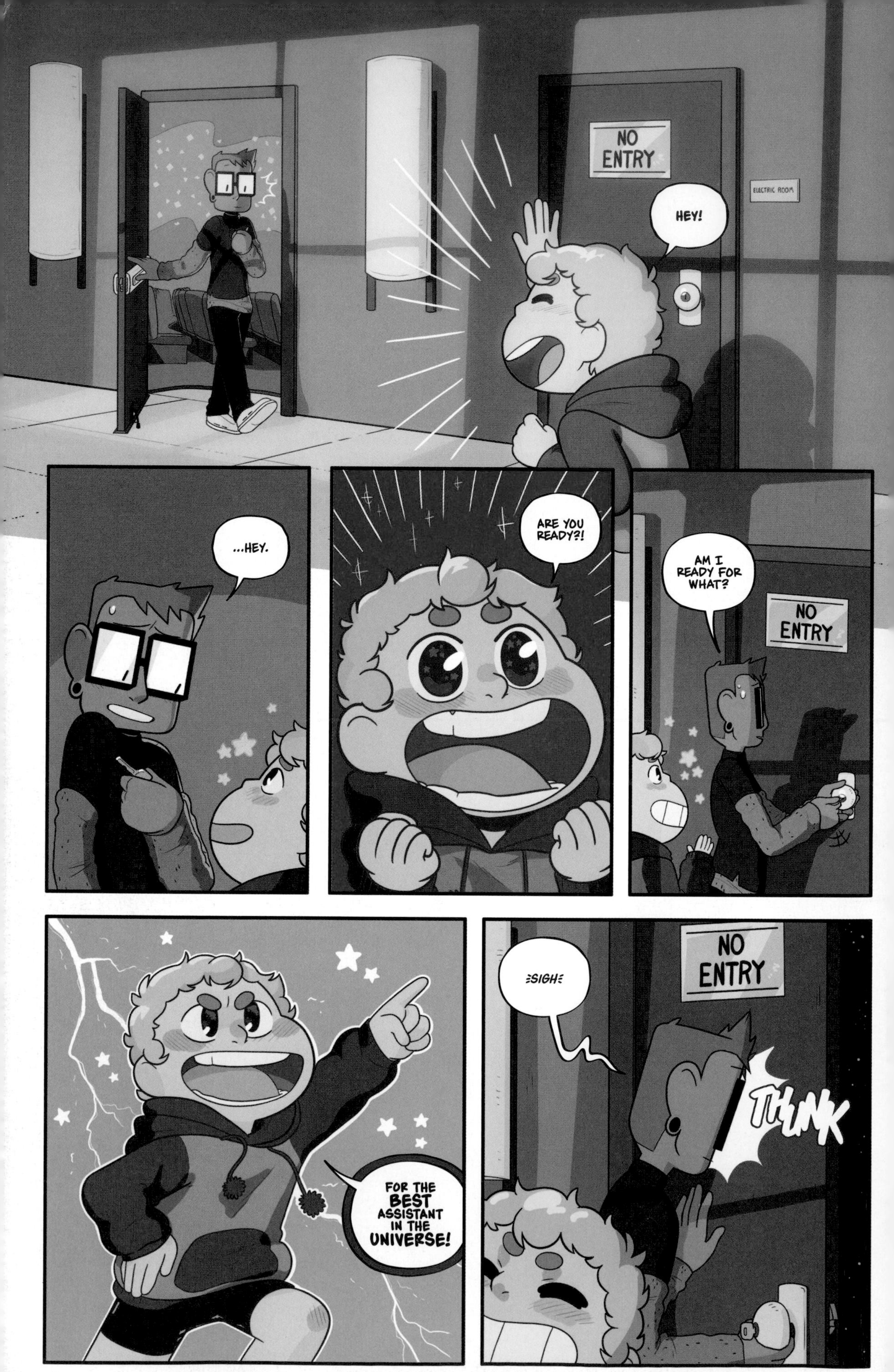
NO ENTRY
ELECTRIC ROOM
HEY!
...HEY.
ARE YOU READY?!
AM I READY FOR WHAT?
NO ENTRY
FOR THE BEST ASSISTANT IN THE UNIVERSE!
NO ENTRY
SIGH
THUNK

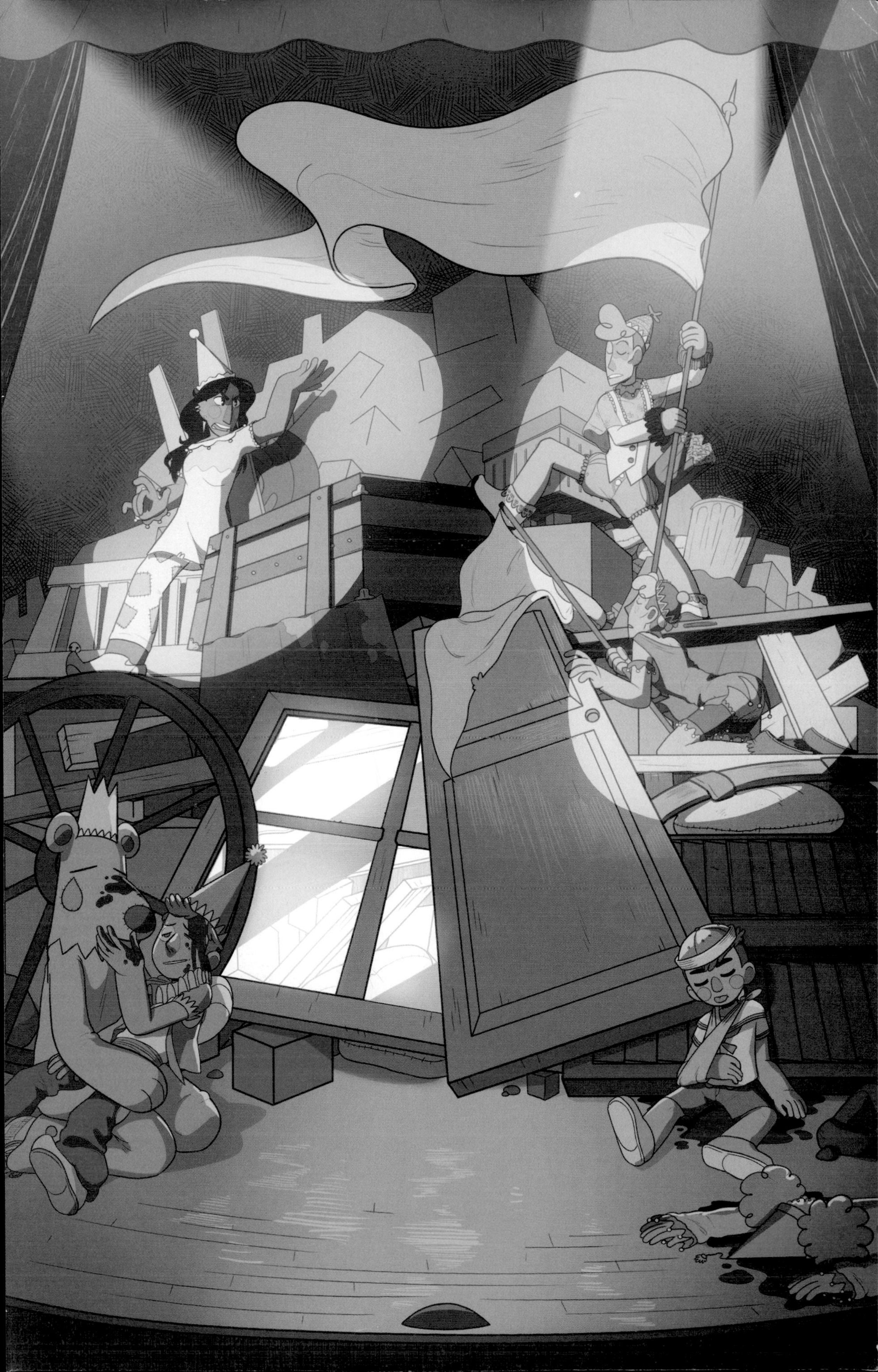

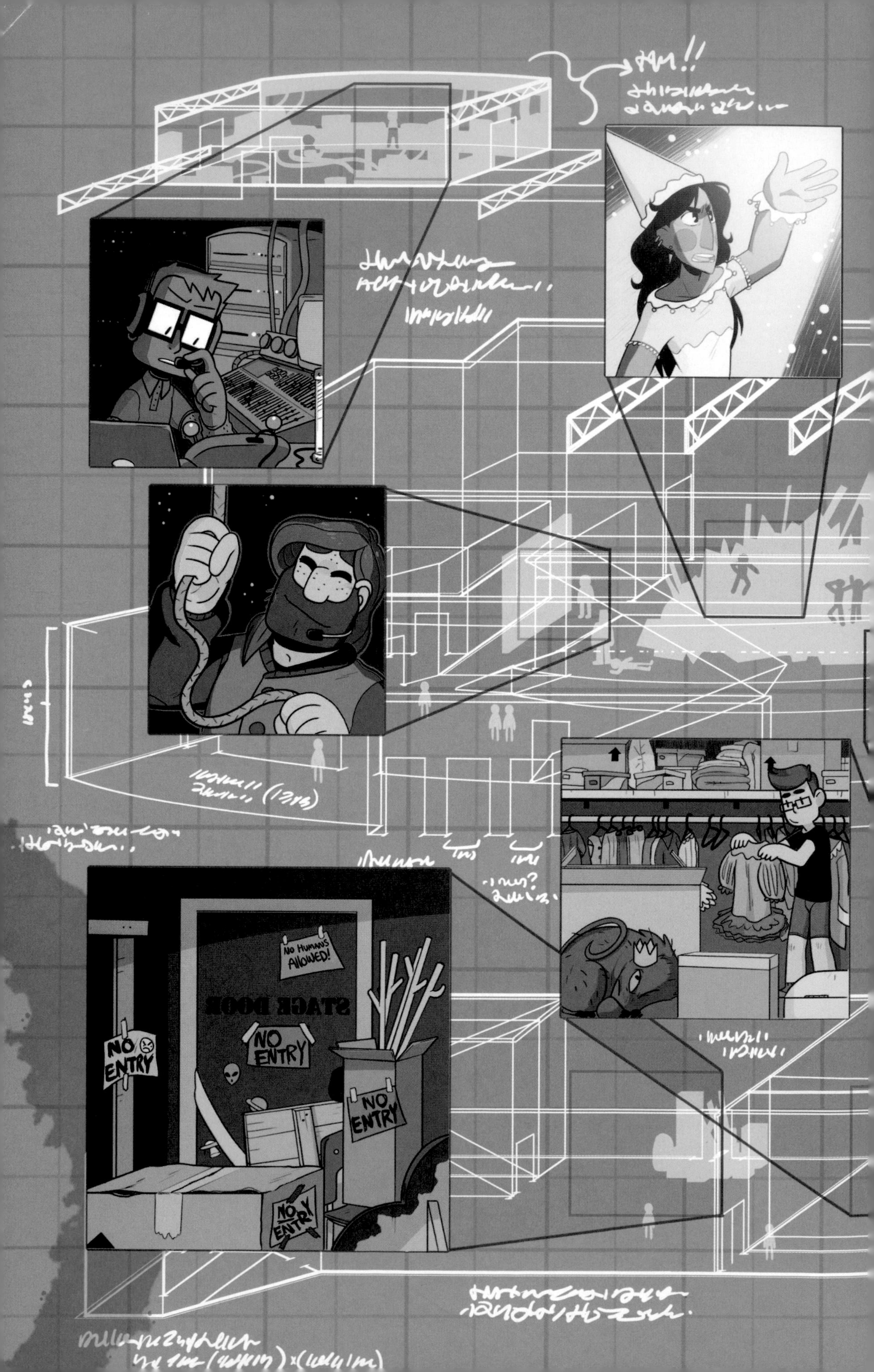
NO HUMANS ALLOWED!
STAGE DOOR
NO ENTRY
NO ENTRY
NO ENTRY
NO ENTRY

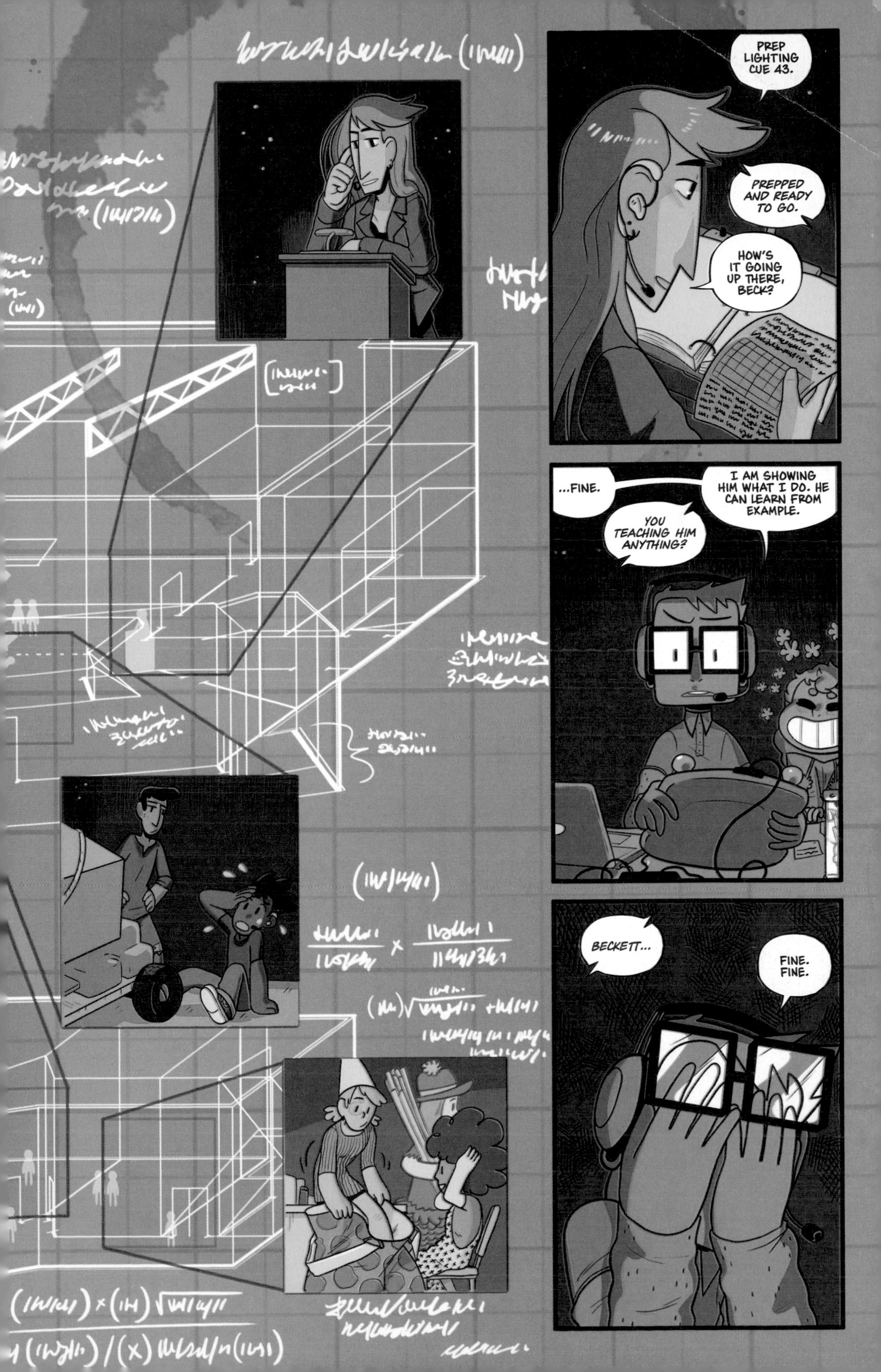
PREP LIGHTING CUE 43.
PREPPED AND READY TO GO.
HOW'S IT GOING UP THERE, BECK?
...FINE.
YOU TEACHING HIM ANYTHING?
I AM SHOWING HIM WHAT I DO. HE CAN LEARN FROM EXAMPLE.
BECKETT...
FINE. FINE.

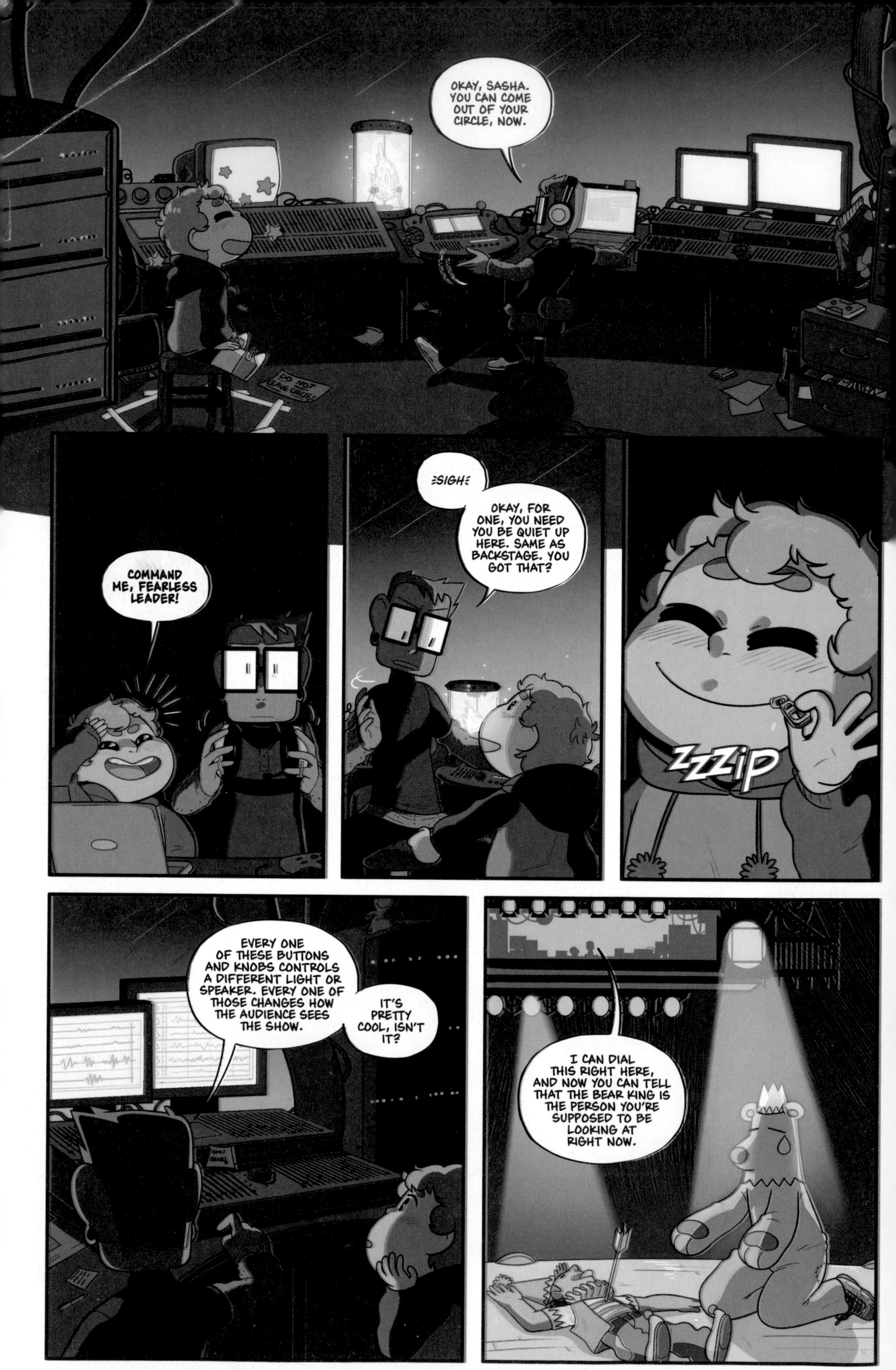
OKAY, SASHA. YOU CAN COME OUT OF YOUR CIRCLE, NOW.
DO NOT LEAVE CIRCLE!
COMMAND ME, FEARLESS LEADER!
SIGH
OKAY, FOR ONE, YOU NEED YOU BE QUIET UP HERE. SAME AS BACKSTAGE. YOU GOT THAT?
ZZZIP
EVERY ONE OF THESE BUTTONS AND KNOBS CONTROLS A DIFFERENT LIGHT OR SPEAKER. EVERY ONE OF THOSE CHANGES HOW THE AUDIENCE SEES THE SHOW.
IT'S PRETTY COOL, ISN'T IT?
I CAN DIAL THIS RIGHT HERE, AND NOW YOU CAN TELL THAT THE BEAR KING IS THE PERSON YOU'RE SUPPOSED TO BE LOOKING AT RIGHT NOW.

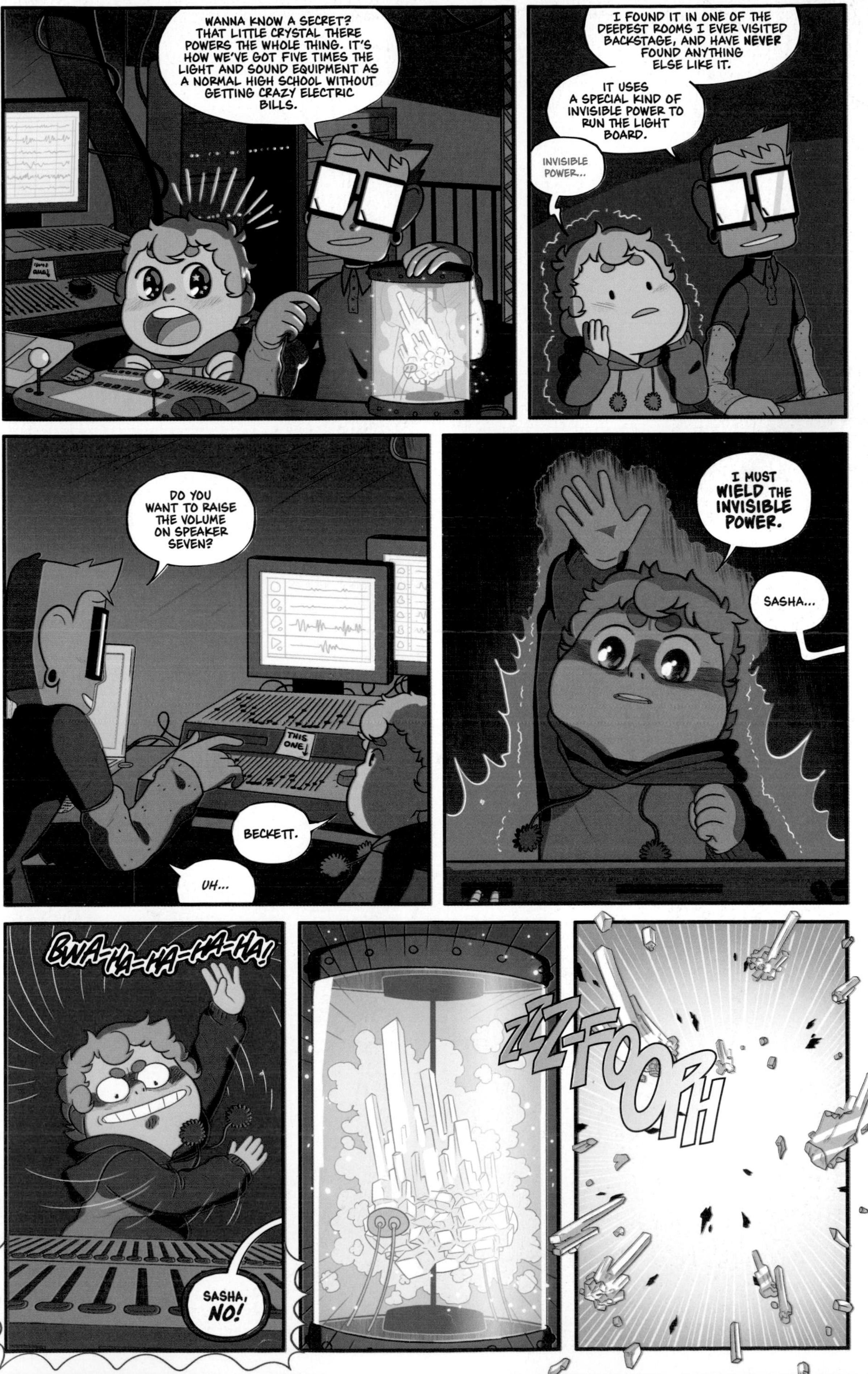
WANNA KNOW A SECRET? THAT LITTLE CRYSTAL THERE POWERS THE WHOLE THING. IT'S HOW WE'VE GOT FIVE TIMES THE LIGHT AND SOUND EQUIPMENT AS A NORMAL HIGH SCHOOL WITHOUT GETTING CRAZY ELECTRIC BILLS.
I FOUND IT IN ONE OF THE DEEPEST ROOMS I EVER VISITED BACKSTAGE, AND HAVE NEVER FOUND ANYTHING ELSE LIKE IT.
IT USES A SPECIAL KIND OF INVISIBLE POWER TO RUN THE LIGHT BOARD.
INVISIBLE POWER...
DO YOU WANT TO RAISE THE VOLUME ON SPEAKER SEVEN?
THIS ONE
UH...
BECKETT.
I MUST WIELD THE INVISIBLE POWER.
SASHA...
BWA-HA-HA-HA-HA!
SASHA, NO!
ZZZ-FOOPH

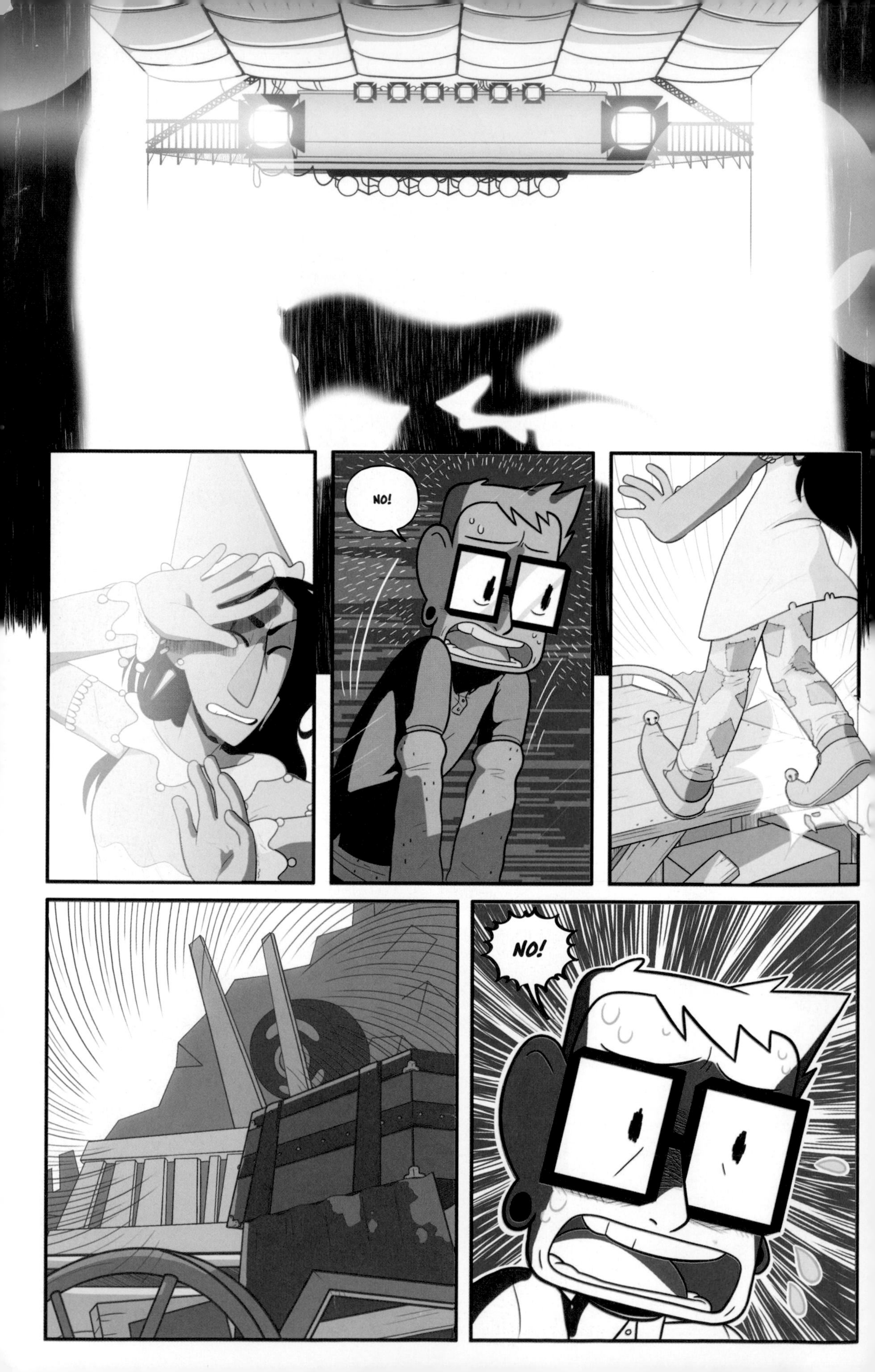
NO!
NO!

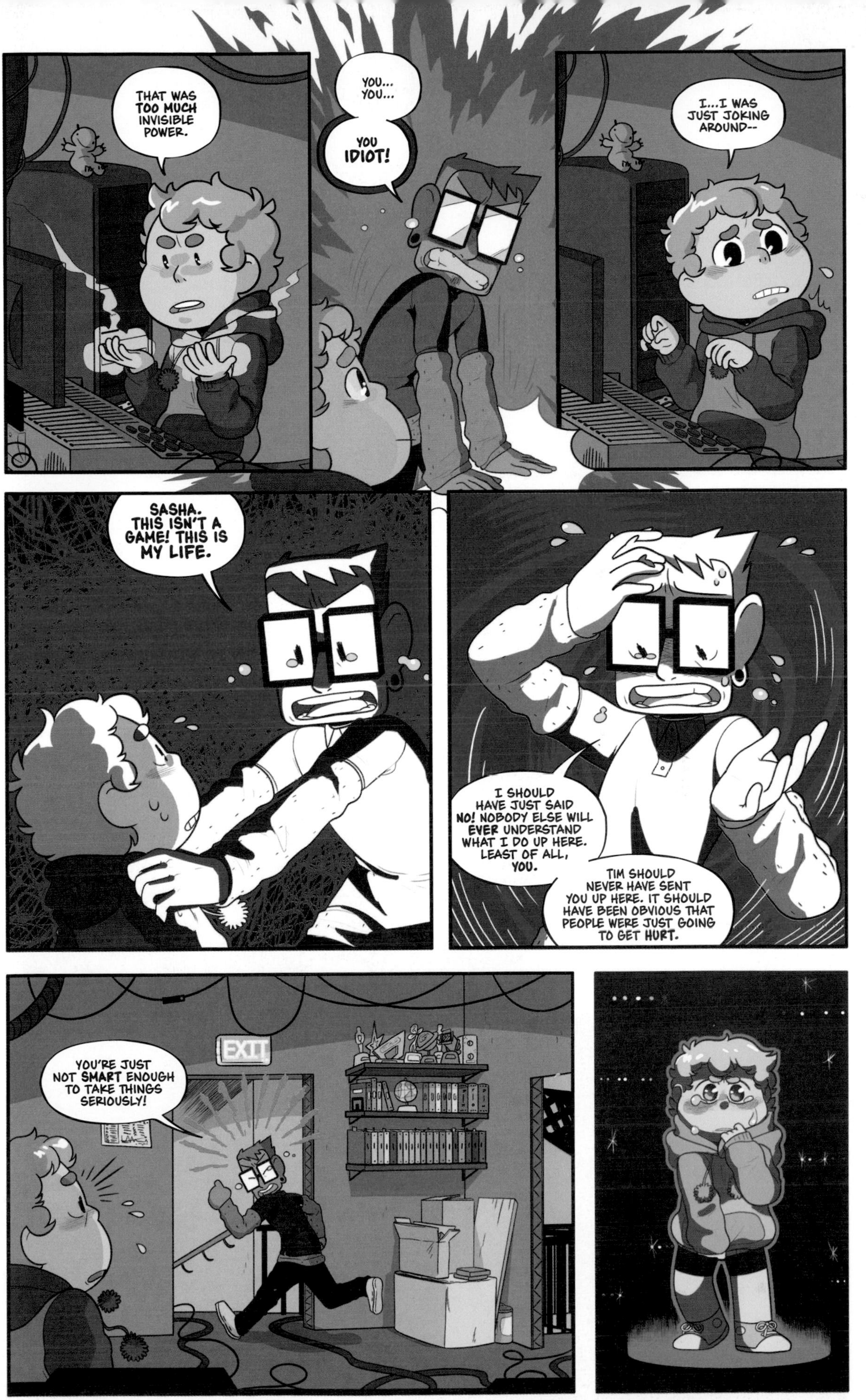
THAT WAS TOO MUCH INVISIBLE POWER.
YOU... YOU...
YOU IDIOT!
I...I WAS JUST JOKING AROUND--
SASHA. THIS ISN'T A GAME! THIS IS MY LIFE.
I SHOULD HAVE JUST SAID NO! NOBODY ELSE WILL EVER UNDERSTAND WHAT I DO UP HERE. LEAST OF ALL, YOU.
TIM SHOULD NEVER HAVE SENT YOU UP HERE. IT SHOULD HAVE BEEN OBVIOUS THAT PEOPLE WERE JUST GOING TO GET HURT.
EXIT
YOU'RE JUST NOT SMART ENOUGH TO TAKE THINGS SERIOUSLY!

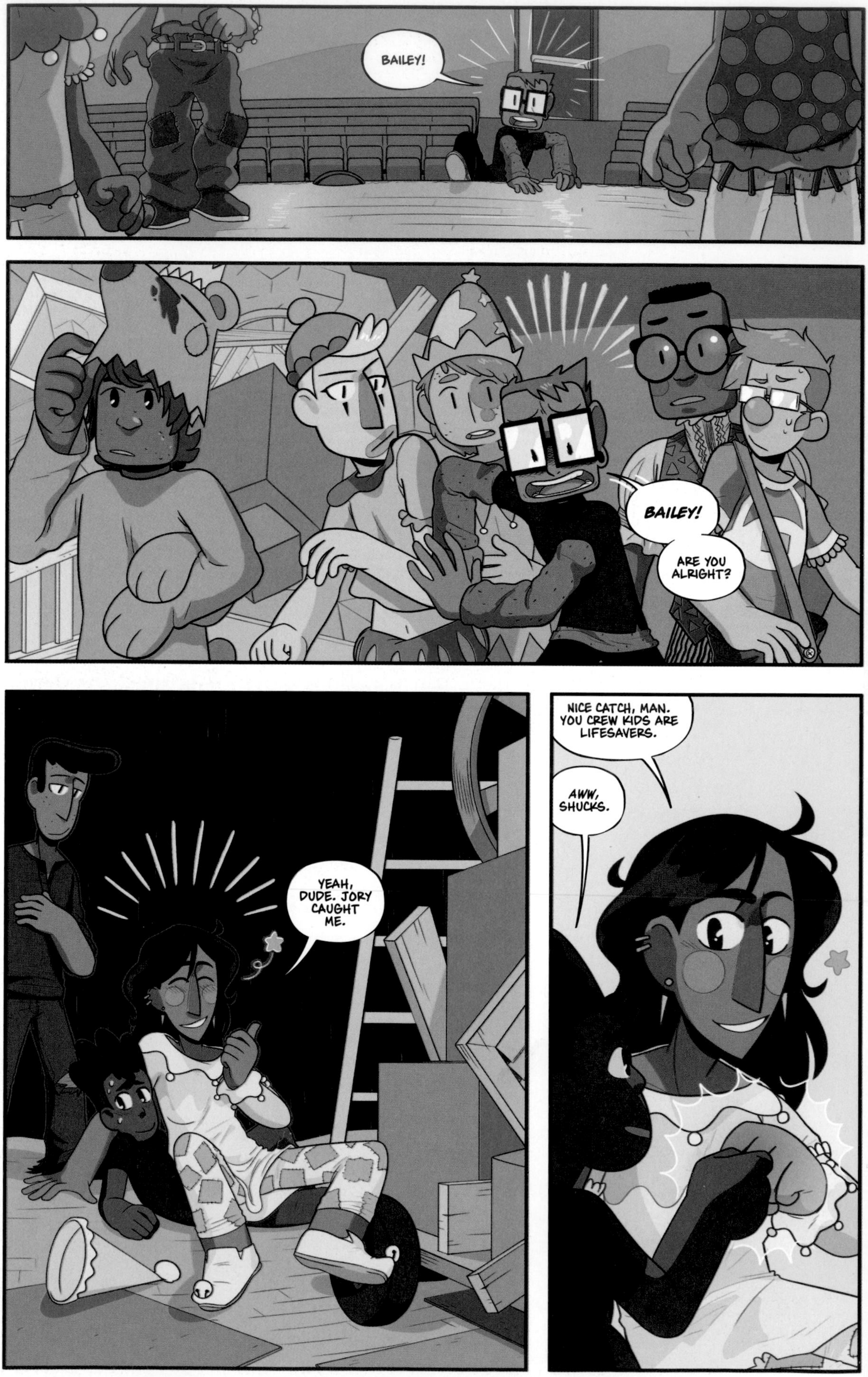
BAILEY!
BAILEY!
ARE YOU ALRIGHT?
YEAH, DUDE. JORY CAUGHT ME.
NICE CATCH, MAN. YOU CREW KIDS ARE LIFESAVERS.
AWW, SHUCKS.

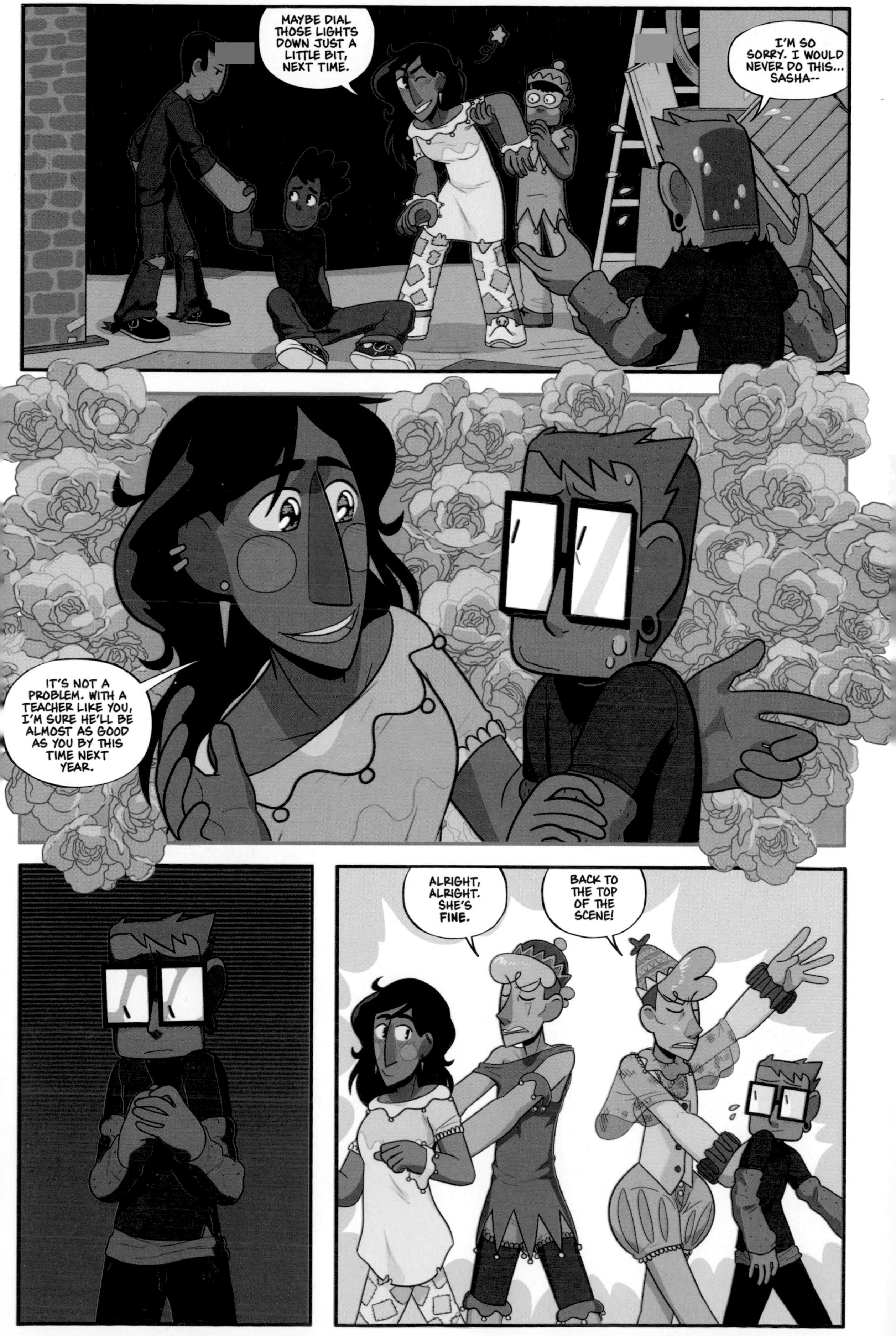
MAYBE DIAL THOSE LIGHTS DOWN JUST A LITTLE BIT, NEXT TIME.
I'M SO SORRY. I WOULD NEVER DO THIS... SASHA--
IT'S NOT A PROBLEM. WITH A TEACHER LIKE YOU, I'M SURE HE'LL BE ALMOST AS GOOD AS YOU BY THIS TIME NEXT YEAR.
ALRIGHT, ALRIGHT. SHE'S FINE.
BACK TO THE TOP OF THE SCENE!

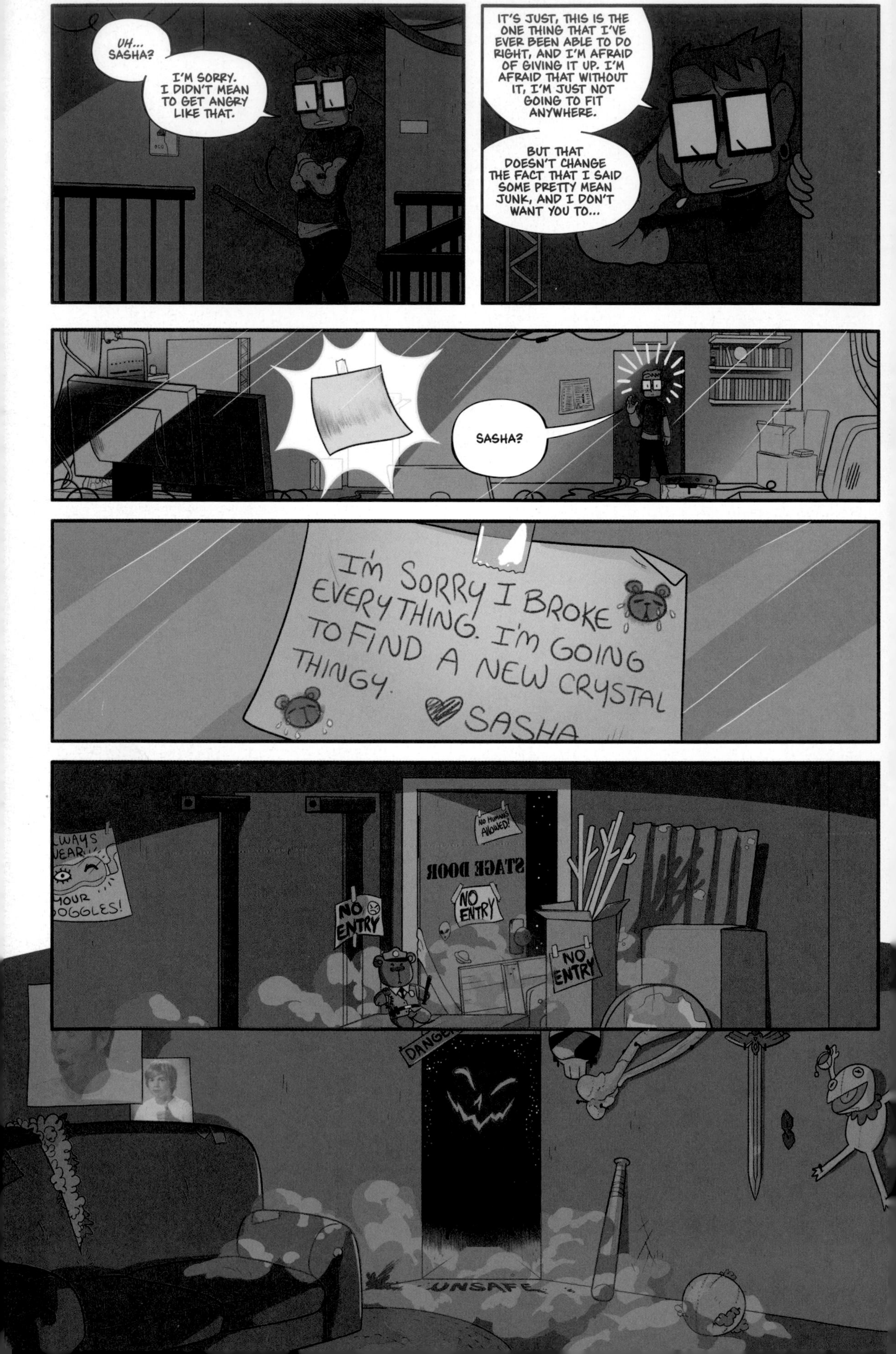
UH... SASHA?
I'M SORRY. I DIDN'T MEAN TO GET ANGRY LIKE THAT.
IT'S JUST, THIS IS THE ONE THING THAT I'VE EVER BEEN ABLE TO DO RIGHT, AND I'M AFRAID OF GIVING IT UP. I'M AFRAID THAT WITHOUT IT, I'M JUST NOT GOING TO FIT ANYWHERE.
BUT THAT DOESN'T CHANGE THE FACT THAT I SAID SOME PRETTY MEAN JUNK, AND I DON'T WANT YOU TO...
SASHA?
I'M SORRY I BROKE EVERYTHING. I'M GOING TO FIND A NEW CRYSTAL THINGY. SASHA
ALWAYS WEAR YOUR GOGGLES!
NO HUMANS ALLOWED!
STAGE DOOR
NO ENTRY
NO ENTRY
NO ENTRY
DANGER
UNSAFE

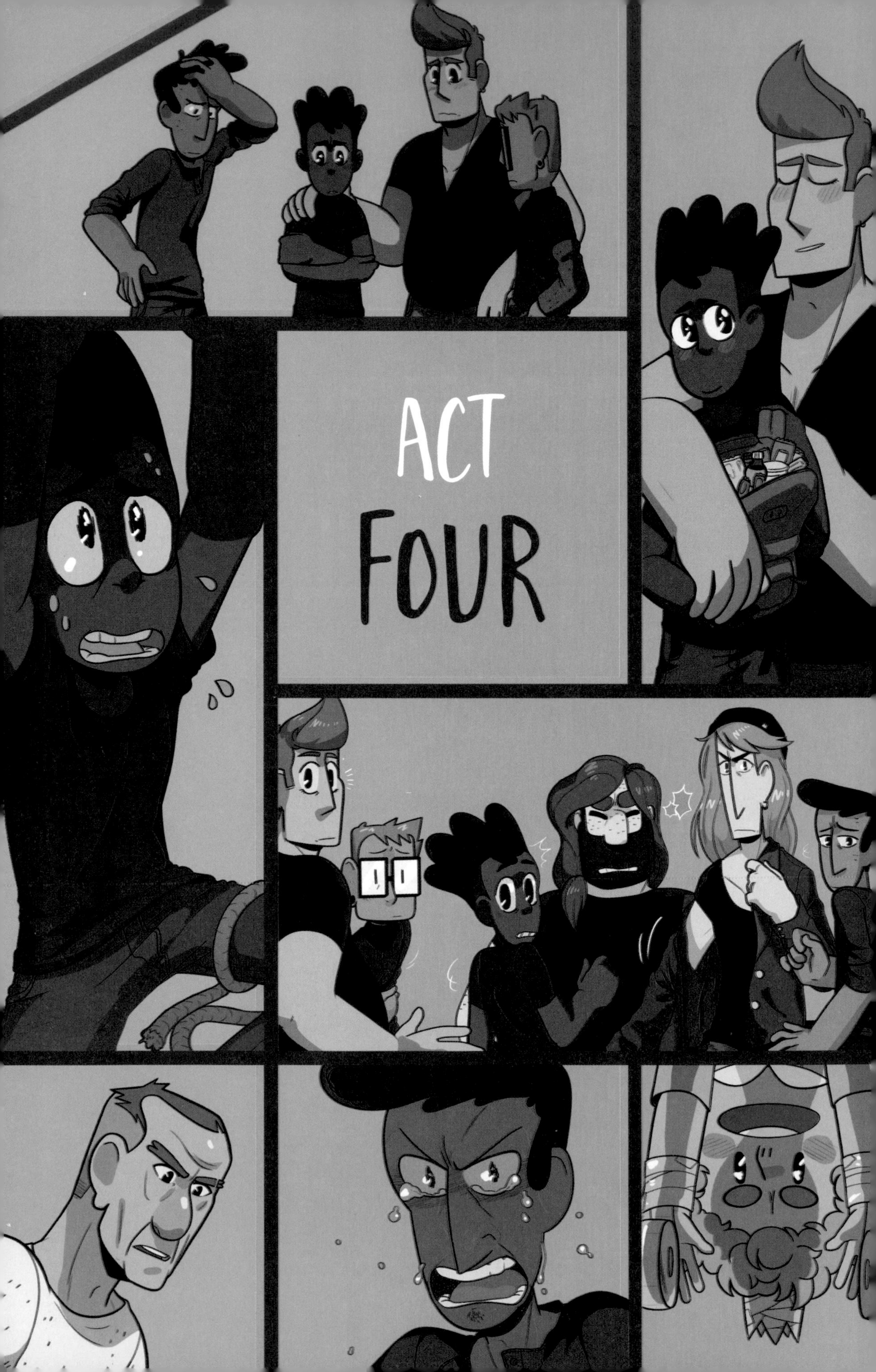
ACT
FOUR

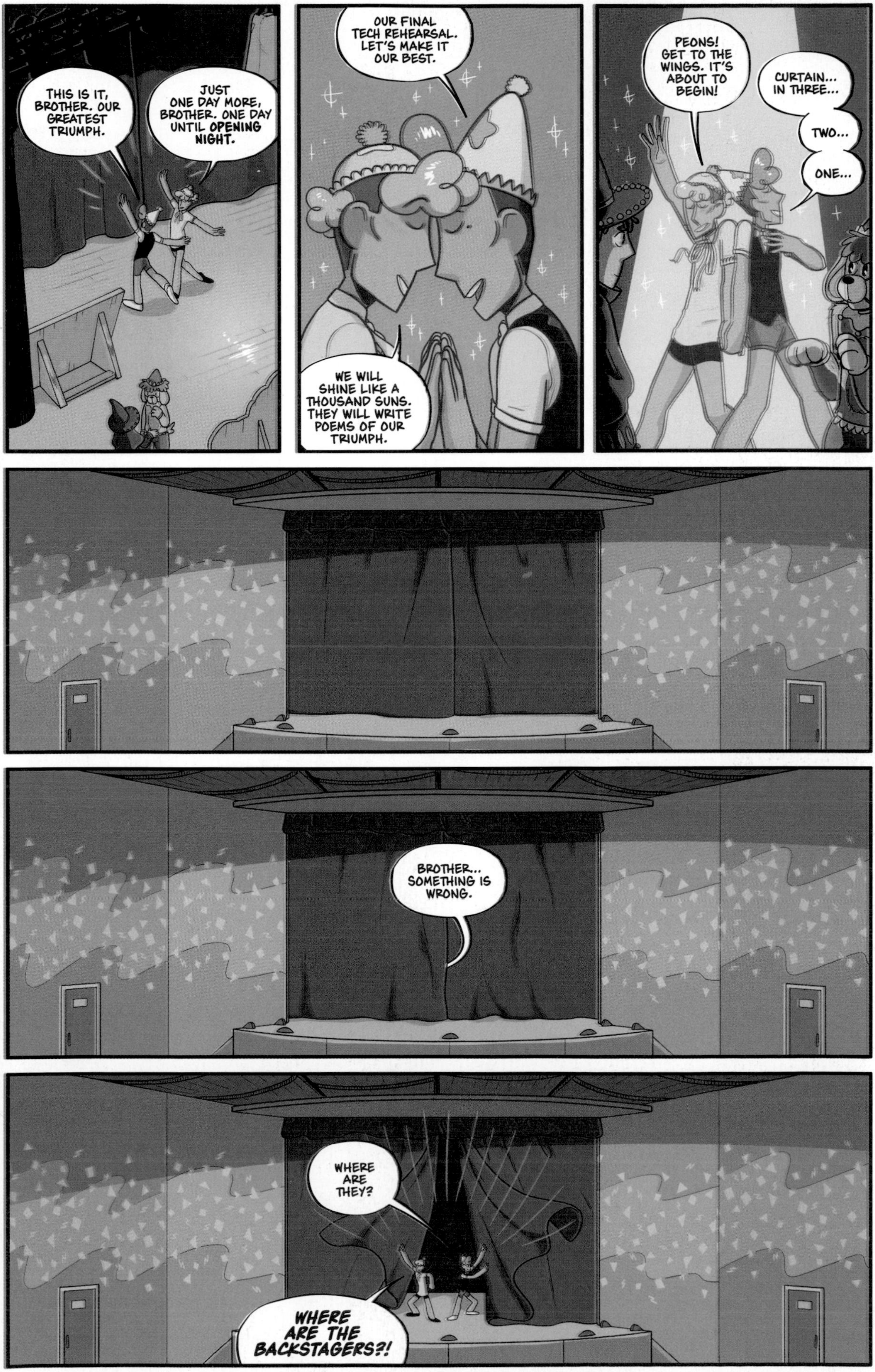
THIS IS IT, BROTHER. OUR GREATEST TRIUMPH.
JUST ONE DAY MORE, BROTHER. ONE DAY UNTIL OPENING NIGHT.
OUR FINAL TECH REHEARSAL. LET'S MAKE IT OUR BEST.
WE WILL SHINE LIKE A THOUSAND SUNS. THEY WILL WRITE POEMS OF OUR TRIUMPH.
PEONS! GET TO THE WINGS. IT'S ABOUT TO BEGIN!
CURTAIN... IN THREE...
TWO...
ONE...
BROTHER... SOMETHING IS WRONG.
WHERE ARE THEY?
WHERE ARE THE BACKSTAGERS?!

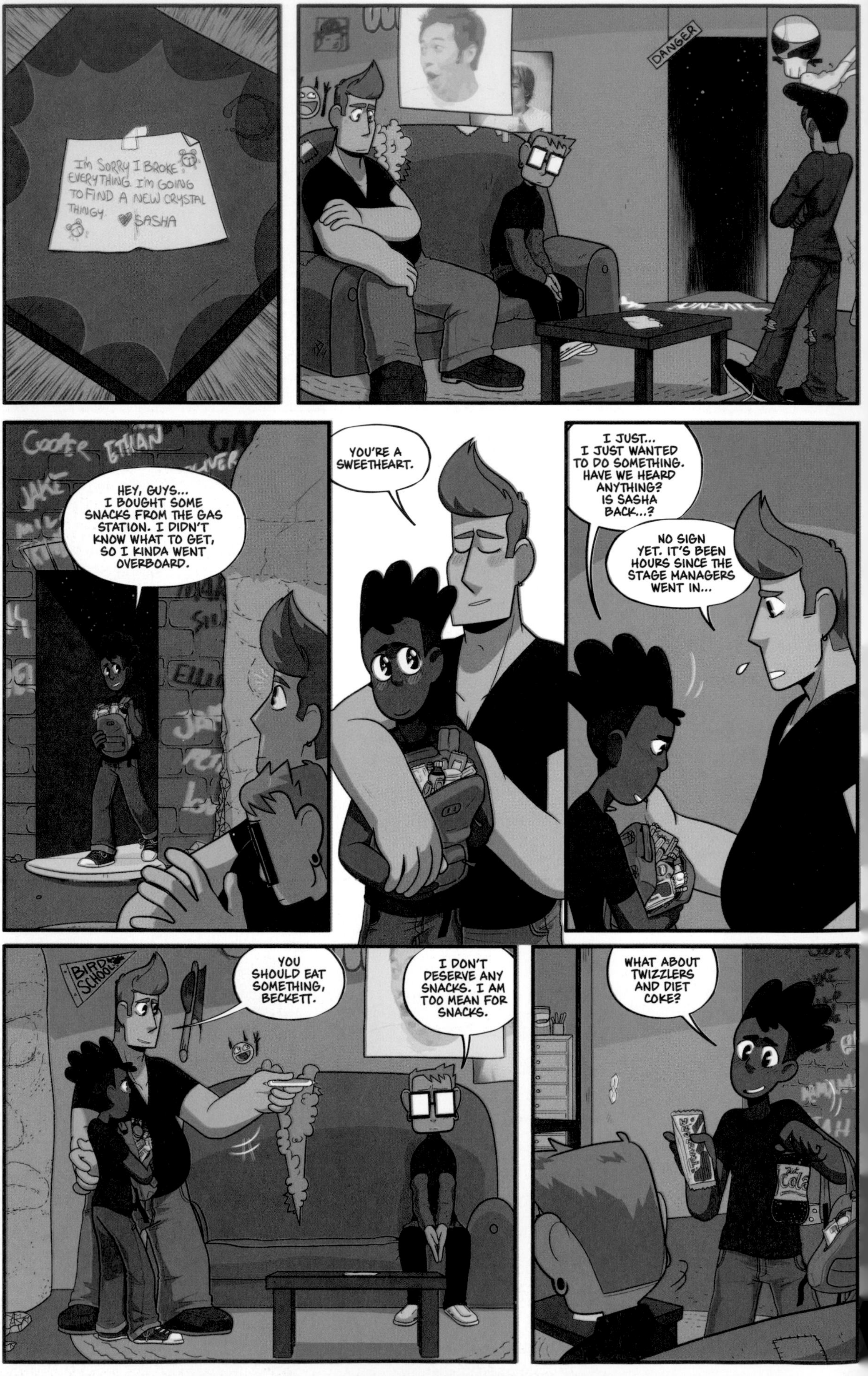
I'M SORRY I BROKE EVERYTHING. I'M GOING TO FIND A NEW CRYSTAL THINGY. SASHA
DANGER
COOPER
ETHAN
JAKE
HEY, GUYS... I BOUGHT SOME SNACKS FROM THE GAS STATION. I DIDN'T KNOW WHAT TO GET, SO I KINDA WENT OVERBOARD.
YOU'RE A SWEETHEART.
I JUST... I JUST WANTED TO DO SOMETHING. HAVE WE HEARD ANYTHING? IS SASHA BACK...?
NO SIGN YET. IT'S BEEN HOURS SINCE THE STAGE MANAGERS WENT IN...
BIRD SCHOOL
YOU SHOULD EAT SOMETHING, BECKETT.
I DON'T DESERVE ANY SNACKS. I AM TOO MEAN FOR SNACKS.
WHAT ABOUT TWIZZLERS AND DIET COKE?

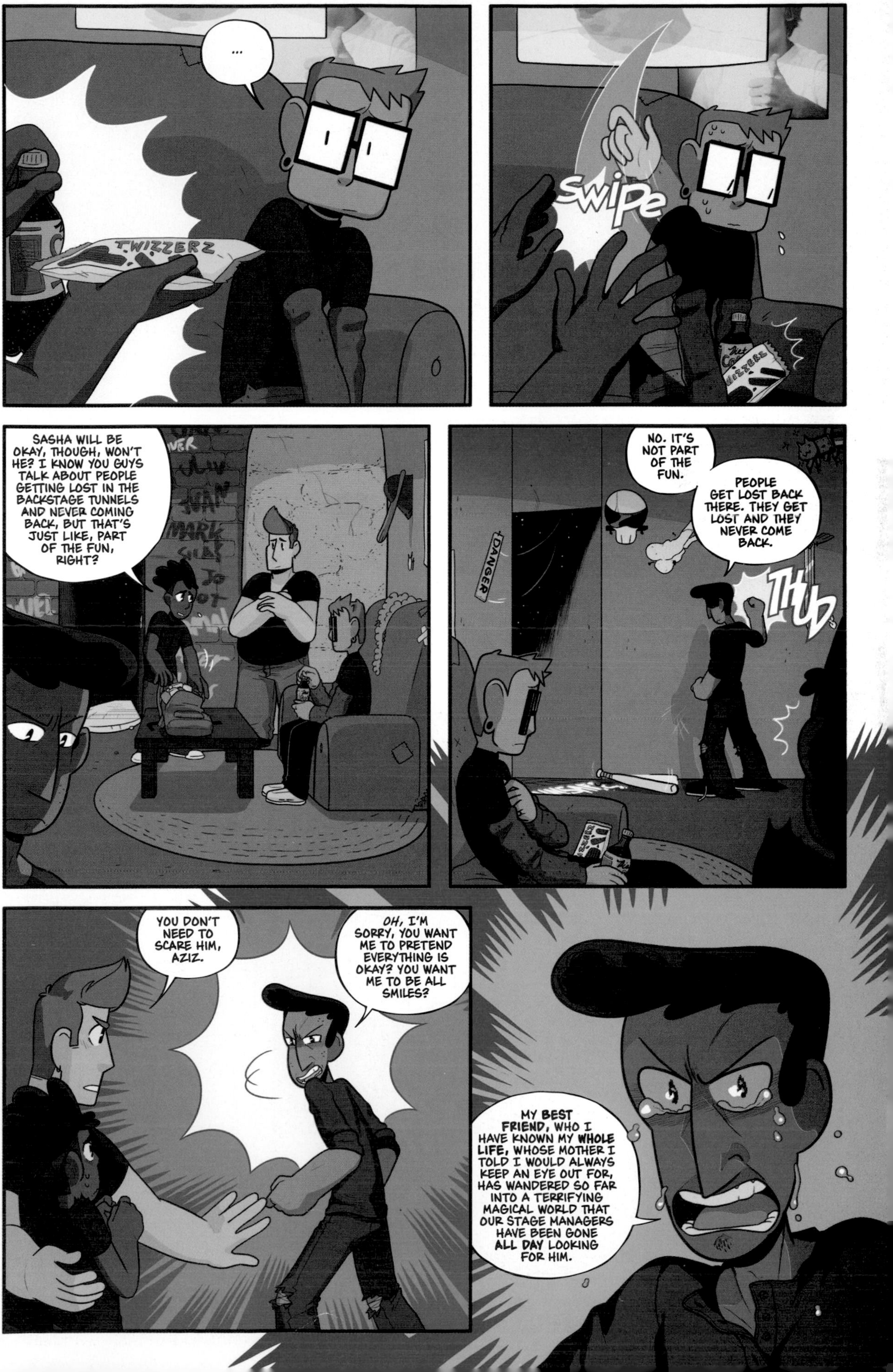

...
TWIZZERZ
SWIPE
SASHA WILL BE OKAY, THOUGH, WON'T HE? I KNOW YOU GUYS TALK ABOUT PEOPLE GETTING LOST IN THE BACKSTAGE TUNNELS AND NEVER COMING BACK, BUT THAT'S JUST LIKE, PART OF THE FUN, RIGHT?
NO. IT'S NOT PART OF THE FUN.
PEOPLE GET LOST BACK THERE. THEY GET LOST AND THEY NEVER COME BACK.
DANGER
THUD
YOU DON'T NEED TO SCARE HIM, AZIZ.
OH, I'M SORRY, YOU WANT ME TO PRETEND EVERYTHING IS OKAY? YOU WANT ME TO BE ALL SMILES?
MY BEST FRIEND, WHO I HAVE KNOWN MY WHOLE LIFE, WHOSE MOTHER I TOLD I WOULD ALWAYS KEEP AN EYE OUT FOR, HAS WANDERED SO FAR INTO A TERRIFYING MAGICAL WORLD THAT OUR STAGE MANAGERS HAVE BEEN GONE ALL DAY LOOKING FOR HIM.

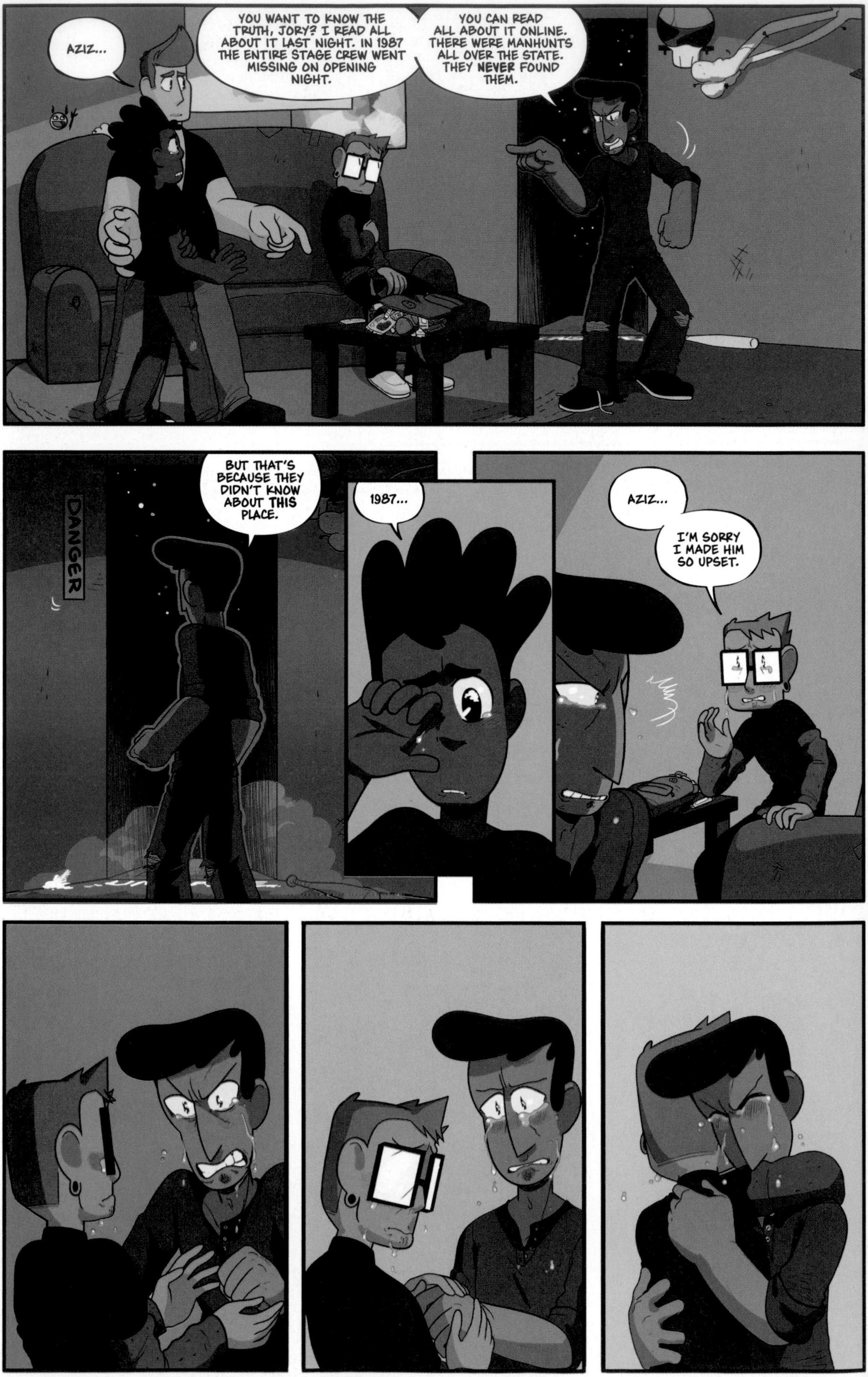
AZIZ...
YOU WANT TO KNOW THE TRUTH, JORY? I READ ALL ABOUT IT LAST NIGHT. IN 1987 THE ENTIRE STAGE CREW WENT MISSING ON OPENING NIGHT.
YOU CAN READ ALL ABOUT IT ONLINE. THERE WERE MANHUNTS ALL OVER THE STATE. THEY NEVER FOUND THEM.
DANGER
BUT THAT'S BECAUSE THEY DIDN'T KNOW ABOUT THIS PLACE.
1987...
AZIZ...
I'M SORRY I MADE HIM SO UPSET.

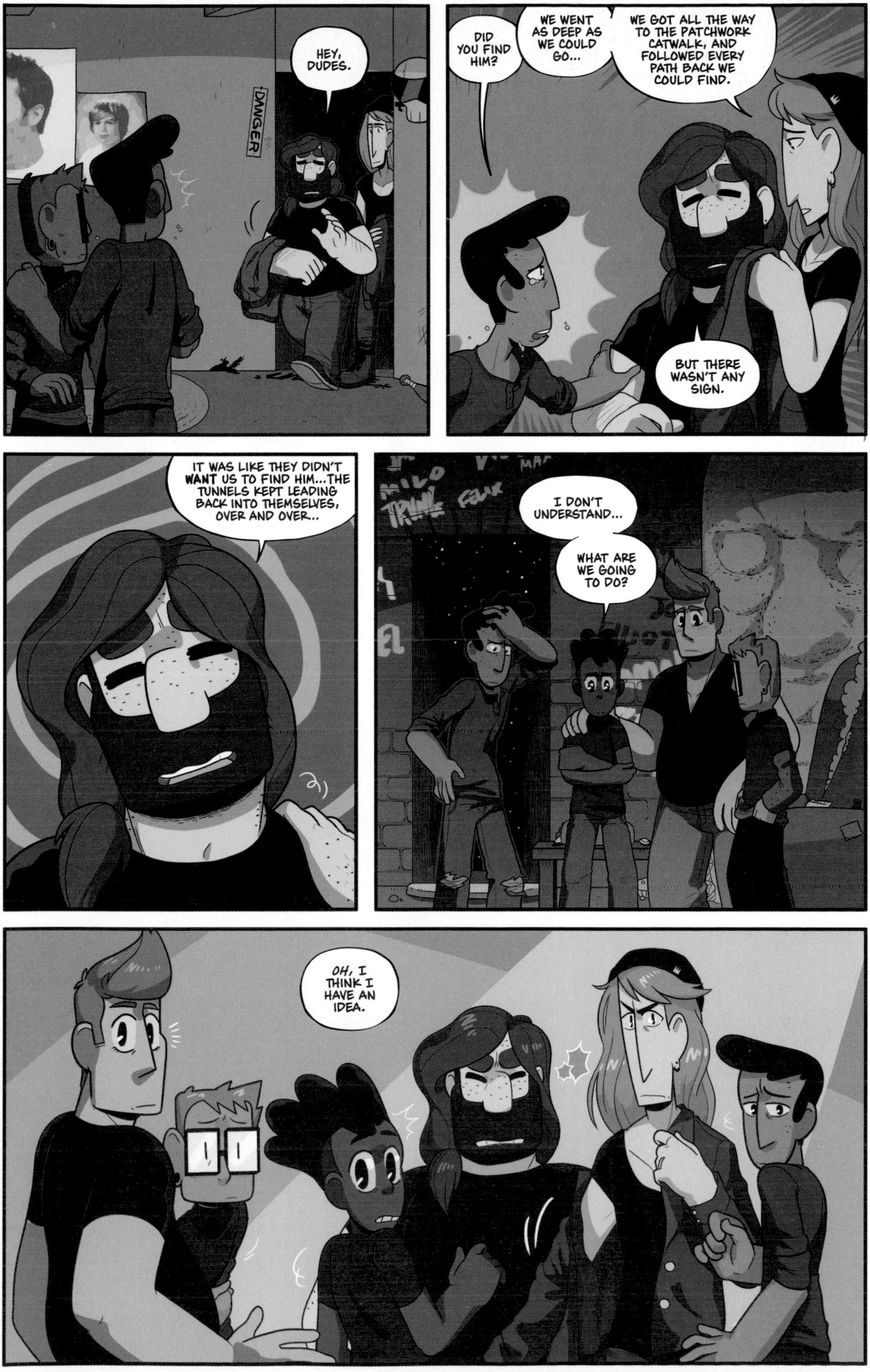
HEY, DUDES.
DANGER
DID YOU FIND HIM?
WE WENT AS DEEP AS WE COULD GO...
WE GOT ALL THE WAY TO THE PATCHWORK CATWALK, AND FOLLOWED EVERY PATH BACK WE COULD FIND.
BUT THERE WASN'T ANY SIGN.
IT WAS LIKE THEY DIDN'T WANT US TO FIND HIM...THE TUNNELS KEPT LEADING BACK INTO THEMSELVES, OVER AND OVER...
I DON'T UNDERSTAND...
WHAT ARE WE GOING TO DO?
OH, I THINK I HAVE AN IDEA.

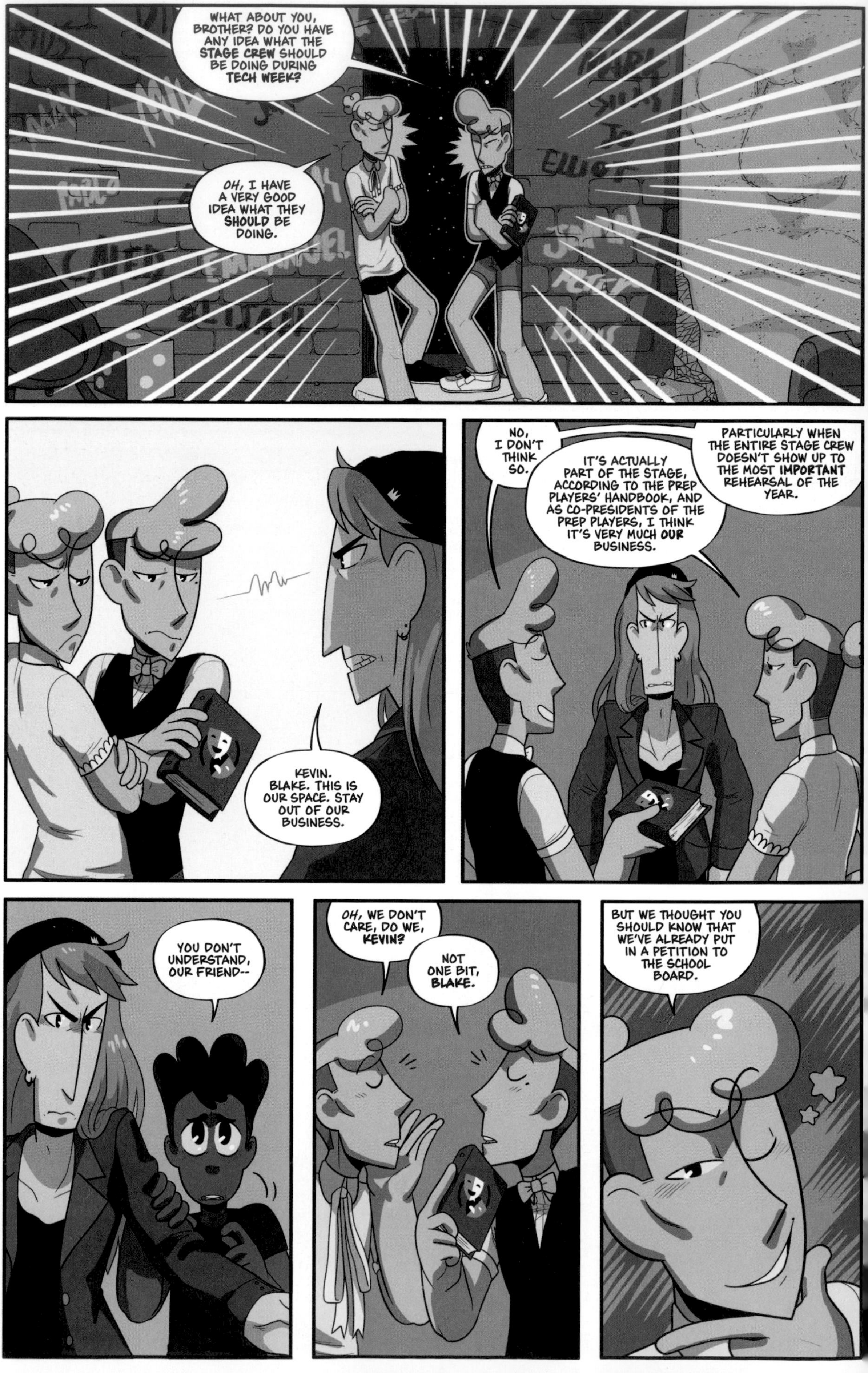
WHAT ABOUT YOU, BROTHER? DO YOU HAVE ANY IDEA WHAT THE STAGE CREW SHOULD BE DOING DURING TECH WEEK?
OH, I HAVE A VERY GOOD IDEA WHAT THEY SHOULD BE DOING.
KEVIN. BLAKE. THIS IS OUR SPACE. STAY OUT OF OUR BUSINESS.
NO, I DON'T THINK SO.
IT'S ACTUALLY PART OF THE STAGE, ACCORDING TO THE PREP PLAYERS' HANDBOOK, AND AS CO-PRESIDENTS OF THE PREP PLAYERS, I THINK IT'S VERY MUCH OUR BUSINESS.
PARTICULARLY WHEN THE ENTIRE STAGE CREW DOESN'T SHOW UP TO THE MOST IMPORTANT REHEARSAL OF THE YEAR.
YOU DON'T UNDERSTAND, OUR FRIEND--
OH, WE DON'T CARE, DO WE, KEVIN?
NOT ONE BIT, BLAKE.
BUT WE THOUGHT YOU SHOULD KNOW THAT WE'VE ALREADY PUT IN A PETITION TO THE SCHOOL BOARD.

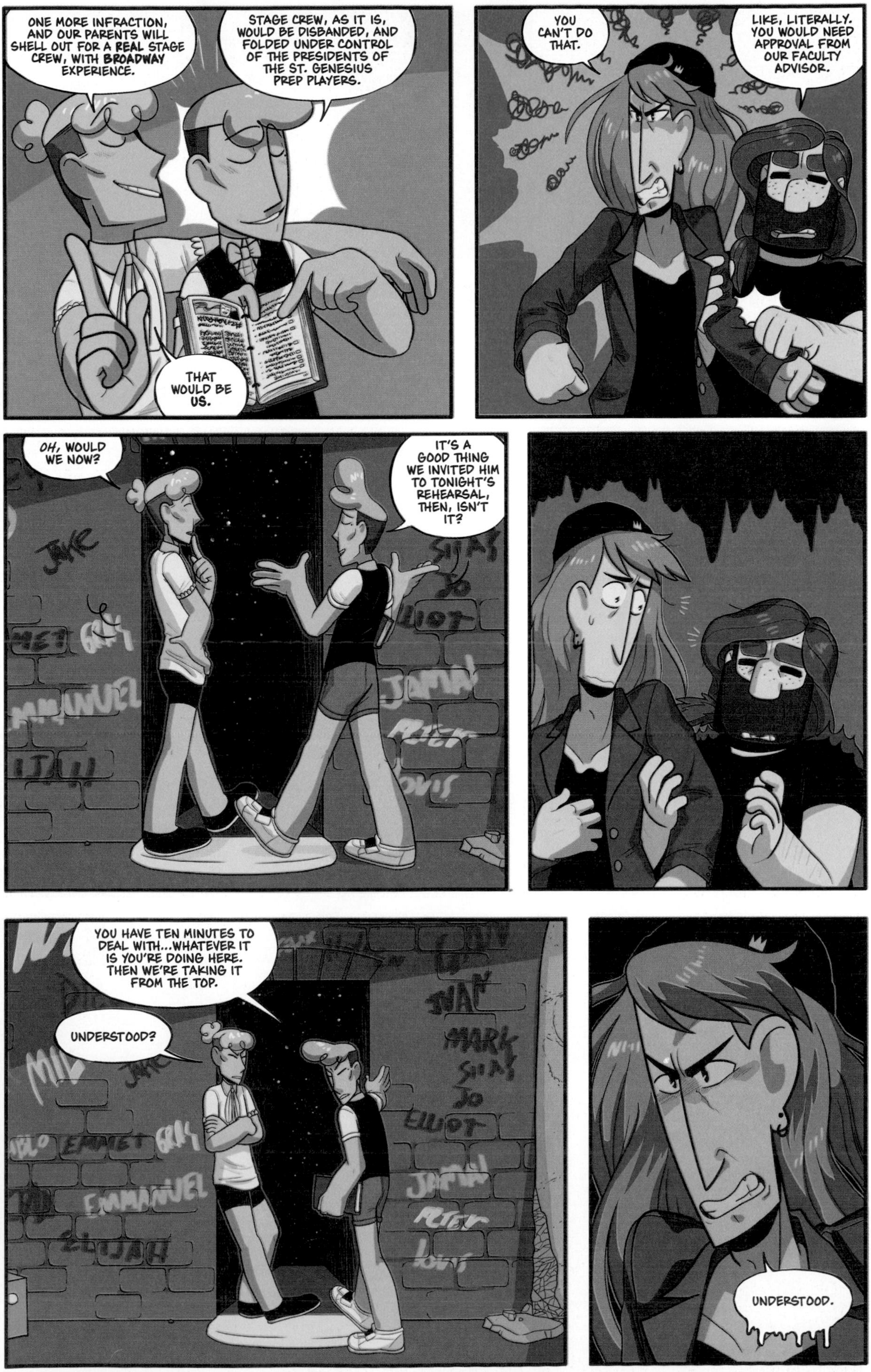

ONE MORE INFRACTION, AND OUR PARENTS WILL SHELL OUT FOR A REAL STAGE CREW, WITH BROADWAY EXPERIENCE.
STAGE CREW, AS IT IS, WOULD BE DISBANDED, AND FOLDED UNDER CONTROL OF THE PRESIDENTS OF THE ST. GENESIUS PREP PLAYERS.
THAT WOULD BE US.
YOU CAN'T DO THAT.
LIKE, LITERALLY. YOU WOULD NEED APPROVAL FROM OUR FACULTY ADVISOR.
OH, WOULD WE NOW?
IT'S A GOOD THING WE INVITED HIM TO TONIGHT'S REHEARSAL, THEN, ISN'T IT?
YOU HAVE TEN MINUTES TO DEAL WITH...WHATEVER IT IS YOU'RE DOING HERE. THEN WE'RE TAKING IT FROM THE TOP.
UNDERSTOOD?
UNDERSTOOD.

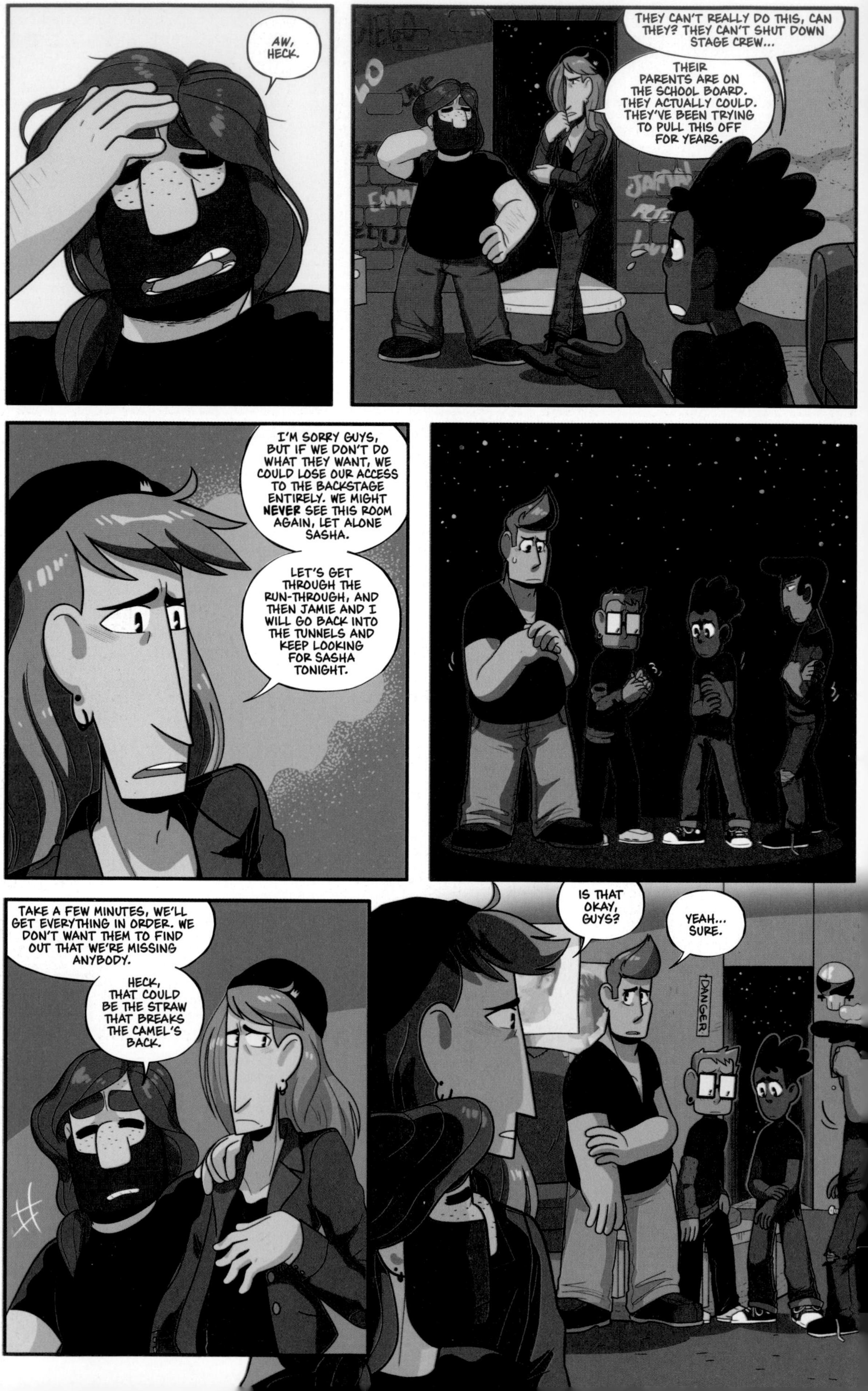
AW, HECK.
THEY CAN'T REALLY DO THIS, CAN THEY? THEY CAN'T SHUT DOWN STAGE CREW...
THEIR PARENTS ARE ON THE SCHOOL BOARD. THEY ACTUALLY COULD. THEY'VE BEEN TRYING TO PULL THIS OFF FOR YEARS.
I'M SORRY GUYS, BUT IF WE DON'T DO WHAT THEY WANT, WE COULD LOSE OUR ACCESS TO THE BACKSTAGE ENTIRELY. WE MIGHT NEVER SEE THIS ROOM AGAIN, LET ALONE SASHA.
LET'S GET THROUGH THE RUN-THROUGH, AND THEN JAMIE AND I WILL GO BACK INTO THE TUNNELS AND KEEP LOOKING FOR SASHA TONIGHT.
TAKE A FEW MINUTES, WE'LL GET EVERYTHING IN ORDER. WE DON'T WANT THEM TO FIND OUT THAT WE'RE MISSING ANYBODY.
HECK, THAT COULD BE THE STRAW THAT BREAKS THE CAMEL'S BACK.
IS THAT OKAY, GUYS?
YEAH... SURE.
DANGER

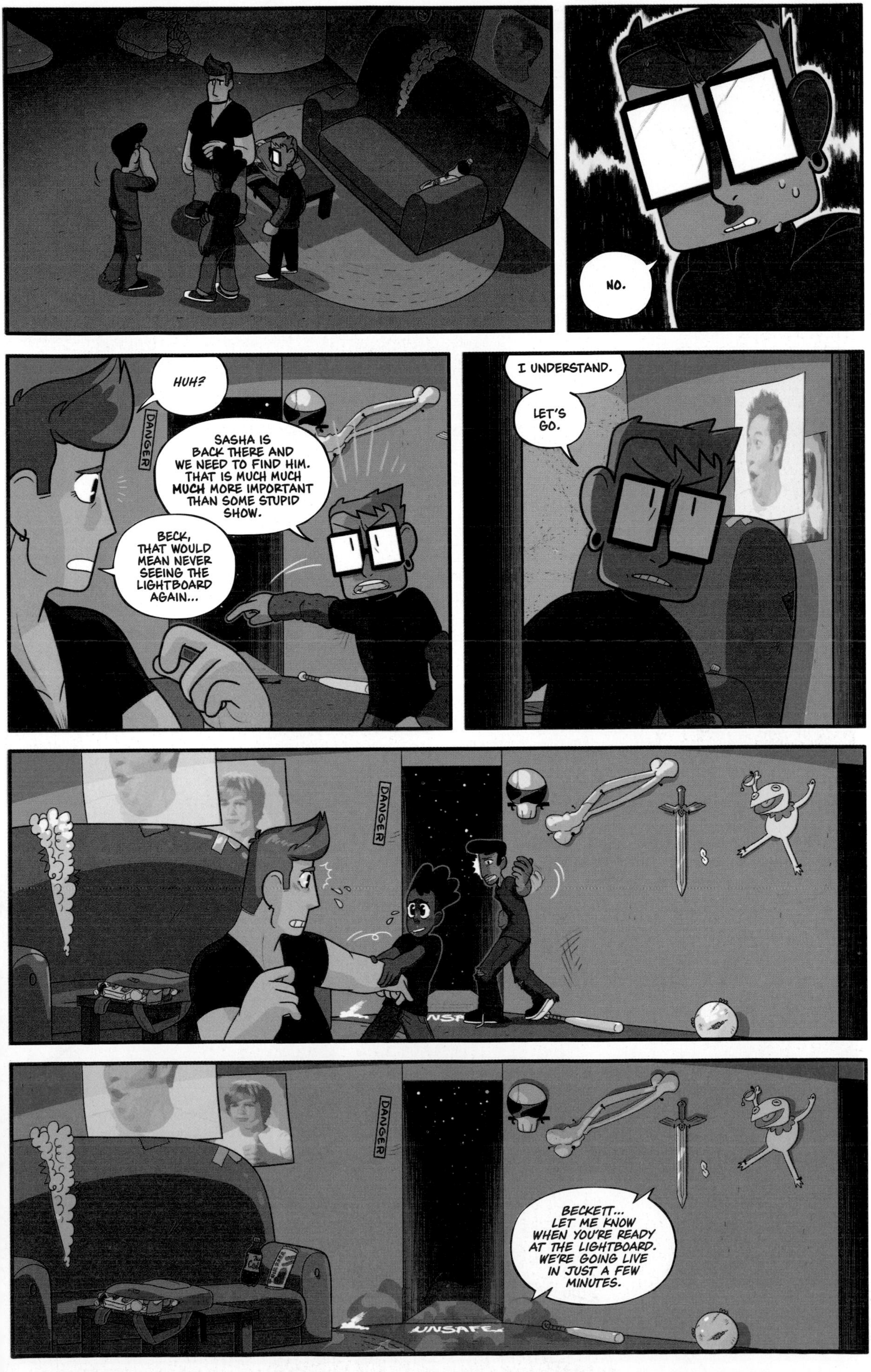
NO.
HUH?
DANGER
SASHA IS BACK THERE AND WE NEED TO FIND HIM. THAT IS MUCH MUCH MUCH MORE IMPORTANT THAN SOME STUPID SHOW.
BECK, THAT WOULD MEAN NEVER SEEING THE LIGHTBOARD AGAIN...
I UNDERSTAND.
LET'S GO.
DANGER
DANGER
BECKETT... LET ME KNOW WHEN YOU'RE READY AT THE LIGHTBOARD. WE'RE GOING LIVE IN JUST A FEW MINUTES.
UNSAFE

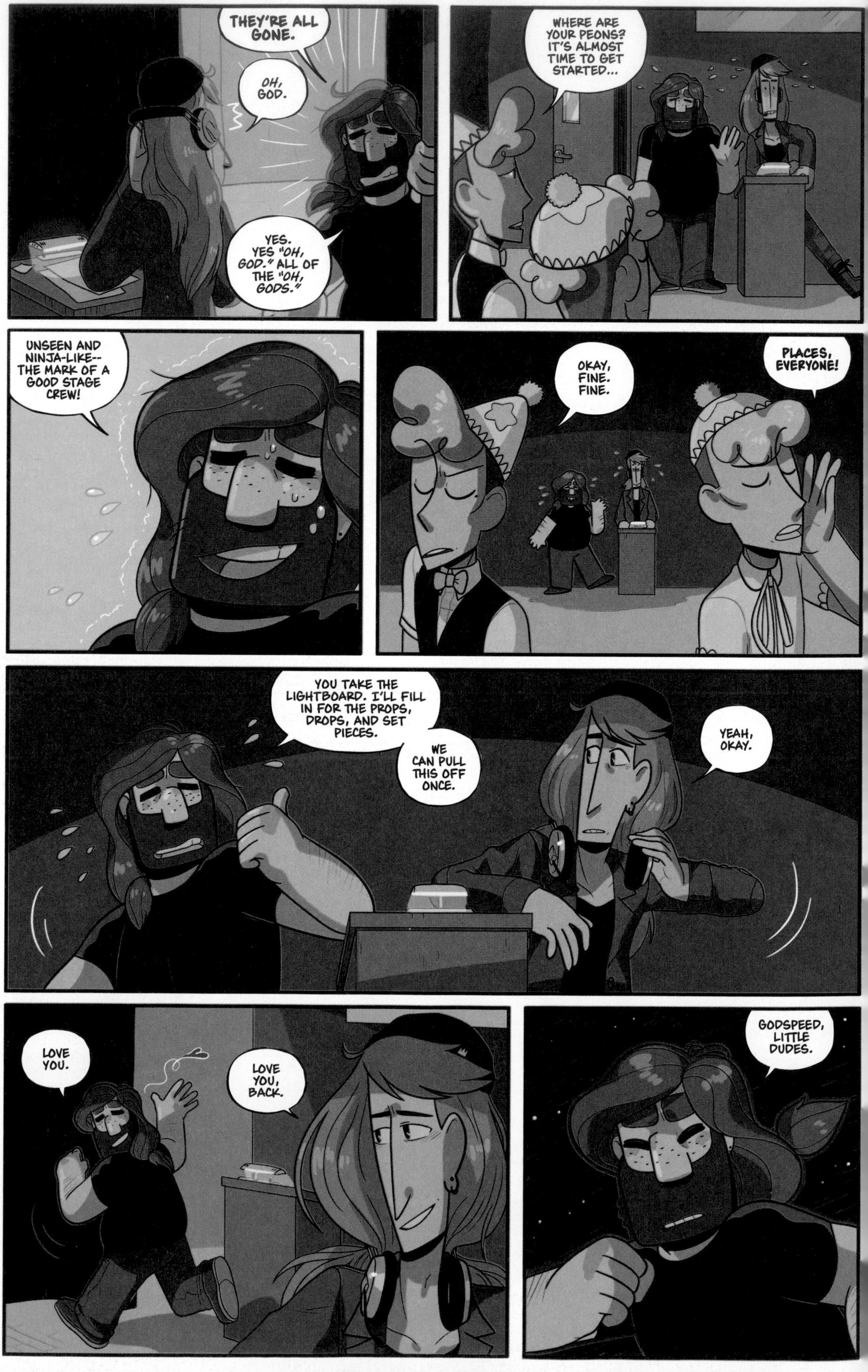

THEY'RE ALL GONE.
OH, GOD.
YES. YES "OH, GOD." ALL OF THE "OH, GODS."
WHERE ARE YOUR PEONS? IT'S ALMOST TIME TO GET STARTED...
UNSEEN AND NINJA-LIKE-- THE MARK OF A GOOD STAGE CREW!
OKAY, FINE. FINE.
PLACES, EVERYONE!
YOU TAKE THE LIGHTBOARD. I'LL FILL IN FOR THE PROPS, DROPS, AND SET PIECES.
WE CAN PULL THIS OFF ONCE.
YEAH, OKAY.
LOVE YOU.
LOVE YOU, BACK.
GODSPEED, LITTLE DUDES.

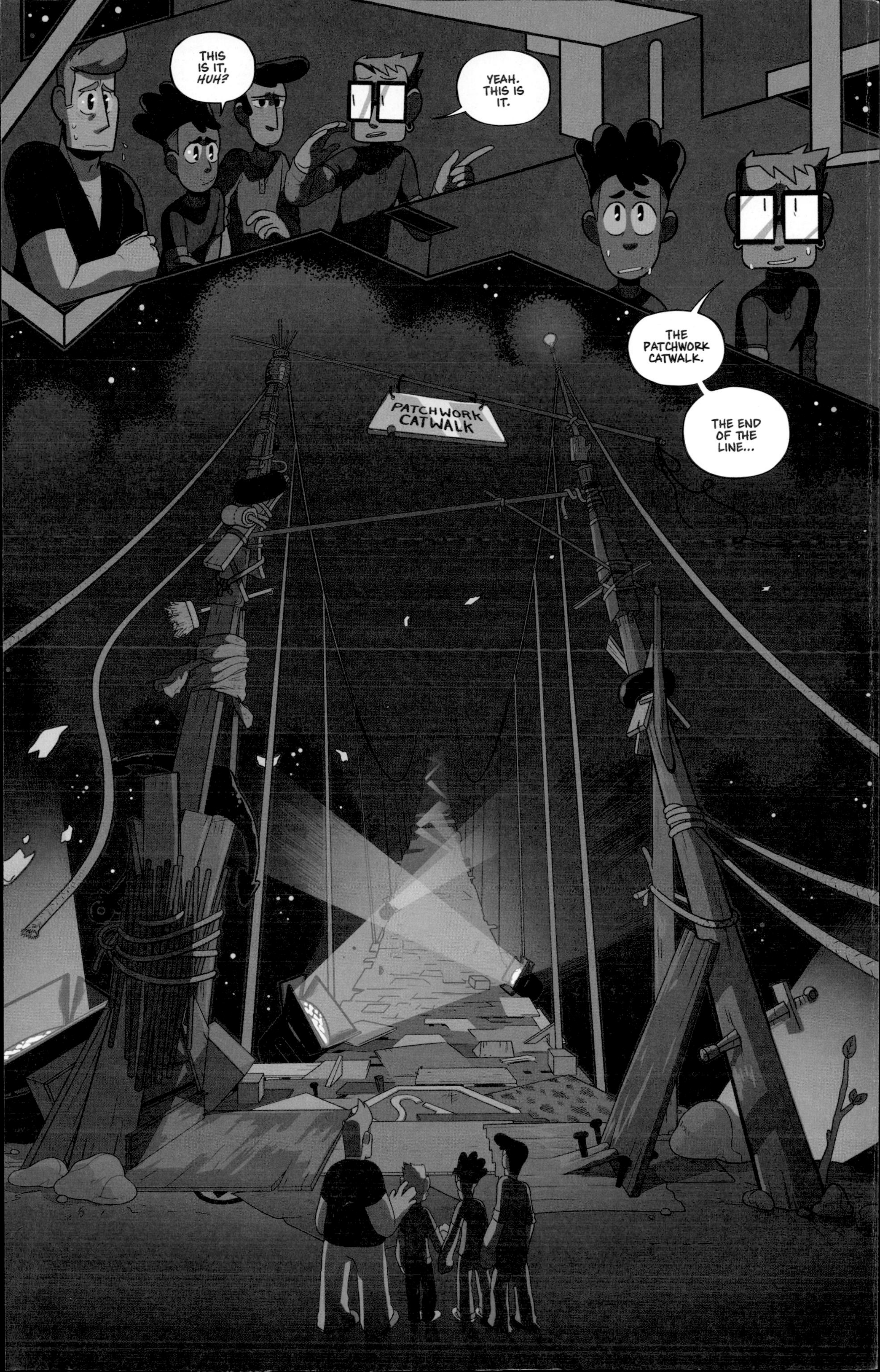
THIS IS IT, HUH?
YEAH. THIS IS IT.
PATCHWORK CATWALK
THE PATCHWORK CATWALK.
THE END OF THE LINE...

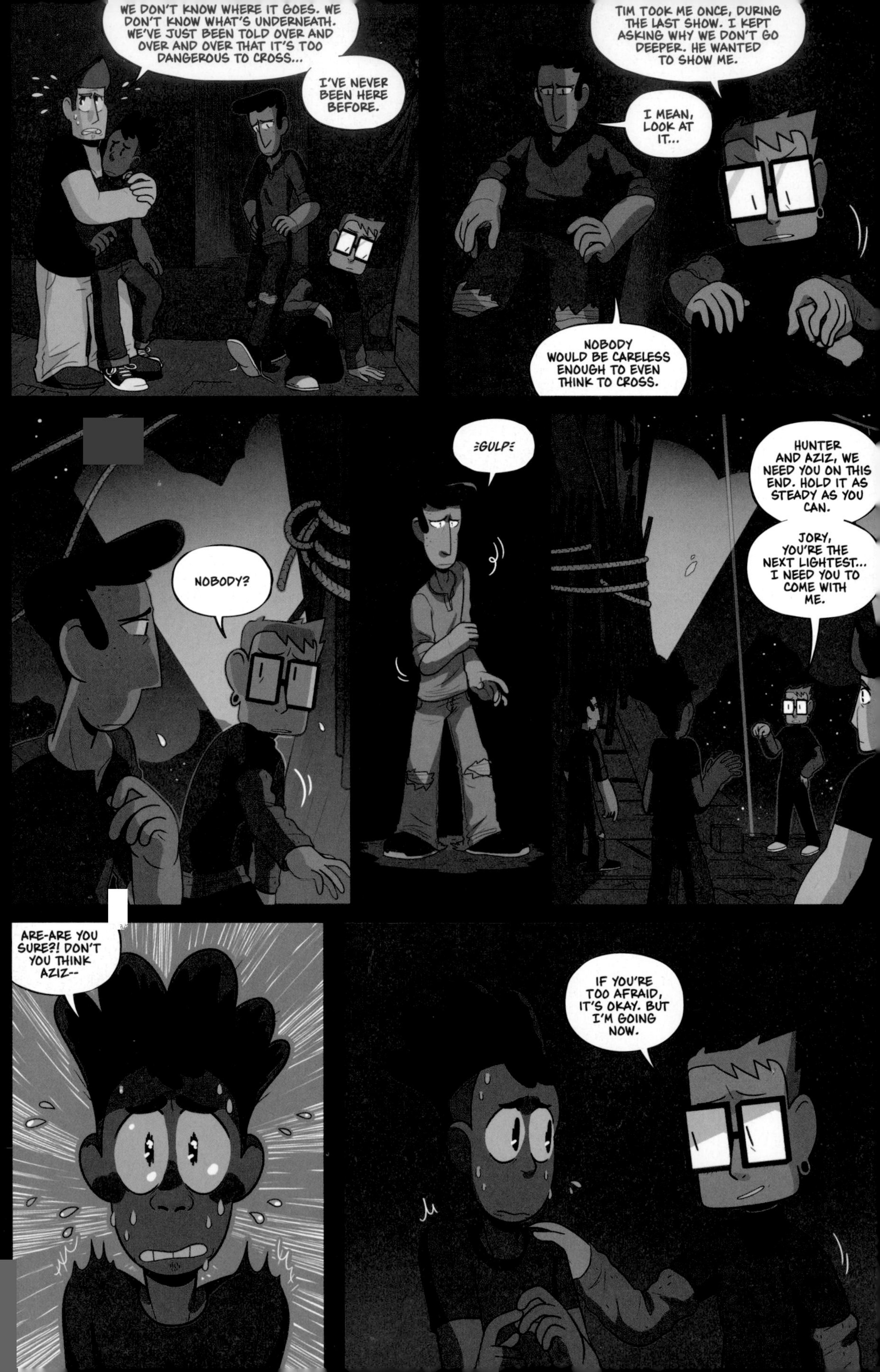

WE DON'T KNOW WHERE IT GOES. WE DON'T KNOW WHAT'S UNDERNEATH. WE'VE JUST BEEN TOLD OVER AND OVER AND OVER THAT IT'S TOO DANGEROUS TO CROSS...
I'VE NEVER BEEN HERE BEFORE.
TIM TOOK ME ONCE, DURING THE LAST SHOW. I KEPT ASKING WHY WE DON'T GO DEEPER. HE WANTED TO SHOW ME.
I MEAN, LOOK AT IT...
NOBODY WOULD BE CARELESS ENOUGH TO EVEN THINK TO CROSS.
NOBODY?
GULP
HUNTER AND AZIZ, WE NEED YOU ON THIS END. HOLD IT AS STEADY AS YOU CAN.
JORY, YOU'RE THE NEXT LIGHTEST... I NEED YOU TO COME WITH ME.
ARE-ARE YOU SURE?! DON'T YOU THINK AZIZ--
IF YOU'RE TOO AFRAID, IT'S OKAY. BUT I'M GOING NOW.

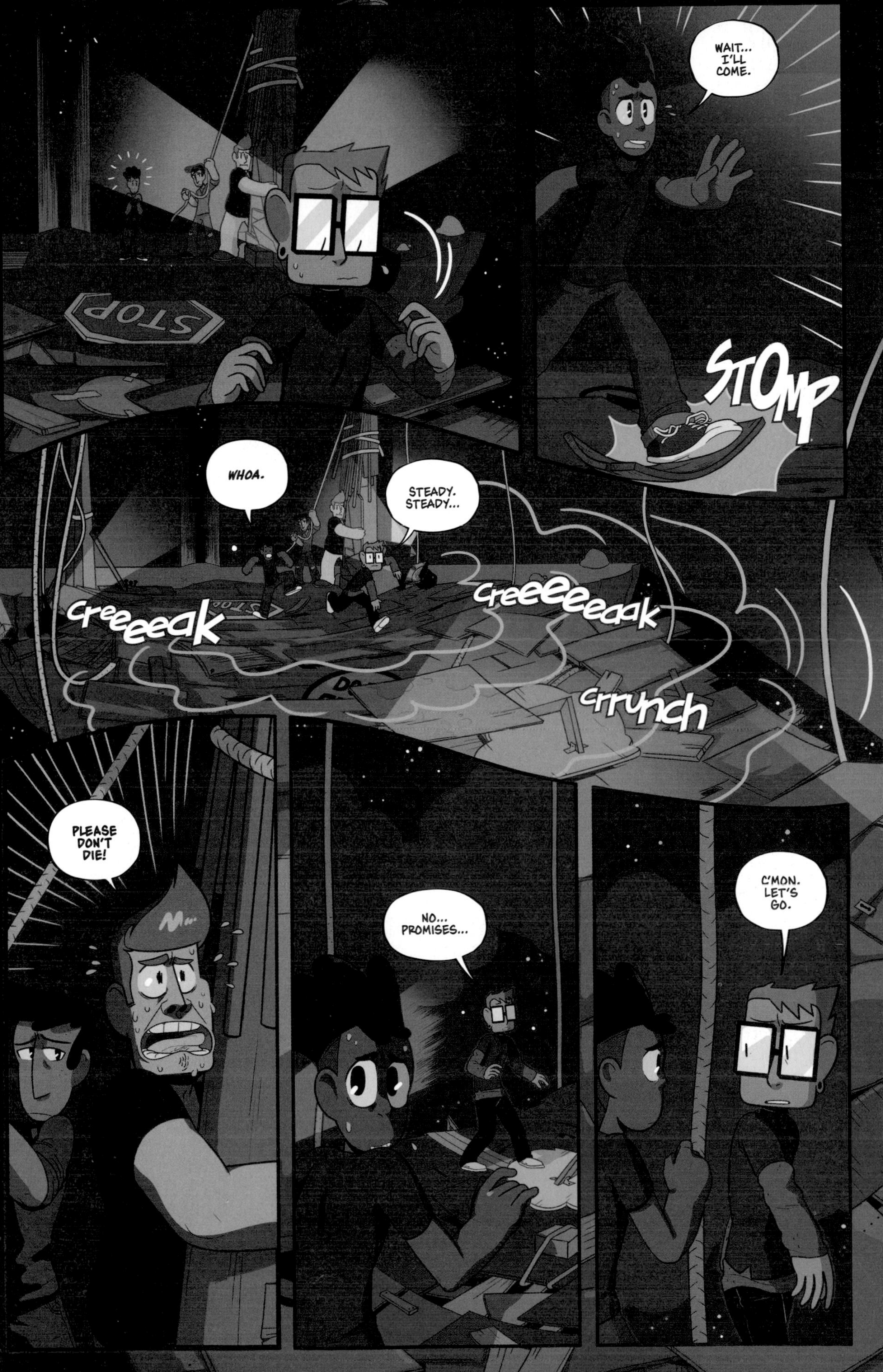
WAIT... I'LL COME.
STOMP
WHOA.
STEADY. STEADY...
creeeeak
creeeeeeaak
crrunch
PLEASE DON'T DIE!
NO... PROMISES...
C'MON. LET'S GO.

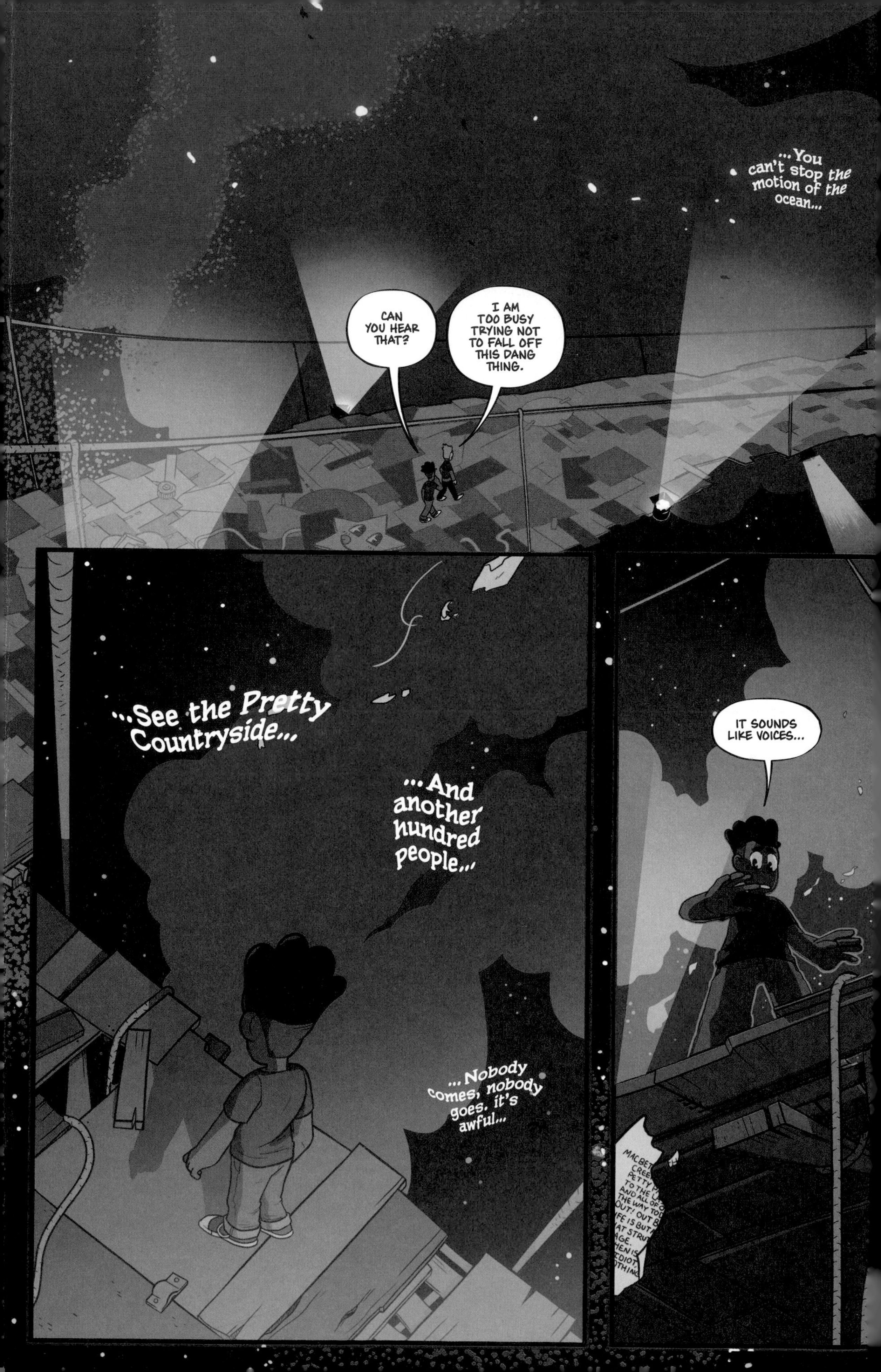
...You can't stop the motion of the ocean...
CAN YOU HEAR THAT?
I AM TOO BUSY TRYING NOT TO FALL OFF THIS DANG THING.
...See the Pretty Countryside...
...And another hundred people...
...Nobody comes, nobody goes, it's awful...
IT SOUNDS LIKE VOICES...

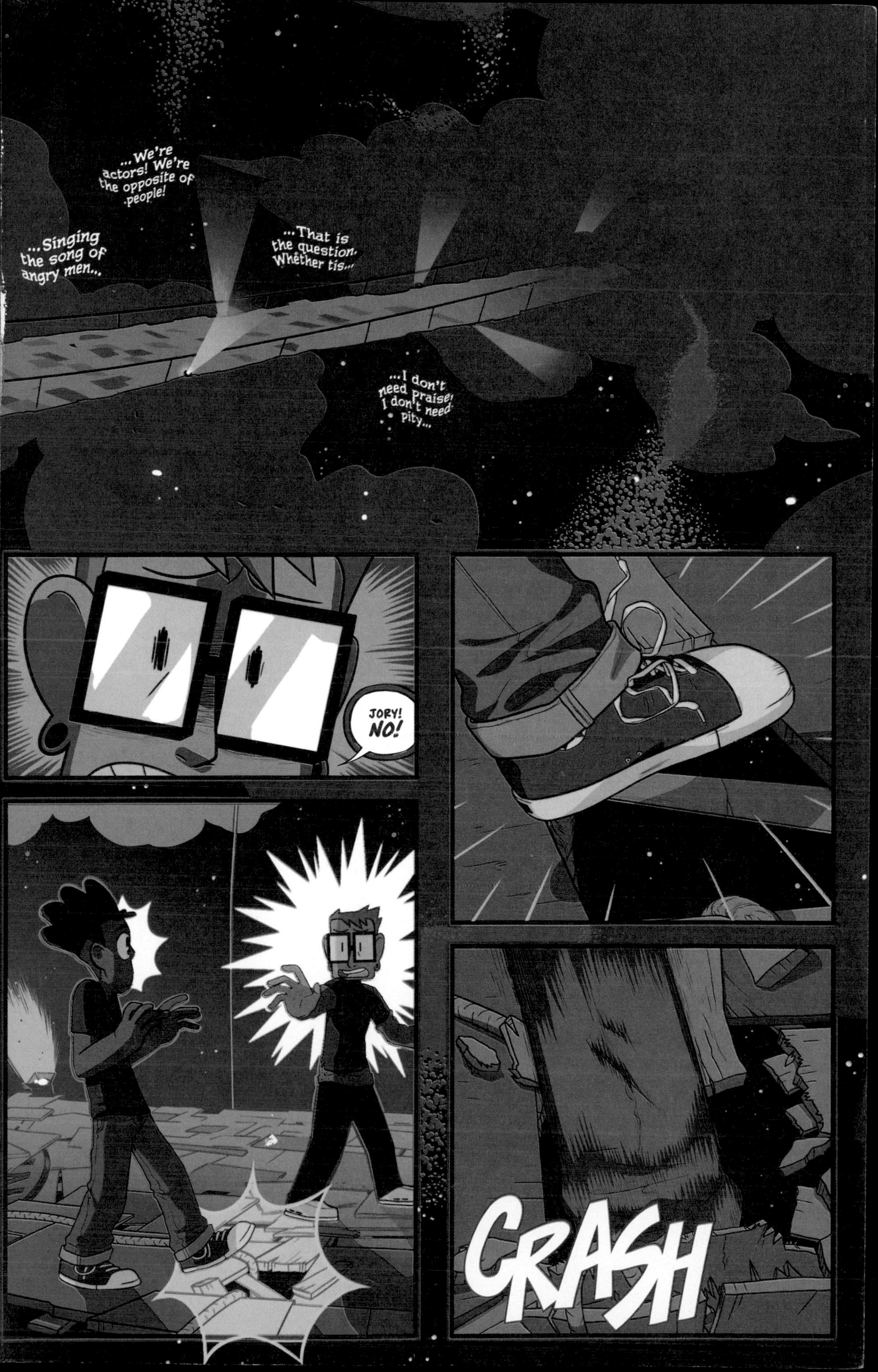
...We're actors! We're the opposite of people!
...Singing the song of angry men...
...That is the question. Whether tis...
...I don't need praise! I don't need pity...
JORY! NO!
CRASH

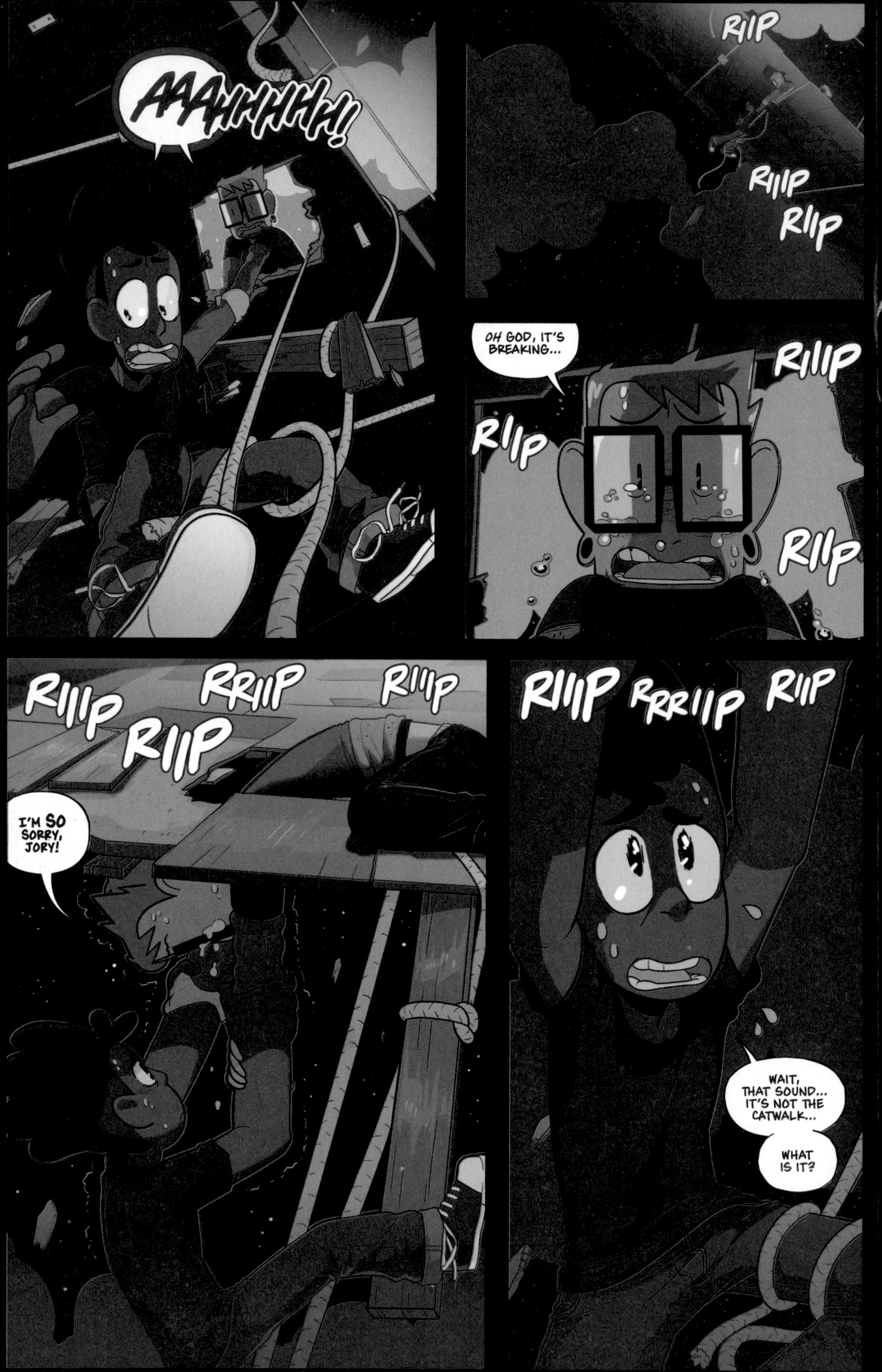
AAAHHHHH!
RIIP
RIIIP
RIIP
OH GOD, IT'S BREAKING...
RIIIP
RIIP
RIIP
RIIIP
RRIIP
RIIP
RIIP
I'M SO SORRY, JORY!
RIIIP
RRRIIP
RIIP
WAIT, THAT SOUND... IT'S NOT THE CATWALK...
WHAT IS IT?

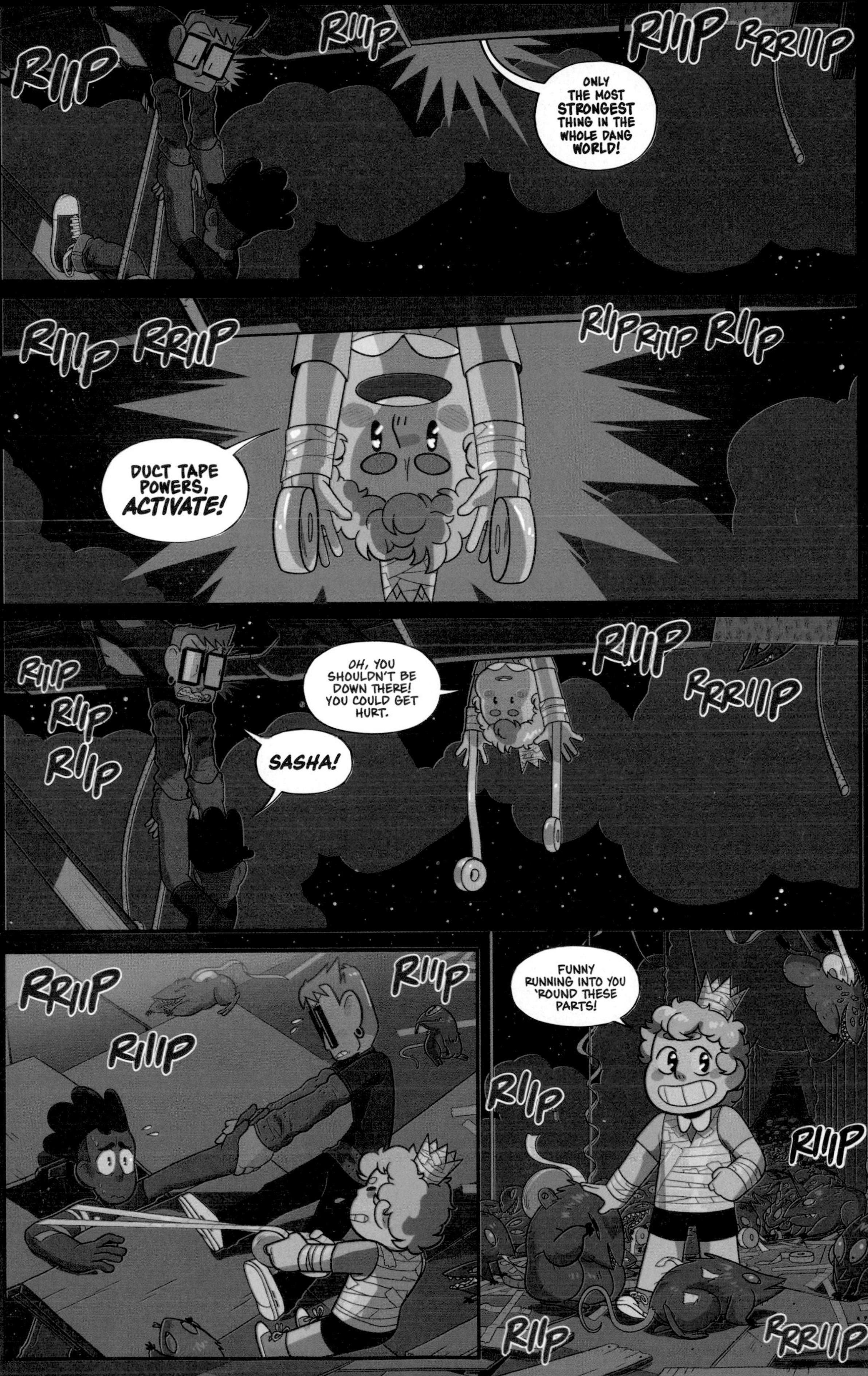
RIIP
RIIP
ONLY THE MOST STRONGEST THING IN THE WHOLE DANG WORLD!
RIIP
RRRIIP
RIIP
RRRIIP
RIIP RIIP RIIP
DUCT TAPE POWERS, ACTIVATE!
RIIP
RIIP
RIIP
RIIP
OH, YOU SHOULDN'T BE DOWN THERE! YOU COULD GET HURT.
RRRIIP
SASHA!
RRIIP
RIIP
RIIP
FUNNY RUNNING INTO YOU 'ROUND THESE PARTS!
RIIP
RIIP
RIIP
RRRIIP

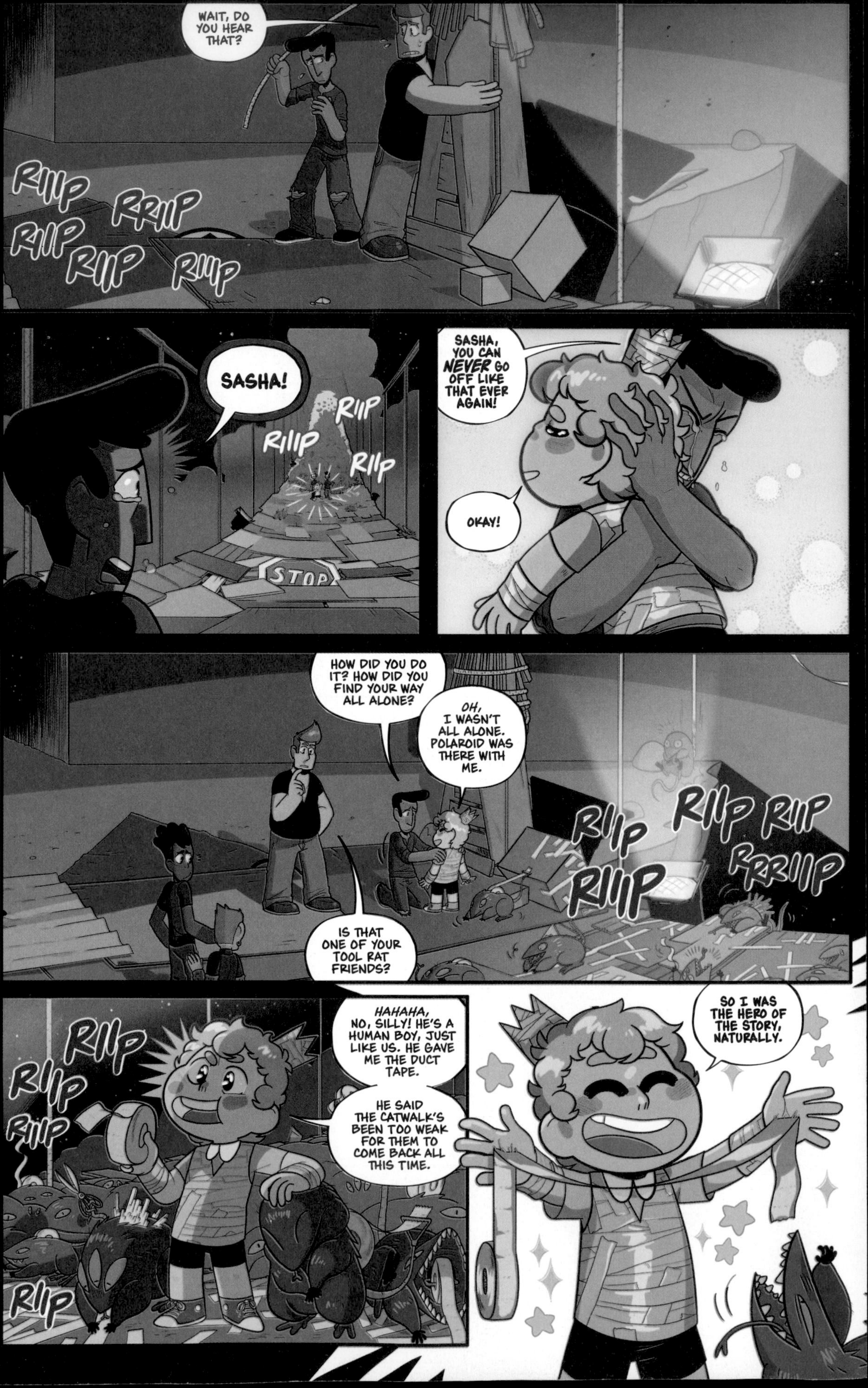
WAIT, DO YOU HEAR THAT?
RIIP RRIIP RIIP RIIP RIIP
SASHA!
RIIP RIIP RIIP
STOP
SASHA, YOU CAN NEVER GO OFF LIKE THAT EVER AGAIN!
OKAY!
HOW DID YOU DO IT? HOW DID YOU FIND YOUR WAY ALL ALONE?
OH, I WASN'T ALL ALONE. POLAROID WAS THERE WITH ME.
IS THAT ONE OF YOUR TOOL RAT FRIENDS?
RIIP RIIP RIIP RIIP RRRIIP
HAHAHA, NO, SILLY! HE'S A HUMAN BOY, JUST LIKE US. HE GAVE ME THE DUCT TAPE.
HE SAID THE CATWALK'S BEEN TOO WEAK FOR THEM TO COME BACK ALL THIS TIME.
RIIP RIIP RIIP RIIP
SO I WAS THE HERO OF THE STORY, NATURALLY.

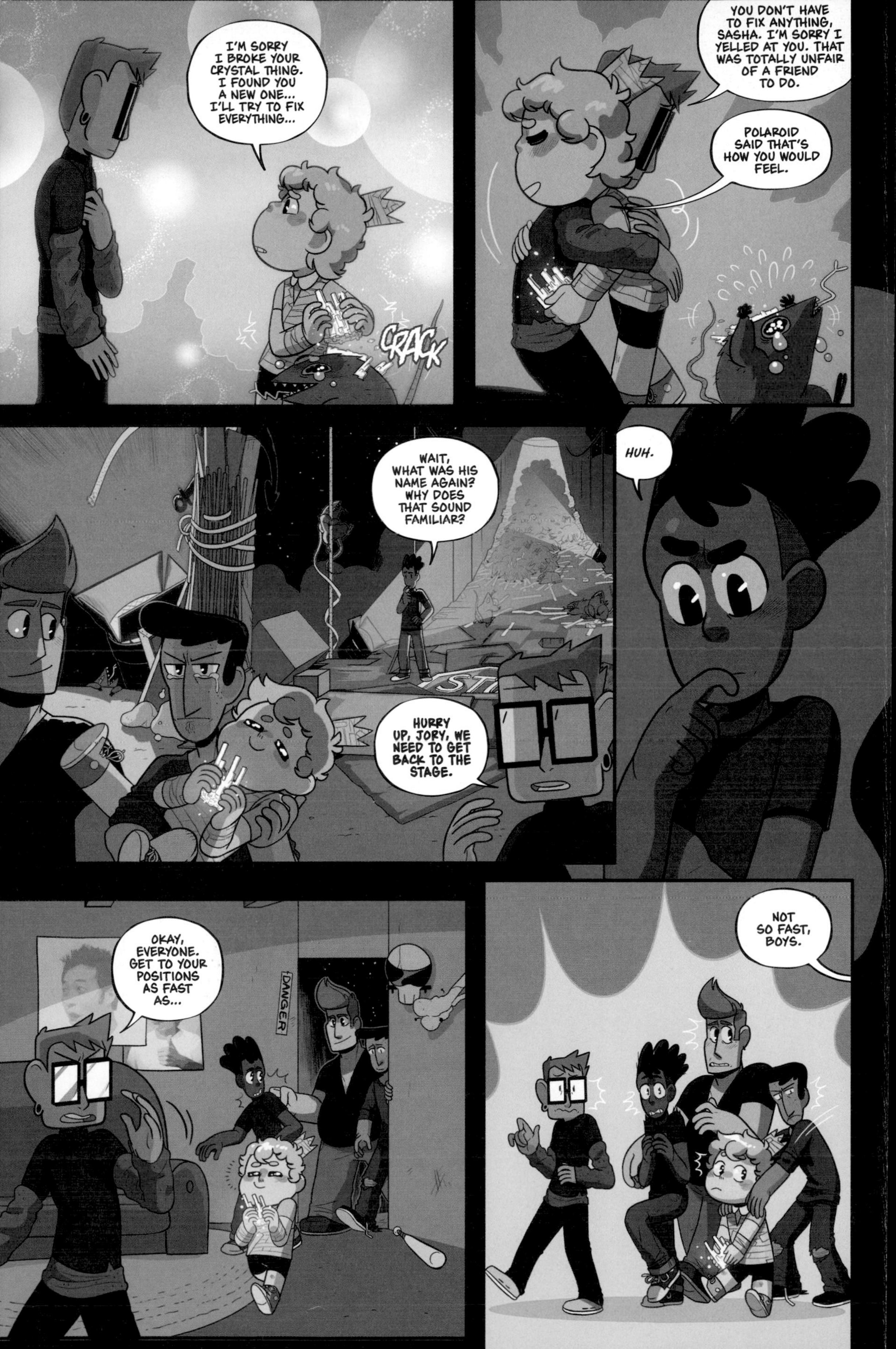
I'M SORRY I BROKE YOUR CRYSTAL THING. I FOUND YOU A NEW ONE... I'LL TRY TO FIX EVERYTHING...
CRACK
YOU DON'T HAVE TO FIX ANYTHING, SASHA. I'M SORRY I YELLED AT YOU. THAT WAS TOTALLY UNFAIR OF A FRIEND TO DO.
POLAROID SAID THAT'S HOW YOU WOULD FEEL.
WAIT, WHAT WAS HIS NAME AGAIN? WHY DOES THAT SOUND FAMILIAR?
HURRY UP, JORY, WE NEED TO GET BACK TO THE STAGE.
HUH.
OKAY, EVERYONE. GET TO YOUR POSITIONS AS FAST AS...
DANGER
NOT SO FAST, BOYS.

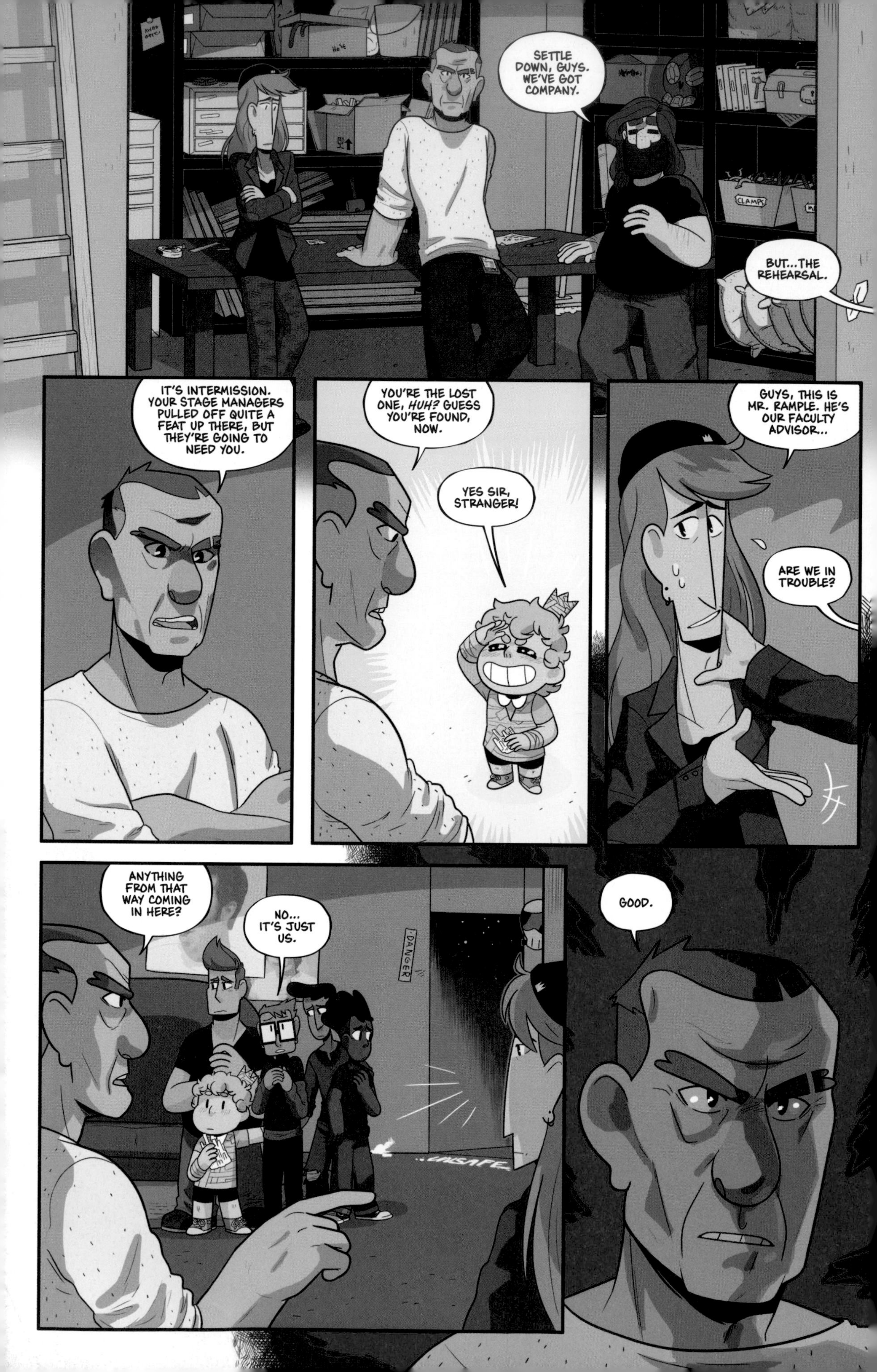
SETTLE DOWN, GUYS. WE'VE GOT COMPANY.
BUT...THE REHEARSAL.
IT'S INTERMISSION. YOUR STAGE MANAGERS PULLED OFF QUITE A FEAT UP THERE, BUT THEY'RE GOING TO NEED YOU.
YOU'RE THE LOST ONE, HUH? GUESS YOU'RE FOUND, NOW.
YES SIR, STRANGER!
GUYS, THIS IS MR. RAMPLE. HE'S OUR FACULTY ADVISOR...
ARE WE IN TROUBLE?
ANYTHING FROM THAT WAY COMING IN HERE?
NO... IT'S JUST US.
DANGER
UNSAFE
GOOD.
CLAMPS

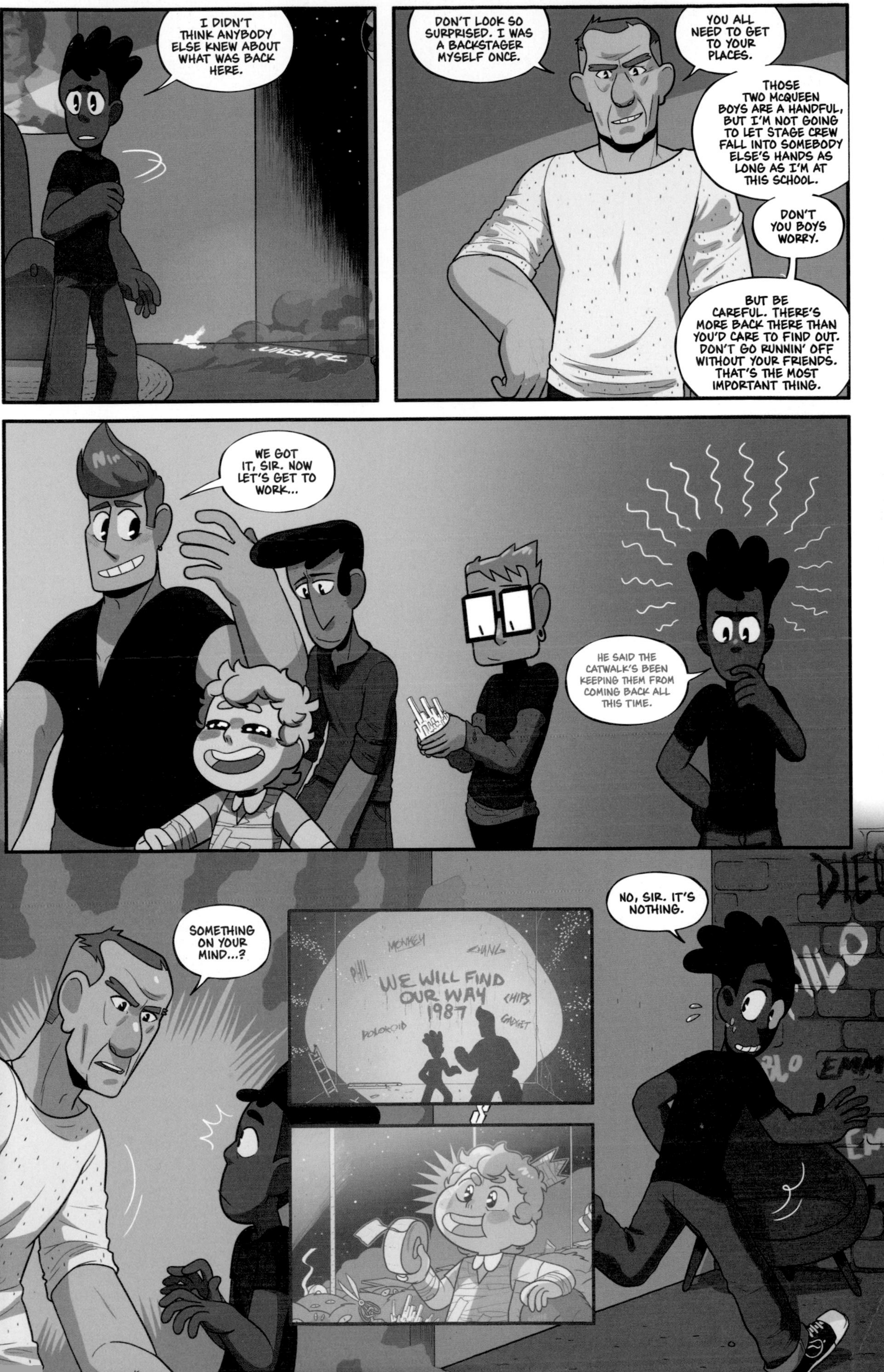
I DIDN'T THINK ANYBODY ELSE KNEW ABOUT WHAT WAS BACK HERE.
UNSAFE
DON'T LOOK SO SURPRISED. I WAS A BACKSTAGER MYSELF ONCE.
YOU ALL NEED TO GET TO YOUR PLACES.
THOSE TWO McQUEEN BOYS ARE A HANDFUL, BUT I'M NOT GOING TO LET STAGE CREW FALL INTO SOMEBODY ELSE'S HANDS AS LONG AS I'M AT THIS SCHOOL.
DON'T YOU BOYS WORRY.
BUT BE CAREFUL. THERE'S MORE BACK THERE THAN YOU'D CARE TO FIND OUT. DON'T GO RUNNIN' OFF WITHOUT YOUR FRIENDS. THAT'S THE MOST IMPORTANT THING.
WE GOT IT, SIR. NOW LET'S GET TO WORK...
HE SAID THE CATWALK'S BEEN KEEPING THEM FROM COMING BACK ALL THIS TIME.
SOMETHING ON YOUR MIND...?
MONKEY
CHANG
PHIL
WE WILL FIND OUR WAY 1987
CHIPS
POLOROID
GADGET
NO, SIR. IT'S NOTHING.

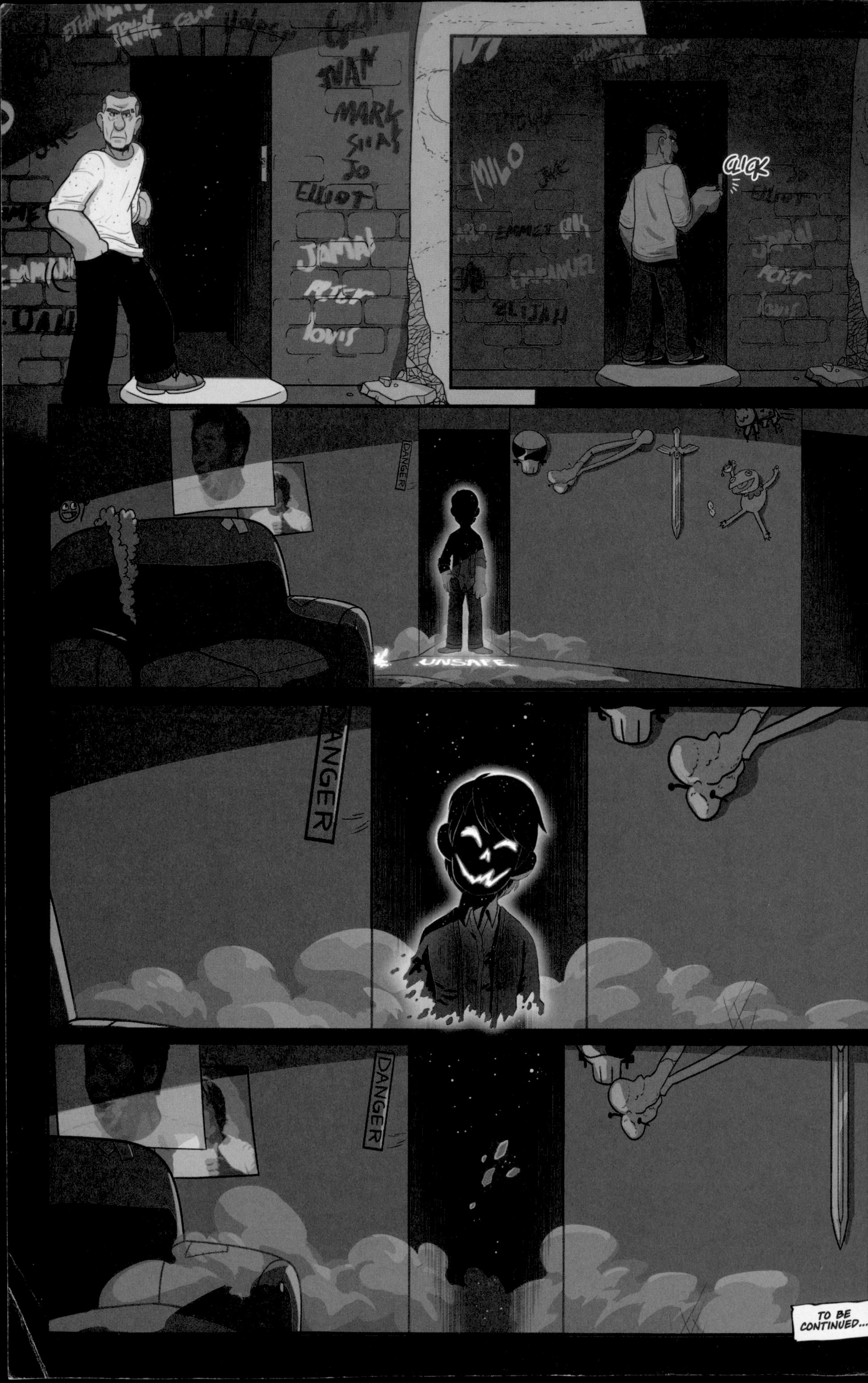
MARK
JO
ELLIOT
MILO
CLICK
DANGER
UNSAFE
DANGER
DANGER
TO BE CONTINUED...

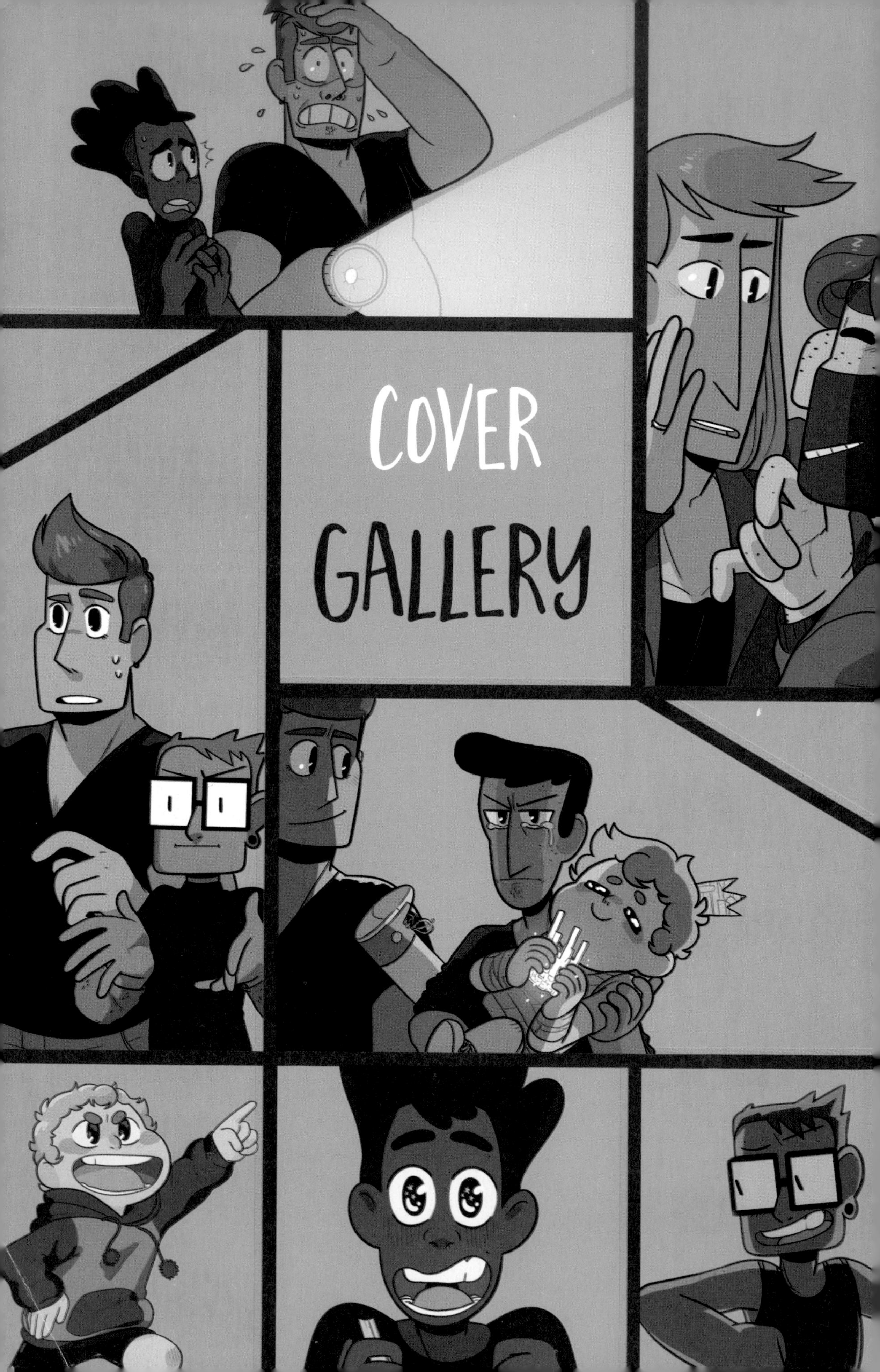
COVER
GALLERY

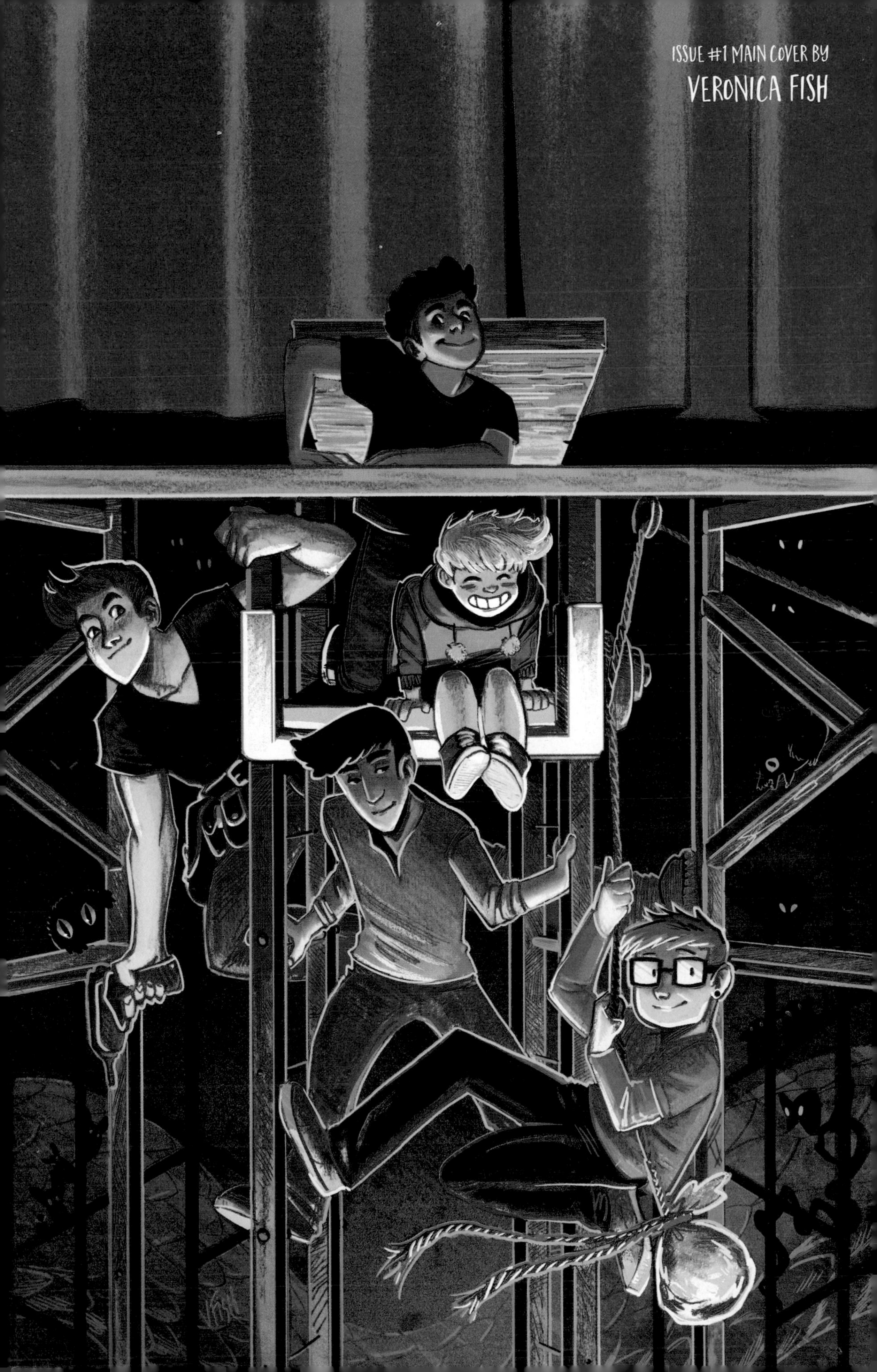
ISSUE #1 MAIN COVER BY
VERONICA FISH

The BACKSTAGERS

ST. GENESIUS PREPARATORY HIGH SCHOOL THEATRE

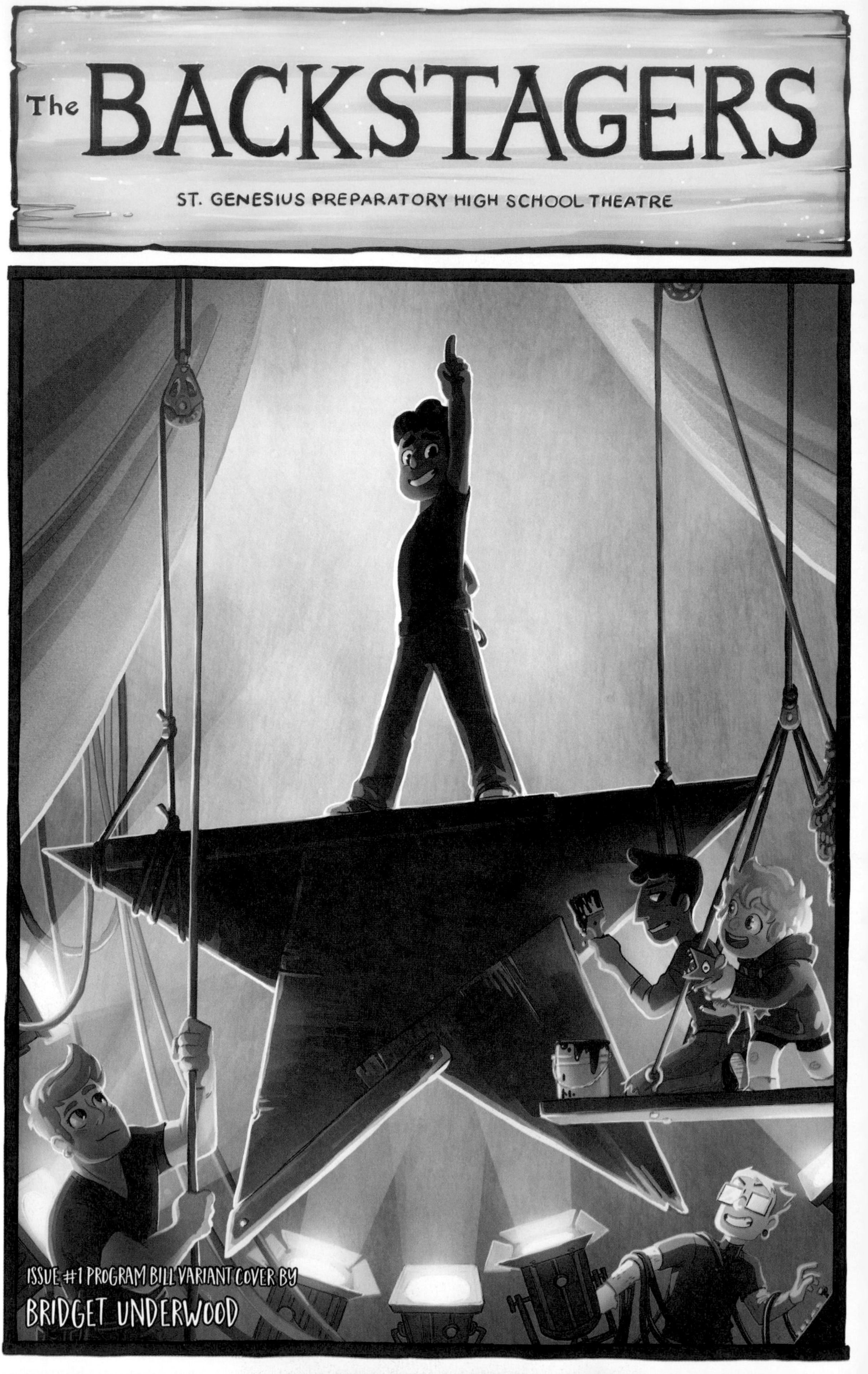
ISSUE #1 PROGRAM BILL VARIANT COVER BY
BRIDGET UNDERWOOD

ISSUE #1 VARIANT COVER BY

ROB GUILLORY

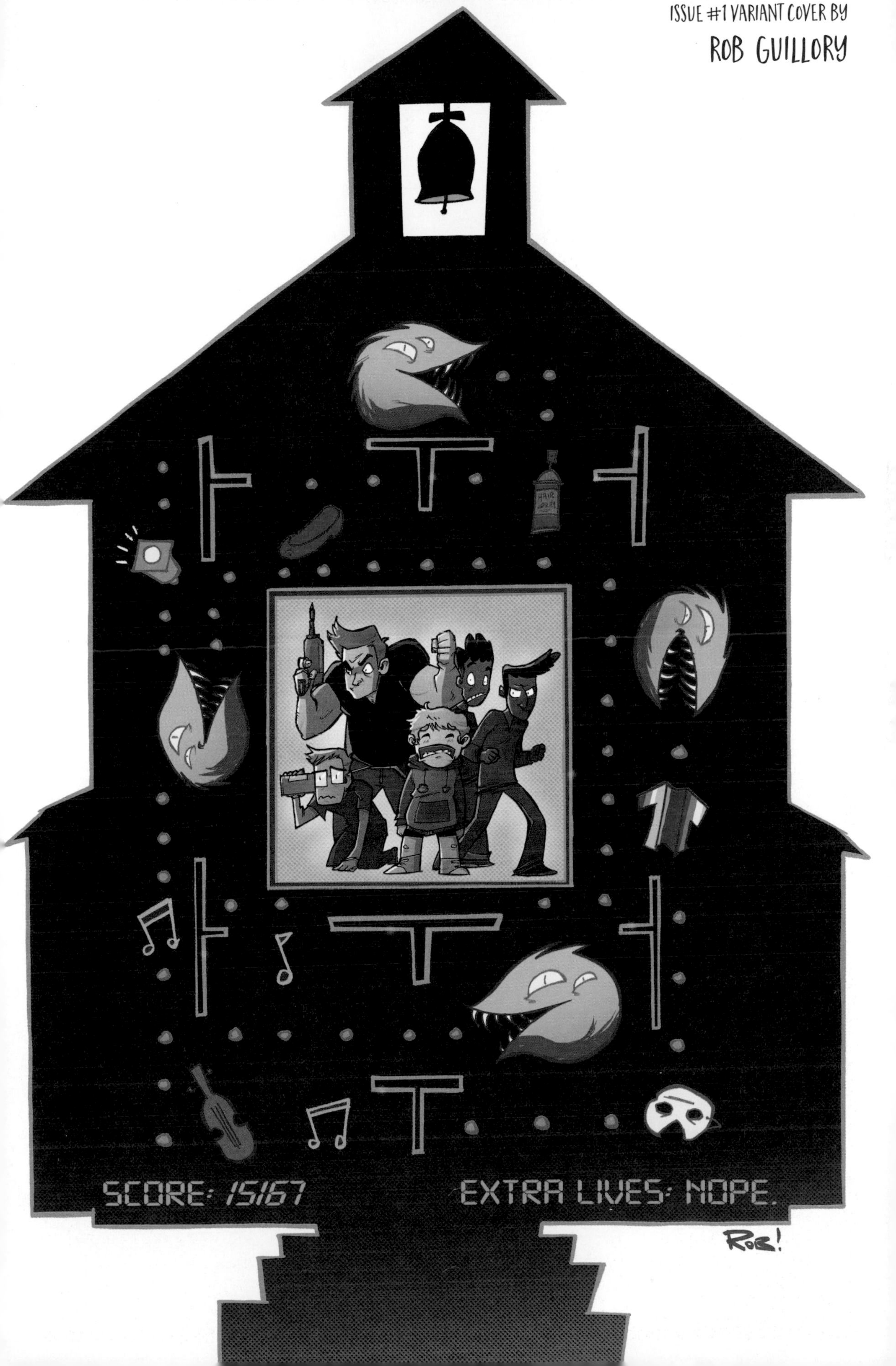
HAIR SPRAY
SCORE: 15167
EXTRA LIVES: NOPE.
ROB!

ISSUE #1 NEW YORK COMIC-CON
EXCLUSIVE COVER BY

MICHAEL DIALYNAS

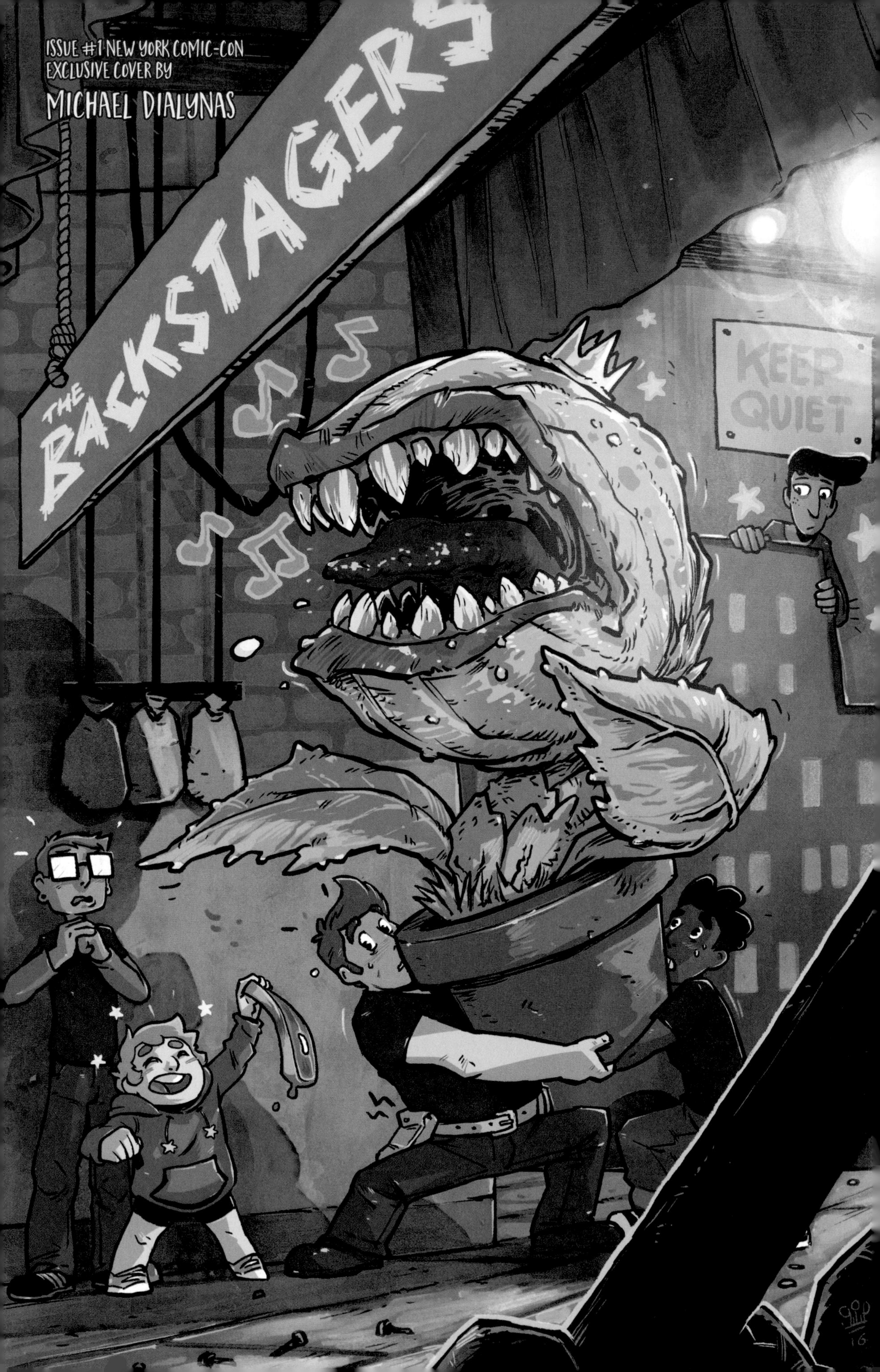
THE BACKSTAGERS
KEEP QUIET

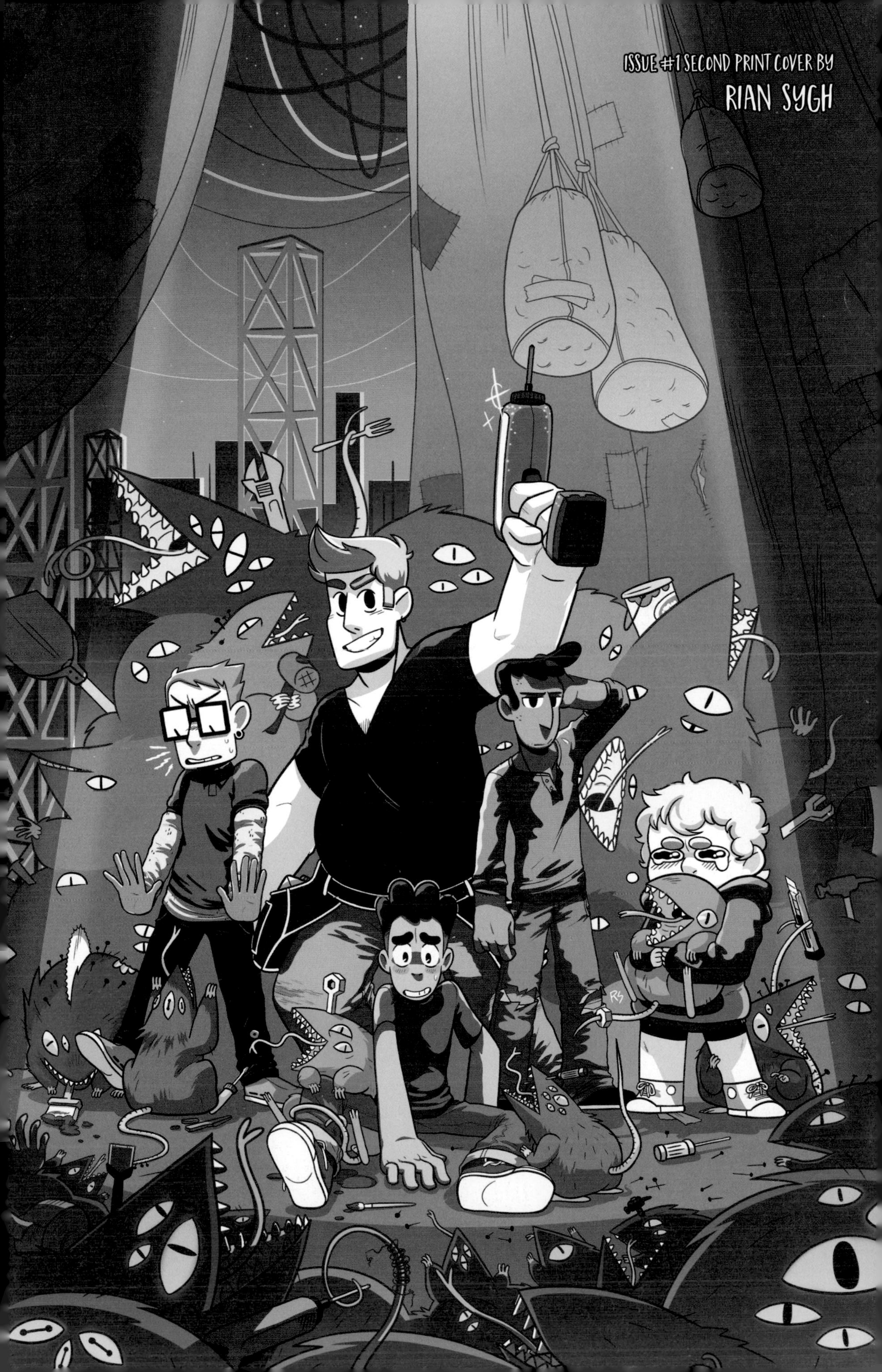
ISSUE #1 SECOND PRINT COVER BY
RIAN SYGH

ISSUE #2 MAIN COVER BY

VERONICA FISH

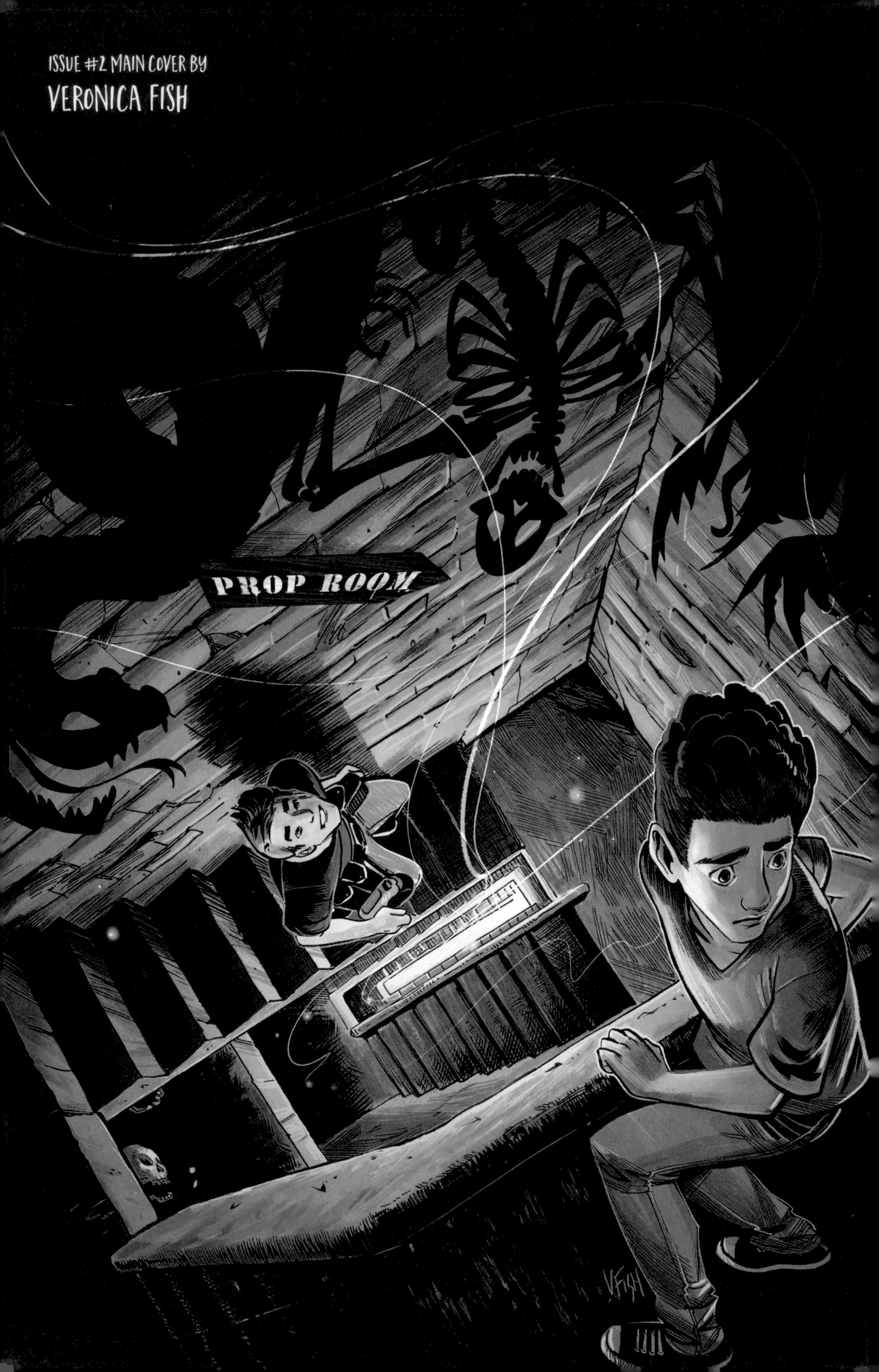
PROP ROOM
VFISH

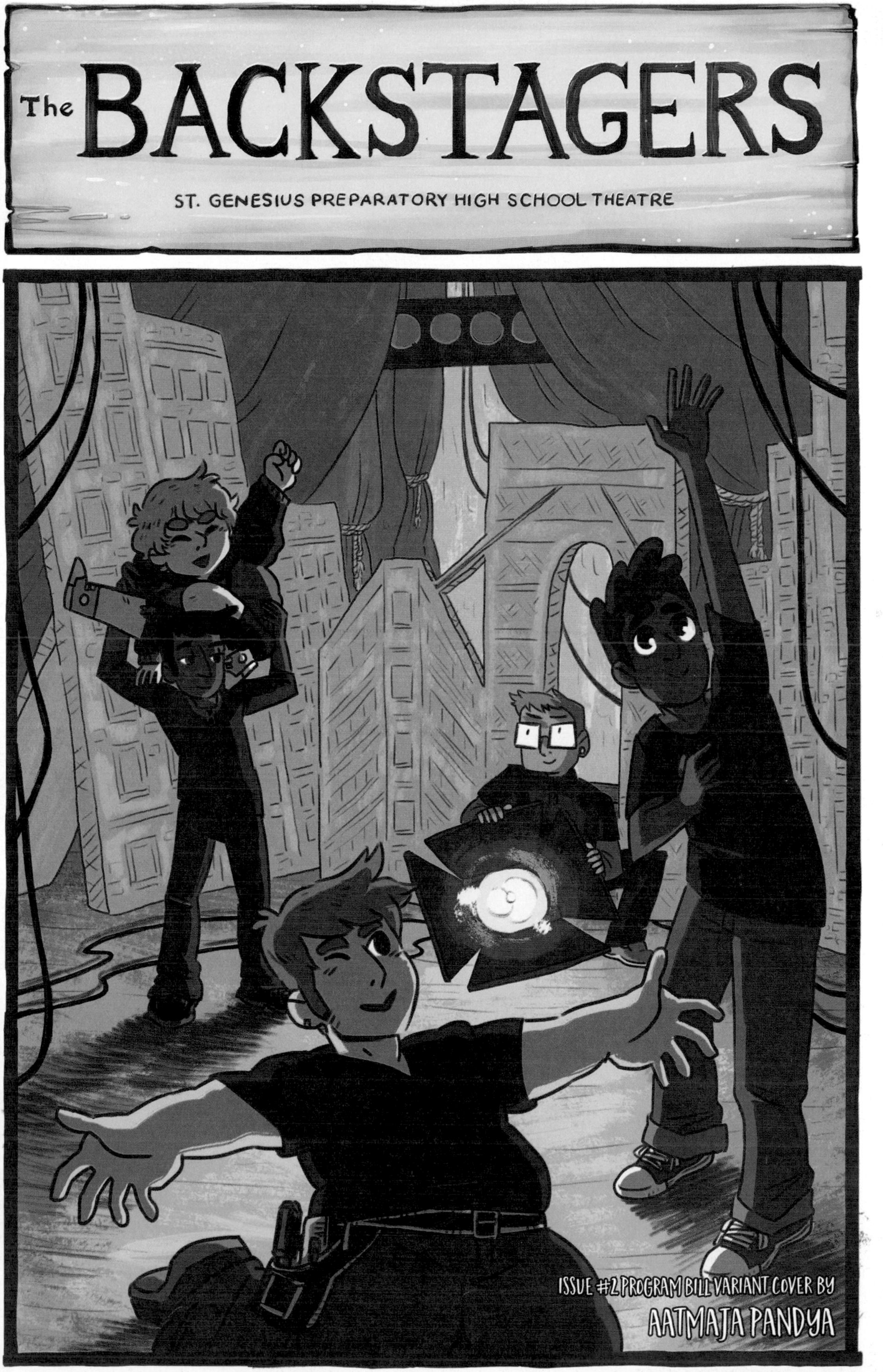
The BACKSTAGERS
ST. GENESIUS PREPARATORY HIGH SCHOOL THEATRE
ISSUE #2 PROGRAM BILL VARIANT COVER BY
AATMAJA PANDYA

ISSUE #3 MAIN COVER BY

VERONICA FISH

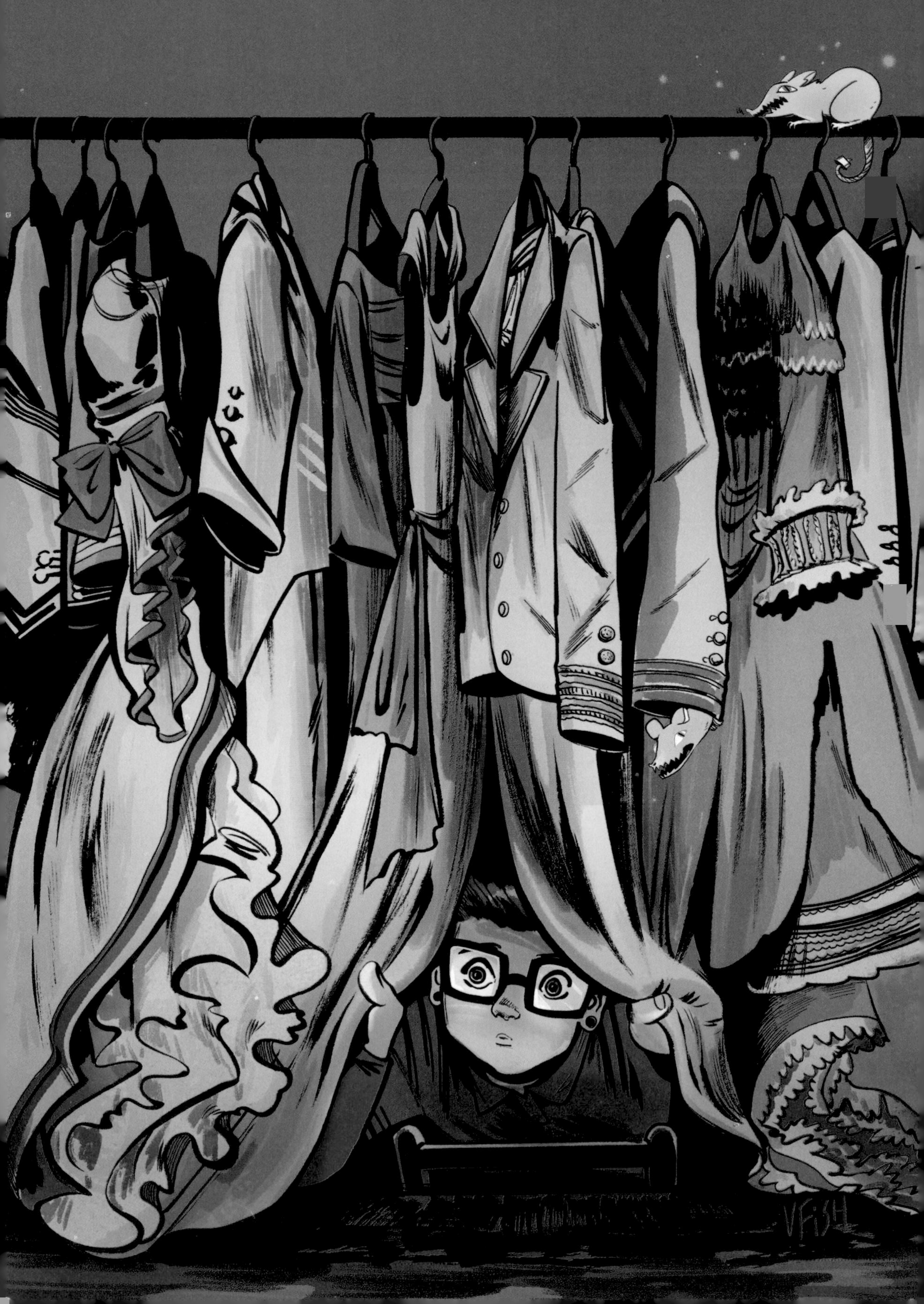
VFISH

The BACKSTAGERS

ST. GENESIUS PREPARATORY HIGH SCHOOL THEATRE

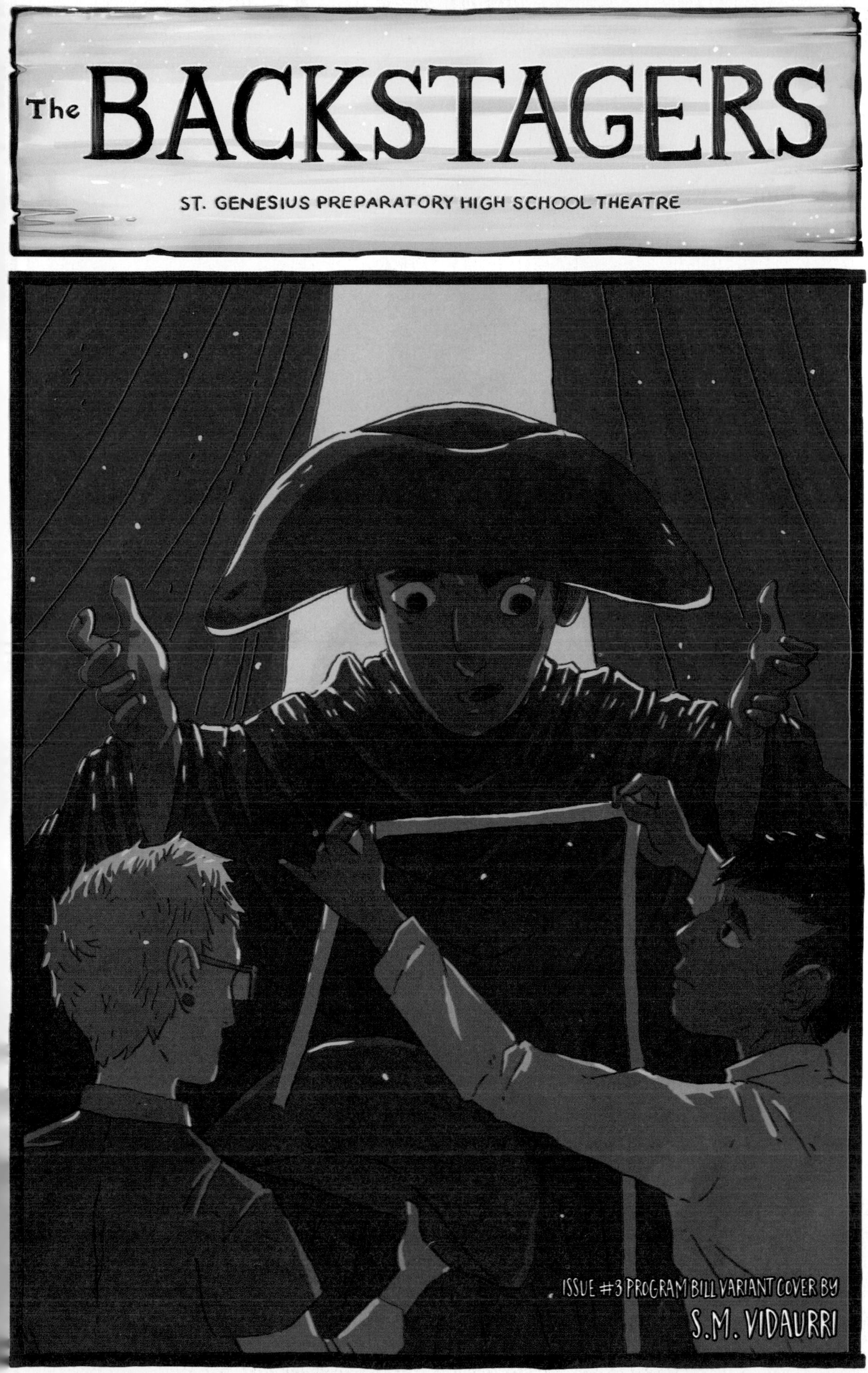
ISSUE #3 PROGRAM BILL VARIANT COVER BY
S.M. VIDAURRI

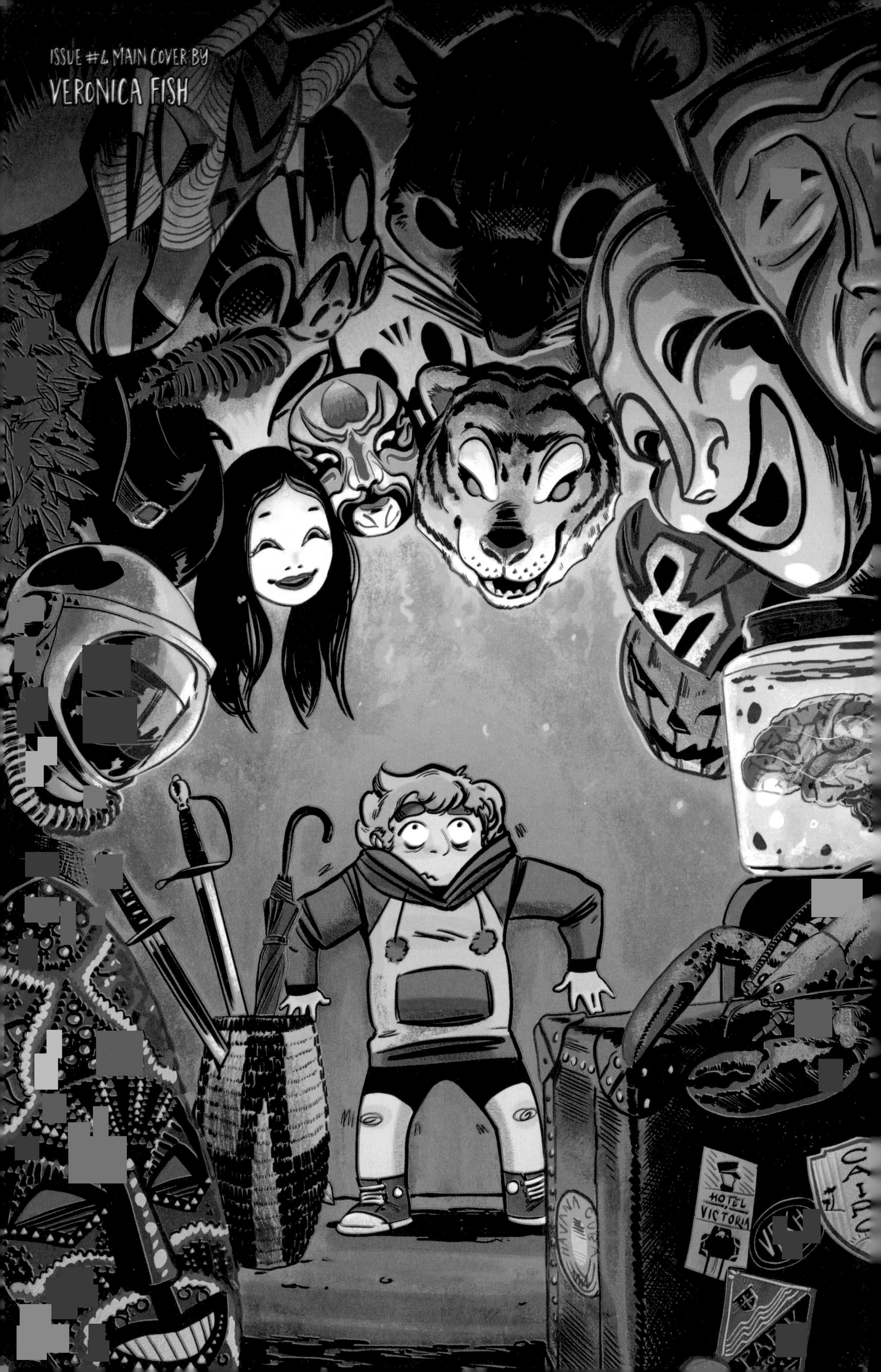
HOTEL VICTORIA
HAVANA CUBA

ISSUE #4 MAIN COVER BY VERONICA FISH

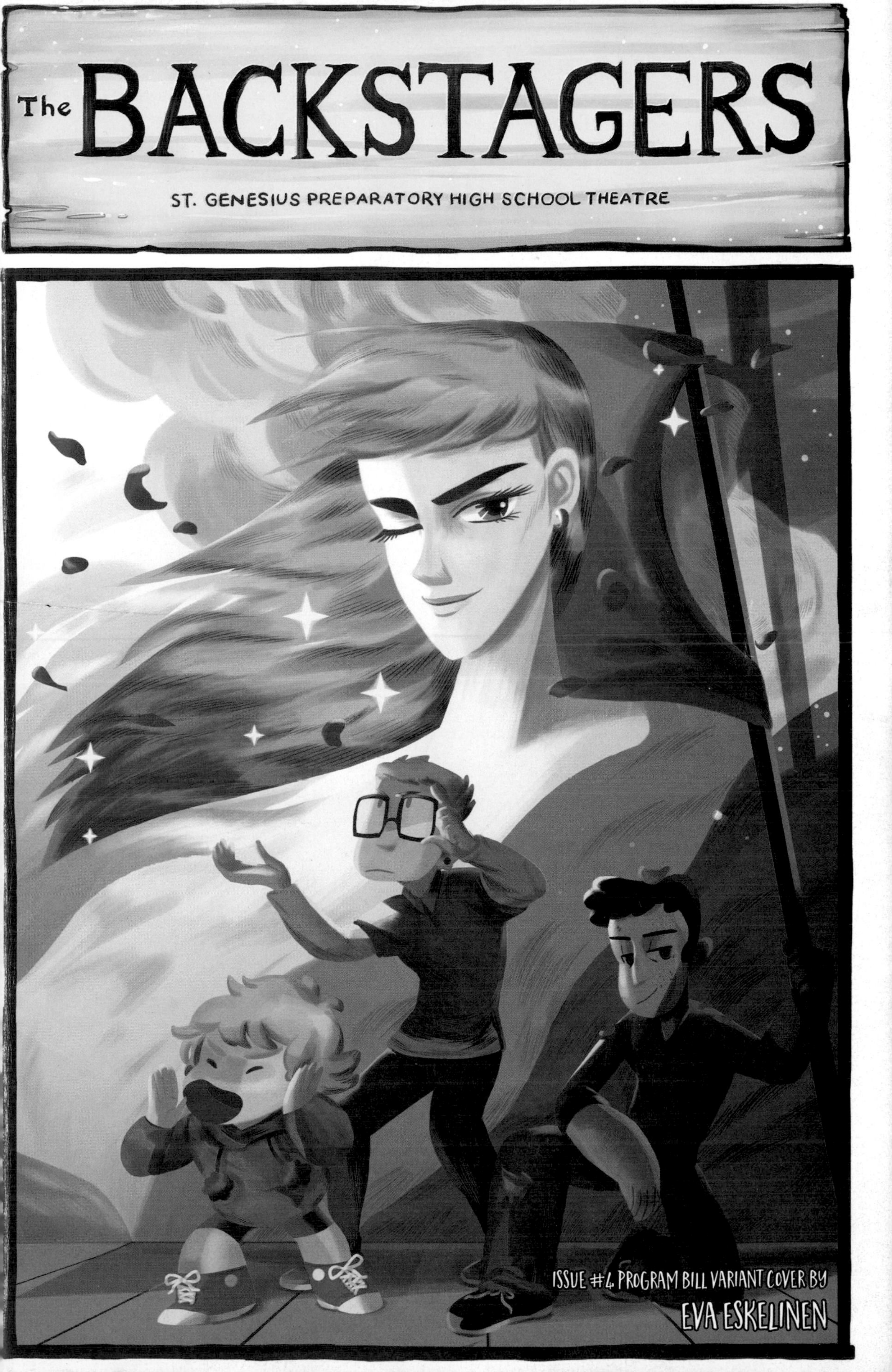
The BACKSTAGERS
ST. GENESIUS PREPARATORY HIGH SCHOOL THEATRE
ISSUE #4 PROGRAM BILL VARIANT COVER BY
EVA ESKELINEN

DISCOVER
ALL THE HITS

STEVENSON · ELLIS · WATTERS · ALLEN
LUMBERJANES
BEWARE THE KITTEN HOLY
NEW YORK TIMES BESTSELLING SERIES

Allison + Treiman + Cogar
GIANT DAYS
VOLUME ONE

From a writer of Disney's Moana
RIBON · FISH · PEER
SLAM!
VOLUME ONE

Hope Larson · Brittney Williams · Sarah Stern
GOLDIE VANCE
"Scoot over Nancy Drew..."
—Los Angeles Times
Volume One

JAMES TYNION IV · RIAN SYGH · WALTER BAIAMONTE
THE BACKSTAGERS

TYSON HESSE'S
DIESEL
IGNITION

Lumberjanes
Noelle Stevenson, Shannon Watters, Grace Ellis, Brooke Allen, and Others

Volume 1: Beware the Kitten Holy
ISBN: 978-1-60886-687-8 | $14.99 US

Volume 2: Friendship to the Max
ISBN: 978-1-60886-737-0 | $14.99 US

Volume 3: A Terrible Plan
ISBN: 978-1-60886-803-2 | $14.99 US

Volume 4: Out of Time
ISBN: 978-1-60886-860-5 | $14.99 US

Volume 5: Band Together
ISBN: 978-1-60886-919-0 | $14.99 US

Giant Days
John Allison, Lissa Treiman, Max Sarin

Volume 1
ISBN: 978-1-60886-789-9 | $9.99 US

Volume 2
ISBN: 978-1-60886-804-9 | $14.99 US

Volume 3
ISBN: 978-1-60886-851-3 | $14.99 US

Jonesy
Sam Humphries, Caitlin Rose Boyle

Volume 1
ISBN: 978-1-60886-883-4 | $9.99 US

Volume 2
ISBN: 978-1-60886-999-2 | $14.99 US

Slam!
Pamela Ribon, Veronica Fish, Brittany Peer

Volume 1
ISBN: 978-1-68415-004-5 | $14.99 US

Goldie Vance
Hope Larson, Brittney Williams

Volume 1
ISBN: 978-1-60886-898-8 | $9.99 US

Volume 2
ISBN: 978-1-60886-974-9 | $14.99 US

The Backstagers
James Tynion IV, Rian Sygh

Volume 1
ISBN: 978-1-60886-993-0 | $14.99 US

Tyson Hesse's Diesel: Ignition
Tyson Hesse

ISBN: 978-1-60886-907-7 | $14.99 US

Coady & The Creepies
Liz Prince, Amanda Kirk, Hannah Fisher

ISBN: 978-1-68415-029-8 | $14.99 US

BOOM! BOX™

AVAILABLE AT YOUR LOCAL COMICS SHOP AND BOOKSTORE

To find a comics shop in your area, call 1-888-266-4226

WWW.**BOOM-STUDIOS**.COM

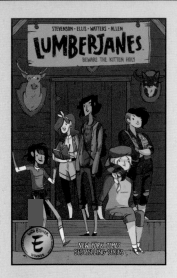

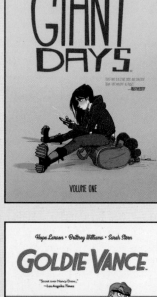

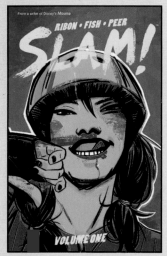

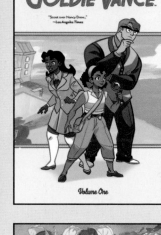

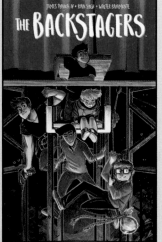

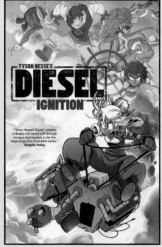